The Clock Winder

Anne Tyler is one of America's most acclaimed novelists, and in 1994 was nominated 'greatest living novelist writing in English' by Roddy Doyle and Nick Hornby. Her fiction includes the Pullitzer Prize-winning novel *Breathing Lessons* and *The Accidental Tourist*, which was made into a major film. Her most recent novels are *Ladder of Years,* the bestselling *A Patchwork Planet* and *Back When We Were Grownups.*

Anne Tyler was born in Minneapolis in 1941, but has lived for many years with her family in Baltimore, where her novels are set.

ALSO BY ANNE TYLER

Anne Tyler

THE CLOCK
WINDER

V

VINTAGE

Published by Vintage 1991

13 15 17 19 20 18 16 14

First published in Great Britain by
Chatto & Windus Ltd 1973
Published by Hamlyn Paperbacks 1983
Arena edition 1987

Vintage
The Random House Group Limited
20 Vauxhall Bridge Road, London SW1V 2SA

Random House Australia (Pty) Limited
20 Alfred Street, Milsons Point, Sydney,
New South Wales 2061, Australia

Random House New Zealand Limited
18 Poland Road, Glenfield,
Auckland 10, New Zealand

Random House (Pty) Limited
Endulini, 5a Jubilee Road, Parktown 2193, South Africa

The Random House Group Limited Reg. No. 954009

www.randomhouse.co.uk

A CIP catalogue record for this book
is available from the British Library

ISBN 009 946960 X

Papers used by Random House are natural, recyclable
products made from wood grown in sustainable forests.
The manufacturing processes conform to the
environmental regulations of the country of origin.

Printed and bound in Denmark by
Nørhaven Paperback A/S, Viborg

1

The house had outlived its usefulness. It sat hooded and silent, a brown shingleboard monstrosity close to the road but backed by woods, far enough from downtown Balti- more to escape the ashy smell of the factories. The upper- most windows were shuttered; the wrap-around veranda, with its shiny gray floorboards and sky-blue ceiling, remained empty even when neighbours' porches filled up with children and dogs and drop-in visitors. Yet clearly someone still lived there. A pile of raked leaves sat by the walk. A loaded bird-feeder hung in the dogwood tree. And in the side yard, Richard the handyman stood peeing against a rosebush with his profile to the house and his long black face dreamy and distant.

Now out popped Mrs Emerson, skin and bones in a shimmery gray dress that matched the floorboards. Her face was carefully made up, although it was not yet ten in the morning. Whatever she planned to say was already stirring her pink, pursed lips. She crossed the veranda rapidly on clicking heels. She descended the steps gingerly, sideways, holding tight to the railing. 'Richard?' she said. 'What is that I see you doing?'

'Just cutting back the roses is all,' Richard said. His back was turned to her. He waved a pair of pruning shears behind him, hip-high.

'I meant what you're doing at this *moment*, Richard.'

'Oh, why, nothing,' Richard said.

It was true. He was zipped up by now, free to turn and beam and click his shears on thin air. Mrs Emerson stopped in front of him and folded her arms.

'Don't try to get around *me*, Richard. I looked out my

5

window and saw you. I thought, *Richard? Is that Richard?'*

'I was preparing to cut back the roses,' Richard said.

'Is that what you call it?'

Richard had a special set of gestures he made when embarrassed – pivoting on his heels with his head hanging down, working something over in his hands. He twisted the rubber grips on his shears and said, 'It's getting time, now. Fall is coming on.'

'That house you are standing by is Mrs Walter Bell's,' said Mrs Emerson. 'In full clear view of her dining room window. Don't think that I won't hear about this.'

'*I* wasn't doing nothing, Mrs Emerson.'

'Oh, hush.'

'I was only cutting back the roses.'

'Just hush. I don't know, I really don't know,' said Mrs Emerson.

'You're just distraught nowadays, that's all.'

'Distraught? Why would I be distraught?' said Mrs Emerson. 'Oh, give me those shears, hand them over. You're fired.'

Richard stopped twisting the shears. He looked up at her with his mouth open, his face jutting forward as if he had trouble seeing her. 'Ah, now,' he said.

'I'll cut back my own damn roses.'

'Now Mrs Emerson, you know you don't mean that. You'd never just *fire* me. Why, I been working here twenty-five years, not counting the war. Planted them roses myself, watered them daily. Do I have to tell you that?'

'I don't know what kind of watering you're talking about,' said Mrs Emerson. 'but you're leaving anyway. Don't expect wages, either. It's only Monday, and you were paid Friday. You've been here not half an hour yet and most of that time ill-spent. Oh, I looked out that window and thought I was seeing things. I thought, What have we come to, after all? What's it going to be next? First Emmeline, letting my transistor radio run down, and then no sooner do I let *her* go than *you* start in. Well, you can send your new employers to me for a reference but don't expect me to cover up for you. "Works well," I'll say, "but tinkles on the flowers." Maybe *some* won't mind.'

'Couldn't you just take a little longer over this?'

6

Mrs Emerson raised her chin and looked past him, twiddling with the empty sleeves of her sweater. She said, 'Longer? Why should I take longer? I've made up my mind.'

'But if you gave it your thought, some. Who could you find that would work as good as me?'

'Whole multitudes,' said Mrs Emerson, 'but I won't be looking. I'm too disappointed. Everywhere I turn there is someone failing me. Well, that's the end of that. From now on I'll do it all myself.'

'Paint the shutters? Keep that creaky old plumbing fixed? Climb up to clean the gutters in them little spiky shoes?'

Mrs Emerson had already turned to go. She paused, lifting one hand to test a curl. It was a sign of uncertainty and Richard knew it, but then he had to go and ruin it for himself. 'You'll be calling me back, Mrs E.,' he said. 'You'll call.'

'Never,' said Mrs Emerson.

Then she went off on tiptoe, to keep from sinking into the lawn.

She kept a pack of playing cards on her dining room table. She sat down on the edge of a chair, smoothing her skirt beneath her, and reached for the cards and began laying out a game of solitaire with sharp little snaps. Her breathing was too rapid. She made a point of slowing it, sitting erect, aligning the cards carefully before she started playing. But unfinished questions kept running through her head. Should she have – ? How could he – ? Why had she – ?

The sun from the bay window fuzzed the edges of the sweater draping her shoulders, lit the flecks of powder across the bridge of her nose. She had once been very pretty. She still was, but now that her children were grown there was something brave about the prettiness. She had started having to work for it. She had to fight the urge to spend her days in comfortable shoes and forget her chinstrap and let herself go. Mornings, patting a pearly base coat over her cheekbones, she noticed how she seemed to be falling into separate pieces. Her face was a series of pouches tenuously joined by transparent skin, reminding her of the tissue-covered frames of model airplanes that her sons used to make. Her close-set blue eyes were divided by minute cracks. Her mouth had bunched in upon itself so that she permanently wore the sulky look she had once had as a child. All she had left was color – pink, white, blond, most of it false. Weekly she went to the hairdresser and returned newly gilded, with her scalp feeling tight as if it were drawing away from her face. She dressed up for everything, even breakfast. She owned no slacks. Her thin, sharp legs were always in ultra-sheer stockings, and her closet was full of those spike-heeled shoes that made her arches ache. But when her children visited and she stood at the door to meet them, wearing pastels, holding out smooth white hands with polished nails, she had seen how relieved they looked. Relieved and a little disappointed: she had survived their desertion, she had not become a broken old lady after all.

She put the red seven on the black eight. Now the six could go up. She looked across the table, out the bay window, and saw Richard standing exactly where she had left him. His shoulders were slumped. The pruning shears were dangling from one hand. Would still more be expected of her? But as she watched he dropped the shears and started off toward the toolshed behind the house. She would have to put the shears away herself, then. She had no idea where they went.

She turned an ace up. Then another. Along came Richard, carrying an old suit jacket, a brown paper bag, a thermos bottle. He was plodding, that was the only word for it. Thinking she was watching. Well, she wasn't. She snapped the last card down, checked for possibilities one more time, and then hitched her bracelets back and gathered the cards into a deck again. When she next looked out the window, Richard was gone.

This house was full of clocks, one to a room – eight-day pendulum clocks that struck the hour and half-hour. Their striking was beautifully synchronized, but the winding was not. Some were due to be wound one day, some another. Only her husband had understood the system. (If there *was*

8

a system.) When he died, three months ago, she considered letting all the clocks run down and then restarting them simultaneously, so that she could stop puzzling over which day to wind which one. But the symbolism involved – the tick, pause, tock, the pause and the final tick of the grandfather clock in the hall, the first to go – made her so nervous that she abandoned the plan. Anyone else would have just wound them all tightly on a given day, and carried on from there. Mrs Emerson didn't. (Wasn't there something about overtight mainsprings? Wouldn't her husband have done that years ago, otherwise? Oh, what was in his mind? What was the meaning of these endless rooms of clocks, efficiently going about their business while she twisted her hands in front of them?) Evenings she wandered through the house bewildered, opening the little glass or wooden doors and reaching for the keys and then pausing, her fingertips to her lips, her eyes round and vague as she counted back over the days of the week. She was not a stupid woman, but she was used to being taken care of. She had passed almost without a jolt from the hands of her father to the hands of her husband, an unnoticeable sort of man who since his death had begun to seem much wiser and more mysterious. He knew answers to questions she had never thought of asking, and kept them to himself. He had wound the clocks absentmindedly, on his way to other places; he had synchronized their striking apparently without effort, without even mentioning it to her – but how? The grandfather clock in the hall was now a quarter-minute ahead of the others, and that was as close as she could get it after half a morning spent irritably shoving the hands back and forth, waiting for the whir of the little hammer as it prepared to strike.

It struck now. Then after a pause the others began: ten o'clock. And here she was with nothing to do, no one to talk to, alone in a sealed house with the last of her supports sent away. She rose from the table, touching a hand to her hair, and went to the front hall. On the bureau was a vase of marigolds which she spent minutes rearranging, changing nothing. She smoothed the linen runner beneath the vase. Then she opened the front door, intending to stir the dim, dust-flecked air. She was about to close it again when she

9

caught sight of the outdoor furniture, which spilled in an uneven line down the veranda and on around the corner of the house. It would stay there year-round; it always had. No wonder this house was so depressing. She remembered how dismal the wicker loveseats looked in winter, the seams of their soggy cushions harboring wisps of snow; how the aluminum chairs dripped icicles and the rattan ones darkened and split and overturned in the wind. The picture came to her like an answer: everything would change for the better, if she moved the furniture before fall set in.

She rushed out with her skirt swirling around her, picked up the round metal tea-table and clicked down the front steps with it. Then around to the back yard – more forest than yard, slanting downward as steeply as a mountainside all the way to the garage,which was out of view. She passed two empty trellises, a toolshed, a rotting gazebo, a stone bench, countless frayed, cut-off, cruel-looking ropes her children had once climbed and swung by. Spongy moss gave way beneath her heels, and brambles snagged her stockings. Birds started up from bushes as if she had no right to come this way. When she reached the garage she found that the side door was stuck. She gave it a kick with the pointed toe of her shoe. Then she heaved the table inside and started back up the hill. Already she was out of breath.

Next came a loveseat, bulky and awkward. She flung the sleeves of her sweater behind her and bent to tug at one wicker arm, but the legs kept catching on the floorboards. When she had pulled it to the steps she stopped to rest. Then someone on the street said, 'Need a hand?'

She turned. A tall girl in dungarees was watching her. 'I could take the other end,' she was saying.

'Oh, *would* you?' said Mrs Emerson.

She stepped to the side, and the girl moved past her to scoop up one end of the loveseat. 'It's not heavy but it's *clumsy,*' Mrs Emerson told her. The girl nodded, and followed her down around the house with the base of the love-seat resting easily in her hands. She certainly didn't believe in wasting words. Every time Mrs Emerson looked back at her to smile apologetically (she really should have warned her about the distance they had to cover), all she saw was the top of a bent head – dark yellow hair hanging straight to her shoulders, a style Mrs Emerson considered drab. The girl didn't comment on the steepness, or the brambles, or the fact that it seemed ludicrous to cart furniture through an apparently endless forest. When they reached the garage she disappeared inside, righted the tea-table, and reached out for the loveseat. 'Any more going in?' she asked.

'Yes,' Mrs Emerson said.

'Well, then,' said the girl, and she moved the two pieces of furniture down to the far end, opposite the car, making more space. Mrs Emerson waited outside with her arms folded. She could use this breathing spell. Now, should she offer a tip? But that might be an insult. And there was always the question of how *much* to offer. Oh, where was her husband, with his desk-size checkbook and his bills on a spindle and his wallet that unfolded so smartly whenever she was sad, offering her money for a new outfit or a trip to Washington?

The girl emerged from the garage, wiping her hands on the seat of her dungarees. 'I certainly do appreciate this,' Mrs Emerson told her. 'I hope I haven't held you up too much.'

'Didn't you say there was more?'

'Oh, yes, all that's left on the veranda.'

'I'll stay and help you finish, then.'

'Well, goodness,' said Mrs Emerson. She was glad of the help, but she wondered what kind of person would let herself get so sidetracked. Weren't there any fixed destinations in her life? As they climbed back up the slope she kept glancing sideways at the girl's face, which was pretty enough but Mrs Emerson thought it would take a good eye like her own to notice. Not a trace of make-up. What a nice bright lipstick could have done! She wore brown moccasins, shapeless and soft-soled. Ruining her arches. Her white shirt was painstakingly ironed, the creases knife-sharp across the shoulders and down the sleeves. A mother's work, for certain – some poor mother wondering right this minute where her daughter had got to. But she hadn't the strength of character to send her on her way. The girl looked so capable, hoisting up two chairs at once when

11

they reached the veranda and swinging through the side yard with them. 'Any time you get tired, now,' said Mrs Emerson, compromising, 'or have to be somewhere, or meet someone – ' The girl was already too far down the path to hear her.

When they were climbing the slope again Mrs Emerson said, 'I *used* to have a handyman. Did until this morning. He would have made short work of this. Then I caught him mistaking the nearest rosebush for the men's room.' The girl laughed – a single, low note that made Mrs Emerson look up at her, started. 'Well, I fired him,' she said. 'I can't have *that.*'

The girl said nothing. They rounded the house, climbed the front steps side by side. There seemed to be more furniture now than before; they hadn't made a dent in it. 'Where did they all *come* from?' Mrs Emerson said, poking a chair with her foot. 'I can't remember ever buying any of this.'

'Outdoor furniture is capable of reproducing,' said the girl. Which made Mrs Emerson pause for a moment before she went on with her own train of thought.

'Our family was once so big, you know,' she said. 'Seven children, all grown now. One married. And a grandchild. When they were still home these chairs got filled soon enough, believe me. Children and friends and boyfriends and neighbors, all just having a grand time.' She was staring vaguely at a wooden rocker, although the girl was already halfway down the steps with her own load. 'Ask anyone in these parts, they all know my children,' she said. 'It's the Emersons,' they'd tell each other, when we'd go sailing past in the car with everybody sitting in everybody's lap. I am Pamela Emerson, by the way.'

'I'm Elizabeth Abbott,' said the girl.

She had stopped on the grass. She waited while Mrs Emerson dragged the rocker down the steps. Mrs Emerson said, 'Abbott? It's funny, I can't remember seeing you here before.'

'I haven't *been* here. I come from North Carolina.'

'Oh, I have cousins in North Carolina,' said Mrs Emerson. 'Not to know personally, of course. Are you just visiting?'

'I'm going to see these people about a job.'

'A job. Goodness,' Mrs Emerson said, 'and here you are moving furniture. Do you usually go at things in such a roundabout way?'

Elizabeth smiled. The whole of her face smiled. 'Always,' she said.

'I just hope you won't arrive late, that's why I asked. The last thing I'd do is interfere but *I* have daughters, working daughters, and I can't help telling you: first impressions are all-important. Promptness. Neatness.'

She was looking at Elizabeth's shirt-tails, but Elizabeth didn't notice; she had moved off now with her chairs. 'They don't know to expect me, anyway,' she called back. 'I saw their ad on a bulletin board in a thrift shop. I like getting jobs from bulletin boards. What they want is a mother's helper, and I need to find out if that means housework or babysitting. Babysitting wouldn't be good at all. I don't like children.'

'Is that right?' Mrs Emerson said. She was trying to remember if she had ever heard anyone else admit to such a thing. She puffed along with the rocker, taking short rapid steps to keep up. 'Now, I would have thought you were still in school.'

'I am. I'm earning money for my senior year at college.'

'In September?'

'I'm taking a year off.'

'Oh, that's terrible!' said Mrs Emerson. They had reached the garage by now. She set down the rocker to stare at Elizabeth, who seemed undisturbed. 'Interrupting like that! It's terrible. Why, one thing may lead to another and you may never get back. I've known that to happen.'

'It's true,' Elizabeth agreed.

'Couldn't you get a scholarship? Or a loan?'

'Oh, my grades were rotten,' she said cheerfully.

'Still, though. It's no good to have to stop something in the middle. What does your father do, dear?'

'He's a minister.'

'Nothing wrong with *that*. Although a lot depends on the denomination. What denomination is he?'

'Baptist.'

'Oh.'

13

'If this job is babysitting,' Elizabeth said, 'I'll just have to find me another bulletin board. But the friend that dropped me here said Roland Park was the likeliest neighborhood.'

She stacked her chairs inside the garage and reached for the rocker. Mrs Emerson said, 'Do you know the people's name? The ones you're going to see?'

'O'Donnell.'

'O'Donnell. Well, I've never heard of *them* before. If it's people I don't know they're generally young. New young people buying up these old houses for a song and moving in with children. But *children* aren't so bad. What is it you have against them?'

'I don't like people you can have so much effect on,' Elizabeth said.

'What? Goodness,' said Mrs Emerson.

They climbed back up the hill. It seemed to have grown steeper. Mrs Emerson's palms were sore, and two finger-nails had broken, and her stockings were in shreds. 'If only my boys were home,' she said. 'If only I'd thought of this sometime when they were visiting. They'd have been glad to help. But I just never did, and then I asked myself, Why wait until they come? Why not do it myself, while the weather's still warm and the sun so nice?'

She paused to catch her breath, one hand clamped to the small of her back. Elizabeth stopped too. 'Would you like me to finish up for you?' she asked.

'No, no, I wouldn't hear of it.'

'It'll only take a minute.'

'I'm all right.'

They gathered up the next load and started back down. Mrs Emerson's heels kept slipping on dead leaves. This was all Richard's fault. He couldn't even rake properly. Slick brown leaves were scattered here and there, with moss or smooth earth beneath them instead of the grass he should have been growing. The chair she carried was knocking against her knees. Mean little tangled bramble bushes kept snatching her sweater off her shoulders. What would her husband say, if he could look down now and see how her life was turning out? She sighed raggedly, hitched the chair higher, wiped her forehead on her upper arm.

Then when they were just descending the steps to the

14

garage, Mrs Emerson caught her heel and fell. She landed on top of the overturned chair, scraping both knees and the palm of one hand. 'Ooops, there!' she said, and gave a little tinkling laugh. Tears were stinging her eyelids. She reached for Elizabeth's hand and struggled to her feet. 'Oh, how ridiculous,' she said.

'Are you all right?'

'Of course I am.' She jerked her hand away and began brushing her skirt. 'I just caught my heel,' she said.

'Maybe you should rest a while.'

'No, I'm fine. Really.'

She lifted the chair again and one of its legs fell off – a white metal tube, rust specks seeping through a sloppy paint job. It clattered down the rest of the steps. She felt the tears pressing harder. 'It's broken,' she said. 'Isn't that ridiculous? It's just not my day. And Richard gone, too.' She fixed her eyes on the chair leg, which Elizabeth had picked up and was examining. 'If I had fired him *tomorrow*, now. Stayed in bed where I should have and kept my head under the covers and fired him tomorrow instead. Some days just anything I do is certain to bring ruin.'

'It can easily be mended,' Elizabeth said.

'What? Oh.'

'The screw must be somewhere around. I can fix it.'

'Yes, but – *why* did I fire him? What got into me?'

'You said – ' Elizabeth began.

'Oh, that. He's been tinkling on the roses for twenty-five years, not counting the war. Everybody knows that. It was just his flaw, something we avoided mentioning. Well, I *would* have, but I was uncertain how to bring it up, you see. What phraseology to use.'

'Now, was there a washer to this, I wonder?' Elizabeth said. 'Or just the screw.'

'I certainly never meant to *fire* him for it!' said Mrs Emerson. 'I didn't even know I was going to.'

She dropped to the steps, pulling a flowered handkerchief from her belt with shaky hands. By now the tears had spilled over, but she smiled steadily and kept a tight rein on her voice. 'Well, I'm being very silly,' she said.

'Could you move your feet a minute?' said Elizabeth. She was patting the ground in search of the screw. Her face was turned slightly away; possibly she had not even noticed the tears. Mrs Emerson straightened her back and blew her nose, silently. '*All* help is difficult, I suppose,' she said.

Elizabeth's hands were square and brown, badly cared for, the nails chopped-looking and the knuckles scraped. But their competence, as they located the screw and fitted it into the chair, was comforting to watch. Mrs Emerson blinked to clear her blurred eyes. 'Emmeline was another one,' she said. 'The maid. Now I'm having to make do with a girl from State Employment, a shiftless sort that chews tobacco. Half the time I can't even count on her to come. And the house! I'm ashamed to look at it too closely. Oh, it seems I've just been left all alone suddenly. No one stayed with me.' She laughed. 'I must be hard to get along with,' she said.

Elizabeth had pulled a red pocketknife from her dungarees. She opened out a screwdriver blade and began tightening the screw. 'My,' said Mrs Emerson, making an effort to lighten her voice. 'Is that the kind with all the different blades? Corkscrew? Can opener?'

Elizabeth nodded. 'It's Swiss,' she said.

'Oh, a Swiss Army knife!' Mrs Emerson blew her nose once more and then folded the handkerchief and blotted her eyes. 'Matthew wanted one of those for Christmas once,' she said. 'My oldest son. He asked for one.'

'They come in handy,' said Elizabeth.

'I'm sure they do.'

But she had given him, instead, a violin and a record player and a complete set of Beethoven's symphonies. Remembering that made her start crying all over again. 'I'm sorry about this,' she said, although Elizabeth still had not looked up at her. 'It must be bereavement. The aftermath of bereavement. I just lost my husband three months ago. At first, you know, things are very busy and there are always people calling. It's only later you notice what's happened. After the people have left again.'

She watched the pocketknife being folded, the chair being set in the garage. 'Goodness, *that* didn't take long,' she said.

Elizabeth returned, dusting off her hands. 'I'm sorry about your husband,' she told Mrs Emerson.

16

'Oh, well. Thank you.'

Mrs Emerson rose from the steps. All her joints ached, and her knees felt tight and stiff where they had been scraped. They started together up the hill. 'My friends say it's often this way,' she told Elizabeth. 'The delayed reaction, I mean. But I never expected it *now*, three months after. I thought I had felt bad enough at the time. Sometimes this terrible idea comes to my mind. I think, if he was going to die, then couldn't he have done it earlier? Before I was all used up and worn out? I could have started some sort of new life, back then. I would have had some hope. Well, *that's* a stupid thing to say.'

'Oh, I don't know,' Elizabeth said.

It was this girl's silence that made Mrs Emerson rattle on so. Mrs Emerson had a compulsion to fill all silences. In an hour she would be wincing over what she had spilled out to a stranger, but now, flushed with the feeling of finally having someone stay still and listen, she said, 'And I *can't* go for comfort to my children. They're not that kind, not at all. Oh, I always try to look on the bright side, especially when I'm talking to people. That makes me tend to exaggerate a little. But I never fool *myself:* I know I'd have to attend my own funeral before I see them lined up on this veranda again talking the way they used to. They are always moving away from me; I feel like the center of an asterisk. They *work* at moving away. If I waited for my sons to come carry this furniture it would rot first, they never come. They find me difficult.' She climbed the front steps and turned to flash a very bright smile at Elizabeth, who was looking at her blankly. 'Those auto rides,' she said, 'with all of us crammed inside. "There go the Emersons," people would say, and never guess for an instant that behind the glass it was all bickering, arguing, scenes, constant crisis –'

'Oh, well,' Elizabeth said comfortably, 'I reckon *most* families work that way.'

Mrs Emerson paused; her thoughts snagged for a second. Then she said, 'They *live* on crisis. It's the only time they're happy. No, they're never happy. They lead such complicated lives I can't keep up with them any more. All I've seen of my grandchild is one minute little black-and-white

17

photo of a bunch of total strangers, one of them holding the baby. A lady I'd never seen before. Elderly. The last time we were all together was by necessity, for the funeral – and they left the baby with his other grandmother. Two of my boys live right in this area, but do I see them? Well, Matthew, when he can get away. Timothy never. The only one just dying to come is Andrew, and him I'm supposed to discourage because he's a little bit unbalanced. He's not supposed to leave his psychiatrist. He's not supposed to come home and expose himself to upset. It's unhealthy of him to want to.'

'It sounds,' Elizabeth said unexpectedly, 'as if he's in somebody's *clutches*.'

For a moment Mrs Emerson, who had already opened her mouth to begin a new sentence, had trouble following her. She looked up, startled, at Elizabeth's earnest, scowling face. Then she laughed. 'Oh, my,' she said, and reached for her handkerchief. 'Oh, my, well . . .'

Elizabeth straightened up from the railing she had been leaning against. 'Anyway,' she said, 'I'll just take this last load of furniture down.'

'Oh, will this be the last?' Mrs Emerson said. She had suddenly stopped laughing.

'There's only these two.'

'Wait, don't hurry. Wouldn't you like to rest a minute? Have some milk and cookies? You said you hadn't made an appointment. You could finish up any time.'

'I just did have breakfast,' Elizabeth said.

'Please. Just a glass of milk?'

'Well, all right.'

Mrs Emerson led her into the house, through the ticking hallway toward the kitchen at the rear. 'My, it's so *dark* in here,' she said, although she was used to the darkness herself. As she passed various pieces of furniture – the grandfather clock, a ladderback chair, the chintz-covered armchair in the kitchen, all of them scuffed and worn down around the edges from a lifetime with children – she reached out to give them little pats, as if protecting them from a stranger's eyes. But Elizabeth didn't even glance at them. She seemed totally unobservant. She pulled an enamelled stepstool toward the table and sat down on it, doubling her knees so as to set her feet on the top step. 'I just don't want to hit the O'Donnells at lunch,' she said.

'No, no, you have plenty of time,' said Mrs Emerson.

She poured out a tall glass of milk. Elizabeth said, 'Aren't you having any?'

'Oh. I suppose so.'

Ordinarily she never touched milk. She only kept it for cooking. When she settled herself at the table and took the first sip she had the sudden sense of being back in her mother's house, where she used to have milk and cookies to ease all the minor tragedies. The taste of milk after tears, washing away the gluey feeling in the back of her throat, was the same then as now; she stared dreamily at a kitchen cabinet, keeping the taste in her memory a long time before taking another sip. Then she set the glass down and said, 'I hope you don't think I'm one of those people that gives notice all the time.'

'Notice?'

'Firing people.'

'Why should I think that?' Elizabeth said.

'Well, all this talk about Richard. And then Emmeline. But those two have been with me half a lifetime; it's only lately that all this unpleasantness came up. They took advantage, knowing the state I was in. Oh, I don't blame them entirely, I know I haven't been myself. But how could they expect me to be? Ordinarily I'm a marvelous employer, people can't do enough for me. You can tell by their name that family will have too many children.'

'Um –'

'The O'Donnells. Babies and toddlers and little ones in diapers, I'm just sure of it. I believe I know them. Don't I?'

'I thought –'

'They'll run you off your feet over there.'

Elizabeth finished her milk and set her empty glass down. She wiped the back of her hand across her mouth. 'I think you must be offering me a job,' she said.

'A job,' said Mrs Emerson. She sat straighter and placed her palms together. 'That is something to consider.'

'Are you asking if I'd like to work for you?'

'Well, would you?' Mrs Emerson said.

'Sure. I'd make a better handyman than babysitter.'

19

'Handyman!' said Mrs Emerson. 'No, I meant house-work. Taking over for Emmeline.'

'Why not a handyman? It's what you need most. You already have a maid, you said.'

'But *gardening*. Painting. Climbing ladders.'

'I can do that.'

'Well, I never heard of such a thing.'

'Why? What's so strange about it?' Elizabeth said. She had a habit of rarely bothering to look at people, Mrs Emerson noticed. She concentrated on objects – pulling threads from a seam of her dungarees or untangling the toaster cord or examining the loose knob on the pepper-mill, so that when she did look up there was something startling, almost a flash, in the gray of her eyes. 'You wouldn't have to pay me much,' she said, looking straight at Mrs Emerson. 'If you let me live in I could get by on next to nothing.'

'It's true, it scares me just to think of looking for another colored man,' said Mrs Emerson. 'Nowadays you can't tell *what* to expect.'

'Well, I don't know anything about that.'

'But carrying firewood! Digging compost!'

Elizabeth waited, looking perfectly comfortable, picking leaves off the soles of her moccasins.

'I do get nervous at night,' said Mrs Emerson. 'Not that I am *frightened* or anything. But having someone down the hall, just another human being in case of –'

She fell silent and raised a hand to her forehead. This world expected too many decisions of her. The girl's good points were obvious (calmness and silence, and the neat twist of her hands mending the chair) but there were bad points, too (no *vivacity*, that was it, and this tendency to drift into whatever offered itself). She sighed. 'Oh, well,' she said. 'It can't hurt to try you out, I suppose.'

'Done,' said Elizabeth, and reached a hand across the table. Mrs Emerson was slow to realize that she was supposed to shake it.

'Now, I was paying Richard fifty a week,' she said. 'But he wasn't living in. Is forty all right?'

'Oh, sure,' said Elizabeth, cheerfully. 'Anything.' How would she earn her way through college, talking like that?

Then she stood and took her glass to the sink. She said, 'I guess I'll get the last of those chairs taken care of.'

'Fine,' said Mrs Emerson. She stayed where she was. That was her privilege, now that she was paying. She listened to the front door slamming, the chair legs scraping across the veranda. Then she heard Elizabeth crashing through the woods. She thought of living in the same house with her – such a lanky, awkward, flat-chested girl – and she raised her eyes to the ceiling and asked her husband what she had let herself in for.

2

'It's simple,' said Elizabeth. 'That stump is the chopping block. There's the axe. And there sits the turkey, wondering when you'll start. What else could you want?'

'If it's all that simple why ask *me* to do it?' the boy said. He was standing beside her in the toolshed doorway, looking at the turkey in its crate. The turkey paced three steps to one side, three steps to the other, stopping occasionally to peer at them through the slats.

'Look at him, he wants to get it over with,' Elizabeth said.

'Couldn't we call in the butcher?'

The boy was a college senior named Benny Simms – pleasant-faced, beanpole-thin, with a crewcut. He lived two houses down, although his mother was beginning to question that. 'He lives at *your* place,' she told Mrs Emerson on the phone. 'Every weekend home he's out visiting your handman. Handywoman. What kind of girl is she anyway? Who are her people? Do you know anything *about* her?' Elizabeth had heard of this call, and other mothers' calls just like it, from Mrs Emerson, who reported it in a voice that tried to sound amused but came out irritated. 'This is one problem I never had with Richard,' she said. 'I find there are drawbacks that I hadn't foreseen when I hired you.' She was still trying to switch Elizabeth over to housekeeping, which was probably why she sounded irritated. She tapped her fingernails on a tabletop. 'I don't know, people surprise me more all the time. "Above all else, be *feminine*," I used to tell my daughters, and here you are in those eternal blue jeans, but every time I look out the window some new boy is helping you rake leaves.'

'Oh, well, the leaves are nearly gone by now,' Elizabeth said.

'What's that got to do with it?'

'I'll be indoors more. They won't be stopping by so much.'

'It's more likely they'll just start invading my kitchen,' Mrs Emerson said.

Benny Simms picked up the axe that was leaning against the toolshed. He ran a finger down the blade and whistled. 'I just did sharpen it,' Elizabeth told him.

'I guess you *did*.'

'Did you know the Emersons have a whetstone wheel? The old-fashioned kind, that works with a foot pedal. I found it in the basement.'

'Nothing about the Emersons would surprise me at all,' Benny said.

'I like things like that. Things without machinery to them. Machinery is something I don't understand too well.'

'I would've thought you'd know all about it,' Benny said.

'No. *Yard* work now, or carpentry, or plumbing – things that you can see reason to right on the surface . . . '

'Then why can't you kill the turkey?' asked Benny.

'Well.'

He handed her the axe. Elizabeth turned it over several times, studying the glint of the blade very carefully but moving no closer to the turkey. She was wearing what Mrs Emerson called her uniform – moccasins, dungarees, and a white shirt, and a bulky black jacket with a rib-knit waist now that the weather had turned cool. A wind from the east was whipping her hair around her face. She kept brushing it back impatiently without lifting her eyes from the axe. 'I'm

22

not too certain about that bevel,' she said. 'It looks a little bluish. I hope I didn't go and ruin the tempering.'

'I don't know what you're talking about,' said Benny. 'What'd you take this job for, if you can't kill turkeys?'

'Well, how was I to know? Would you expect that to be a part of my job? First I heard of it, in she walked yesterday carrying the crate by the handle. Passed it over to me without even slowing down, walked on through the house peeling off her gloves. Said, "Here you are, Elizabeth, take care of this, will you? Have it ready in time for Thanksgiving dinner." Tomorrow! I didn't know what to say. I suspect,' she said, setting down the axe, 'that she planned it all on purpose, to turn me to housekeeping.'

'Most people get their turkeys from the supermarket,' Benny said.

'Not her.'

'All plucked and wrapped in plastic.'

'Not Mrs Emerson. She won it at a church bazaar.'

'Oh, is that what you win? I've heard of prize turkeys before but I thought they'd have their feathers off.'

'Nope. You do it all yourself.'

'Do you know how to pluck them?'

'Oh, sure,' said Elizabeth. 'The feathers and the innards, *that's* no problem.'

Benny was brushing his crewcut on end, over and over. 'Innards. Jeepers,' he said. 'I'd forgotten them. You'll have to fish out all those half-made eggs.'

'I tend to doubt that,' Elizabeth said. She smiled suddenly and shut the toolshed door, dropping the wooden crossbar into place. 'Oh, well, I don't know why I asked you anyway. If you can't, you can't.'

'I'm awfully sorry.'

'That's all right.'

They started up the hill toward the front yard – Elizabeth ahead, with her hands deep in her jacket pockets, Benny still brushing up his crewcut as he walked. 'What I stopped by for,' he said, 'was to ask if you wanted to come with me this afternoon.'

'I'd love to.'

'I'm going – don't you want to know where you'd be coming with me *to?*'

23

'Where am I coming with you to?'

'I'm going out to the country for my mother. Picking up some pumpkins for pumpkin pie.'

'Oh, good,' said Elizabeth. 'Maybe I'll get Mrs Emerson a pumpkin too. Big as a footstool. Drop it in her lap and say, "*Here* you go, take care of this, will you? Have it ready in time for Thanksgiving." ' She laughed, but Benny didn't.

'I don't know why you stay with that woman,' he said. 'Couldn't you find someone else to work for?'

'Oh, I like her.'

'What for? The whole family's crazy, everyone knows that.'

Elizabeth had stopped to empty bits of leaves from one moccasin. She shook it out, standing one-legged in the grass. 'Other people have said so too,' she said, 'but I don't know yet if they're right. So far I've only seen Mrs Emerson and Matthew.'

'Matthew. Well, he's okay but *Andrew* is stark raving mad. Wait till you see *him.*'

Elizabeth bent to put her moccasin back on, and they continued toward the street. Squirrels were racing all around them, skimming over the grass and up the skeletons of the trees.

'When I was little Mrs Emerson used to scare me to death,' said Benny. 'Also Andrew, and Timothy a little too but that might have been just because he was Andrew's twin. I wouldn't even come in for cookies, not even if Mrs Emerson called me herself with her sweetie-sweet voice. I'd heard stories about them since I was old enough to listen. That Andrew is *violent.* And do you know that Mrs E. went to pieces once because she thought her first baby got mixed up in the hospital?'

'I hear a lot of people have that thought,' Elizabeth said.

'Maybe so, but they don't go to pieces. And they don't try and give the babies back to the hospital.'

Elizabeth laughed.

'I wonder if my mother would care to hire you,' Benny said.

'It's not too likely. Besides, I believe I'd like to stay and meet these people.'

'When would you do that? Some don't come home from

one year to the next.'

'Well, one's coming today, as a matter of fact,' Elizabeth said. 'The one here in Baltimore. Timothy. That's what we're killing the turkey for.'

'I could ask my mother if she needs any carpentry done.'

'Never mind,' said Elizabeth. She tapped him lightly on the shoulder. 'Go on, now. I'll see you this afternoon.'

'All right. I hope you manage that turkey somehow.'

'I will.'

She climbed the steps to the veranda, unzipping her jacket as she went. Inside, the house was almost dark, filled with ticking clocks, smelling of burned coffee. The furniture was scarred and badly cared for. 'Mrs Emerson,' Elizabeth had once said, 'would you like me to feed the furniture?' Mrs Emerson had laughed her tinkling little laugh. 'Feed it?' she had said. 'Feed it what?' 'Well, oil it, I mean. It's drying out, it's falling to pieces.' But Mrs Emerson had said not to bother. She had no feeling for wood, that was why – the material that Elizabeth loved best. The hardwood floors were worn dull, black in some places where water had settled in, the grain raised and rough. In a house so solid, built with such care (six fireplaces, slate in the sunporch, a butler's pantry as big as a dining room, and elegant open inserts like spool-bed headboards above every doorway), Mrs Emerson's tumble of possessions lay like a film of tattered leaves over good topsoil, their decay proceeding as steadily as Mrs Emerson's life. Strange improvements had been tacked on – a linoleum-topped counter, crumbling now at the edges, running the length of the oak-lined breakfast room, dingy metal cabinets next to the stone fireplace in the kitchen. In the basement there were five separate servants' rooms, furnished with peeling metal bedsteads and rolled-up, rust-stained mattresses; on the second floor most of the doors were kept shut, darkening the hall; on the third floor there was an echo; the wallpaper was streaked brown beneath the shuttered windows, the floor outside the bathroom bore a black ring where someone had long ago left a glass of water to evaporate, unnoticed. The two attics off the third-floor rooms were crammed with playpens, cribs, and potty-chairs, bales of mouse-eaten letters, textbooks no school would think of using any more. There was a leak beside one chimney which only Elizabeth seemed concerned about. (Periodically she was to empty the dishpan beneath it; that was all.) Mrs Emerson, meanwhile, set antique crystal vases over the scars of the dining room buffet and laid more and more Persian carpets over the worn spots on the floors. The carpets glowed richly, like jewels, calling forth little sparkles of admiration from the ladies who came to tea. Elizabeth hated Persian carpets. She wanted to banish all their complicated designs to the basement and sand the floors down to bare grain – something she knew better than to suggest to Mrs Emerson.

She climbed the stairs, creaking each step in turn, trailing her hand along the banister. In the hall she stopped a moment to listen to Mrs Emerson, who was in her bedroom talking to the maid. 'Now, Alvareen, if Mr Timothy gets here by lunchtime I don't want you serving any bread. He's gained fifteen pounds since he started medical school. Heart disease runs in the family. Give him Ry-Krisp, and if he asks for bread say we don't have any. Can you understand that? Meanwhile, I want to see a little cleaning done. I don't know how things have been allowed to slide so. The baseboards are just furry. Do you know what Emmeline used to do? She ran along the baseboard crevices with a Q-tip, down on her hands and knees. Now that's *cleaning.*'

'Yes'm,' said Alvareen.

'Are you out there, Elizabeth?'

Elizabeth crossed the hallway to the bedroom. Mrs Emerson was sitting at her little spinet desk, wearing a dyed-to-match sweater and skirt and a string of pearls, holding a gold fountain pen poised over a sheet of cream stationery. She looked like an advertisement. So did everything else in the room – twin beds canopied with ruffles, the lace lampshades, the two flowered armchairs that turned out to be shabby only if you came up close to them. It was hard to imagine that Mr Emerson had lived here too. He had died of a heart attack, people said, in one of the twin beds – almost the only Emerson to do things without a fuss. Now the beds were neatly made and there were little satin

26

cushions arranged at the heads. The only thing out of place was Alvareen, a black hulk of a woman in a gay uniform, standing beside Mrs Emerson with her hands under her apron. 'Mrs Emerson, I'll be going now,' she said.

'Yes, yes, go on. Elizabeth, have you taken care of that turkey?'

'Not yet,' Elizabeth said.

'Why not? I can't imagine what's holding you up.'

'I was just going to fetch an old shirt,' said Elizabeth. 'I don't want to get all bloody.'

'Oh. Now, I'm not interested in the details, I just want him seen to. At one o'clock tomorrow I want to find him stuffed, trussed, and ready to carve. Is that clear?'

'Who's going to cook him?' Elizabeth asked. 'Not me.'

'Alvareen, but I'm having to pay her double for the holiday. No one *else* will do it.'

She smoothed the lines between her eyebrows, looking tired and put-upon, but Elizabeth didn't offer to change her mind about cooking. One piece of housework, she figured, would turn her magically into a maid – and just when Mrs Emerson was getting used to her as a handyman. At teas, catching sight of Elizabeth as she climbed the stairs or passed a doorway, Mrs Emerson would cry, 'Wait! Girls, I want you to see Elizabeth. My handyman, can you imagine?' And the ladies would round their mouths and act surprised, although surely the news was all over Roland Park by now. 'Oh, Pamela, I swear,' one of them said, 'you always find some different way of doing things.' Mrs Emerson beamed, setting her cup soundlessly in its little fluted saucer.

'I've brought you in some firewood,' Elizabeth said, 'and later I'll drive out for the stuffing mix. Would you like a big old pumpkin?'

'Excuse me?'

'A pumpkin. I'm going out to the country with Benny this afternoon.'

'Now what would Alvareen know to do with a pumpkin? She can barely warm up a brown-and-serve pie. I don't remember giving you the afternoon off.'

'I did a full day's work in the morning,' Elizabeth said. 'Carried in the firewood, caulked three window frames,

27

mended the back porch railing, and sharpened all your tools. Also I oiled the whetstone.'

'What whetstone is that?'

'The one in the basement.'

'Oh, I never knew we had one. Well, Richard worked five full days a week. Morning *and* afternoon.'

'Richard wasn't on hand round the clock whenever you called for him,' Elizabeth said.

'Oh, never mind that, can't you just stay? Timothy's coming home.'

'I won't take long.'

Mrs Emerson rose and went to her dresser, where she began going through a little inlaid box full of bobby pins. She dug out bobby pins and put them back in and dug out more, as if some were better than others. Then she began shifting hairbrushes and perfume bottles around. 'I don't know what I depend on you for,' she told Elizabeth. 'You're never here when I need you.'

Elizabeth said nothing.

'And the country, all these trips to the country and anywhere else that comes to mind. Washington. Annapolis. Lexington Market. The zoo. Any place you're asked. It's ridiculous, can't you just stay put a while? Timothy said he might be here by lunch. I was counting on your standing by to help me.'

'Help you do what?' Elizabeth asked.

'Well, maybe we'll need more firewood.'

'I just got through telling you, I brought some in. MacGregor delivered a truckload this morning.'

'What if we burn more than you'd planned on? *Some* problem will turn up. What if we need a repair job all of a sudden.'

'If you do, I'll see to it later,' Elizabeth said. 'And Timothy will be here.'

'To be truthful, Elizabeth, it's nice to have things thinned *out* a little when just one of my children is here. Somebody to lighten the conversation. Couldn't you stay?'

'I promised Benny,' Elizabeth said.

'Oh, *go* then. Go. I don't care.'

When Elizabeth left, Mrs Emerson had started opening all her bureau drawers and slamming them shut again.

*

Elizabeth's room was across the hall from Mrs Emerson's. The air in it smelled heavily of cigarettes – the Camels Elizabeth chain-smoked whenever she was idle – and there was a clutter of paperback detective stories and orange peels and overflowing ashtrays on the dresser. In the lower drawers were odds and ends belonging to Margaret, who had lived in this room until she left home. Her Nancy Drew mysteries were still in the bookcase, and her storybook dolls lined one wall shelf. The other children's rooms were stripped clean; Margaret's was different because she had left in a hurry. Eloped, at sixteen. Now she was twenty-five, divorced or annulled or something and drawing ads for a clothing company in Chicago. 'And moody, so terribly moody,' Mrs Emerson said. 'The few times she's been back I've wondered if she'd go into a depression right before my eyes.' Mrs Emerson had a way of summing up each child in a single word, putting a finger squarely on his flaw. Margaret was moody, Andrew unbalanced, Melissa high-strung. But coming from her, the flaws sounded like virtues. In Mrs Emerson's eyes anything to do with nerves was a sign of intelligence. Other people's children were steady and happy and ordinary; Mrs Emerson's were not. They were special. On the bookshelf in the study Margaret's pale, pudgy face scowled out from a filigree frame, her lipstick a little blurred, her lank hair a little mussed, as if being special she must have seemed as out of place as Elizabeth, who sat on the satin bedspread in her dungarees and scattered wood chips across the flowered carpet whenever she was whittling.

Wood chips marked the doorway to the room, and trailed across the hall and down the top few stairsteps. 'You must think you're Hansel and Gretel,' Mrs Emerson once said. 'Everywhere you go you drop a few shavings.' She had seen Elizabeth's carvings – angular, barely recognizable figures, sanded to a glow – and not known what to make of them, but apparently they had settled her mind. Before then she kept asking, 'What are you going to do, in the end? What will you make of your life?' She liked to see plans neatly made, routes clearly marked, beelines to success. It bothered her that Elizabeth had just bought a multi-purpose electric drill that would sand, saw, wire-brush, sink screws, stir paint — *anything* — which she kept the basement for her woodworking. 'How much did that thing cost? It must have taken every cent I've yet paid you,' Mrs Emerson said. 'At this rate you'll never get to college, and I have the feeling you don't much care.' 'No, not all *that* much,' Elizabeth said cheerfully. Mrs Emerson kept nagging at her. That was when Elizabeth showed her the woodcarvings. She dragged them out of her knapsack, along with a set of Exacta knives and a sheaf of sandpaper. 'Here you go, I'm planning to set up a shop and make carvings all my life,' she said. 'Are you just saying that?' Mrs Emerson asked. 'Or do you mean it. It's a mighty strange choice of occupations, and I never knew you to plan so far ahead. Are you just trying to quiet me?' But she had turned the carvings over in her hands, looking at least partly satisfied, and after that she didn't nag so much.

Elizabeth pulled the knapsack out of her closet and dug down to the bottom of it, coming up finally with a man's ragged shirt that was rolled into a cylinder. She shook it out and put in on over her jacket. Down the front of the shirt were streaks of paint in several different colors, but no blood. She had never even killed a chicken before. Not even a squirrel or a rabbit, and that at least would have been killing at a distance.

Across the hallway Mrs Emerson was talking into her dictaphone. 'This is going in Melissa's letter. Melissa, are you sure you don't need that brown coat with the belted back that's hanging in the cedar closet? Something else, now. What was it I wanted to say?' There was a click as the dictaphone was shut off, another click to turn it on again. 'Yes, Mary. Now, the last thing I want is to offend that husband of yours. I'm not any ordinary mother-in-law. But would you be able to use my old fur coat that I got four years ago? I never wear it, I was just going through my winter things this morning and stumbled across it. Young men can't generally afford fur coats so I thought – but if you feel he'd be offended, just say so. I'm not any ordinary . . .'

Elizabeth stood by her window, flattening the rolled sleeves of her paint-shirt and wondering what she would do if it took more than one chop to kill the turkey. Or could

30

she just refuse to do it at all? Say that she had turned vegetarian? But that would give Mrs Emerson an excuse to clap her into housework. Elizabeth had nothing against housework but she preferred doing things she hadn't done before. She liked surprising herself.

'Andrew, I understand about Thanksgiving but on Christmas I set my foot down,' Mrs Emerson said. 'I'm not thinking of myself, you understand. I'm managing quite well. But Christmas is a *family* holiday, you need your family. Tell your doctor that. Or would you rather I did? It doesn't matter to *me* what he thinks of me.'

She could go on like this all night, sometimes. To Elizabeth it seemed like so much busywork. If she couldn't write those messages right then, or bother remembering them, were they worth committing to tape? Maybe she just liked pressing all those buttons on her little beige machine. But Mrs Emerson said, 'I take pride in my correspondence, letter-writing is a dying art. I refuse to turn into one of those people who sit themselves at a desk to say, "Well, nothing to report at *this* end, everything is going as usual . . . " ' At two or three in the morning, waking just enough to shut her window or reach for another blanket, Elizabeth would hear sudden, startling sentences floating across the dark hallway. 'I resent what you said in your last letter, Melissa. Everyone knows I am not the sort of mother who interferes.' 'Where is that necklace I lent you? I never said you could *keep* it.' Her voice was clear and matter-of-fact, the ordinary daytime voice of a woman who had been awake for hours. 'How could you just hang up on me like that? I've been thinking and thinking, the older you get the less I understand you.' 'Do you have Emily Barrett's address?' 'Someday *you* will be alone.' 'Where is the photograph you promised?'

On the student desk in the corner sat Elizabeth's own mother's letter, weeks old, sheets and sheets of church stationery hoping for an answer.

  . . . Honey if you were going to be gone so long you should have said so when you left. We would never have let you for one thing and for another we would have cooked you a finer last meal and made a bigger to-do. I could just cry

31

*thinking of that plain old meat loaf and succotash I gave you.
But your sister's wedding was still on my mind and I never
knew you were planning anything but hopping off for a short
summer job. I thought sure you would be back for school.
Well the college called and I didn't know what to say, I
remembered you had talked about taking time off but we
never thought you were serious. And we thought you meant
to go by bus like ordinary people, not with just a wedding
guest that none of our side knew. How could you be sure
what he drove like? Nowadays they let just anyone on the
road, all kinds of things can happen. But there you went and
didn't say a word more about it. I don't know if you were
planning to be gone so long or it just happened. You often do
get carried away. Anyway here you are now in Baltimore
you say. You should see all the times I've crossed addresses
out and written new ones in for you since you sat here back in
May eating that meat loaf and succotash.*

*Well there is not too much to report here. Everybody is
fine although as usual your father is working too hard. He
just lets these women walk all over him, taking up his time
for missionary circles and all kinds of lectures and tea-
parties and slide-showings and paltry illnesses and so forth,
when I tell him he should rest more and behave like ordinary
pastors, confine himself to sermons and funerals and maybe
a few deathbeds. He eats it all up, I believe. He wouldn't
know what to do with himself if they would stop pestering
him. Now Mrs Nancy Bledsoe has gone and given him a
dog, a female collie that chews up everything including
magazines and table legs, and you know how scared he is of
dogs and never would have anything to do with them. She
says it is a token of appreciation for all he did while her
mother was dying. He said thank you kindly although I
notice he has no notion what to do with the thing, doesn't
know how to pet it, backs off when it jumps on him, asked
me right out one day after a lot of hemming and hawing what
was wrong with her that she squats to piddle when everyone
else's dogs raise their legs. Now Christmas will be coming up
which is the busy time for all those deaths and melancholies
as well as church services and so on.*

*Polly is looking so sweet and pretty now that she is
married and she is just real active in the Young Wives*

Fellowship. I don't know if she has told you yet about the event they are expecting in March. Me a grandmother, I'm just tickled pink. I always did want to have someone to spoil rotten but hand back when he got to fussing. Honey I just wish you would settle down yourself some, finish at Sandhill College or get married, one. I know you don't like to hear me say that but I just have to tell you what's on my mind. Mrs Bennett talking the other day said there is always one in every family that causes twice as much worry as all the others, not that you would love them any the less for it, well, I knew what she meant although of course I didn't say so.

Dommie Whitehill still comes calling on us and asks all about you, where you are and what you are doing and who you are going around with and so forth. I could just cry for that boy. You will never find anyone sweeter than Dommie, I don't care how far you look, and that is something that is getting mighty hard to find these days and nobody waits forever.

Elizabeth I have oftentimes told your father he should drop you a line. He says it is up to you to write first and take back all you said so I wish you would. Honey he is just so hurt but would never show it for the world, you know how proud he is. Nobody is as strong as they look. I have thought of calling you on the long distance but not knowing how your employer might feel about it I didn't. You could, though. Just one word is all it would take and it would make him so . . .

Elizabeth changed into older dungarees, tattered and spotted and faded white at the seams. She took a leather belt from her dresser, but instead of putting it on she raised it over her head and spun it by the buckle like a lariat, in a huge wide beautiful circle. The tongue of the belt flicked a storybook doll — Margaret's doll but Elizabeth's room, no one's but her own. She awoke here every morning feeling amazed all over again that she had finally become a grownup. Where to go and when to sleep and what to do with the day were hers to decide — or not to decide, which was even better. She could leave here when she wanted or stay forever, fixing things. In this house everything she touched seemed to work out fine. Not like the old days.

When she descended the stairs, threading the belt through her jeans, she found Alvareen in the front hallway wiping the baseboards. 'I'm going to take care of that turkey now,' Elizabeth told her.

'That right?'

'*You* wouldn't like to do it, I don't guess.'

'Not me,' Alvareen sat back on her heels and refolded the dustcloth. 'Honest to truth, you think she could find the money somewhere to *buy* one. What you all have for supper last night?'

'Tuna fish on saltine crackers, open-face, topped with canned mushrooms.'

Alvareen rubbed her nose with the back of her hand, a sign she was amused. She loved to hear what was served up on her sick-days.

'For vegetables she spread oleo on celery sticks, with a line of green olives straight down the middle.'

'You making this up?'

'No.'

'Can't be *anyone* to cook as bad as that by accident,' said Alvareen. 'Must be she wants to discourage your appetite. She's tight with a dime.'

'Elizabeth?'

'Just going,' Elizabeth called up the stairs.

'I thought you'd have left by now.'

'Just on my way.'

She waved a hand at Alvareen and walked out the front door, crossing the veranda briskly but slowing as she reached the yard. There wasn't a person in sight, no one to offer to help. She dragged her feet all the way to the toolshed. When she opened the door the turkey rushed to the back of his crate with a scrabbling sound. Elizabeth squatted and peered inside. 'Chick, chick?' she said. He strutted back and forth within his three-step limit, his wattle bobbing up and down. Away from the light his wings lost their coppery sheen. He looked drab and shabby, his feathers a little ragged, like someone who had slept with his clothes on. 'Well, anyway,' Elizabeth said after a moment. She untwisted the wire that held the crate shut and reached in, carrying out a set of motions that she had rehearsed in her mind. One arm circled his body and pinned his wings down, the other clutched his legs. He struggled at first and then relaxed, and she straightened up with the turkey tight against her chest. 'You surely are a *big* buster,' she told him. There by the chopping block lay the axe, right outside the toolshed door, but it would take her a minute longer to get herself prepared. She set the turkey down. He was too fat to run far. He ambled out the door and down the hill, jerking his neck self-righteously with each step, while Elizabeth followed a few feet behind. She could still grab him up if he started running, but neither of them seemed in any hurry. They walked single file through the trellis, past the blackberry bush, under the rotting roof of the gazebo that showed squares of sky between its warped shingles. Then back again, toward the toolshed. That turkey had no sense at all. He circled the chopping block twice, and still Elizabeth let the axe stay where it was. He headed back through the trellis. They walked like two people filling time, sauntering with exaggerated carelessness, trying to look interested in the scenery. Then the turkey started speeding up. He didn't run, just took longer and longer steps, never losing his dignity. Elizabeth walked faster. Trees and shrubs and the second trellis skated past them, perfectly level. Then they reached the end of the yard and Elizabeth suddenly darted beyond the turkey and skidded down the bank into the alley, heading him off. A car screeched to a stop not two feet from her. The turkey became interested in something on the ground and stayed there, just at the edge of the bank, pecking unconcernedly.

The car was a dirty white sportscar. The driver was a round-faced blond boy wearing an Alpine hat with a feather in it. When he climbed out he bumped his head against the doorframe. 'I wish you would watch where you're going,' he said.

'Sorry,' said Elizabeth. She couldn't give him more than a glance because she had to keep her eyes on the turkey. Without looking around she reached toward a bush behind her, snapped off a switch, and started up the bank. 'Shoo, now, shoo!' she said.

'Out walking your turkey, I see,' said the boy.

'I'm getting up nerve to kill him.'

'I see. Are you Elizabeth? My name's Timothy

Emerson. I knew we were going to have a turkey dinner, but Mother never mentioned it was still on foot.'

'It may be *forever* on foot,' Elizabeth said. 'This whole business is harder than it looks.'

'Can I help?'

But he wore a plaid sports and wool slacks, much too good for killing turkeys in, and even the effort of climbing the bank after her had turned his face pink. 'Just stay where you are, keep him off the road,' Elizabeth told him. 'That's all I need.'

'I could run over him with my car if you like.'

She smiled, but her attention was still on the turkey. She gave a flick of her switch and the turkey moved away, slowly now, still examining the ground. 'What you need is a leash,' Timothy said.

'I can get him to the chopping block easily enough, but then what? I just hate to tell your mother I'm not equal to this.'

'Let him run off,' Timothy said. 'Buy one at the super-market. Mother'll never know.'

Elizabeth bent one ankle beneath her and sank down to the ground, still holding the switch. The turkey moved a few steps further off. 'Is it you that the unicycle in the basement belongs to?' she said.

'Me? Oh, no, that's Peter's. I was never one for exercise. I'm sure he wouldn't mind if you used it, though.'

'I was just hoping to *see* it used,' said Elizabeth. 'I'm not one for exercise either.'

'Really? I thought you would be.'

'How come?'

'I expected to see you out playing football with the little neighborhood boys,' Timothy said.

'What would I want to do that for?'

'Well, you are the handyman, aren't you?'

'Sure,' said Elizabeth, 'but that's got nothing to do with football. I wonder if other people have the same idea? I've been getting the strangest invitations lately. Tennis, bicycling, nature walks – if there's one thing I don't like it's nature, standing around admiring nature. I come home feeling empty-headed.'

'Why go, then? Look, your turkey is heading toward the

road again.'

The turkey was a good twenty feet off, but Elizabeth merely glanced at it and then settled herself more comfortably on the ground. 'I *always* go where I'm asked,' she said. 'It's a challenge: never turn down an invitation. Now, does Peter really know how to ride that unicycle? I mean, bump downstairs on it? Shoot basketballs from it, like they do in the circus?'

'Your *turkey!*'

Elizabeth looked around. The turkey was picking his way down the shallowest part of the bank, talking to himself deep in his throat. 'What about him?' she asked.

'Aren't you afraid he'll get away?'

'Oh, I thought I was going to give up on him and go buy one from the supermarket.'

Timothy stared at her. 'Well, I only said – you didn't seem – I never heard you make up your mind about it,' he said. So that Elizabeth, for the first time giving him her full attention, wondered why he wore such a jaunty feathered hat set at such a careless angle. He sounded like his mother, who was forever tying herself into knots over plans and judgements and decisions. But his eyes must have been his father's – narrow blue slits whose downward slant gave him a puzzled look – and she liked his hair, which stuck out in licked-looking yellow spikes beneath the hat. She smiled at him, ignoring the turkey.

'Are you really going to let him just walk off?' he said.

'Sure,' said Elizabeth, and did – rose and brushed off her dungarees, stood on the edge of the bank to watch the turkey cross the road at an angle and start up someone's back yard. Finally he was only a jerking coppery dot among the trees. 'Now I have to go to the grocery store,' she said. 'Anything you need?'

'Maybe I could take you there.'

'Oh, no, I like to drive. You could get your car off the road, though.'

'Or I might come with you. Is that all right? I'm always on the lookout for something to do while I'm home.'

He hadn't been home at all yet, but Elizabeth didn't bother reminding him. 'Fine,' was all she said, and she reached under her paint-shirt to pull, from her jacket pocket, a set of keys dangling from Mrs Emerson's lacy gold initial.

The car was a very old Mercedes with a standard shift that tended to stick and make grinding noises. Elizabeth was used to it. She drove absentmindedly, keeping the clutch halfway in and watching the scenery more than the road, but Timothy changed positions uneasily every time she shifted gears. He kept one hand tight on the dashboard, the other along the back of the seat. 'Have you been driving long?' he asked her. 'Since I was eleven,' Elizabeth said. 'I haven't had time to get a license yet, though.' She swerved neatly around an oncoming taxi. The roads here in the woods were so narrow that one car always had to draw aside when it met another, but Elizabeth made a game out of never actually coming to a full stop. She ducked in and out of parking spaces, raced other drivers to open sections of the road and then rolled easily toward their bumpers as they backed to let her by. 'I can see that I'm making you nervous,' she told Timothy, 'but I'm a better driver than you realize. I'm trying to save the brakes.'

'I'd rather you saved us,' Timothy said, but he loosened his grip on the dashboard. Then they hit Roland Avenue, and he settled back in his seat. 'I don't suppose you know if Andrew's coming,' he said.

'He's not.'

'I was afraid to ask Mother on the phone. She can go on and on about things like that. But Matthew will be there.'

'Nope.'

'What, no Matthew? He practically *lives* there.'

'He used to,' said Elizabeth. 'Then your mother said he was wasting his life on a dead-end job. Running a dinky country newspaper and getting all of the work but none of the credit. I don't know why.'

'The owner drinks,' Timothy said.

'She said for him to come back when he got a decent job. He never did. It's been three weeks now.'

'Matthew is the crazy one in the family,' Timothy said.

'Oh, I thought that was Andrew.'

'Well, him too. But Matthew is downright peculiar: I don't believe he hears a word Mother says to him. He visits

38

her every week, no matter *what* she's up to. Brings tomatoes he's grown himself, stays an hour or two.'

'Not any more he doesn't,' Elizabeth said. 'Will he get another job, do you think?'

'No.'

'Well, what then? Won't he ever come home again?'

'Oh, sooner or later Mother will give up. Then he'll wander in again and that'll be the end of it.'

'I doubt if he's crazy at all,' Elizabeth said.

She parked haphazardly in a space barely longer than the car, and they climbed out. Standing on the curb she peeled her paint-shirt off, shut it in the car, and brought a curling vinyl wallet from her jacket pocket. 'I wonder how much turkeys cost,' she said.

'Let me pay. It was my idea.'

'No, I have enough.'

'Aren't you saving up for college or something?'

'Not really,' Elizabeth said.

The grocery store was vast and gloomy, even under the fluorescent ice-cube trays that hung from the ceiling. There was a smell of damp wood, cardboard, cracker crumbs. They had barely stepped inside when someone said, 'Timothy Emerson!' – a sharp-edged woman in a fur stole, one of Mrs Emerson's tea guests. 'Don't tell me you're honoring your mother with a visit,' she said. 'Did she recognize you?' She flung out a little peal of laughter. Elizabeth slid past her and went over to the meat counter. 'I'd like a turkey,' she told the butcher. 'Kind of fat.'

'Fifteen pounds? Twenty?'

'I wouldn't know. Could you let me hold one?'

He disappeared into a back room. Mrs Emerson's friend could be heard all over the store. ' . . . never known a braver woman, just so sweet and brave. Disappointments never faze her. I said, "Pamela," I said, "why don't you sell that big old house and find yourself an apartment now that – " "Oh, no, my dear," she told me, "I'll need all that space for my children, if ever they choose to come home." '

The butcher reappeared, carrying three turkeys. 'This one?' he said. 'This one?' He held them up one by one, while Elizabeth frowned and twirled her car keys. 'Let me try that last one,' she said finally. She reached across the counter for it and weighed it in her hands. 'Wait a minute. I'll be back.'

'How is your twin brother, dear?' the friend was saying. 'I understand he's in the care of a doctor again. Now, wouldn't you think he should be in his own home? New York is no place for a, for someone who's . . . '

'Try this,' Elizabeth told Timothy. 'Add intestines and such. Feathers. Feet. Do you think he's about the right size?'

Timothy, who had lit a pipe, stuck the pipe between his teeth and took hold of the turkey. 'Feels okay to *me*,' he said.

Mrs Emerson's friend said, 'It's Elizabeth, isn't it? How are *you* this fine day? Planning for a great many dinner guests?'

'Well, not exactly,' Elizabeth said. 'Forget you saw me buying this.' She left the woman staring after her and went back to the butcher. 'I like it,' she told him, 'but I could do without that piece of metal in his tail.'

'That's to pin his legs down.'

'I'd prefer it without, anyway,' Elizabeth said.

While he was wrapping the turkey she went off in search of stuffing mix. Timothy by now was coasting down the aisle on the back of a shopping cart. He took several long strides and then hopped on the rear axle, leaning far forward to keep his balance. The pipe in his round face looked comical, like a snowman's corncob. 'This is something I've always wanted to do,' he told her when he had coasted to a stop. 'Mother never took us to grocery stores; she telephoned. Up until Margaret ran away with the delivery boy.'

'Telephoned!' Elizabeth said. 'Didn't it cost more that way?'

'Why not? We're rich.'

He wheeled the cart over to the meat counter, where they collected the turkey. Then Elizabeth went off to find snacks for Alvareen's sick-days. Timothy followed, pretending the turkey was a baby in a carriage. 'Who do you think he favors?' he asked, and he lovingly rearranged a patch of the butcher's tape. Then he hopped on the cart and coasted off again. 'I must find Mrs Hewlett,' he called back. 'She has such a consuming interest in little Emersons.' Periodically, in her trips down the aisles, Elizabeth caught sight of him. He whizzed past sober ladies and grim-faced clerks, a flash of yellow hair topped with a red feather. When she met him at the check-out counter he had parked the cart and was carrying a gigantic sack of dog food that hid his face and reached to his knees. All she saw were his hands clutching the sides of it. 'I know we don't have a dog,' he said, poking his head around the sack, 'but I can never resist a bargain, can you?' And he turned to put it back again, his knees buckling, staggering beneath its weight, all to make her smile.

But when they were back in the car his mood had changed completely. He sat hunched in his seat, staring out the side window and fiddling with his pipe but not smoking it. 'I'd have liked to find a turkey with a couple of feathers left,' Elizabeth told him. Timothy didn't answer. Then when they stopped for a light he said, 'Maybe we could just drive around for a while.'

'Where would you like to go?' said Elizabeth.

'I don't know. Nowhere. Home,' he said, and he slouched down in his seat and tapped his dead pipe on his knee all the rest of the ride.

Elizabeth parked in front of the house. The minute the car doors slammed Mrs Emerson appeared on the veranda, stepping forward and then back on the welcome mat with both hands clasped in front of her. 'Timothy!' she said. 'What are you – why – ?'

'My car is down back,' Timothy said. He climbed the steps and bent to kiss her on one cheek. Mrs Emerson's face was tilted up to him, her eyes half closed by the frown she wore, and she kept her hands pressed tightly together. 'I still don't understand,' she said.

'How are you, Mother?'

'Oh, just fine. I'm doing beautifully. I'm managing very well.'

'You *look* well.'

Elizabeth passed them and went into the house, carrying the groceries. As soon as she reached the kitchen she dumped the whole bag in one swoop, stripped the turkey of its wrappings and set it on the counter. Then she put the

41

other items away more slowly and folded the paper bag. Alvareen came in with a scrub pail full of gray water. 'Is that *him?*' she asked looking at the turkey.

'Pretty neat job, wouldn't you say?'

'Then what's that other feller doing, running around out back.'

'Oh, Lord.'

Elizabeth went out the kitchen door and found the turkey squatting by a basement window. 'Shoo!' she said, and clapped her hands. The turkey moved a few feet off before he stopped again. 'Shoo, boy! Shoo!'

Mrs Emerson appeared on the back porch, followed by Timothy. 'Now, how on earth – ' she said. 'I thought I told you to kill that thing.'

'I was just getting set to,' Elizabeth said.

'Then what did I see in the kitchen? What is that creature on the counter?'

Timothy handed his pipe to his mother and came down the porch steps. 'Drive him this way,' he told Elizabeth. 'I'll be here to grab him.'

'I would rather drive him off again.'

'Explain that, please,' Mrs Emerson said. 'I gave you a perfectly simple chore to do, one that Richard would have seen to in five minutes. The only thing in my life I ever won and you shoo him off like a common housefly. Then try to fool me with one from the butcher. That *is* what you did, isn't it? That's where you and Timothy came in from together, looking so smug?'

Because neither Elizabeth nor Timothy felt like answering, they concentrated on the turkey. They closed in on him tighter and tighter, although the last thing they wanted to do was catch him. The turkey did a little mumbling dance with himself, stiff-legged.

'I can't trust anyone,' Mrs Emerson said.

'Oh, Mother. What'd you ask her to do it for, anyway? She's too tender-hearted.'

'Too *what? Elizabeth?*' Mrs Emerson set the pipe down, in the exact center of the top porch step, and folded her arms against the cold. 'It isn't the turkey I mind, it's the deception,' she said. 'The two of you going off like that, laughing at me behind my back. Conspiring. That naked,

42

storebought-looking bird lying on my kitchen counter.'

Timothy had driven the turkey to a spot directly in front of Elizabeth, but Elizabeth made no move to catch him. She was watching Timothy, who was growing pinker and stonier but not answering back. He stood so close to her that she heard the angry little puff of his breath when his mother spoke to him.

'This was *your* idea, wasn't it. Elizabeth never did such a thing before. I always felt I could rely on her. Now I don't know, I just don't know. It isn't enough that you leave me all alone yourself, you have to drive everyone else off too. Isn't that it? Isn't that what you're hoping for?'

'Good God,' said Timothy, and then in one swift lunge he scooped up the turkey and carried it squawking and flapping to the toolshed. He took such long steps that Elizabeth had to run to keep up with him. It seemed that the whole upper half of his body had turned into beating, whirling, scattering feathers. When he reached the chopping block he jammed the turkey down on it and held it there. Then for a moment everything stopped. The turkey held still. His head lay limp on the block, his eyes seemed fixed on some inner thought.

'Timothy? Wait,' Mrs Emerson called.

Timothy reached for the axe without looking at it, hefted it in his hand to get a better grip and chopped the turkey's head off. It took one blow. The turkey's wings began flapping, but with doomed, slow beats that carried the body nowhere. The beady eyes stared at a disc of blood. Mrs Emerson cried, 'Oh!' – a single, splintering sound. Elizabeth said nothing. She stood at Timothy's side with her hands in her jacket pockets, staring out over the trees and pinning her mind on something far away from here.

3

Two weeks before Christmas there was a heavy snowfall. Timothy had a date with Elizabeth, and it took him nearly an hour to make the drive to his mother's house. Downtown was difficult enough, but once he reached Roland Park his was the only car on the road, laying new black tracks which wavered slightly if he traveled at more than a creeping pace. He hunched over the steering wheel and squinted through a fan of cleared glass while handfuls of soft snow floated soundlessly around him. His gloves were lost, his heater was broken, and he had forgotten to have his snow tyres put on. The only comfort was his radio – a news announcer telling him, over and over, that Baltimore was experiencing a heavy snowstorm and traffic conditions were hazardous. 'Exercise extreme caution,' he said. His voice was friendly and concerned. Timothy carried out a token pumping of his brakes, relieved that someone else had noticed these dreamlike puffs of white.

He had begun to have spells lately of worrying that he had died, and that everyone knew it but him.

The lights of the houses along the way were circled with bluish mist. Parked cars were being buried, quickly, and stealthily. 'If you don't have to drive, stay home,' the announcer said. 'Keep off the roads.' Timothy had no need to drive at all, and should have been safe in his own apartment, but he felt like seeing Elizabeth. He had started taking her out two and three times a week. They went to dinner or the movies, or sometimes they stayed home and played whooping, dashing games of chess, with Elizabeth making bizarre moves and sacrificing quantities of pieces whenever she grew bored. Timothy was more scientific about it. He knew all the famous matches by heart, and could solve any chess problem the newspapers offered him.

44

But Elizabeth had a psychological trick of swooping into his territory from some unexpected corner of the board, stunning him with the swift arc of her long arm, so that even when the invasion was harmless he was taken off guard and made some unlikely move to counter hers. Their games ended in giggles. Everything they did ended in giggles. He kept trying to get on some more serious footing with her, but every time they saw each other they went sailing off into some new piece of silliness. He caught it from her; laughter came shimmering off her like sparkles of water. His mother watched them with a puzzled, anxious smile.

The house was lit in every window, casting long yellow squares across the white lawn. He climbed out of the car and braced himself for a trip through the snow without boots, but before he took his first step Elizabeth rounded the house carrying a snow shovel. Sparks of white glinted on her cap, which seemed to be one of those fighter-pilot helmets with ear-flaps that little boys often wear. 'Halt!' she said, and raised her shovel like a rifle. Then she placed herself squarely in front of the steps, set the shovel down at a slant, and started running. A narrow black line followed her magically, pausing each time she was stopped short by the creases between sidewalk squares. The rasping sound brough Timothy's mother to an upstairs window – a silhouette against yellow lamplight. He laughed and waved at her. Then the blade of the shovel arrived at his shoe-tips and Elizabeth faced him, laughing too and out of breath. 'There,' she said, and turned to lead him up the black carpet she had laid for him.

They stamped their feet on the doormat. Elizabeth had on huge rubber boots with red-rimmed soles and flapping metal clasps; he had the feeling they were once his father's. The cuffs of her jeans were stuffed into them, and her jacket collar was turned up so that her hair, streaming from the helmet, fell half inside and half out in honey-colored tangles. Other girls could waft through his mind in chiffon, or silk, or at least ruffled shirtwaists, but not Elizabeth. Elizabeth forever wore that thick, shabby jacket, and wore it badly – hands deep in her pockets, waist hiked up in back, shoulder seams reaching halfway to her elbows and the zippered front bellying out below her chest. He thought of

45

the way she dressed as another joke played on him by the universe. If he was going to get so tied up with her, couldn't she have at least one romantic quality? Couldn't she smell like flowers, or be as light on her feet as a snowflake? But she smelled of wood shavings. When she stamped her boots, gleaming drops shot out to dampen his trousers all the way to the knees.

'We still going to the party?' she asked.

'If you want to. It's still on. But you didn't have to clear the walk for me, it'll only get snowed under again.'

'Oh, snow-shoveling's my favorite job,' she said.

So she would probably have done it anyway; it wasn't for him at all.

They stepped inside, into a blast of hot air. While Elizabeth bent to take her boots off Mrs Emerson came down the front stairs. She kept her head perfectly level, one hand weightless on the banister. 'Timothy darling, I can't imagine why you tried driving on a night like this,' she said. She came up to him and took one of his hands between her own, which were so warm they stang him. 'Mercy! Where are your gloves?' she said. 'Where are your boots?'

'I must've lost them.'

'You're surely not going out again. Are you? Stay here at home.'

'Well, there's this party I want to hit.'

'Fiddlesticks,' said his mother.

She drew him into the living room, skirt swirling as she turned. If anyone looked dressed for a party tonight, it was she. Surely not Elizabeth, who had taken off her jacket to expose a shirt that seemed to have mechanic's grease down the front. 'In a minute we'll have the fire built up,' Mrs Emerson said. 'Matthew's out getting more wood.'

'Oh, is Matthew here?'

'He got some time off.'

'From what? Did he change out of the dead-end job?'

His mother looked uncomfortable, but only for a minute. She picked up a poker and rearranged a pile of embers. 'No,' she said, 'but I had him come anyway. I hated to think of him out in that shack of his. He's going to be working over Christmas, did you ever hear of such a thing? Well, no one *else* there could get a paper out.'

'Are any of the others spending Christmas here?'

'Andrew is, but not for long. Just two days.' She put the poker in its stand and began pacing in front of the couch, where Elizabeth was sitting now to slide her moccasins back on. 'Mary will be with her in-laws. Margaret I haven't heard from yet. Melissa,' she said, and frowned briefly but then shook it off, 'is traveling with someone to Bermuda. It worries me *who*, I think I have some right to know these things, but in her last letter she ignored all my questions and she doesn't answer her telephone. Peter's going skiing with his roommate in Vermont.' She had ticked off the names on her fingers, like a hostess planning a dinner party. Now she looked over at Timothy, one last finger waiting to be tapped. '*You* will be here,' she said.

'I guess so.'

She settled herself in a wing chair. At the back of the house a door slammed, a log crashed to the floor and rolled with a splintery sound. Matthew appeared in the living room doorway with an armload of firewood. 'Hello, Timothy,' he said, and crossed the room to shake hands. He was trailing clumps of wet snow, and had to reach awkwardly around a stack of logs that rose to his chin. Depend on Matthew to find the hardest way to do anything. When he dumped the wood beside the fireplace, bark and dead leaves flew across the rug. More bark clung to the front of his jacket, which was a plaid logger's shirt whose sleeves did not cover his wristbones. No sleeves covered his wristbones. He was the longest, lankiest, knobbiest man Timothy had ever known. His face was bony and sad-looking, with clear-rimmed glasses forever slipping down his narrow nose. His straight black hair had last been cut months ago, probably by himself. If any jeans could be more faded than Elizabeth's, his were, and when he hunkered down to build the fire Timothy saw that his ankles were bare, red and damp-looking above soggy gray sneakers. 'Jeepers, Matthew,' he said. 'It makes me uncomfortable just *looking* at you.'

Matthew only smiled and went on laying logs in the fireplace. He worked so deliberately that the others fell silent. They were willing sparks not to fly, logs not to slide, kindling not to sift through the grate. That was what

Matthew's way of moving did to people. In a family full of noise and confusion and minor accidents, he was the quiet one. He touched everything as gently and awkwardly as if he had broken some precious object years ago that he would never forget; yet he had always been that way. The only fuss he caused was the irritation his family felt when they watched him hold his fork too cautiously, smooth down too kindly a rug he had just stumbled over, stack each stick of wood so meticulously with his long, bony fingers when he was laying a fire.

'Why don't you let Elizabeth do that?' Timothy asked.

'I didn't want her out in the snow.'

'How come? She was just now shoveling the walk.'

Matthew lowered a stick of wood that he had almost set in place. He looked over at Elizabeth.

'It's nice out there,' she told him.

He set the stick on the top of the pile. It fell off again.

'In a few days,' Mrs Emerson said, 'Elizabeth goes off to New York for her vacation. I tell her it's a mistake, especially if the snow sticks. I want her to spend Christmas with us.'

'Bus or train?' Timothy asked Elizabeth.

'Car,' she said.

'Car? You're driving?'

'A fellow named Miggs is. I got him off a bulletin board.'

'Elizabeth is so devoted to bulletin boards,' Mrs Emerson said. 'I never even knew they existed. She finds them everywhere – laundromats, thrift shops, university buildings. She always knows who is driving where and who has lost what and who is selling their old diamonds off.'

'In this weather a train would be safer,' Matthew said.

'I prefer cars,' said Elizabeth. 'They give you the feeling you can get off whenever you like.'

'But why would you want to get off?' Timothy asked.

'Oh, I wouldn't. I just like to know I can.'

Matthew said, 'Did this man Miggs show you any references?'

Timothy stopped lighting his pipe and looked at him.

'He's only a student,' said Elizabeth. 'He goes to Hopkins. On the phone he sounded very nice.'

The fire had caught. It blazed up, spitting as it reached

the snowy logs, and Matthew squatted back to watch it with his hands dangling between his knees. 'My, isn't that lovely,' Mrs Emerson said. 'Isn't this pleasant. Why would anyone want to go out on such a terrible night?'

She was cuddled between the wings of her chair, with the firelight turning her face pink and soft. Timothy imagined that a struggle was going on within her: Should she be rejoicing that he was coming by so much lately, or should she be worrying over his choice of dates? (Such a shambling sort of girl, not at all like the ones he usually went out with.) 'Aren't you going to stay longer?' Mrs Emerson would ask, and instead of his usual evasive answer Timothy could say, 'No, but I'll be back day after tomorrow. I'm taking your handyman to the movies' – choosing the word 'handyman' on purpose, gleefully watching the two different reactions tangling her smooth face. (The *handyman?* But he did have to come home, after all, to get her.) Whenever she saw them off at the door she would fuss over Elizabeth, offering to retie her scarf or lend her a lipstick, 'something to brighten your face just a little, a touch of color is always nice although of course you're looking very pretty as it is.' Then Timothy, in the midst of enjoying himself, would shoot a glance at Elizabeth and suddenly wonder: did she have to wear that wristwatch *everywhere*, with its huge luminous dial and its paint-spattered leather band? Even on a date? Even dressed up? He was split between wanting to defeat his mother's expectations and wanting to live up to them. He would rock on his heels, blank-faced, hoping for Elizabeth and his mother to settle things without him. 'Maybe next time you could borrow my curlers,' Mrs Emerson would say. 'A tidy hairdo is always nice for special occasions.' Elizabeth never seemed bothered by her. *Nothing* bothered Elizabeth; that was part of her charm. It was also very irritating. He sighed and looked over at her, where she sat on the couch peacefully curling the red cellophane strip from a cigarette pack. Matthew had taken the seat beside her. The two of them looked something alike, both scruffy and ragged and lost in their separate trances. 'We should be going,' Timothy said.

'Oh, is it time?'

'But it wouldn't hurt to put a dress on.'

49

Elizabeth shrugged and uncoiled from the couch. 'All right, back in a minute,' she said, and padded out of the room in her rundown moccasins. She left behind her a silence that spread and hardened, until Mrs Emerson came to herself and sat straighter in her chair.

'I was just thinking,' she said. 'This is the first Christmas we'll be spending without your father.'

'That's true,' said Timothy.

'He always did love Christmas so. Just like a child.'

'I remember he did.'

Matthew said nothing at all, although he was the one who had been closest to their father. Sometimes Timothy had trouble even picturing what their father had looked like. He was a forgettable man. He had come up from nothing, from nowhere, married a Roland Park debutante and made a fortune in real estate – a line of work so beneath notice that no one had ever thought of suggesting it for his sons, least of all Mr Emerson himself. Only strangers considered him important. 'At the settlement on our house,' Timothy had once heard someone say, 'things got so tangled I thought they never *would* straighten out. Fortunately I happen to know Billy Emerson personally. I just popped in his office and said "Billy – " ' as if Billy Emerson were a name worth dropping. That conversation had made Timothy stop and think. Was there something about his father that he had overlooked? Something he should reconsider? But his father's only talent, after all, was for making money. Money sprang up around whatever he touched, a fact that he seemed to take for granted. He never mentioned it, at least not to his family. 'Money is essential,' Mrs Emerson said, 'but not important.' Her children had no trouble understanding her.

'When you were all little,' Mrs Emerson said now, 'he used to take you to visit Santa Claus. Do you remember that? Urging you all to make lists beforehand, practically sitting in Santa's lap himself just to overhear what you asked for. And all of you so hard-headed you never believed in Santa for an instant, not a one of you. Remember, Matthew?'

But if Matthew remembered he didn't say so. He was slumped in one corner of the couch, examining the helmet

50

Elizabeth had left behind. He straightened the chin-strap, tucked the ear-flaps in, pulled them out again and then held the helmet up on the tip of a finger to frown at it.

'He would have had that yard lit up like the Fourth of July, if I hadn't begged him not to,' Mrs Emerson said. 'Always so fond of Randolph. Rudolph. The reindeer. I don't know why. And birthdays! How he loved birthdays!' She narrowed her eyes at Timothy, who shifted his weight uneasily. 'I don't suppose you remember what day it is tomorrow,' she said.

'It's my birthday,' said Timothy.

'It's your birthday. Andrew's and your birthday. Will you be spending it with us?'

'I don't think so, Mother.'

'*Andrew* likes birthdays.' She pulled off a ruby ring and twisted it in the firelight. 'He always sends me a dozen roses, thanking me for having him.'

'How do you know? Maybe he's congratulating you.'

'*You* would be.' She shoved the ring back on. 'I used to give you double birthday parties, remember that?'

'Yes,' said Timothy, and remembered Andrew, thin and frantic and overexcited, aiming a sputtery breath at his side of the cake, suffering even then from some jerkiness of mind which Timothy had feared a twin could catch like a cold.

'I sent him his presents in plenty of time,' said Mrs Emerson. 'How is school going, dear?'

For what *she* feared was that twins had to split a single share of intelligence between them – something she had read in a long-ago ladies' magazine and never forgotten, even after the twins had turned out to be the brightest of her children. Timothy had spent too long assuming she was right to be able to laugh it off. 'You asked me that *yesterday*,' he said.

'Oh, did I?'

'Do you imagine you should still be signing my report cards?'

'Timothy dear, I was only interested.'

'That's more than I am,' Timothy said. 'I think it's all a bore.'

'Oh, how can you *say* that? *Medical* school?'

'It's a bore.'

'Well, it was your decision, not mine. I was never the kind of mother to interfere in her children's lives.'

'Oh, Lord.'

'Now, let's just sit and enjoy the fire. Shall we? You've done a very good job with it, Matthew. I believe the last time you built a fire you left the flue shut.'

The last time Matthew had built a fire was when their father died, in June, and their mother kept insisting the house was cold. Oh, everything she said nowadays was attached to other things by long gluey strands, calling up other days, none of them good, touching off chords, opening doors. All he could do was tip his head back against his chair and sink into his own private tunnel while she pattered on.

'I'm ready,' Elizabeth said.

She had changed into a bulky wool dress that fit haphazardly, and nearly all of her hair was caught up by one flaking gilt barrette. Her nylons were wrinkled at the ankles and her squashed-looking black pumps curled at the toes. She swung her vinyl handbag like a waitress just getting off work. Mrs Emerson looked up at her and sighed, sharply. But Matthew gave Elizabeth a happy smile, and she stood in front of him smiling back until Timothy rose abruptly and took her hand. 'Come on, come on,' he said. 'We're late already.'

'Elizabeth, dear, your hair is falling down,' Mrs Emerson said.

They had a long drive ahead – past the city limits, out on a super highway filmed with slippery snow. Elizabeth had to keep clearing the mist off the inside of the windshield. When she wasn't doing that she was switching radio stations – from one song to the other, in the middle of a note, which was something Timothy rarely did himself. He felt an obligation to hear songs through to the end, even if he didn't like them. He also finished books that bored him, and had never in his life walked out on a movie. The fact that he and Elizabeth were so different, even on this small point, deepened the sense of uneasiness that had been growing in him all evening. Here they were out on a snowy road, probably driving to their deaths, and he didn't know anything about this girl. Everything he asked her was batted back at him, or turned into a joke. 'Elizabeth,' he said, 'why is it we never have a serious conversation?'

'Why should we? she asked.

'You never say anything you mean. Never talk about your family, or that place you're from — what's-its-name — '

'Ellington.'

'Ellington. Have you got something against it?'

'Oh, no. I like it,' said Elizabeth, and she smiled at a lone house swaddled with blue Christmas lights. Then she began tracing spirals on her window, and just when he thought the conversation had reached a dead end she said, 'I probably would be there still, if my father didn't get so het up about reincarnation.'

'About what?'

'He doesn't believe in reincarnation.'

'Well, who does?'

'I do,' said Elizabeth. Then she giggled and said, 'This week, anyhow.'

'You couldn't possibly,' Timothy said.

Elizabeth only sat back in her seat, tucking her hands in her sleeves for warmth.

'*Do* you?' he asked.

'Oh, well. It was one of those last-straw deals,' she told him. 'I was enough of a thorn in his side not being religious. Reincarnation was the end.'

'What do you want to go and believe in a thing like *that* for?' Timothy said.

'I just think it's a nice idea. You can stop getting so wrought up about things once you know it's not your last chance. Besides. It gives me something to say when old ladies tell me I shall pass this way but once. "Oh, well, or twice, or three times . . . " I tell them.'

'How far do you carry this business?' Timothy asked. 'Do you think you were once a high priestess in Egypt? Do you feel we knew each other in Atlantis?' He was hoping for her to give some crackpot answer, something that would disenchant him, but it wasn't that easy. 'Who knows?' was all she said. 'What would it matter, anyway?'

'You just thought this up to irk your father.'

53

'Well, maybe so,' she said cheerfully.

'And he wouldn't have started a fight over a little thing like that.'

'Of course he would. Besides, he didn't like this boy I was seeing.'

'Oh,' said Timothy. 'What was wrong with him?'

'He just considers me a trial. Always has. You can't really blame him.'

'No, I mean the boy.'

'Oh. Well, nothing, to the naked eye. He was just a State College student. Then he got arrested for robbing laundromats.'

Timothy swerved to avoid an abandoned car. 'You certainly know some funny people,' he said.

'Why do you say that?'

'Did he tell you what he was doing? Did you know?'

'Oh, no, just that he was working. I wondered what at.'

'You could have guessed, if he wouldn't say. I could have guessed. You could have been a little more curious, and maybe stopped him.'

'I would never change someone else's affairs around,' Elizabeth said.

That kept him silent for a full five minutes; he couldn't think of a thing to say. He concentrated on driving, which was growing more difficult. The road felt like cotton beneath his wheels. The few cars he met were barely creeping along, shapeless white igloos eerily glowing beneath a white sky. 'How can you see? I can't,' Elizabeth said, and Timothy said, 'I don't understand you. Fighting with your father! And here I thought you were Miss Easy-Going. Miss Fix-It. I wondered how your family was managing without you to patch the plaster.'

'At home I break things more than fix them,' said Elizabeth.

Then she rolled the window down with a jerk, which was unnecessary. Their breaths seemed likely to freeze in front of their faces. A new wave of mist fogged Timothy's vision and he hunched forward, peering for the turnoff. 'Can't see a thing,' he said, but he found it, anyway – an overhead sign swinging and whipping in the wind – and turned blindly.

'I thought they had snowplows up north,' Elizabeth said.

'Well, this burglar,' said Timothy. 'Are you supposed to be visiting him or anything? Waiting until he gets out?'

'Waiting for what?'

'Well, to get married, maybe.'

'He wasn't going to be in *that* long, it was only laundromats.'

'The reason I'm asking all this,' Timothy said carefully, 'is that you and I seem to be going out together a lot. I wanted to know if you were committed in any way.'

'Committed?'

'Not tied to this burglar or someone.'

'Why do you keep calling him a burglar?' Elizabeth said. 'He was a chemistry major. We hardly even knew each other.'

Timothy gave up. 'Would you like to go out to dinner tomorrow?' he asked.

'I can't. I'm going to see Matthew's house.'

'Matthew?' He turned to stare at her. 'How did *he* get into this?'

'Why not? I like him.'

So this was where all the uneasiness had been going: Matthew. 'Break it, can't you?' he said.

'No,' said Elizabeth. 'I want to see his house. Besides, I never turn down an invitation.'

'Do you *have* to keep *telling* me that?'

Then he slammed into the Schmidts' driveway and cut the engine and piled out. He didn't open the door for Elizabeth. She followed on her own, calmly swinging her handbag and shuffling up the narrow groove of cleared sidewalk. Timothy waited on the front porch with his back turned, ignoring her. She didn't seem to notice.

It was Ian Schmidt who opened the door – a classmate of Timothy's. He said, 'Oho! We thought you weren't coming. This is Elizabeth, isn't it? We met one night at a play.'

'That's right,' Elizabeth said.

He showed them into a living room papered with travel posters. Guests sat around in clumps, not yet at ease, and a small, square baby was being passed from lap to lap. 'That's Christopher Edward. Our son,' Ian said. 'Today's his six-month birthday.' He was so proud of that that he kept them standing in the doorway, fully wrapped and shedding snowflakes, while he scooped the baby up and brought him over. 'Say hello, Christopher, say hello.' The baby stared, poker-faced, at Elizabeth. She stared back. 'Hmm,' she said finally, and began tugging her boots off. Lisa Schmidt appeared to show her where to put her jacket. As they passed each group of guests she stopped for introductions, and Elizabeth nodded gravely once the names were said. The profile view of her, with her chin-strap dangling and her stiff, cold hands clutching her purse, sent a sudden stab of love through Timothy that left him feeling tired and puzzled. He bent toward the baby politely and let him clutch an index finger.

The party was a small one, only five couples. Others had been kept away by the storm. People sat on floor cushions and canvas butterfly chairs, with spaces between them that seemed reserved for absent guests. There were spaces in the conversation, too. When Elizabeth had returned from a back room, stripped off her jacket and helmet, a silence had fallen. Timothy still stood in the doorway with Ian, carrying his coat draped over his arm. He ignored Elizabeth (let her manage for herself, if she was so independent) and she settled right away beside a boy with a mustache. 'I rode down here with you last fall,' she said. 'You gave me a ride from Philadelphia, remember?'

The boy brightened; up till now he had been glumly snapping his watchband. 'Oh, Mike's friend!' he said. 'I didn't know you with your hair up. How is Mike?'

'Fine, I guess.'

'Did you find a job all right?'

'The very first day,' Elizabeth said. 'I miss Philadelphia, though.'

'Take it from me, there's nothing to miss about Philadelphia.'

'I thought there was. I might never have left, if they hadn't fired me.'

Timothy wanted to hear who had fired her, and for what, but now other people had pounced on the subject of Philadelphia. Conversation started darting around the room again, with Elizabeth at the center of it looking

56

perfectly comfortable. She didn't need Timothy at all. He went off to find a drink.

The Schmidts were serving hot mulled wine. They were on a budget. Timothy sniffed gloomily at the kettle on the kitchen stove, and then he filled two mugs. He would have preferred something stronger. He had what he thought of as the medical-student syndrome – overworking and over-drinking, alternately, studying all one night on Dexedrine and drinking all the next to rid his mind of that heavy feeling. Hot mulled wine wasn't much good for getting drunk on. Standing by the stove he drank one of the mugs straight down, refilled it, and went back to the living room. The boy with the mustache had returned to the subject of Mike. Whoever Mike was. 'If he would only put that Honda out to pasture,' he was saying. 'It's held together with paper clips. But you know Mike, he's too soft-hearted.' Timothy handed Elizabeth a mug and passed on by.

He went to sit beside a blond girl whose turn it was to hold the baby. He was trying to think of her name; she had come to cook him dinner twice last spring. Now she had been passed on to another medical student, and probably at the next party she would come with still another. She turned the baby to face him and said, 'Say hello, Chrissy, say hello.'

'He did, he did,' Timothy said. Jean, maybe. Or Betty. One of those plain names. She looked like half the girls he knew – feathered cap of hair, bright lipstick and blue eye-shadow, fine-boned figure that fit very tidily into a nurse's uniform. The other half of the girls he knew were from Roland Park, and their hair was smoother and hung gleaming to one side and they wore their clothes with a sloping, casual elegance. But they all had one thing in common: they treated Timothy like a teddy bear. They couldn't seem to take him seriously. Was it because of his round face, or the curling-up corners of his mouth? 'Show how you play patty-cake,' the girl told Christopher. 'Isn't he adorable?' Her tone was the same for Timothy as for the baby; it wasn't clear who she thought was adorable.

'I believe he's throwing up,' Timothy said.

'That's not throwing up, he's just spitting a little milk.

Tell him, Chrissy. Say, "Don't you know anything about *babies,* fellow?" '

What he really wanted (and thought of whenever one of these girls showed off with a baby or a frying pan) was to get married and settle down, have two or three children. He had been planning on that all his life, even when he was in the girl-hating stage and when, much later, he had turned into a Hollywood-style bachelor with an apartment full of dim lights and soft music always waiting on the record player. Only he seemed to keep choosing the wrong girls. Even Elizabeth was wrong, and look at him: still tagging after her, still mulling her over all day and half the night until he grew weary at the thought of her. Elizabeth took him no more seriously than any of the others did. She could have, once, maybe at the beginning. He thought she had been swayed by public opinion. He imagined his family and a whole string of girls drawing her aside, one by one, to say, 'You know that Timothy is a clown, of course. Always good for a laugh. Never really *feels* anything.' Now she was as gay and careless with him as if he were a brother. When he took her home after a date she gave him a companionable good-night kiss and slid out of his hands like water. When he said something important to her she ignored it, or dodged it, or laughed it off. Why did he keep on seeing her, anyway? She would make someone a terrible wife. She was too lackadaisical. There was something frustrating about her. Any plan involving Elizabeth was bound to fall to pieces in a stream of irrelevent side trips, senseless delays, wild goose chases. 'Why don't you get *organized?*' he had asked her once. 'What for?' she said.

What did she care?

He finished off his wine and let Lisa Schmidt ladle him another mugful. She was passing around the room barefoot with the steaming kettle. Jean or Betty, whoever she was, untangled her beads from the baby's fingers and said, 'How's your cute little gerbil, Timothy?'

'I got rid of him,' he said.

'Oh, why?'

'He was getting on my nerves.'

'Well, I wish you'd've told me. I thought he was adorable. Who'd you give him to?'

'I flushed him down the toilet.'

'Flushed – you didn't.'

He nodded.

'You didn't really.'

'Would I lie? Last I saw of him he was scrabbling with his little paws, trying to climb back out. Then *whoosh!* down he went.'

'If that's really true,' the girl said, 'and not something you just made up, I think you should be reported.'

'Probably hell on the plumbing,' said Timothy.

'You don't deserve another animal as long as you live. I hope they blacklist you at all the pet shops.'

'Now I have ants,' he said.

'That's all you're worthy of.'

'They come in a glass tray, you can watch them dig tunnels. After a while it gets boring, though. And even ants are a trouble. They're always asking for syrup, and every now and then a drop of water. You have no idea how silly it makes you look with the neighbors. "I'll be out of town a few days, could you water my ants?" '

'That cute little roly-poly gerbil,' the girl said. 'What's the matter with you? You must like to think you're funny. Well, you don't hear *me* laughing.'

'Oh, don't take it to heart,' Timothy said. 'I gave him to one of the intern's wives.'

She rested her chin on the baby's head and stared across the room, slit-eyed.

'Honest I did. He's much happier there. Got married and had a family.'

'I don't know which to believe,' she said, 'but I'd hate to see the inside of that head of yours. How could you even make up a thing like that? Scrabbling with his little hands?'

'I have a cruel streak,' Timothy said.

'Take another look. That's no streak, it's a yard wide.'

Then she rose to pass the baby on, as if she didn't trust Timothy too close to him.

Elizabeth and three other people had progressed to the subject of jobs, all the odd summer jobs they had held down. Someone had worked in a funeral parlor. Someone had made hairbrushes. Elizabeth, whom he had imagined coming directly here from home, turned out to have

59

wandered through various northern cities stuffing envelopes, proofreading text-books, and substituting for mailmen. And been fired from every one. She had sent out a thousand empty envelopes by mistake, let horrendous errors slip by her in the textbooks, and on the mail route (her favorite job) given everybody the wrong letters, consistently. How was that possible, when he had seen her keep track of a dozen tiny wheels and screws while dismantling and reassembling the kitchen clock? He thought of her with her family, breaking more things than she fixed. None of it fitted with what he saw of her here.

He stretched out on the floor with another mug of wine and imagined a federal law ordering everybody to switch parents at a certain age. Then butter-fingered Elizabeth, her family's cross, could come sustain his mother forever and mend all her possessions, and he could go south and live a happy thoughtless life assisting Reverend Abbott at Sunday vespers. There would be a gigantic migration of children across the country, all cutting the old tangled threads and picking up new ones when they found the right niche, free forever of other people's notions about them. He stared up at the ceiling with a blank smile while words buzzed over his head. His damp, stockinged feet were poked under a radiator. Elizabeth was next to him, and when the ceiling started whirling he turned to watch her hands clasped around her mug. His eyes became fixed on them. He sank into the grainy texture of her skin, he thought he could taste on his tongue the sharp, scraped knuckles. Who else would have hands in such terrible shape? There must be some special meaning to them. On her left wrist was a deep, slow-healing cut, running diagonally across the radial artery. She had done that in his presence. He had seen the knife flash too far along the grain of a carving, watched blood spurt instantly across the kitchen table. 'Find the pressure point. Here,' he had said, and wound a dishtowel around it and bundled her into his car. 'Keep it tight. Push down harder.' He had sped her to old Dr Felson's office, frantically honking his horn. The dishtowel grew bright red. Elizabeth pressed beneath it with sawdust-covered fingers and watched the scenery through her side window. 'What on earth?' she said once.

She was looking at a man and woman struggling beside a bus stop, the man flailing his fists and the woman taking swipes at him with her pocketbook. Timothy slammed on his brakes, cursed, and speeded up again. He hadn't known Elizabeth very well at the time. He had thought her unconcern was due to a misguided faith in medical students – people who could supposedly take charge of these things. Responsibility weighed on his head as if she had dumped it there. He was unable to tell her that for him, medicine was only so many words in a textbook; that humans were fragile, complicated networks encased in envelopes nearly as transparent as the diagrams made them out to be; that faced with blood, his stomach froze and his throat closed up and he wondered why his mother expected so much of him.

An image of his mother's house rose up, cupped in his own hands like the Allstate insurance ad.

Now Elizabeth was trying to convince some stranger that the length of a person's forearm was always exactly the length of his foot. 'It's a scientific fact,' she said (more earnestly than she had said anything else this evening, especially to him), and the boy said, 'That's ridiculous.' But he tried it, anyway – took off a shoe and knelt on the floor with his arm flat alongside his foot. All over the room, other people were trying it too. The place was turning into a contortionists' convention. Timothy felt like the lone human being in a jumble of machinery, intricate wheels and gears and sprockets, all churning busily. He closed his eyes and sank away, following green fluorescent threads that criss-crossed behind his lids.

Then Elizabeth was saying, 'Timothy? Wake up, it's time to go.' When he opened his eyes everyone was smiling down on him. He struggled to his feet, shaking his head, and let someone bundle him into his coat. The other guests were leaving too. The room had a ragged, broken look as they stood around in knots saying goodbye. Elizabeth led him over to Ian and Lisa, and then through the swamp of galoshes by the door. As she was pulling on her boots she said, 'You want me to drive?'

'Why? Do you think I'm not able? I'm stone cold sober.'

And he was, as soon as he hit fresh air. He stood on the sidewalk a moment, tilting his face into the falling snow while other people stepped around him and clapped him on the back and wished him good night. A headache started up and ran like a crack from one temple to the other, waking him fully. 'I have never in my life let a girl drive me home,' he said.

'Oh well, all right.'

The car was buried. Timothy dragged handfuls of snow off the front windshield while Elizabeth, who seemed unable to do the simplest thing in a routine way, drew vertical and horizontal lines across the rear window until it looked like a stretch of plaid. Then, 'Zzzip!' she said, and swooped off all the white squares in between and was settled in her seat by the time he had opened his door. 'I had a very good time,' she told him.

'Did you?'

He started the engine, and the wheels spun a moment before getting a grip. When he turned his head to back into the street he had a glimpse of Elizabeth peacefully chewing her chin-strap, unaware of the arrows of irritation he was sending her across the dark.

The snow was worse. Although the roads had been cleared, by now they were filling up again, and the soft flakes had grown smaller and faster. He inched along, screwing his face up with the effort of finding his way. When Elizabeth reached toward the radio button he said, 'Do you *mind?*' She settled back in her seat. She jingled a boot-clasp with her fingernail and hummed a program of her own.

Once inside the city limits he thought he could relax, but in Roland Park the roads were deep with snow and rutted so that his car kept wavering. The engine made whining, straining noises like a sewing machine. '*Freen, freen,*' said Elizabeth, imitating it. Ordinarily he would have answered with a sound effect of his own. That was one thing they had in common: an ability to fry like bacon, whine like mosquitos, jingle like his mother's bracelets, always fading into giggles while anyone around them looked baffled. It wasn't the kind of talent other people could appreciate. ('What's this?' Elizabeth had once asked, and then given a creak and said, 'A tree growing. Ever put your ear to a treetrunk?' And the two of them had collapsed against each other, laughing not at the treetrunk but at Mrs Emerson's bewildered face.) But now Timothy only scowled at a gust of white that slammed agianst the windshield. 'Who was that character you were talking to so long?' he asked.

'Bart Manning, his name was.'

'How come you know him?'

'He gave me a ride here. His mother'd just died; he worried all the way down because they put the wrong color eyes on her death certificate.'

She sometimes offered him these sudden jewels, tacked to the end of dull facts. He nearly smiled, but then he rubbed the windshield with his coat sleeve and said, 'Are you breaking that date with Matthew tomorrow?'

'No,' she said.

Nothing tacked to the end of *that*.

'Well, in that case, Elizabeth – '

'Turn toward the skid,' she told him.

But he couldn't. The car had started sliding in a slow, dreamy semicircle, and all he seemed able to do was hang on tight to the wheel. He had the sense of watching from far away, with only a passing interest, curious as to how this would all come out. When they stopped they were at right angles to the road. The nose of the car pointed into a bank. The headlights lit tall scrubby weeds growing from dimples in the snow.

'Looks like we get to walk off the wine,' Elizabeth said.

Walk? In this weather? It was easily a mile or more. He thought of the other possibilities – sit here hoping for a police car to pass, go wake one of those sleeping houses and phone his family or an all-night service station. But he was too tired suddenly to bother framing the words out loud. And while he was looking at the houses – all of them huge and silent beneath a glowing sky, drinking in snow and giving back not so much as a gleam of lamplight – he began to feel unreal. It seemed possible he would die here. With somebody foreign, not even related to him. It seemed possible he was already dead.

'Elizabeth,' he said, 'did you ever get the feeling you had just died?'

'In a *skid?*'

'Did you ever think you might be making all this up –

63

everyday life, the same as usual – and meanwhile your family had your body in a coffin and your funeral all arranged?'

Elizabeth seemed to need time to think that over. He watched her closely, as closely as his mother did when she was waiting for Elizabeth to solve all her problems. '*Did* you?' he asked.

'Oh, well, it must be the sign of a happy nature,' Elizabeth said.

'What? A what?'

'Must be, if you think heaven is just everyday life.'

'No, you don't – '

'And anyway, it's not such a bad idea,' she said. 'I never did think much of those streets of gold and pearly gates. Wouldn't you like to just go on like this forever? With something always about to happen and someone new always showing up? Oh, wouldn't that make dying all *right*? I prefer reincarnation myself, more chance of surprise, but there's not all that much difference.'

Then she turned up her jacket collar and climbed out of the car. After a moment Timothy followed. He was about to poke fun at her – 'Is *that* what you think? Is that how well you understand? Are *you* the one my mother is leaning on to patch her life together?' But something about the way she walked ahead of him, with her shoulders hunched against the cold and her shiny stockinged legs plowing awkwardly through the drifts, made him keep still. He caught up with her and trudged alongside, protecting her with his silence. The tight, closed line of his mouth was a gift to her; his hand, guiding her onto the curb, cradled her shoulder as gently as if she were some sad little glass figurine that he could break in an instant.

But at the first streetlight she stopped, bent to take one boot off, and handed it to him. 'It's for you,' she told him. 'Wear it and we'll be even.' He put it on. When they set off again their footsteps had a drunken, slaphappy rhythm – a shoe squashing, a boot flopping, another shoe squashing. Their shadows tilted from side to side, limping and draggled but comical, so that when Elizabeth pointed them out Timothy had to smile. Then he started laughing, and she joined in, and they walked the rest of the way strung out across the sidewalk holding hands stiff-armed, like tottering black paperdolls on a field of white.

4

1961

'No fats, no butter,' Mrs Emerson said. 'That I could stand for, I've always been a picky eater. I cut the fat off my meat as a matter of course. But no eggs, he said! Stop eating eggs! What will I do for breakfast?'

Elizabeth glanced in the rear-view mirror and watched Mrs Emerson straighten her hat, which was circled with spring flowers. They were returning from a heart specialist that old Dr Felson had recommended. Ordinarily Mrs Emerson drove herself, but today she must have been nervous over the appointment. She had risen at five-thirty, and collected her gloves and hat two hours ear y. Then at the last moment she had looked at the cloudless April sky and said, 'Will it rain, do you think? You'd better drive me, Elizabeth.' So Elizabeth had put on the chauffeur's cap, once black but now gray with mildew, which she had found on a rafter in the garage the month before. 'Oh, *must* you?' Mrs Emerson always said when she saw it. Elizabeth thought it was a wonderful cap. Whenever she wore it she made Mrs Emerson sit in back. If there had been a lap-robe she would have tucked it in; if it hadn't looked silly with jeans she would have liked a gold-buttoned jacket and driving gloves. Only Mrs Emerson would never have entered the spirit of it. 'Sometimes,' she said now, 'I feel you are making fun of me, Elizabeth. Did you have to stand at attention when I came back to the car? Did you have to click your heels when you shut my door?'

'I thought that was what I was *supposed* to do,' Elizabeth said.

'All you're supposed to do is be a help, and it would have helped much more if you'd come in with me as I asked. Taken off that silly hat and come been a comfort in the waiting room.'

'I tend to develop symptoms in waiting rooms,' Elizabeth said. She drove lazily, one arm resting on the hot metal frame of the open window. Her hair whipped around her neck in the breeze, and sometimes she had to reach up and steady her cap. 'Isn't it funny? If I go into a waiting room sick all my symptoms disappear. If I'm well it works the other way.'

'Thank goodness there were no *real* chauffeurs around,' said Mrs Emerson. 'I would have found you all playing poker, I'm sure. Discussing carburetors.' But she watched the scenery as she spoke, as if her mind were only half on what she was saying. During these last eight months, her life and Elizabeth's had come to fit together as neatly as puzzle pieces. Even the tone of their voices was habit now – Mrs Emerson's scolding, Elizabeth's flip and unperturbed. Outsiders wondered how they stood each other. But Mrs Emerson, as she talked, kept dexterously erect in spite of Elizabeth's peculiar driving, and Elizabeth went on smiling into the sunlight even when Mrs Emerson's voice grew creaky with complaints. 'How will I manage *breakfast* now?' Mrs Emerson asked.

'He say no eggs at all?'

'No more than two a week. A precautionary measure, he said. He kept comparing me to clocks and machines and worn-out cars, and the worst of it was that it all made sense. You keep *hearing* about the body being a machine, but have you ever given it any real thought? Here I am, just at the stage where if I were a car I'd be traded in. Repairs growing more expensive than my value. Things all breaking down at once, first that bursitis last winter and now my chest grabbing, only it's worse than with a machine. All my parts are sealed in, airtight. No replacements are possible.'

'That's true,' said Elizabeth.

She tried picturing Mrs Emerson as a machine. Sprung springs and stray bolts would be rattling around inside her. Her heart was a coiled metal band, about to pop loose with a twang. Why not? Everything else in that house had come apart. From the day that Elizabeth first climbed those porch steps, a born fumbler and crasher and dropper of precious objects, she had possessed miraculous repairing powers; and Mrs Emerson (who had maybe never broken a thing in her life, for all Elizabeth knew) had obligingly presented her with a faster and faster stream of disasters in need of her attention. First shutters and faucets and door-knobs; now human beings. A wrist dangled suddenly over her shoulder. 'See, how knobby?' Mrs Emerson said. 'Nobody ever *told* me to expect varicose *bones*.'

Elizabeth touched the wrist and returned it, unchanged.

'Could it be all those pregnancies?' said Mrs Emerson, sitting back. 'Eight of them, Elizabeth. One born dead. People are always asking if I'm Catholic, but the truth is I'm Episcopal and merely had a little trouble giving up the habit of a baby in the house. Could *that* harm my health?'

Elizabeth drove slowly, changing lanes in long arcs when the mood hit her. Buttery sunlight warmed her lap. The radio played something that reminded her of picnics.

'It doesn't seem just that I should be getting old,' Mrs Emerson said.

She removed her gloves and took a cigarette from a gold case – something she rarely did. Elizabeth, hearing the snap as she shut it, looked in the rear-view mirror. 'Oh, don't *frown* at me,' Mrs Emerson said.

'I wasn't.'

'I thought you were. The doctor told me not to smoke.'

'It's all right with *me* if you smoke.'

'I plan to stop, of course, but not till I get over this nervous feeling.' She flicked a gold lighter which sputtered and sparked and finally rose up in a four-inch flame that blackened half the cigarette. She took a puff, not inhaling, and held it an an awkward angle with her elbow tight against her side. 'What a beautiful day!' she said, just noticing. 'It's nice to be driven places.' And then, after a pause, she cleared her throat and said, 'I don't know if I ever mentioned this, Elizabeth, but I appreciate having you here.'

She had stepped far enough out of the pattern so that Elizabeth had to look at her again in the mirror. 'That's all right,' she said finally.

'No, I mean it. If I talked to my children this way they would get upset. Tell *them* I'm getting old, they'd feel forced to convince me I wasn't.'

'Oh, well, getting old is one of the things I'm looking forward to,' Elizabeth said. 'I'd like the insomnia.'

'The what?'

'The early-morning insomnia. I could have a lot more fun if I didn't sleep so much.'

'Oh,' said Mrs Emerson. She took half a puff from her cigarette. 'Now, a little worry wouldn't hurt the other children at all, but don't mention this new doctor to Andrew. He's subject to anxiety as it is. Sometimes he calls long distance asking if I'm sure I'm all right, wondering about things so specific you know they must have come to him in a dream, either waking or sleeping: have I had any falls recently? am I careful around blades? Well, nowadays we all know what *that* means, but even so, I don't want you giving him any grounds for concern.'

'I don't even know Andrew,' Elizabeth said.

'Yes, but this weekend he's coming for a visit.'

'No problem, then. I won't be here.'

'Oh, but you *have* to be here!' Mrs Emerson said.

'I'm going home.'

'What? Home?' Mrs Emerson fumbled her cigarette, dropped it, and caught it in mid-air. 'Not for *good,*' she said.

'No, I just promised my mother I'd visit.'

'Well, that's impossible,' said Mrs Emerson. 'I mean it. Impossible. I won't let you go.'

'I've put it off for months now. I can't do it again.'

'You'll have to.'

'I can't,' said Elizabeth, and she crammed her cap down tight on her head and began driving with both hands.

'You never asked *me* about this. I never heard a word.'

'My weekends are my own,' Elizabeth said.

'Oh, listen to you. You're as set in your ways as an old maid,' said Mrs Emerson. She ground out her cigarette and then braced herself as they zoomed away from a traffic light. 'I should have know better than to rely on you. You or *anyone.* I should have let Billy buy me a lingerie shop on Roland Avenue, sat there all day the way my friends are

68

doing, drinking gin and writing up the losses for income tax. *Much* too busy to see my children. Then they'd come home every week; just watch. They only take flight if you show any signs of caring.'

Elizabeth coasted past little Japanese trees that flowered pink and white on the grassy divide. She kept time in her head to faint music from the radio.

'This is all taking place because I mentioned something about appreciating you,' said Mrs Emerson. 'I am cursed with honesty. And where does it get me?'

'What would you want me for anyway?' Elizabeth asked. 'I've kept even with all my work.'

'No, you don't understand. I need a – Andrew and I manage better when there's a buffer, so to speak. Somebody neutral. His brothers are no help at all. Matthew is always in a daze, anyway, and Timothy just flies off somewhere. These two weeks he's having a run of tests, isn't that typical? I believe he arranged it that way, so that I'd be left alone with – oh, nothing that I say is what I mean. I *love* Andrew, sometimes I think I might love him best of all. And he's so much better now. He's not nearly so – he doesn't have that – nothing's really *wrong* with him, you know.'

Elizabeth peered into her side mirror.

'Why don't you say something?'

'Just trying to change lanes,' Elizabeth said, and she leaned out of the window. 'How come this mirror is at such a funny angle?'

'I can't put the visit off,' said Mrs Emerson, 'because he likes to come when things are in bloom. He's already missed most of it. I wonder why Timothy can't study at home? Talk to him, Elizabeth. Make him change his mind.'

'I'm against things like that,' Elizabeth said. 'What if I changed his mind and he stayed home and got run over by a truck? What if the house burned down?'

'What?' Mrs Emerson passed a hand across her forehead. 'I'm not in the mood for an outline of your philosophy, Elizabeth. I'm worried. Oh, wouldn't you think my children could be a little *happier?*' She waited, as if she really expected an answer. Then she said, 'I suppose you're going home with someone from a bulletin board.'

'Well, no.'

'You're taking the train?'

'I'm going with Matthew,' Elizabeth said.

'Matthew?'

'That's right.'

'Matthew *Emerson?*'

Elizabeth laughed.

'Well, I don't know all the Matthews you might know,' Mrs Emerson said. 'I don't understand. What would Matthew be going to North Carolina for?'

'To take me home.'

'You mean he's going especially for you?'

'I invited him.'

'Oh. You're taking him to meet your family.'

'Yes,' said Elizabeth, and flicked her turn signal.

'Does that have any significance?'

'No.'

'This is so confusing,' Mrs Emerson said.

Which made Elizabeth laugh again. The spring air gave her a light-headed feeling, and she was enjoying the drive and the thought of taking a trip with Matthew. She didn't care where the trip was to. But Mrs Emerson, who misinterpreted the laugh, sat straighter in her seat.

'I *am* his mother,' she said.

'Well, yes.'

'I believe I have some right to know these things.'

Elizabeth braked at a stop sign.

'That would explain Timothy's strange mood,' Mrs Emerson said.

'He doesn't know about it yet.'

'Well, what are you doing? Are you playing off one brother against another? Lately you've seen so much of Matthew, but you still go out with Timothy. Why is that?'

'Timothy invites me,' Elizabeth said.

'If you tell me again that you accept all invitations, I'm going to scream.'

'All right.'

'I didn't want to mention this, Elizabeth, because it's certainly none of my business, but lately I've worried that people might think there's something *easy* about you. You can never be too careful of your reputation. Out at all

70

hours, dressed any way, with any poor soul who happens along – and I can't help noticing how Timothy always seems to have his hand at the back of your neck whenever he's with you. That gives me such a *queasy* feeling. There's something so – and now Matthew! Taking Matthew home to your parents! Are you thinking of marrying him?'

'He never asked,' Elizabeth said.

'Don't tell me you accept all invitations to marry, too.'

'No,' said Elizabeth. She wasn't laughing any more. She drove with her hands low on the wheel, white at the knuckles.

'Then why are you taking him home?'

Elizabeth turned sharply into the garage, flinging Mrs Emerson sideways.

'Elizabeth?'

'I *said* it had no *significance,*' Elizabeth said.

Then she cut the motor and slammed out of the car. She didn't open the door for Mrs Emerson. She snatched her cap off her head and threw it in a high arc, landing it accidentally on the same rafter where she had found it. Was that how it got there in the first place? She stopped and stared up at the rafter, bemused. Behind her Mrs Emerson's door opened and closed again, hesitantly, not quite latching.

'Elizabeth?' Mrs Emerson said.

Elizabeth turned and went out the side door, with Mrs Emerson close behind.

'Elizabeth, in a way I think of you as another daughter.'

'I'm already somebody's daughter,' Elizabeth said. 'Once is enough.'

'Yes. I didn't mean – I meant that I feel the same *concern*, you see. I only want you to be happy. I hate to see you wasting yourself. I mentioned what I did for your own good, don't you know that?'

Elizabeth didn't answer. She was climbing the hill so fast that Mrs Emerson had to run to keep up with her. '*Please* slow down,' Mrs Emerson said. 'This isn't good for my chest. If you must play chauffeur, couldn't you have dropped me at the front door?'

'Oh, is that what they do?'

'It's just that you seem so – aimless. You don't make any

distinctions in your life. How do I know that you won't go wandering off with someone tomorrow and leave me to cope on my own?'

'You don't,' said Elizabeth. But she had slowed down by now, and when they reached the back door she held it open for Mrs Emerson before she entered herself.

It was one of Alvareen's sick-days, and she had left the kitchen a clutter of dirty dishes and garbage bags that they had to pick their way through gingerly. Then when they reached the front hall they heard someone upstairs. Slow footsteps crossed a room above them. Mrs Emerson clutched Elizabeth's arm and said, 'Did you hear that?'

'Someone upstairs,' Elizabeth said.

'Well, do you – should we – could you find out who it *is*?'

Elizabeth tilted her head back. 'Who is it?' she shouted.

'*I* could have done *that*,' Mrs Emerson said.

Then Timothy appeared in the upstairs hall, stuffing something into his suit pocket. 'Hi there,' he said.

'Timothy!' said his mother. 'What are you doing here?'

'I was in my room.'

'We thought you were a burglar. Well, it's fortunate you've come, I have a favor to ask you.'

She climbed the stairs with both hands to her hat, removing it as levelly as if it were full of water. 'Now, about this weekend – ' she said.

'I thought we'd been through all that.'

'Will you let me finish? Come with me while I put my things up.'

Mrs Emerson crossed the hall and entered her bedroom, but Timothy stayed where he was. When Elizabeth reached the top of the stairs he opened his mouth, as if he were about to tell her something. Then his mother said, 'Timothy?' He gave one helpless flap of his arms and followed his mother.

Elizabeth went into her own room. She was fitting together a rocking horse that had arrived unassembled, a present for Mrs Emerson's grandchild. He might be visiting in July. 'Fix it up and put it in Mary's room,' Mrs Emerson had said. 'I plan to be a grandmother well-stocked with toys, so that he looks forward to coming. In time maybe he can visit alone, they say it's quite simple by air. You tag the child like luggage and tip the stewardess.' The rocking horse had been packed with the wrong number of everything – too many screws, too many springs, not enough nuts. Elizabeth had spread it on the floor of her room, and now she sat down on the rug to look at the diagram. Across the hall, behind a closed door, Mrs Emerson murmured endlessly on. When the words were unintelligible she always sounded as if she were reading aloud. It was the positive way in which she put things, without breaks or fumbles. From time to time Timothy's voice rode over hers, but it never slowed her down.

Elizabeth emptied out a mayonnaise jar full of stray nuts from the basement. She picked up one after another, trying to fit them to the extra screws. 'Now, this for this one,' she said under her breath. 'This for this. No.'

'I already *told* you – ' Timothy said.

Mrs Emerson went on murmuring.

'Don't you ever take no for an answer?'

Elizabeth shoved the nuts aside and went back to the diagram. She already knew it by heart, but there was something steady and comforting about printed instructions. 'First assemble all parts, leaving screws loose. Do not tighten screws until entire toy has been assembled.' The author's voice was absolutely definite. Timothy's was frazzled at the ends. What was she doing here, still in Baltimore? She should have left long ago. She awoke almost nightly to hear the tape-recorder voice – 'Why don't you write? It's not that I care for my own sake, I just think you'd wonder if I were dead or alive' – and she lay in bed raging at Mrs Emerson and her children too, all those imagined ears putting up with such a loss of dignity. She kept promising herself she would leave. But never see Matthew again? Never play chess with Timothy? Lose the one person who leaned on her and go back to being a bumbler? She set a deadline: at the first mistake, the first putty knife through a windowpane, she would move on. *That* shouldn't take long. But her magic continued to hold. What she couldn't solve the hardware man down on Wyndhurst could, and there was always *The Complete Home Repairman* in her bureau drawer. All she had to do was

73

disappear for a moment and refer to it, like a doctor keeping his patient waiting while he thumbed through textbooks in some hidden room. At this rate she would stay here forever. And always knowing, to the end of her days, that she should be out in the world again.

'You mistake the kind of twins we are,' Timothy said. 'Did you think we were Siamese?'

'Fit tab A into slot B, making sure that . . .'

'We're not even identical. Not even close to identical. We were an accident of *birth!*'

Elizabeth sighed and dropped the diagram. She rose to circle her room, twice, and then she padded out the door and down the stairs. In the kitchen, where she had meant to stop for milk, the clutter seemed like an extension of the argument above. She went through without slowing and continued on down to the basement. There everything was dim and silent, flickering like a pool of water in the sunlight that sifted through dusty windows. Dark, battered doors closed off the old servants' rooms, with transoms above them that reminded her of school corridors and church fellowship halls. In the central part were tangled metal cast-offs, bicycles, a workbench, hunks of monster household appliances. There was a cabinet door laid across the zinc laundry tubs, with two huge canning kettles on top of it. Elizabeth and Matthew were making wine together. They had split the cost of the ingredients and shared the work, but it was up to Elizabeth to stir up the dregs once a day. She took a long-handled spoon from a nail, rolled the cheesecloth off the first kettle and dipped the spoon deep inside. A yeasty, spicy smell rose up, with bubbles that churned and snapped in a film across the surface.

'Where will we get the grapes?' Matthew had asked, and Elizabeth said, 'Oh, grape wine we can *buy*. Just look in this recipe book – tomato wine, dandelion wine. Let's make something different. Is there such a thing as mushroom wine?' And she had laughed at his expression. He was slow, thorough, too serious; she provided the lightness for him. What answering glimmers she found in him she nourished along, and then he would surprise her by laughing too and losing that dark, baffled look on his face. He was the only Emerson she knew of who was short of

74

money. She seized on that as a base for all the flights she took him on – painting, wine-making, installing a shower in his cracked old bathtub. Once they mixed up a week's supply of something called sludge that they found in a cookbook for the poverty-stricken. With Timothy it would have ended in silliness; sludge might have been rolled into balls and flung all over the kitchen. Well, that was fun too, of course. But Matthew enjoyed it in his own way, following a plan systematically with that knotted gaze he turned on everything, giving his slow smile when it was done.

They had made a batch of orange wine and another of wheat. They had chopped oranges, lemons and raisins endlessly, baked wheat on cookie sheets in the oven until a musty golden smell filled the kitchen, all while Mrs Emerson was out at a meeting. (She might not take to having a brewery in her basement, and they had never bothered about a government permit. Matthew was all for sending off for one but Elizabeth was too impatient to begin.) They had lugged the kettles down the stairs and filled them with buckets of water and sacks of sugar. 'It may turn out too sweet,' Matthew said gravely. 'It may,' said Elizabeth. They never talked much. When he found she was planning a visit home he said, 'I'll miss you,' and Elizabeth, instead of answering as she would to someone else ('*Miss* me, what for? I'm only going for the weekend'), said, 'I'll miss you too. Want to come with me?' 'That would be better,' he said, 'and you won't have to ride with strangers.' He was forever protecting her, but not in that fretful way that wore on her nerves. He lent her his rain-hat, and scooped her hair out of the way when she shrugged herself into her jacket. On walks through the woods to his house he would let her go single-file, unhampered by hand-holding or the troublesome etiquette of briars held back for her and roots pointed out; but once inside, in a living room splintery with cold, he might come up behind her to stand motionless and silent, his arms folded around her and his chin resting on her head, warming the length of her back.

'Any time the basement door is open there's the strangest smell coming up,' Mrs Emerson once said. 'Have you noticed?' She thought it was a new kind of detergent Alvareen was putting in the washing machine. Elizabeth

75

never told her anything different.

She twirled the spoon dreamily, resting her head against a shelf, listening to the fizz of the bubbles. Up in one corner a spider spun a web between two waterpipes, but the strands looked like another slant of sunlight. Leaves that had sifted through the grate rustled in the window-well, as dry and distant as all the past autumns that had dropped them there.

Footsteps crossed the kitchen. 'Elizabeth?' Timothy called.

'Down here.'

He came to the doorway above the basement steps; she saw the darkening of the patch of light on the floor. Then he snapped a switch on, paling the sunbeams. 'Where?' he said.

'Here by the tubs.'

While he descended the stairs she uncovered the second kettle and began stirring it. It had a burned, toasty smell. She was afraid they might have overbaked the wheat. She lowered her head and breathed deeply, inches from the wine. 'Ah,' said Timothy. 'Eye of newt. Toe of frog.' But the scene upstairs must still be hanging over him; his voice was as heavy as the hand he laid on her shoulder. 'What *is* it, anyway?' he asked.

'Just wine.'

'You handymen certainly have some odd chores.' He moved toward the window, and peered up at the spider in its web. 'I came to see if you wanted to take a drive. Have lunch at my place or something.' He poked at the web and the spider scuttled higher, a fat brown ball with wheeling legs. 'Are you scared of spiders?'

'Nope.'

He turned away, hands back in his pockets. 'I hear you're going home,' he said.

'That's right.'

'But just for the weekend.'

'That's right.'

Elizabeth straightened up. She hung the spoon on its nail, pulled the cheesecloth back over the kettles and knotted the strings that held it there. When she turned to go, she found Timothy just taking something from one pocket: a pistol, bluish-black and filmed with grease. 'What

76

on *earth*,' she said. He shifted it in his hands, as carelessly as if it were a toy.

'Evil-looking, isn't it?' he said. 'I found it in Andrew's room.'

'Is it real?'

'Well, probably. How can you tell? I would break it open but I'm scared of the thing.'

'Put it down, then,' Elizabeth said. 'Stop tossing it around like that, will you?'

'Me? Two-Gun Tim?' He set his feet apart like someone in a western, one thumb hooked in the pocket of his slacks, and tried to whirl the pistol by its loop but failed. When it dropped they both sprang away and stared at it, as if it might explode spontaneously. Nothing happened. Timothy bent to pick it up, holding it this time by the barrel, firmly, the way his mother must have taught him to hold scissors. 'Ah, well,' he said.

'What would Andrew want with a gun?'

'He collects them.'

'Well, that's a very silly hobby,' said Elizabeth, and she led the way to the stairs, making sure to keep out of the pistol's aim.

'Oh, I don't mean *collects*. I don't mean as a hobby. I mean he collects them like a boat collects barnacles; they flock to him. What are you laughing at? I'm serious. When Andrew takes a walk he finds guns under bushes, when he goes to the attic he stumbles over them, when he answers the doorbell it's a mailman with the wrong package, and what's in the package? Guess. He's never bought a gun in his life, he wouldn't think of it. He's the gentlest soul you can imagine. He spends all his days in the New York Public Library doing research for professors, but when he comes out to go home what does he find in the litter basket? A gun among the orange peels, handle up. It's crazy.'

'He wouldn't have to *accept* them,' Elizabeth said.

'Why not? It's fate.'

'Then what does he do with them?'

'Oh, stows them away.'

They were in the kitchen now. Timothy had forgotten all his caution; he dropped the gun in his pocket, carelessly, and then gave the pocket a pat. 'We don't mention this to

77

Mother, you understand,' he said. 'I come pistol-hunting before every visit, just to be on the safe side. Not that he would *do* anything. I don't want you thinking – oh, there *was* a sort of accident once, someone got shot through the foot. But you're an outsider here. You don't know what Andrew's really like. He felt terrible about it. He was just –'

'Oh, stop, I'm not interested,' Elizabeth said, although up till then she had been. She had the sudden feeling that troubles were being piled in front of her, huge untidy heaps laid at her feet, Emersons stepping back waiting for her to exclaim over the heaps and admire them. She headed out the back door, toward the toolshed. Timothy followed. When he came up beside her she saw that one of his pockets hung heavier than the other. She thought of an old Sunday comic strip: Dick Tracy's crimestopper's textbook, warning against men with lopsided overcoats. 'You be careful you don't get yourself arrested,' she told him. Then she reached inside the toolshed for a hoop of hose, closing the subject.

But Timothy said, 'The worst is getting rid of the damn things. You'd never believe how hard it is. The last one I sent out with the garbage, under the coffee grounds. Elizabeth?'

'What,' said Elizabeth. She backed across the lawn, feeding out coils of hose.

'I cheated on a test.'

Another trouble, added to the heap. 'Did you?' she said.

'This is serious, Elizabeth.'

'Well, why tell *me* about it?' she said. 'It's always something. Tomorrow it'll be something else. Go tell a professor, if it bothers you so much.'

'I can't,' Timothy said. 'I've already been caught.'

Elizabeth looked over at him.

'I was just walking past his desk, after it was over. He said, "Emerson, I'd like to have a word with you," and I knew, right then. I knew what he would say. It felt as if my stomach had dropped out.'

'What will happen?' Elizabeth said.

'I'll be expelled.'

'Well, maybe not.'

'Of course I will. Those guys are tough as nails. And you

78

know something? I knew that answer I cheated on. I didn't have a shadow of doubt about it. I wrote it down, and I turned to my left, and I read off the other guy's answer just as cool as you please. It was like I forgot where I was, suddenly. I forgot the customs of the country. I just wanted to see if Joe Barrett knew the answer too.'

'Maybe if you told them that,' Elizabeth said.

'Not a chance. It wouldn't help.' He kicked at the hose. 'Come on, will you? It's getting to be lunchtime.'

'The grass is drying up. If I don't – '

'Look,' said Timothy. 'I've been walking around by myself ever since this happened. Can't you just drop everything and come with me?'

'Oh, well. All right. Let me go and tell your mother.'

'Call from my place. Don't go back in, she already knows something is wrong. Oh Lord, this is going to kill her.'

'I doubt it,' said Elizabeth.

But she didn't go back in, even so.

Timothy's apartment was downtown, in a dingy building with a wrought-iron elevator. All the way up to his floor, with the cables creaking and jerking above them, Timothy stood in the corner staring at his shoes. His face reflected the bluish light, giving him a pale, sweaty look. His silence was heavy and brooding. But once they entered his apartment, where tall windows let the sun in, he seemed to change. *'Well* now,' he said. 'What shall we eat?' And he went off to the little Pullman kitchen while Elizabeth settled herself on the couch. His apartment had a smothered look. It was curtained, carpeted, and upholstered until there were no sharp corners left, and in the evenings carefully arranged lamps threw soft, closed circles on the tabletops. Elizabeth felt out of place in it. She shucked off her moccasins and curled her legs beneath her, but everything she looked at was so padded and textured that she couldn't keep her eyes on it long. Finally she closed them, and tipped her head back against the couch.

'Here,' said Timothy. 'Corned beef on rye. All right?'

'Well, thanks,' said Elizabeth, sitting up. She took the plate and peered between the slices of bread. 'Corned beef is what we had two weeks ago. Is this the selfsame can?'

79

'I don't know.'

'Can you get food-poisoning from canned corned beef?'

But Timothy, in a chair opposite her with his sandwich halfway to his mouth, stared into space.

'Timothy.'

'What.'

'Look, it's not so bad. Find something else to do.'

'Like what, for instance,' he said.

'Well, *I* can't tell you that.'

'Why not? Say *something* can't you? Give me a treatise on reincarnation, convince me I'm full of lives and can afford to throw one away. Convince my mother too, while you're at it.'

'Well, it is a point,' Elizabeth said.

'Ha.' He took a swig from his beer can. 'Women have it easy,' he said. 'You can work or not, nobody minds. Men are expected to be responsible. There's no room for variation.'

'Maybe you should make a *big* switch. Lumberjack? Fur-trapper? Deck-swabber?'

'I could answer one of those DRAW ME ads on the matchbooks,' Timothy said. He laughed.

'You could be a state hog inspector.'

But then he leaned forward, his elbows on his knees, his sandwich still untasted. 'I can't seem to picture a future any more,' he told her. 'There's nothing I hope for. No one I want to be. Yet I started out so promising, would you believe it? In grade school they thought I was a genius. No one but Andrew even knew what I was talking about. I invented weird gadgets, I played chess tournaments, I monitored Stravinsky on an oscilloscope that I rebuilt myself. Did you know that?'

'No,' said Elizabeth. 'I don't even know what an oscilloscope is.'

'Why is everything you say so *inconsequential?* Can't you understand when something serious is going on?'

But it was hard to take him seriously when he looked so much like the child he had been talking about. There was one of him in every classroom Elizabeth had ever sat in – chubby and too clever, pale and scowling, wearing an old man's suit and cracking elderly jokes that made his classmates uneasy. She could picture him scuffing around the playground with his hands in his pockets while the others chose up softball teams; his name would come up by default, at the end, and he would play miserably and dodge the ball when it crossed the plate and then hit some pathetic, ticked-off foul and fling his bat in a panic and run toward first base anyway, hunched and desperate, until the hoots and curses called him back. 'Oh, aren't you glad you're not still *there?*' she asked suddenly, for in spite of the traces of that child on his face he had at least grown into his suit, and his friends had grown into his jokes. He had passed the age for softball and learned when not to sling long words around. But Timothy, off on some track of his own, merely blinked.

'Elizabeth,' he said. 'Don't go home this weekend. Let's take a trip together.'

'Oh, well, no.'

'We could start off for anywhere! Drive without a plan. Stop when we felt like it.' He paused, having just then heard her answer. 'What's the matter with you? You love sudden trips. Are you worried what people might think?'

'I just –'

'I never thought you would be, somehow.' He looked down at his sandwich, and began tearing pieces out of it and dropping them on his plate. 'We would have separate rooms, of course,' he said.

'No, you see –'

'If *that's* what's bothering you.'

'No.'

The sandwich had turned into a pile of shreds. 'Maybe you think – we wouldn't *have* to have separate rooms,' he said. 'I just meant – I don't know what you expect of me. What do you want, anyway? What am I supposed to be doing? Just tell me, can't you? I don't know why I should be making such a mess of saying this.'

'Oh, well, that's all right,' Elizabeth said helplessly. What she wanted to say was, 'Of *course* I'll come.' When would she learn not to plan ahead, when always at the last minute she felt tugged by something different? 'I'm sorry,' she said. 'I really would like to.'

'Or take me home with you.'

'I don't think I can.'

'Why not? If you want I could stay in a hotel, I wouldn't be bothering your family then. Would that be better?'

'You see, Matthew is coming,' Elizabeth said.

He stared at her.

'I invited him.'

'But why *Matthew?* Why does he always keep popping up like this?'

'I like him,' she said. And she decided she'd better go on with what she had planned to tell him earlier: 'While we're on Matthew, Timothy, I thought I should say something about –'

'You are going to turn into a very objectionable old lady, Elizabeth. You know that. The opinionated kind. "I like this, I don't like that," every other sentence – it's fine now, but wait a while. See how it sits on people when you've lost your looks and you're *croaking* it out.'

'That is something to think about,' said Elizabeth, glad to change the subject.

'Call up Matthew. Tell him *I'm* the one that *needs* to go.'

'Timothy, I've been up since six o'clock this morning and every single minute there's been some Emerson dumping crisises on me.'

'Crises,' Timothy said into his beer can.

'Picking and bickering and arguing. Raking up all these disasters and piling them in front of me. Well, I've had my quota. I don't want any more. I'm going to call your mother, and then I'm going off for an afternoon on my own and not coming back till supper.'

'Wait, Elizabeth –'

But she left. She went into the bedroom, sat down on the edge of the bed, and lifted the telephone from the table. Then she couldn't remember Mrs Emerson's number. All this chaos was disrupting her mind. There were tatters of old arguments in the air around her, and she had a restless, hanging-back feeling as if there were something she had not done well. She listened to the dial tone droning in her ear and watched Timothy pace back and forth in the living room with his eyes averted, his face pink and rumpled-looking. Then Mrs Emerson's number flashed before her, and she leaned forward to dial.

The telephone rang four times. (Was Mrs Emerson in some new frenzy, twirling through the house wringing her hands and far too upset to answer?) The fifth ring was cut off in the middle. 'Hello!' Mrs Emerson said.

'It's Elizabeth.'

'Elizabeth, where are you? There's a man here delivering big sacks of something.'

'Oh, that'll be the lime.'

'What will I do with it. Where will I tell him to put it? I thought you were around the house somewhere.'

'The lime goes in the toolshed,' Elizabeth said. 'I'm at lunch. I may be late getting back, I'm spending the afternoon downtown.'

'Downtown? What – and I can't find Timothy. One minute he was here and the – now, don't take *all* afternoon, Elizabeth.'

'Okay,' Elizabeth said. 'Bye.'

She hung up. Timothy was leaning against the doorframe, watching her. 'Now call Matthew,' he said.

'I'm through with that subject.'

'That's what *you* think.'

He took a step back and slammed the door between them, with a noise that shook the room. She heard the key in the lock. '*Call* him!' he shouted from the other side.

'Oh, for –'

She stood up and went to try the door. It was firmly locked. Timothy was standing so close behind it that she heard his breath, which came in short puffs. '*Timothy,*' she said. He didn't answer. She gave the door a kick and then turned an oval knob at eye level that locked it from inside – a useless move, but the final-sounding click was a satisfaction. Then she flung herself on the bed again and lay back to stare at the ceiling.

When she had been there a few minutes she began to see some humor in the situation. She got off the bed and circled the room, stopping to look out the window. 'I'm stripping your bed, Timothy,' she called. 'Now I'm tying the sheets together. Now I'm tying the blankets. I'm knotting them to the headboard, I'm hanging them out the window. Whee! Down I go.'

Timothy said nothing. She imagined him waiting aimlessly, feeling sillier by the minute but unable to back down.

She went over to the bureau, found two military brushes, and brushed her hair with both at once. She picked up a text book and went back to the bed with it and looked at a diagram of the circulatory system. There seemed no point in memorizing it. She went through her pockets, hoping to find something time-consuming – a scrap of sandpaper, maybe. Timothy's windowstill was scarred and peeling. But all she came up with was a rubber band, an unwrapped stick of chewing gum, six wooden matches and an envelope flap with a number on it. The rubber band she flipped into a light fixture on the ceiling, and the gum she dusted off and popped into her mouth. The matches she struck one by one on the windowsill and them held in her fingers, testing to see if telepathy could make a flame go out before it burned her. It couldn't. She was relieved to see the flickering knot of blue proceed steadily downward, unaffected by anything so substantial as her thought waves, which flickered also, veering from the match in her hand to the silent figure behind the door. When she had blown the last match out, and wiped the sting from her fingers, she dialed the number on the envelope flap. 'Hardware,' a man said. She dialed again, choosing the numbers at random. 'I'm sorry, we are unable to complete your call as dialed,' someone told her disapprovingly. 'Please hang up and dial again, or ask your operator for assistance. This is a – ' Elizabeth slammed the receiver down. 'Timothee,' she said, in the tone she might use for the cat, 'I'm ready to come *out* now.'

'Did you call Matthew?'

She blew a strand of hair out of her face and tried another number. This time she hit on one that existed. A woman said, 'Hello? Barker residence.'

'Oh, Mrs Barker,' Elizabeth said, shifting her chewing gum to the back of one cheek. 'This is Miss Pleasance calling, from Baltimore Gas and Electric? Your name has been referred to us for an in-depth study. Would you care to answer a question?'

'Why, surely,' Mrs Barker said.

'Could you tell me if – '

'But first, I want to say that I just love the little leaflets you send out. The ones with the bills? Your recipe-of-the-month *is* especially helpful and of course I'm always interested to see what new appliances are out. Why, every time the bill comes I just sit right down and read every word.'

'You do?'

'Oh, my yes. And try the recipes. Living on a budget, you know, I especially appreciate those meals-in-a-skillet. Rice and what-not. Of course my husband prefers straight meat. "I'm a meat-and-potatoes man," he says, but I say, "Joe, you supply the money and then I'll supply the meat. Until then," I say, "it's meals-in-a-skillet for *you*, my friend." Well, he's very good-natured about it.'

'Mrs Barker,' Elizabeth said, '*is* your – '

'One thing I might mention, though – '

'Is your *refrigerator* running, Mrs Barker?'

'Oh, you're preparing for summer, aren't you. I read what the leaflet said about summer: don't leave your icebox door open and then come crying to *us* if the bill is high. Well, you don't have to worry, Miss Pleasance. I know how you people are working to save us money and I do try to co-operate in every way I can. One thing I might mention, though, is the amount you depend on tomato sauce in your recipes. I wouldn't bring it up except you did ask, and I feel it might be helpful for you to know. My husband doesn't like tomato sauce. He says it's too acid. I don't know about other families, maybe they *love* tomato sauce, but it's something for you people to think over. Have you considered chicken broth? Look, I'm so glad you called. Any time, any questions at all, you just feel free to give me a ring. I'm home all day. I don't go out much. We just moved here and we don't find Baltimore very friendly, although I hope I'm not stepping on your toes when I say that. But I just know we'll settle in. And I take a great deal of pride in my home and feel sure I could tell you just anything you want to know about the typical housewife's opinions. Are you concerned about your meter-reading service?'

'Well, not just now,' Elizabeth said.

'Any time you are, then – '

'Fine,' said Elizabeth. 'Thank you very much, Mrs Barker.'

'You're very welcome.'

Elizabeth hung up. 'Oh, my,' she said, and pressed her index fingers to her eyelids. Then she rose and went over to the door. She knocked. 'Timothy, I want to come out,' she said.

'Did you call Matthew?'

'This is getting silly.'

'Call Matthew.'

She went back to the telephone. With the receiver to her ear she stared vacantly out the window a minute, popping her chewing gum, and then she smiled. She dialed the operator. 'I'd like to make a long-distance call,' she said, 'to Ellington, North Carolina. Person-to-person. First class. Any *other* special charges you can think of.' Then she settled back, still smiling, unraveling a thread from the ribbing of one sock.

It was her mother who answered. 'Oh, Elizabeth, what now,' she said.

'What?'

'Aren't you calling to put off your visit again?'

'Not that I know of,' Elizabeth said.

'What is it, then?'

'I'm just saying hello.'

'Oh. Hello,' her mother said. 'It's nice to hear your voice.'

'Nice to hear *yours*.'

'Do you have enough money to be spending it like this?'

'That's no problem,' Elizabeth said. 'How *is* everything? Everybody fine? Spring there yet? Trees in bloom?'

'Well, of course,' said her mother. 'Bloomed and finished. You're using up your three minutes, Elizabeth.'

'How's that dog getting along? Pop used to her yet?'

'You know he doesn't like you calling him Pop.'

'Sorry. Well. Is Dommie still hanging around?'

'Elizabeth, that's the saddest thing. I told you how often he's asked after you, well, then Sunday he came to church with a red-headed girl. I didn't think anything of it at the time, she could have been his cousin or something. But *now* what I hear: they're engaged. Planning a fall wedding. Well, I suppose you could care less, I know you're bringing home some Baltimore boy, but I always *hoped*, don't you know, just way in the back of my – '

86

Oh, Dommie was good for a full fifteen minutes. Elizabeth stretched out on the bedspread and listened, every now and then sliding in a question to keep the flow going. When that was exhausted they talked about her father. ('I feel I ought to warn you,' her mother said, 'that he looks upon this visit as a sign of some turning point in your faith. What are you laughing at? I won't have you hurt his feelings for the world. He expects you to have changed some, and if you haven't I don't want to hear about it.') Then Polly's new baby. ('Her hair is brown, and I believe it's going to curl. I'm so glad she *has* some, I never could warm to a bald-headed baby. Her eyes are a puzzle to me. They're blue but may be turning, there's that sort of opaque look beginning around the – ') Once, in mid-sentence, the bedroom doorknob rattled. What would happen if she said, 'Excuse me, Mother, but I just wanted to say that I've been taken prisoner'? The connecting of her two worlds by a single wire made her feel disoriented, but when her mother ran out of conversation Elizabeth said, 'Wait, don't hang up. Isn't anyone else there who would like to talk?'

'Have you lost all common sense? How much is this going to cost you?'

'I don't know,' Elizabeth said.

But she found out, as soon as the call was finished. She dialed the operator, who said, 'Eighty-sixty,' and then 'Ma'am?' when Elizabeth laughed. 'Ho, there, Timothy,' she said. 'Can you hear me? I just made an eighty-sixty phone call.'

Silence.

'Timothy? Now I'm going to call California station-to-station. I'm going to tell some store they delivered the wrong package, and get switched from department to department to – '

Something was thrown against the door. Then he kicked the door until it shook, and then he turned the key and rattled the knob. It was still locked from inside, but Elizabeth didn't open it. 'Damn it, let me in,' he said.

'You're beginning to get on my nerves,' she told him.

'Do I have to break the door down? I want to talk to you.'

'Say please.'

'I'm warning you, Elizabeth.'

'Pretty please?'

There was a pause. Then he said, 'I'm pointing a gun at you.'

'Ho ho, I'm scared stiff.'

'I'm pointing Andrew's gun. I'll shoot straight through the door.'

'Oh, for goodness sake,' Elizabeth said. She slid off the bed and went over to open the door. 'You're lucky I'm not the hysterical type,' she said, brushing past him. 'How do you know that's not loaded? Put it down. Send it out with the garbage.'

She stopped off by the couch to slip into her moccasins, and then she headed out to the entrance hall. It was a pity she had no money; she would have to thumb her way home. Or take a taxi, and have Mrs Emerson pay for it.

Behind her there was a click, a metallic, whanging sound. She wheeled around.

'Stop there,' Timothy said.

But it wasn't at her the gun was pointing, it was at himself, at an upward angle near the center of his chest. His wrist was turned in a sharp, awkward twist. 'Timothy Emerson,' she said. 'Did you just pull that trigger? What if there'd been bullets in it? Of all the – '

'No,' Timothy said, 'I think I took the safety catch off.'

She started walking toward him, slowly and steadily. Timothy kept his eyes fixed on her. His hand was shaking; she saw a glimmer trembling on the gun barrel. 'Stop there,' he said. But an edge of something was moving into his face, and she could tell that in a moment there would be a shift in the way he saw all this: he would laugh. Didn't he always laugh? So she kept chewing her gum all the way across the room, the eternal handyman, unafraid. 'This family is going to drive me up a wall someday,' she told him. 'What did you do before I came along? What will you do when I'm gone?' Then she lunged.

Her hand closed on his. She felt the short blond hairs prickling her palm. There was an explosion that seemed to come from somewhere else, from inside or behind him, and Timothy looked straight at her with a face full of surprise and then slid sideways to the floor.

5

It was all up to Matthew. It was Matthew who made the funeral arrangements, brought his mother endless cups of tea that he had brewed himself, met his brother and sisters at the airport and carted them home, answering their questions as he drove. 'But why – ?' 'How could he – ?' 'I really don't know,' Matthew said. 'I'll tell you what little I've pieced together, that's all I can do.'

Peter came from college, looking young and scared with his hair slicked back too neatly. Mary flew out from Dayton with her little boy; Margaret came home from Chicago and Melissa from New York. Andrew had not been told. He would arrive on Saturday, as he had planned before all this happened. Then they could sit him down and lay comforting hands on his shoulders and tell him gradually, face to face. The funeral would be over by then, but just barely, which made Matthew picture his family burying Timothy in haste. They didn't really, of course. This was the usual waiting period, with the usual tears and boredom and the sense that time was just creeping until they could get this business finished. They wore out the subject of Timothy; they began to feel bruised and battered at the sound of his name. People kept paying formal calls, requiring them to make hushed and grateful conversation that did not sound real even though it was. No one ate regular meals. No one went to bed at regular hours. Any room Matthew went into, at any time of day, he might find several members of his family sitting in a silent knot with coffeecups on their knees. Sometimes a piece of laughter broke out, or an accidental burst of enthusiasm as they veered to other subjects. Then they caught themselves, checked the laughter, dwindled off in mid-sentence, returning to a silence that swelled with inappropriate thoughts.

It used to be Elizabeth who managed this family. Matthew had never realized that till now. She was the one they had leaned on – he and his mother and Timothy, and the house itself, whose rooms had taken on her clear sunny calmness and her smell of fresh wood chips. Only now, when she was needed most, Elizabeth had changed. With the others present she looked bewildered and out of place, like any ordinary stranger who had stumbled into the midst of a family in mourning. Mrs Emerson called on her continually, but she answered with her mind on something else. Her caretaking had descended to the most literal kind: errand-running, lawn-sprinkling, lugging down more toys for Mary's Billy. At twelve o'clock one night Matthew found her on a stepladder in the pantry, changing light-bulbs. She wandered through crowded rooms winding clocks or carrying table-leaves, her face set and distant, and while Father Lewis was in the parlor offering his condolences she stayed on the sunporch, yanking weather-stripping from all the windows.

'Why are you working so hard?' Matthew asked her.

'This is my job,' she said, and dumped tangles of cracked stripping into a garbage can that she had brought in from outside.

'So that's Mother's famous handyman,' said Mary. 'Is she always so grim?'

'No, not ever,' Matthew said.

Then he removed his glasses and rubbed the inner corners of his eyes. Mary looked at him a moment but said nothing more.

Late Friday afternoon, Elizabeth came into the kitchen while Matthew was making a sandwich. She was in her oldest jeans, carrying a curved pruning saw that she set on a counter. 'I thought you would be the one to tell,' she said. 'After the funeral I'm going home for good.'

Matthew spread jam over peanut butter and patted another slice of bread down on top of it. Then he said, 'I don't know what I'd do if you left.'

'I think I'd better.'

'Is it because of the trouble with the police?'

'No.'

'Mother's going to rely on you to keep her going, these

next few months.'

'I don't want to be relied on,' Elizabeth said.

Matthew laid the sandwich carefully on a plate and offered it to her. She shook her head. He set the plate on the drainboard. 'If you would just give it a little more thought,' he said.

'I have.'

'Or if you held off till things here were settled. Then I could come with you. I'm still planning on it.'

'No,' she said.

'Well, all right. Not now. But as soon as you want me to.'

She said nothing. He laid a hand over hers, over cool rough knuckles, and she kept still until he removed it. Then she picked up her saw and left.

'Where is Elizabeth?' Mrs Emerson said. 'Why don't I see her around any more?'

'She's out cutting that hanging branch, Mother.'

'*That's* not what I need her for.'

'Shall I call her?'

'No, no, never mind.'

He set a tray on her nightstand, tea and a perfectly sectioned orange, and then straightened to watch his mother pace between the bed and the window. There was nothing broken about her, even now. She continued to wear her matched skirts and sweaters and her string of pearls, her high-heeled shoes, her bracelet with the names of all her children dangling on gold discs. She spoke when spoken to, in her thin, bright voice, and she kept in touch with the arrivals and the sympathy cards and the funeral arrangements. It was true that she spent more time alone in her room, and there were sometimes traces of tears when she came downstairs, but she was one of those women who look younger after crying. The tears puffed her eyes slightly, erasing lines and shadows. Her skin was flushed and shining. She moved with the proud, deliberate dignity she had had when her husband died. Once, months ago, Matthew had asked Elizabeth if she found his mother hard to put up with. 'No, I like her,' she said. 'Think what a small life she has, but she still dresses up every day and holds her stomach in. Isn't that something?' Now that Elizabeth seemed so removed, Matthew tried to take over for her. He shielded his mother from visitors, and answered her telephone, and brought her food that she never ate. When she paced the room he watched with his hands slightly flexed, as if he were preparing to leap forward any minute and catch her if she stumbled, or prevent her from ricocheting from wall to wall.

He was the one who broke the news to her. Elizabeth had called him from the police station and asked who should do it: he or she. 'I should,' he told her. 'I couldn't decide,' she said. 'I thought, you're her son after all, she might prefer it. Then I thought no, it's something I should do' – as if she saw herself as a culprit, duty-bound to face in person someone whose dish she had broken or whose message she had forgotten to deliver. He couldn't understand that. Everyone knew she was not to blame. He had called for her at the police station, searching her out through long flaky corridors and finding her, finally, pale and stony-faced in a roomful of officials. 'Wait in the hall,' they told him, but instead he crossed to stand behind her chair, one hand on the back of it. He had waited through the endless questions, the short, stark answers, the final re-reading of her statement. The policeman who read it stumbled woodenly over her words, so that it sounded as if she herself had stumbled although she hadn't. His voice was bored and dismal; he was like someone reciting lists. Even her useless repetitions had been conscientiously recorded – 'I don't know. I don't know,' which she must have said before Matthew came in, and surely not in such a despairing drone. She would have been quick with it, flicking it off her tongue like a dismissal, the way she always did when she felt cornered. The thought made Matthew want to move his hand from the chair to her shoulder, but he kept still.

On the telephone he had not even asked her the cause of death, but when it came out at the police station he wasn't surprised. He had assumed it was suicide from the start. Now he wondered why. He had never known that he expected such a thing of Timothy. Why not a car accident? He was a short-tempered driver. Why not a hold-up man, a hit-and-run, one of those senseless pieces of violence that happened in this city every day? He couldn't answer. When he fixed an image of his brother in his mind, trying to understand, he found that Timothy had already grown flat and unreal. 'He had a round face,' he told himself. 'He had short blond hair, sticking out in tufts.' The round face and blond hair materialized, but without the spark that made them Timothy.

He had driven Elizabeth home and left her outside, sitting on the porch steps facing the street, while he went into the house. He found his mother writing letters in the bedroom. The little beige dictaphone was playing her voice back, as tinny and sharp as a talking doll's: 'Mary. Is Billy old enough for tricycles? Not the pedal kind, I know, but – '

'I have bad news,' Matthew said.

She spun around in her chair with her face already shocked. 'It's Andrew,' she said instantly.

'No, Timothy.'

'Timothy? It's Timothy?' She had dropped the pen and was kneading her hands, which looked cold and white and shaky. 'He's dead,' she said.

'I'm afraid he is.'

'I thought it would be Andrew.'

Behind her the mechanical voice played on. 'Does he have a wagon? A scooter? Ask Peter about his plans for the summer.'

'How did it happen?' she asked.

'He, it was – '

'How did it *happen?*'

Timothy should have to be doing this; not Matthew. It was all Timothy's fault, wasn't it? Anger made him blunter than he had meant to be. 'He shot himself,' he said – flatly, like a child tattling on some dreadful piece of mischief that he himself had had no part in.

'Oh, no, that's so *unfair!*' his mother said.

'Unfair?'

He paused. Nothing he had planned covered this turn in the conversation. Mrs Emerson felt her face with her hands, sending icy trembling sparkles from her rings. 'Mother,' Matthew said, 'I wish there was something I – '

'Did he suffer any pain?'

'No.'

'But how did it come about?' she said. 'What was the cause? Where did he find a gun?'

'I'm not too sure. Elizabeth said –'

'*Elizabeth!*' Her face had the stunned, grainy quality of a movie close-up, although she was across the room from him. She felt behind her on the desk and brought forth an ink-bottle. Without looking at it she heaved it, overhand, in a swift, vicious arc – the last thing he had expected. He winced, but stood his ground. The inkbottle thudded against the curtain on the door, splashing it blue-black and cracking one of the panes behind it. In the silence that followed, the dictaphone said, 'Would Margaret like Mr Hughes to print her up more of those address labels?'

'Oh, I'm so sorry,' Mrs Emerson said.

She flicked the dictaphone off, and then bent to pick up a sheet of stationery that had floated to the floor. 'There was no excuse for that,' she said.

'It's all right.'

'What were you saying?'

'Well – ' He hesitated to mention Elizabeth's name again, but his mother prompted him.

'Elizabeth said?'

'She said she went to eat lunch with him. She was just walking down the hall to his apartment when she heard the shot.'

'Oh, I see,' his mother said.

She never gave any explanation for throwing the ink-bottle. She had Elizabeth replace the pane immediately, and Alvareen washed the stain from the curtain. And in restless moments, pacing the bedroom or waiting out some silence ⌐among her family, she still said, 'Where is Elizabeth? Why isn't she here with us?' Matthew watched closely, less concerned for his mother than for Elizabeth herself, but if anything she seemed closer to Elizabeth than before. He saw her waiting at the kitchen window for Elizabeth to come in from staking roses; he saw her reach once for Elizabeth's hand when they met in the hallway, and hold onto it tightly for a second before she gave a little laugh at herself and let it go. The inkbottle settled out of sight in the back of Matthew's mind, joining all the other unexplainable things that women seemed to do from time to time.

He didn't believe what Elizabeth had told the police.

Too many parts of it failed to make sense. It came out very soon that she and Timothy must have driven downtown together, and then a neighbor of Timothy's said she had heard people quarreling, and the police discovered a long distance call that had been made to Elizabeth's family. 'I was with him but left, then came back,' Elizabeth said. Well, that was possible. If they had had an argument she might have stormed out and then changed her mind later and returned. But what would they argue about, she and Timothy? And when had she been known to leave in a huff? And if she did leave, was she the type to come back?

One of the things he had long ago accepted about Elizabeth was that she didn't always tell the truth. She seemed to view truth as a quality constantly shifting, continually reshaping itself the way a slant of light might during the course of a day. Her contradictions were tossed off gaily, as if she were laughing at her stories' habit of altering without help from her. With the police, now, she confined herself to a single version, remodelled only once when they discovered her earlier visit. Yet there were points at which she simply shut up and refused to answer. 'You apparently don't realize that you could be in serious trouble over this,' the policeman said. But that was where they were wrong. She must have realized, to have stopped so short rather than spin whatever haphazard tale came to mind.

'Where did he get the gun?' they asked.

'I don't know.'

'It just came out of nowhere? What were you two arguing about?'

'Arguing?'

'Why were you shouting?'

'Shouting?'

'*Miss.*'

Elizabeth looked at them, her face expressionless.

'Why did you call home?'

'To say hello.'

'Was that during the earlier visit?'

'Of course.'

'Did the argument arise from that phone call in some way?'

'Argument?'

95

They gave up. There was no doubt it was a suicide – they had the powder burns, the fingerprints, the statement of his professor providing motivation. Elizabeth was only the last little untied thread, and although they would have liked her to finish wrapping things up they had never thought of her as crucial. They layered death over with extraneous interviews and coroners' reports and legal process until Timothy himself was all but forgotten. Then, almost as an afterthought, they declared the case closed. The deceased could be buried, they said. That was the end of it.

'Mother,' Matthew said, 'come drink this tea.'

'In a minute.'

She was standing by the window, moving a plant into a pool of sunlight.

'I've been talking with Elizabeth,' Matthew told her.

'Oh?'

'She wants to leave her job.'

Mrs Emerson's hands dropped from the flowerpot. She straightened her back, so that her sharp shoulderblades suddenly flattened.

'She's going to wait till after the funeral, though,' he said.

'But leaving! Why? What did she say about me?'

'Well, nothing about *you*.'

'Did she say I was the cause.'

'Of course not.'

'She must have given you a reason, though.'

'No. Not really,' Matthew said.

His mother turned. Her eyes, when she was disturbed, never could rest on one place; they darted back and forth, as if she were hoping to read her surroundings like a letter. 'And why tell *you?*' she said. 'I am her employer.'

'I guess she thought it was a bad time to bother you.'

'No, she blames me for something. But *now!* To leave now! Why, I've been thinking of her as one of the family. I took her right in.'

'Maybe you could talk to her,' Matthew said.

'Oh, no. I couldn't.'

'If she knew how you felt about it –'

'If she wants to leave, let her go,' said his mother. 'I'm not going to beg her to stay.'

Then she settled herself in a flowered armchair,

96

arranging her skirt beneath her, and pushed her bracelet back on her wrist and leaned forward with perfect posture to pour herself a cup of tea.

Matthew went downstairs and into the kitchen, where he found Peter eating the sandwich that had been on the drainboard. 'Oh, sorry,' Peter said. 'Was this yours?'

'I didn't want it.'

'Just got to needing a little snack,' Peter said. He gulped down one more bite and then set the rest of the sandwich aside, as if he felt embarrassed at being hungry. He was forever embarrassed by something, or maybe that was just his age – nineteen, still unformed-looking, clomping around in enormous loafers bumping into people and saying the wrong things. He had come at the tail end of the family, five years after Melissa. The others had no more than a year between them and some of them less; they were a bustling foreign tribe, disappearing and reappearing without explanation, while Peter sat on the floor beside his rubber blocks and watched with surprised, considering eyes. Then the oldest ones were given quarters on the third floor, into which they vanished for all of their last years at home. They read in bed undisturbed, visited back and forth in the dead of night, formed pacts against the grownups. Peter stayed in the nursery, next door to his parents. No one ever thought to change the pink-and-yellow wallpaper. He grew up while their backs were turned, completely on his own, long after the third floor was emptied and echoing. Now when he came home on visits he bumped into doors and failed to listen when he was spoken to, as if he had given up all attempts at belonging here.

'Mother's upset because Elizabeth is leaving,' Matthew said, trying to draw him into the family.

'Gee, that's too bad. Who's Elizabeth?'

'*Elizabeth*. The handyman.'

'Oh. I guess she must think we're a bunch of kooks after all that's happened.'

'No, she –'

'Is that Elizabeth? I thought her name was Alvareen.'

'No – what? *Whose* name? Oh, never mind.'

Matthew left, bypassing the living room. He was tired of talk. He went out through the sunporch, a quiet place lit with diagonals of dusty orange light. Alvareen stood ironing a table cloth while tears rolled down her cheeks. (She had shown up two days in a row, on time, impressed by tragedy.) Margaret was curled on the windowseat reading a book and chewing on tight little cylinders that she had made from the page corners. Neither of them looked up as he passed.

'Elizabeth,' he said, standing under the poplar tree.

'Here I am.'

She sat on a branch above the one she had just cut off, leaning sideways against the trunk.

'Shall I help you down?'

'I like it here.'

'I'm going home now. I'm not coming back until the funeral.'

'Oh. All right.'

'Could you come down? I'd like to talk some things over with you.'

'No, I don't think so.'

'Well, would you rather I stayed here? What do you want to do?'

'I want to sit in this poplar tree,' Elizabeth said.

He nodded, and stood around for a while with his hands in his pockets. Then he left.

Matthew's house was out in the country, part of a rundown old farm that his father had somehow come into possession of. His family called it a shack, but it was more than that. It was a tiny two-story house, the front a peeling white, the other three sides unpainted and as gray as the rick-rack fence that separated it from the woods behind. To get there he had to leave the highway and drive down a rutted road that rattled the bones of his old car. At the end of the road he parked and walked through new, leafy woods up to the front yard, which was a floor of packed earth. A rotting tyre hung from an apple tree. A Studebaker rusted on concrete blocks out back. His mother had come here only once and, 'Oh, Matthew,' she had said, looking at the porch with its buckling slat railings, '*I* can't go in there. It would make me too sad.' But she had, of course. She had perched uneasily on a squat rocking chair and accepted Oreos and lemonade. Her hair and the glass lemonade pitcher had been two discs of gold beneath the high smoked ceilings. Then forever after that she begged him to find some place nicer. 'I'll pay for it myself, don't think about the money,' she said. 'I'll fix it up for you. I'll shop for what it needs.' When he refused she settled for buying what she called 'touches' – an Indian rug, homespun curtains, cushions from Peru. She comforted herself by imagining that the house was meant to be Bohemian, one of those places with pottery on the windowsills and serapes draped over the chairs. Matthew didn't mind. He had chosen to live here because it was comfortable and made no demands on him, and all the cushions in Peru couldn't change that. His father had been happy to give his permission. (He liked to see every last thing put to use.) Then at his death he had willed Matthew the house outright. The others got money; Matthew got the house, which was what he really wanted.

He walked through the front room, where each board creaked separately beneath his feet. He went into the kitchen and took a roll of liverwurst from the yellowed refrigerator. Leaning against the sink, paring off slices with a rusty knife, he ate liverwurst until he stopped feeling hungry and then put it away again. That was his supper. There was a table, of course, and two chairs, and a whole set of dishes in the cupboard (his mother's gift, brown earthenware), but he rarely used them. Most meals he ate standing at the stove, spooning large mouthfuls directly from the pot to save dishwashing. Once when Elizabeth came for supper he had started to do that – dipped a fork absentmindedly into the stew pot, before he caught himself – and all Elizabeth did was reach for the potato skillet and find herself another fork. Halfway through the meal they traded pans. If he narrowed his eyes he could see her still, slouched against a counter munching happily and cradling the skillet in a frayed old undershirt that he used for a pot-holder.

Then sometimes, when living alone depressed him, he set the table meticulously with knife, fork and spoon and a folded napkin, plate and salad plate, salt and pepper shakers. He served into serving dishes, and from them to his plate, as if he were two people performing two separate

99

tasks. He settled himself in his chair and smoothed the napkin across his knees; then he sat motionless, forgetting the canned hash and olive-drab beans that steamed before him, stunned by the dismalness of this elaborate table set for one. What was he doing here, twenty-eight years old and all alone? Why was he living like an elderly widower in this house without children, set in his ways, pottering from stove to table to sink? The carefully positioned salad plate and the salt and pepper shakers, side by side in their handwoven basket, looked strained and pathetic. He went back to eating at the stove, with salt from a Morton's box and pepper from an Ann Page pepper tin.

In the living room he picked up old *Newsweeks* and placed them in a wooden rack. He straightened the rug. He aligned the corners of the slipcover on the daybed. Then, since it was growing dark, he lit a table lamp and sat down with that morning's paper. Words jerked before his vision in scattered clusters. He felt like a man in a waiting room before a dreaded appointment, reading sentences that skipped along heartlessly in spite of the sick feeling in his stomach. He raised his eyes and looked at the walls instead – tongue-and-groove, shiny green, with an oval photograph of someone long dead leaning over the fireplace. The fireplace itself was black and cold, in spite of the chill in the air. A brown oil burner fed its pipe into one side of the chimney, and clanked periodically as if its metal were still contracting after all the winter months it had tried to heat this room.

'Aren't you *freezing?*' his mother had asked. And Elizabeth had said, 'You want to go hunt firewood?' His father, rocking in that chair with a glass of warm bourbon, had said, 'When I was a boy, rooms were always this cold. We were healthier, too.' His father had come visiting often, mumbling something about business carrying him in this direction. He had supplied the bourbon himself, and occasionally fresh vegetables or a slab of bacon – country things, which he had purchased in the city to bring out here. He liked to have the fire lit. He liked to rock in silence for hours. 'Now, this is the way to live,' he said. 'At heart, I'm a simple man,' but there had been nothing simple about him. Every quality he had was struggling with another its exact

100

opposite. If he rocked so contentedly here, in the city he was a whirlwind. Always selling, pushing, buying, bargaining, sometimes bending the law. 'Remember this,' he kept telling his children. 'If you want to rise in the world, smile with your eyes. Not just your mouth. It gets them every time.' His children cringed. Momentarily, they hated him. (Yet every one of them, blond and dark both, had his pure blue eyes that curled like cashew nuts whenever they smiled.) He mourned for weeks when Mary refused to be a debutante, and he joined the country club on his own and played golf every Sunday although he hated it. 'What do I go there for?' he asked. 'What do I want with those snobs?' He was made up of layers you could peel off like onion skins, each of them equally present and real. The innermost layer (garage mechanic's son, dreaming of a purple Cadillac) could pop up at any time: when he watched TV in his undershirt, when he said, 'like I said' and 'between you and I,' when he brought home an old tyre to whitewash and plant with geraniums. 'Oh, Billy,' his wife said of the tire, 'people just don't — oh, how can I explain it?' He was hurt, which made him brisker and more businesslike, and he stayed late at the office for weeks at a time. Then he bought her a ruby ring too big to wear under gloves. Then he took all his sons hunting although none of them could shoot. 'I like the natural life,' he told them. 'I'm a simple man, at heart.'

Matthew's father was clearer in this room than Timothy; his death seemed more recent, more easily mourned. He had gone unwillingly, after all — taken unawares, in his sleep, probably looking foward to tomorrow's wheelings and dealings. But how could you mourn a suicide? Complications arose every time Matthew tried. On top of the oil burner was a sheaf of photographs he had been puzzling over the night before: Timothy in his mother's yard, last summer when Matthew was trying out his new camera. He had not yet learned how to use it. The focus was blurred, and in every print Timothy's laughing face had extra outlines around it, as if he had been moving, lunging toward the lens, as if laughter were some new form of attack. However, Matthew tried to imagine him sober-faced, he couldn't. He pulled up images in his mind, one by one:

101

Timothy laughing with that girl he had brought to dinner once, his arm around her shoulders; Timothy laughing with his mother, with Melissa, with his father at his college graduation. Then a new picture slid in, clicking up from the back of his head: Timothy quarreling with Elizabeth. Only what was it about? Had she broken a date? Refused one? Shown up late for something? All he remembered was that it had happened on the sunporch, over the noise of a TV western. 'If you persist,' Timothy said, 'in seeing life as some kind of gimmicky guided tour where everyone signs up for a surprise destination – ' and Elizabeth said, 'What? Seeing what?' 'Life,' said Timothy, and Elizabeth said, 'Oh, *life*,' and smiled as fondly and happily as if he had mentioned her favorite acquaintance. Timothy stopped speaking, and his face took on a puzzled look. Wispy lines crossed his forehead. And Matthew, listening from across the room, had thought: It isn't Timothy she loves, then. He hadn't bothered wondering how he reached that conclusion. He sat before the television watching Marshall Dillon, holding his happiness close to his chest and forgetting, for once, all the qualities in Timothy that were hard to take (his carelessness with people, his sharp quick tongue, his succession of waifish girls hastily dressed and combing their hair when Matthew came visiting unannounced). He forgot them again now, and with them the picture of Timothy triumphantly cocking his pistol and laughing in his family's face. All he saw was that puckered, defeated forehead. He cleared his throat. He felt burdened by new sorrows that he regretted having invited.

That night he dreamed that Elizabeth had gone away. She was *long* gone, she had been gone for years, she left behind her a dark blue, funnel-shaped hollow that caused his chest to ache. Then his mother died. She lay on a table with her head slightly propped and he stood beside her reading a newspaper. All the headlines contained numerals. '783 SUNK; 19 SURVIVORS; 45 BURIED IN MINE DISASTER,' he read, but he understood that this was her will leaving everything to Elizabeth. It made sense; on the table his mother had changed into a frail, lavender-dressed old lady, the kind who would make eccentric wills in favor of pets

102

and paid companions. He began searching for Elizabeth, combing through long grasses with his fingers and coming up with nothing. She never appeared. Her absence caused an echoing sound, like wind in the tops of very tall pines. 'What shall I do about the money?' he asked the old lady on the table. 'If you fail to find the beneficiary it must be buried with me,' she said. '*You'll* never get it.' He let the money float into the coffin. He was crying, but it wasn't because of what she had said; it was the wastefulness, the uselessness, the lost look of all that fragile green paper waiting forever for Elizabeth to come home.

At the funeral the immediate family filled one pew – Mrs Emerson, her three daughters, two of her sons, and her sister Dorothy, who was barely on speaking terms but always showed up for disasters. In the pew behind sat Mrs Emerson's two cousins, Mr Emerson's strange brother, and Elizabeth. Matthew felt uncomfortable so close to the front. He had entered with his eyes lowered, guiding his mother by the elbow, and because it was his first time here since his father died he was uncertain of anything that lay behind his own pew. He disliked sitting in places that he had not taken measure of first. Once he turned partway around, but his sister Mary jabbed him in the side. She was staring straight ahead, with her plump, pretty face set in stern lines. Little pockets of irritation shadowed the corners of her mouth.

Irritation was the mood of this whole funeral, for some reason. All down Matthew's pew, exasperated jerks travelled like ripples. Margaret tore triangles off the pages of her hymn-book, until Melissa slammed it shut. Aunt Dorothy tapped Peter for cracking his knuckles. Matthew shoved his glasses higher for the dozenth time and received another jab in the side. His mother, listening to the generalities of the service, twisted restlessly in her seat, as if she wanted to jump up and make additions or revisions. Even Father Lewis seemed annoyed about something. He was deprived of most of the phrases he liked to use – fruitful lives and tasks well done, happy deaths and God's design – and when he had finished the few vague sentences left to him he briskly aligned two sheets of paper on his pulpit, heaved a sharp sigh, and frowned at someone's cough. Before him lay the pearly gray casket, hovering, weighing down the silence, waiting for something more that never came.

By the time they returned from the cemetery it was nearly one o'clock. Three limousines left them at the door. People alighted in straggling lines, and unbuttoned their gloves and removed their hats and commented and argued and agreed all the way up the walk. 'He never liked that hymn, he would have poked fun at us for singing it,' Melissa said. Mrs Emerson's two cousins climbed into their car, murmuring soft sounds that might not even have been words. It looked as if only the immediate family and Aunt Dorothy were staying to dinner. 'You'll stay, Uncle Henry,' Mary told Mr Emerson's strange brother, but Uncle Henry (who was strange because he never talked, not ever, but merely bobbed his Adam's apple when confronted with direct questions) waved one red, bony hand and went off stiff-legged to his pickup truck. 'We'd better tell Alvareen,' Mary said. 'Eight for dinner, if she hasn't yet fed Billy.'

'But how about Elizabeth?' Mrs Emerson said.

'Elizabeth, oh. Does she eat with us?'

'I'll get something later,' Elizabeth said. She was zigzagging across the front lawn, gathering the debris left by last night's rainstorm. In church, in her beige linen dress, she had looked like anyone else, but there was nothing ordinary about her now when her arms were full of branches and rivulets of barky water were running down the wrinkles in her skirt.

'Is that girl all *right?*' Mary said. 'You'd think she'd change clothes first.'

Billy was waiting on the top porch step, guiding his mother back with his intense, unswerving stare. Alvareen stood behind him in a shiny black party dress. 'Dinner's set,' she called. 'Come on in, you poor souls, I got everything you'd wish for right on the table.' When Mrs Emerson came near enough Alvareen patted her arm. 'Now, now, it's finished now,' she said. Mrs Emerson said, 'I'm quite all right, Emmeline.'

'Shows you're not,' said Alvareen. 'I'm Alvareen, not

104

Emmeline, but don't you mind. Come on in, folks.'

Then she led the way into the house, shaking her head and moving her lips, no doubt preparing what she would say to her family when she got home: 'Poor thing was so tore up she didn't know me. Didn't know who I was. Called me Emmeline. Didn't know me.' Behind her, Melissa stumbled against a step and laid one hand on Matthew's arm, but so lightly that the stumbling seemed artificial. Margaret followed, swinging a weed that she had yanked from the roadside. Mary bent to scoop up Billy, and at the end of the line came Aunt Dorothy, talking steadily to Peter although he didn't appear to be listening. 'Now what I want to know is, who made the arrangements? Don't you people believe in the old-fashioned way of doing things? First no wake, no one at the funeral home, just the remains waiting all alone. Then that scrappy little service with hymns I surely never heard of, and the casket closed so that I couldn't pay my — why was the casket closed?'

'I asked it to be,' Matthew said. 'I thought it would be easier.'

'Easier!' She paused in the doorway, her mouth open, a wrinkled, scrawny caricature of Mrs Emerson. 'Easier, you say! My dear Matthew, death is never going to be easy. We accept, we endure. We *used* to put them in the parlor. Now you're telling me – or was he, um, I hope the bullet didn't – '

Nobody rescued her. She closed her mouth and entered the house, leaving Peter horror-struck behind her. 'Did it?' he whispered, and Matthew said, 'No, of course not. Go on in.' (And pictured, clearer than Peter there before him, Timothy's dead, toneless face, so solemn that it had to be a mockery – much worse than blood or signs of pain, although he never could have explained that to Peter.)

Alvareen stood scolding in the dining room. Nobody was coming straight to the table. They were milling in the hallway, or heading for bathrooms, or going off to put away hats and gloves. 'You're breaking my heart,' Alvareen said. 'Here, little Billy, *you'll* pay me mind.' She hoisted him into a chair with a dictionary on it and tied a napkin around his neck. He ducked his round yellow head to examine the tablecloth fringe. There was always something he was checking up on – as if he considered himself the advance scout for the grandchildren yet to be born. He peered at people suspiciously, drew back to study Mrs Emerson when she kissed him, cautiously surveyed all offerings from his aunts and uncles. Sometimes he repeated whole conversations between his relatives, word for word, out of context, as exact as a spy's tape recording. " 'Where you going, Melissa?" "Out for a walk, can't stand it here." "When'll you be back?" "'Spect me when you see me." ' ' "Why don't I ever hear from you, Peter?" ' he said now, and then frowned at his silverware, as if turning the question over for all possible implications.

When they were finally seated, their elbows touched. No one would have guessed how many people were missing. Alvareen had chosen her own menu: ham and roast beef, three kinds of vegetables, mashed potatoes and baked potatoes and sweet potatoes. 'Oh my,' Mrs Emerson said, and she sighed and refolded her napkin and sat back without taking a bite. Only Margaret had any appetite. She ate silently and steadily – a lanky-haired, pudgy, flat-faced girl. Beside her, Billy whacked his fork rhythmically against the table edge. 'In a bottom drawer, under the tea-towels,' he chanted. 'In a bottom – ' 'Cut that out, mister,' Mary said. She buttered a roll and laid it on his plate. 'Eat up and hush.'

'In a bottom – '

'It was nice of Father Lewis to do the services,' Mrs Emerson said.

'*Nice?*' said Mary.

'Well, he could have refused. He had the right, in a case of . . . case like this.'

'I'd like to see him try,' Mary said. She had changed since the days when she lived at home. She looked calmer, softer around the edges, especially now when she was expecting another baby. Her face, with its lipsticked mouth and pale eyes, was settling along the jawline, and she wore her dark hair medium-length, average-styled, marked with crimplines from metal curlers. Yet while her looks had softened, her opinions had hardened. She passed judgment on everything, in her mother's sharp, definite voice. She was forever ready to turn belligerent. Motherhood had affected her in the way it did she-bears, but not only in matters

106

relating to her child. 'You know what I'd have said if he refused,' she said. 'I'd have marched straight up to him. Oh, he'd be sorry he ever mentioned it. Quit that, Billy. Give it to Mother. "Father Lewis," I'd say, I'd say straight to his face –'

'But he didn't,' Margaret said.

'What?'

'What's the point?'

'Oh, Margaret, where are you, off in a daze some place? We were talking about –'

'*I* know what you were talking about. What's the point? He didn't refuse, he never said a word about it. He went right ahead and performed the services.'

'Well, I was only –'

'Funerals are for the living,' said Mrs Emerson. 'That's what all the morticians' ads say.'

'Of course, Mother,' Mary said. 'No one denies it.'

'Well, Father Lewis was very kind to me. Very thoughtful, very considerate. I don't want to disappoint you children in any way, but the fact is that I have never felt all that religious. I just didn't have the knack, I suppose. Now, Father Lewis knows that well but did it stop him? No. He came and spent time, he offered his sympathy, he never even mentioned the manner of Timothy's going. He was no help at all, of course, but you can't say he didn't try.'

'No, of course not,' Mary said.

'The trouble with ministers,' said Mrs Emerson, 'is that they're not women. There he was talking about young life carried off in its prime. What do I care about the prime? I'm thinking about the morning sickness, labor pains, colic, mumps – all for nothing. All come to nothing. You have no idea what a trouble twins are to raise.'

'Can't we get off this subject?' Melissa said.

'Well, it is on my mind, Melissa.'

'I don't care, you're making me nervous. All this talk about Timothy, who has just played a terrible trick on us and left us holding the bag. Hymns. Sermons. Religion. Why do we bother?'

'*Melissa!*'

'What. There's nothing *wrong* with what he did, it was his own life to take. But we don't have to sit around discussing it forever, do we?'

'That's quite enough,' said Mrs Emerson, and then she set her glass down and turned to Alvareen, who was just coming in with more rolls. 'Everything is delicious, Alvareen.'

'How can you tell? You ain't eat a bite.'

'Well, it *looks* delicious.'

'It is,' said Mary, taking over. 'You must give me the recipe for the gravy, Alvareen. Is it onion? Is this something you get from your people?'

'All I done was – '

'Matthew,' Mrs Emerson said, 'I have to know. Was death instantaneous?'

Everyone froze. Instantaneous death, which sounded like something that happened only around police lieutenants and ambulance drivers, seemed undesirable; and before Matthew had thought her question out he said, 'No, of course not.' Then when their eyes widened he realized his mistake. 'Oh,' he said. 'No, it *was* instantaneous. I didn't – '

'Which is it? Are you keeping something from me?'

'Oh no, I just, you see – '

'Elizabeth? Where's Elizabeth?'

'Here we go again,' Mary said.

'Here we go *where* again?'

'You'd think you could get along five minutes without Elizabeth.'

'Mary, for heaven's sake,' Margaret said.

'She *was* on the *scene*,' said Mrs Emerson.

'Ha,' Mary said.

'Just what does that mean?'

There was a silence. Alvareen, who was propped against the wall with her arms folded as if she never planned to leave, suddenly spoke up. 'All I done with the gravy,' she said, 'was throw in a pack of onion soup mix. Lady I used to work for taught me that. You might like to write it down.'

'Oh, is that what it was,' said Mary. 'Thank you very much.'

The silence continued. Forks clinked on plates. Billy's head slid slowly sideways and his eyes rolled, half-shuttered, fighting sleep.

'I do lot of extries,' said Alvareen. 'Sometimes I cater for parties, I mention that in case you're interested. I spread cream cheese over Ritz crackers, I dye it however they want. Green, like, to match the carpet. Pink or blue, to go in with the decor. Little things is what makes them happy.'

She went out through the swinging door, hands under her apron, probably telling herself she had done all that could be expected to liven this funeral party. Mary said, 'I believe Alvareen is even stranger than Emmeline.'

'There was nothing wrong with Emmeline,' said Mrs Emerson.

'What'd you fire her for, then?'

'What I mind about Elizabeth – ' said Melissa.

Margaret said, 'Oh, can't we get off Elizabeth?'

'She's creepy,' Melissa said. 'Never says anything. I distrust people who don't take care of their appearance.'

'Wake up, Billy,' said Mary. 'Eat your beans. Well, I'll say this about her and then we'll drop it: I hate to see people taking advantage. It seems to me, Mother, that girl knows a good thing when she stumbles on it – settled down to live off a rich old lady forever, she thinks, and you should make it plain to her that you have children of your *own* to rely on. Plenty of your own without – '

'Well, I like her,' Margaret said.

'What do you know about it?'

'I've had to share a room with her, haven't I? She talks to *me.*'

Melissa said, 'I don't hear Matthew speaking up.'

'What about?' said Matthew, pretending not to know.

'Aren't you always hanging around Elizabeth?'

She smiled at him from across the table – a cat face, sharp and bony, with that thin, painful-looking skin that some blondes have. Who could have foretold that modeling agencies would consider her a beauty? Matthew decided suddenly that he disliked her, and the thought made him blink and duck his head. 'Anyway, she's going,' he said.

'Aren't you going to mope around, or follow after her or something?'

'Stop it,' Mrs Emerson said.

They looked up at her, with the same stunned, pale eyes.

'Oh, what makes you act like this?' she said. 'They say

it's the parents to blame, but what did *we* do? I'm asking you, I really want to know. What did we do?'

No one answered. Billy slumped against Margaret, his lids glued shut, exhausted from having so much to watch out for. Peter speared beans with all his concentration, and Aunt Dorothy began examining her charm bracelet.

'Just loved you and raised you, the best we knew how,' Mrs Emerson said. 'Made mistakes, but none of them on purpose. What else did you want? I go over and over it all, in my mind. Was it something I did? Something I didn't do? Nights when you were in bed, clean from your baths, I felt such – oh, remorse. Regret. I thought back over every cross word. Now it's all like one long night, regret for anything I might have done but no fresh faces to start in new upon in the morning. Here I am alone, just aching for you, and still I don't know what it was I did. Was it me, really? Was it?'

'Mother, of course not,' Mary said.

'Then sometimes I think you were all in a turmoil from birth, nothing I did could have helped. Can you deny it?'

'Mother –'

'What about Andrew? What about Timothy? I was such a *gentle* person. Where did they get that from?'

Her face was blurring, crumpling, dissolving. And all the movements made toward her were bluffs. Some cleared their throats and some leaned suddenly in her direction, but nobody did anything. In the end, it was Matthew who stood up and said, 'I guess you'd like to rest now, Mother.'

'*Rest!*' she said, with her mouth pressed to a napkin. But she allowed herself to be led away. The others scraped their chairs back and stood up. Alvareen, bearing a hot apple pie, stopped short in the doorway. 'We won't be needing dessert,' Mary told her. 'Now, aren't you an optimist. Have you ever known this family to make it through to the end of a meal?'

'Your mama and Elizabeth always did,' Alvareen said.

The others were filing out of the dining room. Mary bore a sagging, boneless Billy toward a rocking chair by the fireplace. Mrs Emerson, composed again, mounted the stairs with Matthew close behind. 'I'll just turn down the spread for you,' he told her. 'You'll feel better when you're not so tired.'

'It's true I haven't slept much,' said Mrs Emerson.

But instead of going straight to bed, she stopped at the doorway of Margaret's room. Elizabeth was wrapping pieces of wood in tissue paper and stuffing them into a knapsack. 'Elizabeth,' Mrs Emerson said, 'was death instantaneous?'

Elizabeth didn't even look up. 'Oh, yes,' she said, without surprise, and she folded down the flap of the knapsack and buckled the canvas straps.

'Then he didn't have any, say any last –'

'No.'

'Well, thank you. All I wanted was a clear-cut answer.'

'You're welcome,' said Elizabeth.

Matthew took his mother's arm, thinking she would go now, but she didn't. 'You're packing,' she said. 'I never thought you would actually go through with this.'

'Well, there's a lot I need to get done. I have to reapply at the college.'

'Can't you do that by mail?'

'I believe it'd be better just going down there,' Elizabeth said.

She still hadn't looked up. She had started folding shirts into squares and laying them in a suitcase. For once, there was nothing that could sidetrack or delay her. His mother must have seen that too. '*Why*, Elizabeth?' she said. 'Do you blame me?'

'Blame you for what?'

'Oh, well – could you really just leave me like this? Are you going to let me live through these next few months all alone? The *last* time you didn't.'

'I'm sorry,' Elizabeth said.

Mrs Emerson raised a hand and let it fall, giving up. She allowed herself to be led across the hall to her bedroom.

'I never did wholly trust that girl,' she said.

Then she lay down, and shielded her eyes with her forearm. Matthew drew the curtains and left her there.

When he crossed the hall again, Elizabeth's door was closed. It was a message; it seemed meant for him alone. He stood there for a minute, slouched and empty-handed. When she didn't come out he went on downstairs.

Melissa and Peter were playing poker. 'He's very successful,' Melissa was saying. 'He owns his own company. But he nags at me, we fight a lot. You know? Sometimes when he invites me out he makes me change what I'm wearing, just to suit him. He goes charging into my closet and pushes all my dresses down the rod, figuring what he'd like better. What can you do with a person like that?' Peter frowned at his cards. He wasn't even pretending to listen.

Margaret was talking about a man too, but in her own toneless way. She lay on a couch with her feet up, twining a limp lock of hair around her finger and telling Mary about someone named Brady. 'I was planning to bring him home, before this happened,' she said.

'Oh, don't,' said Mary, rocking Billy serenely. 'Everything goes wrong in this house.'

'But he keeps asking me to marry him. Mother would have a fit if she didn't meet him first.'

'Well, coming from someone who *eloped* — '

'Mother met *him* first.'

'Only if you count when he brought in the groceries.' Mary said. 'She's not much for heart-to-heart talks with stray delivery boys.'

'You don't have to be so snide about it.'

'I'm not. Can't we have a normal conversation? I don't know why you want to get married anyway – you're not the type.' She arranged Billy more comfortably, checking his sleep with her mouth tucked in and competent-looking. 'Too disorganized. Any man would be climbing the walls. You must still think marriage is floating around in a white dress. Well, it isn't.'

'*I* know that, I read the ladies' magazines.'

'They expect *you* to take care of *them,* it's not the other way around. Always asking you to pick up, put away, find things for them. Look at Morris – every morning I tell him the butter's kept in the butter bin. He never listens. He opens the refrigerator and panics. "The butter, where's the butter, we've run out of butter again." "It's in the butter bin, dear." Oh, you'd never last through that. I often think of chucking it all myself.'

The telephone rang. Matthew crossed to the armchair and lifted the receiver. 'Hello,' he said.

'Oh, Matthew,' said Andrew.

'Hello, Andrew.'

'What's wrong?'

'Nothing's wrong. Why?'

'You aren't glad to hear from me.'

'Of course I am,' said Matthew.

'I can tell from your voice.'

'Don't be silly,' Matthew said. 'Were you calling about anything in particular?'

There was a chipping sound at the other end of the line – Andrew doing something nervous with the phone. His hands were always busy, twisting or fidgeting or kneading his thumbs, while the rest of him was limp and motionless. Like a rag doll, he tended to remain where he was left – New York, in this case, after a try at college there. It took vast amounts of other people's energy to change his life in any way, and lately no one had felt up to it. What was the use? In New York he lived in a pattern as unvarying as the tracks of a toy train – from rooming house to library to rooming house, lunch every Wednesday with Melissa in the only restaurant he approved of (the only one he had *been* in; someone had once taken him there) and home three or four times a year, shattered and white over the change in his schedule. He distrusted planes (a family trait) and panicked at the swaying of trains, and had never learned to drive. All he had left were buses. Buses, Matthew thought, and started. 'Holy Moses,' he said. 'You're in Baltimore.'

'You forgot,' said Andrew.

'Oh no, I just – '

'You forgot I was coming. Would you rather I just went back again?'

'No, Andrew.'

'There are plenty of buses out of here.'

'I knew you were coming. I just never heard what time,' Matthew said. 'I'll be right down.'

'Oh, well – '

'Wait there.'

'Well, if you're sure you're expecting me,' said Andrew.

'We are. *Stay* there, now. Bye.'

He hung up and started out of the room immediately. 'I have to get Andrew,' he said.

'Oh, Lord,' said Melissa. 'This is too much at once.'

113

'I'll be back in a while.'

'Tell him in the car, Matthew. Get it over with.'

'Are you crazy?' Mary asked. 'Why did we keep it from him, if we're just going to dump it on him now? Don't you say a word, Matthew. Bring him on home. Maybe we'll wait till tomorrow.'

'I think I'm going to throw up,' Melissa said. 'I have a nervous stomach.'

Matthew left. In the hallway he met Elizabeth, who was just coming down the stairs with her suitcase and knapsack. Her burdens made her look lopsided. She still wore her church dress, with pieces of damp bark down the front. When she saw him, she stopped on the bottom step. He had an urge to trap her there, under glass, complete with her baggage and her peeling handbag and her falling-down hairdo, until life was sorted out again and he could collect what he wanted to say to her. 'Can't you wait?' he asked. 'Don't go yet. Won't you just wait till I get back from the bus station?'

'Oh, the bus station,' Elizabeth said. 'That's where I'm going.'

'What for?'

'Well, I'm catching a bus. You could give me a lift.'

'Oh, I thought – I had pictured you getting a ride.'

'Not at such short notice,' Elizabeth said.

She handed him the suitcase. Of all the sad things going on today, it seemed to him that the saddest was that single motion – Elizabeth flashing the luminous inner side of her wrist, with its bulky leather watchstrap, as she passed him her suitcase. Where were her bulletin board drivers, those laughable old cars full of Hopkin students that used to draw up at the door? Where were her blue jeans, and her moccasins with the chewed-looking tassels, and her impatient, brushing-away motion when he tried to help her with loads that looked too heavy?

'Are you waiting for something?' Elizabeth said.

'No.'

'Let's go, then.'

'But – so fast? You haven't said goodbye yet. Mother's still in her room.'

'I'll write her a bread-and-butter letter.'

114

'Well, if that's the way you want to do it,' Matthew said.

They hurried down the sidewalk, with Elizabeth's turned-up pumps making clopping sounds and her knapsack swinging over one shoulder. 'Hop in,' Matthew said. 'We have to get to Andrew before he takes the next bus out again.'

'Oh, Andrew,' said Elizabeth, but her voice was dull and tired. It sounded as if she had had enough of Emersons.

All the way downtown, Matthew kept choosing words and then discarding them, choosing more, trying to make some contact with Elizabeth's cold, still profile. He drove absentmindedly, and had to be honked into motion at several traffic lights. 'You won't get to see how those new shrubs make out,' he told her once. Then later, 'Will August be a good time for me to visit you?' She didn't answer. 'I get my vacation then,' he said. Elizabeth only drew a billfold from her handbag and started counting money. 'Do you have enough?' he asked her.

'Sure.'

'Did Mother ever pay you for this past week?'

'Pay me?'

When Elizabeth answered questions with questions, it was no use trying to talk to her.

They passed dark narrow buildings that had suddenly brightened in the spring sunlight, old ladies sitting on crumbling front stoops taking the air, children roller-skating. In the heart of the city, in a tangle of taverns and pawnshops and cut-rate jewelers, black-jacketed men stood on the sidewalks selling paper cones of daffodils. Matthew drew up in front of the bus station, where he parked illegally because he was afraid of losing both of them, Andrew and Elizabeth, if he took more time. 'Don't get away from me,' he told Elizabeth. 'Wait till I find Andrew. Don't leave.'

'How could I? You're carrying my suitcase.'

'Oh.'

They went through the doors and toward the ticket counter. Only two people were waiting in line there, and the first was Andrew. 'Andrew!' Matthew called. He ran, but he had sense enough to keep hold of Elizabeth's suitcase. Andrew turned, still offering a sheaf of bills to the

115

man behind the counter. He was nearly as tall as Matthew, but blond and pale and fragile-looking. His suit hung from him in loose folds. His face was long and pinched. 'I'm arranging to go back,' he said.

'You can't do that.'

'I can if I want to.'

'This is all a misunderstanding,' Matthew said. He took hold of Andrew's sleeve, and the ticket agent folded his arms on the counter and settled down to watch. 'They're waiting for you at home,' Matthew said. 'They expect you any time now.' Then, to the ticket agent, 'He won't be going.' He pulled Andrew out of the line, and the fat lady behind him moved up to the counter with a huffy twitch of her shoulders.

'Now you've lost my place,' Andrew said.

'You know yourself you're acting like a fool.'

'Oh, am I?' Andrew said. 'Why didn't she think to tell you, then? Did she forget I was coming? Or did she remember and *you* forgot. Did you decide just not to bother?'

His eyes seemed deeper in their sockets than usual, and closer together. His arm, still in Matthew's grasp, was struggling away, and he was moving by fractions of inches back to the counter. Yet if he had really wanted to, he could have shaken Matthew off entirely. Returning to New York was another of his passing impulses, already deserting him, leaving him to fumble on in his course out of sheer inability to back down. All he needed now was some dignified alternative. 'Look,' Matthew said, but Andrew's arm, which was bare and skinny beneath his coat sleeve, seemed to infect him with some of Andrew's shaky tension. He couldn't get his words out. 'You could, could – '

And to make it worse the fat lady at the counter moved away and the person behind her stepped up: Elizabeth. Composed and distant, she unsnapped the clasp of her billfold. 'Ellington, North Carolina,' she said.

'Elizabeth!'

But she wasn't so easily pulled from the line. She went on counting out bills, and the ticket agent gave Matthew a peculiar look from under his eyebrows.

'Elizabeth, too much is going on right now,' Matthew

116

said. 'Will you wait? Will you come back with me, and take a later bus? There are things I want to get settled with you.'

'May I have my ticket, please?' Elizabeth said. The agent shrugged his shoulders and moved off to the ticket rack. Elizabeth spread her money in a fan on the counter. 'I'm in luck, there's a bus leaving right away,' she said. 'I want to get on it.'

'I know you do. I don't blame you at all, but I can't let you go yet. I haven't *said* anything to you.'

'There's nothing to say,' Elizabeth said.

There was, but it was difficult with Andrew there. He was standing between them, teetering on his heels and looking curiously from one to the other. 'I don't believe we've been introduced,' he said.

'Elizabeth,' Matthew said, 'I love you. I think we should get married.'

'*Married?*' said Andrew.

'I'm not interested,' Elizabeth said.

'Why not?'

'I just want to get out of here. I'm sick of Emersons. Thank you,' she told the agent, and stuffed the ticket into her bag.

Andrew said, 'How do you know the Emersons aren't sick of you too, whoever you are?'

'Andrew, keep out of this,' Matthew told him.

Andrew turned on his heel and went up to the counter.

'Andrew!' Matthew said. 'Will you come back here?'

'See what I mean?' said Elizabeth.

'Look, you can't refuse to marry me just because I've got a crazy brother. Andrew! Elizabeth, listen to me.'

'It isn't only Andrew that's crazy,' Elizabeth said. 'It's all of you. Oh, I knew I should have left before. How could I make so many mistakes? Give me my suitcase, please.'

'No,' said Matthew. He held onto it. 'Elizabeth – '

She turned and left, walking fast and swinging her knapsack. She was heading out toward the buses, but he couldn't believe she would really go. He still had the suitcase, after all. He was holding it tightly. When Andrew reappeared, waving a ticket, Matthew said, 'Here, take this suitcase. Don't let it go. I'll be back in a minute.' Then he pushed through a crowd of ladies in hats, past a girl with a

French horn case and a tiny old black woman with a caged parakeet. He thought he saw Elizabeth, but he was mistaken; the beige he had his eyes fixed on was a soldier's uniform. He pushed through the doors and outside, where rows of buses were revving their motors and men were rushing by with baggage carts. One bus, already backing out, had stopped to unfold its doors to Elizabeth. 'Wait!' he called. 'I have your *suitcase!*' If she heard, she didn't care. She scrambled up the steps, hoisting her knapsack higher on her shoulder. The last he saw of her was one upturned shoe sole with a wad of pink bubble gum stuck to the toe. Then the doors folded shut again.

When he returned to the terminal, Andrew was waiting meekly beside the suitcase. He touched Matthew's shoulder. 'Let's go home, Matthew,' he said, and the voice was as gentle as a child's after a scolding. 'I wouldn't let it bother me,' he said. 'She looked kind of strange, anyway. Nobody we would have much to do with.'

6

Elizabeth had a nightmare which she couldn't remember. She awoke and sat up, her heart thudding, while vague, malevolent spirits swooped over her head. But the room was warm and sunlit, and a breeze was ruffling the dotted swiss curtains. She lay down and went to sleep again. She dreamed she was mending a quantity of buttons – the finish to every nightmare she had had this month, as boring and comforting as hot milk. She was riffling through a cascade of chipped and broken buttons in a cardboard box. Plastic, glass, leather, gold, mother-of-pearl. She fitted together two halves of a tiny white button that belonged on a shirt collar. She rewove an intricate leather knot from a blazer. She glued a silver shank to a coat button, and a pearl disc back into its round metal frame; she found the missing

118

piece of pink plastic heart from a baby's cardigan. Her hands moved surely and deftly, replacing the gagging horror of the nightmare with a quiet calm. More buttons appeared, in cigar boxes and coffee cans and Band-Aid tins. Sometimes she grew discouraged. Why mend things so fragile? Why couldn't they let her throw them out and buy new ones? But there was some joy in doing her job so well. She worked on, plowing through a torrent of colored discs. She awoke feeling as exhausted as if she had been laboring all night long.

Her mother was out in the kitchen, running the Mixmaster. 'I hope you know what time it is,' she told Elizabeth.

'Eleven-fifteen,' Elizabeth said. She got herself a glass of orange juice and sat down on a stool.

'You never *used* to get up so late. Do you feel all right?'

Mrs Abbot was pouring evaporated milk into the beater bowl. Her face from a distance was young and thin and bright, but close up you could see a network of lines like the creases in crumpled, smoothed-out tissue paper. She wore a gingham dress and canvas slip-ons, and she moved with a quick, definite energy that made Elizabeth feel all the more lumpish. In two swift motions she had scraped down the sides of the beater bowl, slapping the scraper sharply against the bowl's rim. 'Maybe you're coming down with something,' she said.

'I feel all right.'

'You look a mite yellowish.'

'I'm fine.'

But she wasn't. Her head ached, her throat was dry, her eyelids stung. Her joints seemed in need of oiling. She wondered if she were falling apart, like the machine Mrs Emerson had talked about. Maybe, at twenty-three, she had passed her peak and started the long slope downhill. 'Twenty-three,' Timothy said out of nowhere, 'is a woman's sexual prime, and you are going to be very very sorry you didn't take advantage of it.' His voice brushed past her right ear. She flicked it away. Ghosts in the day-time were easily dealt with.

Her mother broke eggs into the beater bowl, and then dumped in an unmeasured amount of salt. Two or three

119

times a year she spent a morning in the kitchen brewing up this mixture – chicken and rice in a pale cream sauce, a dozen portions at once, laid away in the freezer until some church member should sicken or die. The pans were aluminum foil, disposable, to save the bereaved the effort of washing and returning them. How thoughtful can you get? And what would old Mr Bailey say, or that sickly Daphne Knight, if they knew that even now their funeral baked meats were lying in wait for them in the freezer? She watched her mother disjoint a row of stewed chickens on the counter, tossing the slippery gray skin to the collie who fidgeted at her feet. 'This is what you were doing the *last* time I was here,' Elizabeth said. 'They must have been dying off like flies.'

'Oh, they have,' said her mother. 'I made another batch while you were gone.' She sounded cheerful and matter-of-fact. On the surface she was the perfect minister's wife, tilting her head serenely beneath his pulpit on Sundays and offering the proper sympathy in the proper soft, hesitant voice; but underneath she was all bustle and practicality, and if she could have deep-frozen her sympathy ahead of time too she probably would have. She yanked a thighbone from a hen and tossed it toward the garbage bin, but Elizabeth reached out to catch it and offer it to the dog. 'Oh *no*, Elizabeth,' her mother said, and grabbed it back without altering the rhythm of her work. 'No bones for *you*, Hilary,' she told the dog. 'They'll give you splinters.'

'Oh, I doubt it,' Elizabeth said.

'Do you want to pay the vet's bills?'

'Nope, she's not worth it.'

Elizabeth scowled at Hilary, who was beautiful but stupid. She had a white mane and a long sharp nose. Because she was untrustworthy around henhouses she was kept in the house like any city dog, and pent-up energy made her nervous and high-strung. She prowled restlessly around the linoleum with her toenails clicking. 'I don't like you,' Elizabeth told her. Hilary moaned and then zeroed in on a place to lie down.

'Your father's having trouble over tomorrow's sermon,' her mother said. 'He's working on it now, but when he's through he wants to have a talk with you.'

'What about?'

'That's for him to say.'

'Slothfulness,' said Elizabeth. 'Aimlessness. Slobbish-ness.'

'Oh, Elizabeth.'

'Well, that is it, isn't it?'

'If you know what it is,' her mother said, 'why don't you *do* something about it?'

Elizabeth stood up. 'I believe I'll walk the dog,' she said.

'Go ahead. The leash is on the doorknob.'

She stalked through the house, with Hilary leaping and panting and whimpering behind her. There was nothing about this place that made her feel comfortable. Until a few years ago they had lived in an old Victorian frame parsonage, but then the church ladies (always in a flutter over how to make life easier for Reverend Abbott) had arranged to have a brick ranch-house built. It was nearer the church, which was no advantage because the church sat in the middle of a tobacco field out on R.F.D.1. The outline of the house was bland and shallow. Even the sounds there were shallow – wallboard thudding, flimsily, carpets purring, water hissing into a low-slung modern tub. Mr Abbott, who was subject to drafts, loved it. Mrs Abbott hated it, although only Elizabeth guessed that. Mrs Abbott was very much like Elizabeth; she liked wood and stone, she had enjoyed outwitting the bucking hot water heater and the back screen door that was forever sticking shut in the old house. Moving around her new streamlined kitchen, she sometimes stopped to throw a baffled look at the stove that timed its own meals. Then Elizabeth would say, 'We could always move back again.'

'Move *back*? What would the congregation think? Besides, they're tearing it down.'

Elizabeth clipped the leash to Hilary's collar and stepped out the front door. Blazing heat poured down on her. It was only the beginning of June, but in this treeless yard it felt like August. She crossed the flat spread of grass and descended the clay bank to the highway. Just to her right sat the church, raw brick that matched the house, topped by a white steeple. Gravestones and parking space lay in back of it. The Sunday school bus sat beneath a pecan tree at one

side. FAITH BAPTIST CHURCH, its sign read. 'THE DIFFER-
ENCE IS WORTH THE DISTANCE.' She never could get that
phrase straight in her head. At night sometimes it came to
her: The difference is worth the distance, the distance is
worth the difference. Which was it? Either would do. She
stopped to let the dog squat by the mailbox, and then
moved on up the road.

Neat white farmhouses speckled the fields, as far as the
eye could see. Each had its protective circling of henhouses
and pigsties, barns and tobacco barns, toolsheds and
whitewashed fences. Occasionally a little dot of a man
would come into view, driving a mule or carrying a feed-
sack. Nobody seemed to notice Elizabeth. She imagined
that the neighbors thought of her as a black sheep – the
minister's ne'er-do-well daughter who lay in bed till eleven
and then had no better occupation than walking the dog.

There in that green field, where nothing useful grew, a
circus tent rose up every August and a traveling revivalist
came. He stood behind a portable pulpit, sweating from all
his flailing and shouting beneath the bug-filmed extension
lamps. His message was death, and the hell to follow – all
for people who failed to give in to God in this only, only
life. Elizabeth's father sat to one side of him in a folding
wooden chair. 'Wouldn't you be jealous?' Elizabeth had
asked him years ago. 'Having someone else to come and
save your own people?' 'That's a very peculiar notion you
have there,' her father said. 'As long as they arrive at the
right destination, does it matter what road they came by?'
She hadn't taken his words at face value; she never did. She
had watched, in her white puff-sleeved dress on a front row
seat, and come to her own conclusion: the revivalist picked
sinners like plums, and her father stood by with a bushel
basket and smiled as they fell in with a thud. His smile was
tender and knowing. Ordinary Baptist housewives,
stricken for the moment with tears and fits of trembling,
flocked to the front with their children while the choir sang,
'Stand Up, Stand Up for Jesus,' and her father smiled down
at them, mentally entering their names on a list that would
last forever. What if they changed their minds in the
morning? Maybe some did; for the next year they were at
the front once more as if they felt the need of being saved all

over again. A girlfriend of Elizabeth's had been saved three times before she was fourteen. Each time she cried, and vowed to love her mother more and stop telling lies. She gave Elizabeth her bangle bracelets and her bubble-bath, her movie magazines and her adjustable birthstone rings from Dick Tracy candyboxes and all other vain possessions. 'Oh, how could you just *sit* there?' she said, 'With that preacher's voice so thundery and your father so quiet and shining? This has changed my whole life,' she said. Although it never did, for long. But Elizabeth was always stunned by those brief glimpses of Sue Ellen in her altered state, with her face flushed and intense and the centers of her eyes darker. And then at breakfast the next morning there would be her father and the revivalist calmly buttering buckwheat muffins, never giving a thought to what they had caused.

Hilary was begging to run, yelping and shaking with excitement. 'Oh, all right,' Elizabeth told her. They took off across a field. Elizabeth's moccasins sank deep into plowed orange earth. The collie in motion rippled like water, her tail a billowing plume, her white forepaws landing daintily together. But Elizabeth only felt heavy and out of breath, and an ache between her shoulderblades was spreading down her spine. 'Stop, now,' she said. She drew the leash inward and Hilary slowed, still panting, and chose her way between clods of earth. From behind she was bulky-hipped and dignified. The long hair on her hindlegs looked like ruffled petticoats. That should have made Elizabeth smile; why did she want to cry? She studied the petticoats, and the stilt-like legs beneath them – old-lady legs. Mrs Emerson's legs. She saw Mrs Emerson gingerly descending the veranda steps, slightly sideways, with her skirt swirling around her thin, elegant shins. Sun lit her hair and the discs on her bracelet. She was looking down, concentrating on the precise placement of her pointy-toed alligator shoes. Was it worry that puckered the inner corners of her eyebrows?

Pieces of Emersons were lodged within Elizabeth like shrapnel. Faces kept poking to the surface – Timothy, Mrs Emerson, Margaret cheerfully sharing her sawdusty room. And Matthew. Always Matthew, with his dim eyes behind

123

his glasses asking why she had been so curt with him when she left. Why had she? She wanted to do it all over again, take more time explaining to him even if it meant catching a later bus. Take the time to tell Mrs Emerson goodbye, and to put away her tools properly. No one else would. But most of all, what she wanted was to change all those days with Timothy. 'Whatever it was that happened,' Matthew had told her, 'you can't blame yourself for it.' Well, why not? Who else could she blame? She had done everything wrong with him from the very beginning, laughed off all he said to her right up to the moment when the gun went off, misread every word; and what she hadn't misread she had pretended to. She thought of that snowy night when he worried that he had died, and she had acted as if she didn't understand. If she couldn't help him out, couldn't she at least have *admitted* she couldn't?

'Don't mull it over,' Matthew had said. But he was under the impression that they were talking about a straightforward suicide. And he didn't have the picture of death from a bullet wound to struggle against every night of his life.

She tapped Hilary with a loop of leash. 'Let's go,' she said. Then she set off toward the ranch-house, with Hilary trotting beside her casting helpful, anxious glances. Red dust had worked into the stitches of Elizabeth's moccasins. A hot wind stiffened her face. Everywhere she looked seemed parched and bleak and glaring, but at least she was back where she was supposed to be.

When she got home Polly was in the kitchen with her baby, the smallest, fattest baby Elizabeth had ever known. Creases ringed her wrists like rubber bands; she not only had a double chin but double thighs, double knees, double ankles as well. Polly jostled her in her lap absentmindedly, speaking over her wispy head. 'Look at you,' she said. 'I wish *I* could just go tearing off with the dog any time I wanted.'

'Why don't you?' Elizabeth said. 'Leave Julie with Mother.'

'Oh, no,' said Polly. She sighed. She was smaller than Elizabeth, with a heart-shaped face and a tousle of yellow curls like a frilled nightcap. 'You're the one with the cute little sister,' people used to tell Elizabeth. In high school Polly had been Queen of May Day. She had kept to the style of the fifties ever since – spitcurls framing her forehead, her lipstick a pure bright pink. Her flower-sprigged shirtdress was immaculate, except where the baby had just spit down the front. 'Hand me a Kleenex, will you?' she asked Elizabeth. 'What did I take all that Good Grooming for, if this was what I'd come to?'

'If you wore a bibbed *apron* – ' her mother said. 'That's what I always did.' She was laying sheets of foil across the casseroles, which lined one counter from end to end. Without looking around she said, 'Polly brought the mail in with her. What'd you do with that letter, Polly?'

'Here it is.'

From the look Polly gave her as she handed her the envelope, Elizabeth guessed that they had been discussing it before she came in. She made a point of ripping it open in front of them, not even bothering to sit down. It was written in Matthew's looped, rounded hand. *Dear Elizabeth, Why don't you ever answer my letters? Did your suitcase arrive safely? Why do you* – She folded the sheets of paper and replaced them in the envelope. 'What's for lunch?' she asked her mother.

'One of these casseroles.'

'*Funeral* food?'

Polly settled her baby into a new position and studied Elizabeth's face. 'You certainly have been getting a lot of mail these days,' she said.

'Mmm.'

'All from Baltimore. You used to be the world's worst letter-writer. Have you changed? Or is some one an optimist.'

'Oh, you know, these are just people I met,' Elizabeth said vaguely.

'People? They look like mostly one handwriting.'

'Now, Polly, leave her alone,' her mother said. 'Elizabeth, honey, I wish you'd take these down to the freezer for me.'

She stacked foil pans into Elizabeth's outstretched arms. They were still warm, almost hot. Elizabeth rested her chin

125

on the uppermost pan and started for the basement. Behind her, a deep meaningful silence linked her mother and Polly.

Most of the basement was a recreation room, which smelled of asphalt tile. A phonograph sat in one corner. When she was still in secretarial school Polly used to bring her friends here, and they had danced and drunk Cokes and eaten endless bags of Fritos. Then Carl had proposed to her on that vinyl loveseat in front of the TV. Elizabeth remembered the night it happened – Polly making the announcement, smiling up at Carl as she spoke. She was still the younger sister then; it wasn't until she was married that she somehow bypassed Elizabeth and began exchanging those knowing glances with her mother over Elizabeth's head. She had hugged Elizabeth tightly and suggested they have a double wedding. A what? Elizabeth thought she had lost her mind. By then Elizabeth was in her junior year of college, living at home, and she had brought no boys back with her except the laundromat burglar once and you couldn't count poor sweet Dommie. She had never used this recreation room. It affected her the way New Year's Eve parties did: you were supposed to have fun there, you were pressured into it, and the obligation weighted her spirits down.

She crossed to the dark cubicle behind the record player, partitioned off by cinderblocks, containing only a furnace and a freezer. On the floor by the freezer a batch of orange wine was brewing up in a canning kettle. 'What's that stuff you have down there?' her mother had asked the day before. 'It's a new kind of preserves,' Elizabeth said. 'Preserves? What on earth kind of preserves . . . ' Elizabeth had cut all the oranges and lemons herself, regretting it before she was halfway done; every whiff of lemon reminded her of when she and Matthew had done this job together. She had a mind like a tape recorder, an audial version of a photographic memory, and each chop of knife blade against breadboard brought her bits of things that Matthew had said. ' "Two cups raisins, minced" – *how*, when they stick together so?' 'Did you ever go on a picnic. I'll bring a chicken, you bring the wine in some nice, round jug with a cork plugged in . . . ' Now the wine was probably rotting away on the sink, and she would never know how it came out. That was why she was brewing more now – that and sheer devilment. She liked the idea of strong spirits bubbling in Reverend Abbott's basement. She had sent off this time for the special government permit, just so she would know that the parsonage was a licensed brewery even if no one else ever did.

When she had stashed the casseroles away she bent to lift the cheesecloth from the canning kettle. Warm spicy smells rose up. Bubbles stung her nose. Matthew lifted his head and gave her a long, slow, puzzled look from behind his glasses.

It was late afternoon before her father was finished with his sermon. He pushed away the papers on his desk when she came in. 'Every week, the sermon gets harder,' he told her. 'Now I wonder why that should be. I always reach a point where I think I'm beaten, I can't go on, I have finally found a sermon that can't be written.' He smiled and rubbed his eyes with a long angular hand. His face was made of straight lines; his skin was stretched over fine, narrow bones and his fair hair conformed exactly to his skull. When he opened his eyes they were like blue glass globes, but tired veins were traced across the whites. 'I need a vacation,' he said. 'I believe it's showing in my sermons.'

'Take one.'

'Well, but there's always someone needing me, you know.'

'They'll manage,' Elizabeth said.

'Have a seat, will you? Just clear those things off the chair.'

She handed him what she collected – mimeographed pages and a stack of manila folders – and sat down in the captain's chair opposite his desk. He spent some time aligning the corners of the mimeographed pages. Then he cleared his throat and said, 'Well now, Liz, it seems to me we were going to have a little talk.'

'That's what Mom said.'

'Your mother, yes. Now last week you said, if I'm right –'
He slumped in his seat and stared at a letter opener. It always took him some time to get started. In these

127

preliminary stages, before he grew sure of himself, Elizabeth kept feeling she had to help him out. 'I said I would look for a job,' she reminded him.

'Yes. A job.'

'And that –'

'And that you were reapplying to Sandhill. I remember. My point is, do *you*?' He straightened his back suddenly, and stared at her so directly that his eyes seemed to grow square. 'Are you planning to go on like this forever?' he asked. 'The last thing I want to do is pressure you, Liz, but I never *saw* anyone live the way you do. Week after week you rise late and lie around the house all day, your appearance is disorderly and your habits are slovenly, you go nowhere, you see no friends, you stay up till all hours watching television so you can rise late the *next* day – and your mother says you are no help at all.'

'Did Mom say that?'

'She has enough to do as it is.'

'How can she say that? I help out. I did the dishes the last four nights running. Why didn't she come to *me* about it?'

'It's not only the dishes,' said her father. 'It's your general presence. You're disrupting an entire household. Now I suggested, if you remember, that you find something to keep you busy until fall term. "I'm sure you wouldn't want to remain idle all that time," I told you. Well, it seems I was mistaken. You *do* want to. Your mother says you've taken no steps whatever toward finding a job. You haven't even left the house, except to walk Hilary. What kind of life do you call that?'

'I can't think of any job I'd be good at,' Elizabeth said. She drew a pack of Camels from her shirt pocket, causing her father to wince. 'It's not as if I could type, or take shorthand, or do anything specific,' she said, tamping a cigarette on the edge of his desk.

'You know what smoke will do to my asthma,' her father said. 'Liz, honey. I know all about young people. It's part of my job. But you're twenty-three years *old*. We've been waiting twenty-three years for you to straighten out a little. Isn't it time you shaped up? Don't you think you're past the stage for teenage rebellion? It's just not becoming. Why, I would expect you to be married and starting a family by

128

now. Whatever happened to young Dommie?'

'He's engaged,' Elizabeth said. She slid the cigarette back into its pack and studied a double photograph frame on the desk – Polly at eleven, dimpling and looking upward through long lashes; Elizabeth at twelve, an awkward age, with her face sullen and self-conscious and her organdy dress too tight under the arms. 'I bet you were a tomboy,' Timothy once said, but she never had been. She had dreamed of being rescued from fire or water by some young man; she had experimented with lipsticks from the five-and-dime until she realized she would never look anything but garish in make-up. She grimaced, and without thinking took the Camel out again and struck a kitchen match on the arm of her chair. Her father buried his face in his hands.

'I wouldn't worry,' Elizabeth told him cheerfully. 'I'll find something. And school begins in September.'

'*September!*' her father said. 'You'll have rotted away by then.' He raised his head and stared at the photograph. Long deep lines pulled the corners of his mouth down. Was he thinking of when she had been twelve, when he still had some hope she might turn out differently? She suddenly felt sorry for him, and she leaned forward to pat his knee. 'Look,' she said. 'Maybe I could ask if they need help at the newspaper office.'

'I already did.'

'Oh. Did you?'

'I even asked my secretary if she needed an envelope-stuffer. She doesn't. There is something at the hospital, though – a sort of nurse's aide, working on the children's ward –'

'I wouldn't like it,' Elizabeth said.

'How do you know that?'

'Oh, well, seeing all those children with leukemia and things –'

'There's nobody in Ellington with leukemia.'

'And there's so many things you could *cause* there, I mean, giving out the wrong paper pill cup –'

'I'm sure you wouldn't do that.'

'Someone did it to *me* once,' Elizabeth said darkly. 'When I was there having my wisdom teeth cut out.'

'That was only a vitamin, Liz.'

'If I did it, it would be cyanide.'

'Dear heart,' said her father, gathering himself together again, 'I don't know where you get all these thoughts, but if you keep on with them you're going to render yourself immobile. Now, I gather something must have happened up there in Baltimore. All you say is there was a death in the family. Well, it must have been a mighty important death to make you come live here so suddenly, but if you don't want to discuss it I surely won't press you. You know, however, that my job has given me right much experience in – '

'No!' said Elizabeth, surprising both of them.

'Was the person who passed on very close to you?'

Passing on made her think of Matthew, not Timothy. She blinked at Matthew's face, which used to be so warm against her cheek and now made her feel merely cold and shut away.

'Well, we won't go into that if it bothers you,' her father said after a pause. 'But do you know what I would tell you if you were a member of my church? "Young lady," I'd say, "you need to get *outside* yourself a little. Join a group. Do volunteer work. No man is an – " '

'Maybe I could be a garbage collector,' Elizabeth said.

'Please try to be serious a moment. Now, there is one opportunity I haven't brought up yet. A sort of companion for old Mrs Stimson's father. I mention this as a last resort because, frankly, I consider the man beyond need of companionship. His mind is failing. Taking care of him would be a waste of your talents, and I recommend – '

'Would I have to give him pills?'

'Pills? No, I don't – '

'I'll take it,' Elizabeth said.

'Liz, honey – '

'Why not?' She rose and stubbed out her cigarette in a paper clip tray. 'When do I start work?'

'Well, there *is* the matter of an interview,' her father said. 'We'll have to let you talk to Mrs Stimson. But I wonder if you shouldn't think this through a little more.'

'Didn't you tell me to get a job? I'm ready to go any time you are.'

'All right,' her father said. He pulled a leather address

book toward him and leafed through the pages. 'I'll just give her a ring. Meanwhile, could you change?'

'Change?' Elizabeth stared at him.

'Your clothes. Change your *clothes,* Liz. Put on a nice frilly dress.'

'Oh,' said Elizabeth. 'Okay.'

When she left, her father was just reaching for the phone with that broad, sweeping gesture that meant he was back to being a minister again.

She went to her room and changed into the wrinkled beige dress that she had worn home. She slipped her bare feet into ballerina flats and pulled her hair off her face with a rubber band. Then she went out to the living room, where her parents were waiting. They sat side by side on the couch, like a wedding picture. Her mother looked unhappy. 'Elizabeth,' she said immediately, 'I don't think this is the job for you at all.'

'Well, that's what I'm going to find out,' Elizabeth said.

'Honey, Mr Cunningham needs a practical nurse. That's what you'd be doing. Why, they say they can't make sense out of half he says, you'd go out of your mind in a week.'

'It's only till September.'

'John?' Her mother looked at her father, waiting for him to help out – a rare thing for her to do. ('Don't tell your father,' she had once said, 'but it's a fact that from the day they're born till the day they die, men are being protected by women. Here at least. I don't know about other parts of the world. If you breathe a word of this,' she said, 'I'll deny it.') Her father only frowned and smoothed his forehead. 'It's better than wasting away at home,' he said.

'She'd be more wasted there. Here at least she could – oh, I don't know –'

'Walk the dog,' Elizabeth suggested.

'Oh, Elizabeth.'

Her mother went back to her mending, shaking her head. Elizabeth and her father left. Behind them, Hilary yelped anxiously and flung herself at a picture window.

The Stimsons lived in town, in a narrow frame house whose sides were windowless. Wooden curlicues ran under the eaves of the porch. It was Mrs Stimson who answered the door for them. 'Oh, Elizabeth, honey,' she said, 'isn't it

131

nice to see you again. Jerome, *you* remember – '

'Yes, indeed, yes indeed,' said Mr Stimson from behind her. 'And how are you, Reverend?'

He stepped forward to shake hands. He and his wife could have been twins – both small and round, middle-aged. When he shook hands Elizabeth's father laid his other hand on top of Mr Stimson's – a habit he had when greeting church members. 'Good seeing you, Mr Stimson,' he said. 'How's that lumbago doing?'

'Oh, can't complain. Just a twinge now and then, don't you know, when the – '

'Well, let them in, Jerome. Won't you all come in?'

Mrs Stimson led the way into a tiny living room, which had heavily veiled windows and plush furniture with carved legs. Everything wore a settled look, as if it had been there for centuries. Even the seashells and gilt-framed photographs seemed immovable. 'Sit down, won't you?' Mrs Stimson said. 'Elizabeth, I declare, are you still *growing?* Why I remember when you were no bigger than a Coke bottle and *now* look. How tall are you, honey?'

'Five-nine,' Elizabeth said glumly.

'Hear that?' Mr Stimson asked her father. 'Kind of takes you by surprise, don't it?'

'Oh, yes, yes it does. All you have to do is turn your back a minute and – '

'Now tell me about your boyfriends,' Mrs Stimson said. 'I just know you must have dozens.'

'What I really came for was to talk about the job,' Elizabeth said.

She had thrown the conversation out of rhythm. Everyone paused; then her father said, 'Yes, honey, but first I just have to ask, I can't believe my eyes. Mrs Stimson, are those African *violets?* Why, you must have the greenest thumb in Ellington!'

Mrs Stimson smiled into her lap and made tiny pleats in her print dress. 'Oh, pshaw, that's not anything,' she said. 'Well, I do have this love of flowers, I guess you might call it – '

'Now, Ida, don't go being modest,' Mr Stimson said. 'She could make an old stick bloom, Reverend, she's got the damnedest – or, excuse me. But she does have a way

132

with growing things.'

'I can see that,' Elizabeth's father said. 'It's a shame that more people don't have your talent, Mrs Stimson.'

'Oh, nowadays, nowadays,' said her husband. 'Who takes the time any more? Why, I remember back in '48 or '49, over Fayette Road way. Old Phil Harrow, remember him? No kin to Molly Harrow that runs the beauty parlor. He grew melons that could break the table legs, had squash and corn and his own asparagus bed. How many years it been since you see asparagus growing? I believe they make it out of nylon now. And beans. Down to the right, you see – say this rug is Fayette Road – to the right would be the corn, and then *between* the rows, two or three rows of –'

'Jerome, *he* don't want to hear about that.'

'Well, I say he *does*, Ida.'

'This is all very interesting,' Elizabeth's father said. His voice had grown deeper and more southern. His face, when he turned toward Mrs Stimson, had a kindly, faraway smile, as if he were making a mental note to relay to God everything she said. 'There is something truly healing about raising little green things,' he told her.

In the bookcase behind Mrs Stimson's head was a line of pastel paperbacks. If she squinted, Elizabeth could just make out the titles. *Nurse Sue in the Operating Room*, she read. *Nurse Sue in Pediatrics. The Girl in the White Cap. Nancy Mullen, Stewardess. Nurse Sue in Training.* She veered to an enormous spiny conch shell, and was just deciphering what beach it commemorated when Mrs Stimson leaned forward and said, in a whisper that stopped all conversation, 'Elizabeth, I just know you want some Kool-Aid.'

'No, thank you,' Elizabeth said.

'*You* do, Reverend.'

'Why, that would be very nice,' said Elizabeth's father.

'I'll just have it ready in a jiffy, then. You want to come keep me company, honey? *You* don't want to hear about farmland and all.'

Elizabeth rose and followed her out to the kitchen. Everything there was spotless, but orange cats had taken over all the windowsills and counters and linoleum-topped table. 'I'm just a fool about cats,' Mrs Stimson said. 'I guess

133

you can tell. Eleven, at last count, and Peaches here is expecting any minute,' She opened the refrigerator door, dislodging the cat sitting on top of it. 'We never had the fortune to be parents, don't you see. I guess the Lord just didn't will it that way. Jerome says I pour all my love out on the cats, he says I would have made just a wonderful mother if you can judge by how I treat animals.'

She went from cupboard to sink and then back again, mixing up a packet of grape Kool-Aid. Her small cushiony body was packed into some tight undergarment that she kept pulling down secretly at the thighs. Her dress was a church dress, flowers on a shiny black background, and she wore tiny round patent leather pumps. She must have dressed up as soon as she heard the minister was calling. Her husband, who was in a collarless shirt and work pants, would have grumbled over all the fuss and refused to change. Now Mrs Stimson kept stopping work to listen for his voice, as if she worried that he would say something inappropriate. 'Talk?' she said. 'That man could talk the ears off a donkey. Oh, your poor father. Honey, your father is a magnificent human being, don't you ever think otherwise. And when he called today about finding Daddy a companion I thought, Praise be, Reverend Abbott, if you aren't – '

'Well, about that job,' Elizabeth said.

'Oh, it don't pay much, I know, but the hours aren't long and the work is easy, just so you don't mind elderly men. He's well-nigh bedridden, you see. Has to be helped to his chair by the window – that's where he stays. Nice view of the street. I'm gone most of the day, I clerk at Patton's. Ladies' wear. I could get you a discount on your clothing. Jerome's gone too, and *now*, well, I don't feel comfortable leaving Daddy up there alone all day. He's getting on. I won't mince words, his mind is failing. Times he's clear as a bell, other times he thinks I'm Mama who's been gone these twenty years. Or what's worse, his *own* mama. He asks after these names I never hear of, never even knew were in the family. "Daddy," I say, "it's me, it's Ida." Then he'll get right quiet. Then, "Ida," he'll say, "I know I'm slipping. I feel it," he tells me. "Feels like my mind is flickering, feels like I'm a lightbulb just about to burn out.

134

Ida," he says, "tell me straight, am I going to die now?"
Oh, it breaks my heart. I love him so. I've been looking into
those eyes of his for sixty years, and now all of a sudden
there's nobody behind them. You know? Like all he left
with me was their color, and he went somewhere else. Then
when he clears he gets so scared. "Don't let them take me
away," he says, "when I am off like that." "You know I
won't," I tell him. I never would, I'd sooner they take me. I
love him more than ever now that he's so helpless.'

She stirred the Kool-Aid endlessly, her little feet set
apart on the floor and her face pouched with worry. In the
other room her husband said, 'We had what they call a
railroad apartment, I'm sure you know. Say this coffee
table was the hallway. To your left, now, just as you enter,
was the living room. No, wait, the coat closet. *Then* the
living room.' Mrs Stimson sighed and set her spoon down.
'I expect you'd like to see him,' she said.

'Well, yes.'

'Come upstairs, then. I got him sitting by the window. I
told him company might be coming.'

They filed up narrow dark stairs, through a wallpapered
hall and into what was plainly the best bedroom. Light
poured in from a tall window, whitening everything – the
tufted bedspread, the polished floor, the bony old man
sitting in an armchair. A shock of silver hair slanted across
his forehead. He was tilting his face upward, letting the sun
shine on sunken, gleaming eyelids. For a moment Eliza
beth thought he was blind. Then he turned and looked at
her, and his hand fluttered up to make sure his pajama
collar was buttoned.

'Daddy, honey,' Mrs Stimson said.

'They got me in pajamas,' the old man told Elizabeth.
'Used to be I never wore pajamas if there was company
coming.'

'How you feeling, Daddy?'

'Why, I'm all right.' He squinted at his daughter – nothing failing about those eyes of his, which were chips of
bright sharp blue. 'Later I might come down and see the
people.' he said.

'Well, I got someone I want you to meet. This is
Elizabeth Abbott, the preacher's daughter. Remember? I

135

know you must have seen her when she was just a youngster. This is my daddy, Mr Cunningham.'

'How do you do,' Elizabeth said.

Mr Cunningham nodded several times. A metallic flash moved back and forth across his shock of hair. 'I was an usher when the old one was there,' he said.

'The old – ?'

'The *old* pastor, the one before Reverend Abbott.'

'Oh, Mr Blake,' Elizabeth said.

'That's the one. What became of him?'

'He died.'

Mrs Stimson made a sudden clutch in the air with both hands, as if she wanted to grab Elizabeth's words and reel them back in, but Mr Cunningham only went on nodding. '*That's* right,' he said. 'Died. Now I remember.'

'Daddy, the nicest thing – '

'Aren't you the one got married?' Mr Cunningham asked Elizabeth.

'That's her sister, Daddy. The other daughter.'

'Well, anyone could make that mistake.'

'Of course they could,' said Mrs Stimson. 'I'll tell you why she's here, Daddy – '

'I would advise you against the marriage, young lady,' Mr Cunningham said. 'Call it off. Get a divorce. *I* married.' He turned and looked out the window again. 'She aged so,' he said finally.

'Daddy?'

But he went on staring at framed squares of blue, with his hands limp on the arm of the chair. His feet in their leather slippers hung side by side, not quite touching the floor, as neat and passive as a well-cared for child's.

When they had tiptoed out to the hall again Mrs Stimson said, 'Oh, my, I wish you had seen him more at his best.' And then, on the stairs, 'He can be so smart sometimes, you wouldn't believe it. Please don't judge him by this.'

'No, I won't,' Elizabeth said.

'You mean you'll take the job?'

'Sure.'

'Oh, that's *wonderful!*' She beamed and squeezed Elizabeth's arm. Her skin seemed suddenly clearer, two shades lighter. 'You don't know what this means to me,' she said. 'Could you start on Monday? Eight o'clock? I'm not due for work till nine, but I'll want to show you what he eats and all.'

'Okay,' Elizabeth said.

They carried the Kool-Aid in to the men. Mr Stimson was still talking. He broke off to say, 'I was just remarking on the bum, the atom bum. I blame it for the increase in rainfall. *Ida* can tell you. Used to be we could plan a Sunday drive with some hope of carrying it out. Not any more. Bum's changed the cloud formations.'

'What does Reverend Abbott care about cloud formations?' Mrs Stimson asked. She settled herself in her rocker with a tinkling glass. 'Jerome, Elizabeth says she'll come look after Daddy for us.'

'Is that a fact,' said Mr Stimson. 'Well, you surely will be taking a load off my wife's mind there, young lady.'

'And they hit it off just beautifully, Jerome.'

'Is that a fact.'

'Some people,' Mrs Stimson told Elizabeth, 'seem to irritate him, like. I've noticed that. We had a colored girl cleaning up for me on Fridays, he didn't take to her at *all*. Then people with a lot of make-up on, he don't like that. Well, he's just old-fashioned is all. I notice *you* don't wear make-up. I expect that's from being a preacher's daughter.'

'Ah well,' said Elizabeth's father. 'I'm glad things worked out. Any time these little problems come up, Mrs Stimson, that's what I'm here for.'

'I know that,' Mrs Stimson said. 'I don't know what I'd do without you, Reverend. Why, I was about to have a collapse, worrying like I did all the time I was at work. I thought, if I could find *someone* – but I never dreamed your Elizabeth was back in town. I must've missed her in church.'

'I don't go,' Elizabeth told her.

'Oh?'

There was a silence.

'Elizabeth's one of these *modern* young people,' her father said. He laughed lightly. '*She'll* get straightened out. We don't see eye to eye on – what is it this week? Reincarnation.'

'You don't say,' said Mr Stimson. 'Why, I never knew it

137

was in any question. Don't you believe in the reincarnation of Christ on the third day, young lady?'

'It's a thought,' Elizabeth said.

'What?'

'*She'll* get straightened out,' said her father.

'Why, of course she will. Of course she will,' Mrs Stimson said. She beamed at Elizabeth and rocked steadily, holding her Kool-Aid glass level on her knees. Elizabeth's father cleared his throat.

'*Well,* now,' he said. 'I expect we better be moving on. Got a busy day tomorrow.'

'Yes, indeed,' said Mr Stimson. 'We surely do look forward to those sermons of yours, Reverend.'

'That one about pride!' his wife said, 'Well, I can't tell you how much it meant to me. And we appreciate this so much, you helping out about Daddy and all.'

'Glad to do it, glad to do it.'

'Be nice to have a young person about,' Mr Stimson said. 'Never had the fortune to have kids of our own.'

'That's what I said earlier, Jerome.'

'And it takes the burden off Ida some. Old people tend to get difficult sometimes, not that they – ' He grinned and rubbed his chin. 'Dangedest thing,' he said. 'The other day he took me for one of them quack medicine peddlers. Must have been forty years since they been through here last, wouldn't you say? Believe it was back in '21 or '22, I was just a – well, he gave me hell, or heck. Seems I had sold him some little bottle I swore would cure anything. "Where's your conscience?" he asks me. "Can you get up in the morning and look yourself in the eye, knowing how you let a man down?" Well sir, there I stood, wondering who in Hades I was taking the rap for. Probably long dead, by now. Probably died a quarter century ago. Maybe more.'

Nobody said anything. Elizabeth's father sat sharply forward, as if he were about to speak, but all he did was stare into the diamond formed by his knees and his laced hands. One wisp of hair had fallen over his eyes – a single flaw that made him look haggard and beaten. Elizabeth imagined that all his disappointments could be read in the grooves around his mouth: Why couldn't his family see him the way his congregation did? Why had his daughter stayed glued to

138

her seat in the revival tent? What gave him the feeling sometimes that his wife viewed God indulgently, like an imaginary playmate, and that she prepared her chicken casseroles as she would tea-party fare for children on a Sunday afternoon? He shook his head. Elizabeth leaned over to lay a hand on his arm. 'We should go home, Pop,' she said gently.

He flinched, and she remembered too late that she should have called him father.

When she went to bed, fragments of last night's dreams puffed up from her pillow like dust. She lay on her back, clamping her forehead with one hand. She saw a tea-tin spilling out buttons – self-buttons with their fabric frayed, wooden buttons with the painted flowers chipping off, little smoked pearls knocked loose from their metal loops. The self-buttons she cut new circles of material for. The wooden ones she retouched with a pointed paintbrush. She dipped the metal loops in glue and set them into the pearls, holding them there until they dried, pressing them so tightly between thumb and forefinger that she could feel, even in her sleep, the dents they made in her skin.

7

Dear Elizabeth,

I don't understand why you don't answer. I keep thinking up possible reasons, new ones every time. Are you angry? But when you are you generally say so, you don't just fade away like this. I'll keep on writing, anyway. I'll come down in August even if I don't hear from you. I would like to see you before then, maybe for a weekend, but for that I'll wait till you tell me how you feel about it.

Sometimes I imagine you just walking up my path, some

sunny morning. It wouldn't bind you to anything. If you wanted I wouldn't even make a fuss about it – just say hello and peel you an orange to eat on the front steps for breakfast.

Mother is well. She totaled the car last week, which shook her up a little, but she escaped without a scratch. Now she has a Buick. Walked into the car lot and bought one, on sight – said a friend had told her they were all right. I was sorry to see the old Mercedes go. You wouldn't like the Buick at all, you always had such fun maneuvering the gear shift. Whatever happened to your chauffeur's cap? I looked for it in the old car before they took it away. I'd hate to think of it in some auto graveyard.

Andrew has been in a rest home in upstate New York. They expect to release him any day now. I wonder if he shouldn't come back here, but there would be so many difficulties that I haven't suggested it. He claims he'd rather be alone now, anyway; he was very insistent about it. I don't think he has recovered from Timothy. He keeps writing Mother and asking questions and more questions, two letters a day sometimes – all about Timothy, irrelevant things like what he was wearing that day and what he ate and who he was talking to. Mother is very patient about answering him. She says that now that Timothy's gone she doesn't worry so much about Andrew. It's like some quota has been filled.

You said we were all crazy. Maybe you said it just for the moment, not meaning it, but it's all I have to go on so I keep trying to relate it to your not writing. I don't see how it fits in. I do see how it could make you want to leave us. Do you think craziness is catching? It could be, of course. It is, if you still blame yourself for what happened. If that had anything to do with you at all, it was only on the surface.

I just remembered one time when I was downtown with Andrew, Christmas shopping, years ago. We were standing on a corner waiting for a light to change. This car passed us, going very fast, and just as it reached the corner all four doors popped open. One of those fluky things, I just laughed. But Andrew didn't. He got scared. He said, 'I can't understand it. Why do these things happen to me? Why on my corner? I can't grasp the significance of it,' he said. Well, I'm not saying you're like Andrew. But things have been happening to us for years, long before you came along.

Before you were born, even. Look at last summer, when we didn't know you existed. My father died, my mother tangled with a hold-up man, Margaret got engaged to a middle-aged widower but broke it off and Melissa had a ten-day crying jag thinking she was pregnant. That's just what I remember offhand; there's more that got crowded out. We're event-prone. (But sane, I'm sure of that. Even Andrew is, underneath.) Probably most families are event-prone, it's just that we make more of it. Scenes and quarrels and excitement _ but that part's manufactured, just artificial stitches knitting us all together. What would we say to each other if we had to sit around in peace? I may not make scenes myself but I allow them, I go along with them. I see that. It's my way of making connection with my family. Like Andrew's peculiarities. He chose them. Every trouble he causes is just another way of talking. If you look at it like that, doesn't it seem a waste to leave us?

I know I'm talking a lot of bull.

I love you. Why won't you marry me? I think you love me too.

Matthew

JUNE 27, 1961

Dear Elizabeth Abbott:

Having thought it over I am going to kill you

Yours very truly,
Andrew Carter Emerson

Dear Mrs Emerson,

How are you? I'm doing just fine.

I'm writing to see if you could send me my combination drill. It's down on the workbench in the basement. It has a metal box that you can pack it in. I'll be glad to pay the postage.

Thank you.

Sincerely,
Elizabeth

141

Dear Elizabeth,

Well here is half of that ten dollars you loaned me that I bet you thought you seen the last of, ha ha. I would send it all but my nephew's wife is in the hospital getting her nerves fixed and I just didn't have the heart to say 'no.' It seems like this summer we been ailing so. My husband has the arthritis so bad he can't leave the bed and my sister's getting the Change and myself I have the headache alot. Well I shouldn't complain, I can still get around thank the Lord and have a job for what its worth. Mrs Emerson is changing ageing before my eyes and the symptom is parsimonousness. Turning into one of those old ladies that checks on every dime when there's a fortune in the bank. She saves moldy old leftovers and gripes do I take some of the ham for my lunch then goes out and buy herself a Buick. I have talk to her about getting some new handyman as washing outside of windows is not my job but she says 'no' they all steal you blind. Well Elizabeth didn't I was quick to say and she sayd no, that's true. 'I never had to lock up the valubles or the liquor around Elizabeth but she was such a magpie junky things was never safe around her, old doorknobs and screws and caster cups disappearing and coming back in the shape of paperweights and chest men and rubber stamps.' I thought you would want to kow how she is talking about you. She is ever criticizing how I do my work. On the phone she was telling about 'my maid is going to drive me up the wall one of these days.' Lady take care who call yours I wanted to say but held my peace. She is all the time talking like she owns people, my florrist and my pharmacist and my meat man. Well Lord knows that woman has had her share of trouble though. I must close for now as it is hospital visiting hours. I will get that other five to you when my troubles eases up.

Sincerely,
Alvareen

Dear Elizabeth,

I tried to call you this morning but your mother said you were at work. I didn't even know you had a job. Then by evening, I'd changed my mind. You are one of those people who deflect what is said to you and then hang up, bang. But I have seen you reading everything, instructions and Occupant ads and cereal boxes, and I can't imagine you throwing an envelope away without looking to see what's in it. Writing's better.

You must not know what it's like to wait for a letter. I leave for work late, just to catch the postman. I listen for his car on the highway. Cars that aren't his I hate, I despise the way they creep past my eyes taking up road space on trivial errands. Then I go to the back of the house and pretend I'm not interested. It's a superstition. When he comes he's always so cheerful. I reach the end of the driveway before he's finished loading my mailbox and he tells me it's just bills and grins from ear to ear. I pretend that's all I expected. It worries me the sloppy way he handles mail; anything could get lost, fall on the ground or under his car seat and he would never notice. In grade school they showed us a film about how letters travel — canceling machines and sorting machines and finally just the feet of a mailman down a sidewalk. Now that I think about it, there were so many ways those machines could lose a thing.

Mary's baby was born premature, a girl, and she telephoned all in tears at having to leave the baby in an incubator so mother's flown there to keep her company. Margaret has married again, nobody knows who to. I think Mother's going to check him out on the way back. It will do her good to travel a while. I go by the house often, just to make sure Alvareen's taking care of things okay. The place is going to hell — grass turning brown, leaky faucets. You know Mother never got another handyman. She was distrustful of all the people the employment agency sent out to her.

Andrew is back at his old job and doing fine. I called him on his first night home to invite him here, but he says he'd like to be alone awhile.

Mr Smodgett at the paper is drunker than ever and now the linotype operator has taken up drinking too, but come August I'm leaving no matter what. I have two weeks off and I'm spending them with you. Don't tell me not to. I would like to take you back with me. We could live at my house or someplace better, I don't care. If you still don't like children,

143

that's all right. I won't expect you to change in any way. I love you.

Matthew

Dear Elizabeth,

I don't know if you remember me very well or would even be interested in hearing from me, after all the trouble you've been through with my family, but this morning when I was trying to think of someone I'd like to announce my marriage to yours was one of the few names that came to mind –

Not that you would be all that interested in my wedding, I guess, but it seemed like a good excuse to get in touch with you and tell you a lot of other things I've wanted to say –

When you left so suddenly I realized that those last few days must have been hell for you, only none of us thought of it at the time, and I wanted to apologize on behalf of my family and also to thank you for taking such good care of Mother – she used to write about you and she was always so pleased to have something offbeat, like a girl handyman, that could make her feel unconventional right in the safety of her own home –

I hope you aren't too disgusted with us. We are not as unhappy as we must seem. Sometimes when we are all together things start going wrong somehow, I don't know why, and everybody ends up feeling they can't do anything right, and anything they try to do will make it worse. Everybody. Even Mother, maybe. But we love her very much, and we are a very close family, and Matthew is closest of all. I wish I could make you see that.

Well, so I am married – my husband's name is Brady Summers and he's in his last year of law school – next year we'll be moving to New York where he has a job with a corporation –

I'm going to like being so near Melissa and Andrew, who is the most interesting of all my brothers although of course Matthew is very interesting too – we will all have lunch together on Wednesdays at this little restaurant Andrew likes to go to, which will be fun –

I should say also that I'm not a frequent letter writer, so if

144

*it should happen that you'd like to keep in touch I won't be
disappointed if you wait months to answer – then too you
might not want to write at all, which I would understand.
Thank you again –*

> *Sincerely,*
> *Margaret Emerson Summers*

Dear Elizabeth Abbott:
  *I picked a revolver off a policeman at a parade today. It's
for you.*

> *Yours very truly,*
> *Andrew Carter Emerson*

Dear Matthew,
  How are you? I'm doing just fine.
  *I have a job taking care of an old man who I like very
much. I'm having a nice summer.*
  *The reason I'm writing is to tell you not to come in August.
I'm not angry or anything, I just don't think there would be
any point to it.*

> *Sincerely,*
> *Elizabeth*

Dear Elizabeth,
  *What do you mean, point? When did you start caring
whether things had a point?*
  *I'm coming anyway. This is important. You are the first
person outside my family I've ever loved and I'm worried
you may be the last.*

> *Matthew*

Dear Margaret,
  *Congratulations on your recent marriage which I was very
happy to hear about. I'm not much for writing letters but will
try to keep in touch.*
  I know that your family is very nice and I always did like

your mother, only I had to start school again. Thank you for writing.

Sincerely,
Elizabeth

Dear Elizabeth,

I know that my last letter must have sounded rude. I've been thinking things over since then. I woke up last night and suddenly I saw this whole situation in a different light — not me being steadfast and patient but just pushing you, backing you against a wall, forcing a visit on you and talking on and on about love when you don't want to listen. Is that how you see it, too? You're younger than me. Maybe you're just not interested in settling down yet. Maybe I was always afraid of that underneath, or I would have called you on the phone or come down there one of these weekends.

You will have to discuss this with me somehow. I don't know what to think any more.

Mother is back from visiting Mary and Margaret. I don't know that traveling did her that much good after all. She looks tired. When I went to see her yesterday she was just putting the permanent license plates on the new car. She didn't have the faintest idea how to go about it. I suppose Dad or Richard always did it before, and then you last March. Anyway she was just circling the car with them, looking at the plates and then the car and then the plates again and holding a little screwdriver in her hand like a pen. I would have given a million dollars to see you coming across the grass with your toolbox. I even thought you would, for a minute. I kept looking for you. Then when I was putting the plates on for her Mother started crying. Without you we are falling apart. The basement has started seeping at the corners. Mother says she wouldn't even know what to look under in the yellow pages, for a job like that. Elizabeth should be here, she said. She knew the names of things.

I don't know how to think all this through any more, except to ask if you would mind writing and just telling me if

146

*you love me or not, no strings attached. If you don't want me
to come in August, I won't.*

Matthew

Dear Alvareen,
   How are you? I'm doing just fine.
   *I'm writing because I asked Mrs Emerson to send my drill,
but so far she hasn't. Could you do it, please? The combination one, that sands and grinds and all. It's on the
lefthand side of the workbench. There is a metal case you can
put it all into compactly. If you mail it to me you can keep
that other five dollars, I bet the postage will come to nearly
that anyway. Thank you.*

Sincerely,
Elizabeth

JULY 18, 1961

Dear Elizabeth Abbott:
   *The bullet will enter your left temple. Although I prefer the
heart, for reasons which I am sure you understand.*

Yours very truly,
Andrew Carter Emerson

JULY 23, 1961

Dear Elizabeth,
   *Well I have mailed the drill like you asked. It's no surprise
about Mrs E. not sending it as I believe she is mad at you,
also out of town, quite alot. Turning into one of those
visiting mothers. She had a fight with Margaret's new
husband who she didn't hit it off with and came back early.
Now she's off seeing Peter in the summer school. Melissa up
there is going through some kind of breakup with her boy-
friend and always calling on the phone 'where is she, you
think she'd be home the one time I wanted to talk to her.'
Honey I don't know I tell her. I only come in with my key
and dust out these rooms that is seldom used anyway. If I
had the strength I would find me another job. My husband is
so bad with the arthritis he just all the time moans and*

147

*groans. Well the Lord knows what He is doing I suppose. I
must close for now as I am not feeling too well myself these
days.*

Sincerely,
Alvareen

Dear Elizabeth Abbott:
  Now prepare to die.

Yours very truly,
Andrew Carter Emerson

Dear Andrew Carter Emerson,
*Lay off the letters, I'm getting tired of them. If I'm not left
alone after this I'll see that you aren't either, ever again. I'll
fill out your address on all the magazine coupons I come
across. I'll sign you up with the Avon lady and the
Tupperware people. I'll get you listed with every charity and
insurance agency and Mormon missionary between here
and Canada. I'll put you down for catalogue calls at Sears
Roebuck and Montgomery Ward. When they phone you in
the dead of night to tell you about their white sales, think of
me, Andrew.*

Sincerely,
Elizabeth Abbott

8

'This is a story about an outlaw,' Elizabeth said. 'I got it
from the library.'

'Let me see the cover,' said Mr Cunningham.

She held it up for him – a pulpy book too lightweight for

its size, with a picture of a speeding horseman looking over his shoulder. Mr Cunningham nodded and let his head fall back onto his pillow.

He was growing smaller day by day, Elizabeth thought. He reminded her of a fear she used to have: that once grown, free to do what she chose, she might dwindle back into childhood again. Life might be a triangle, with adulthood as it apex; or worse yet, a cycle of seasons, with childhood recurring over and over like that cold rainy period in February. Mr Cunningham's hands were as small and curled as a four-year-old's. His formless smile, directed at the ceiling, had no more purpose than a baby's. He was in bed nearly all the time now. He lay propped on his back exactly as she had placed him, his arms resting passively at his sides. 'I do like westerns,' he said. His S's whistled; his teeth were gnashed helplessly in a glass on his nightstand.

'Chapter one, then,' Elizabeth said.

'Couldn't you just tell it to me?'

'It's better if we read it.'

'I'm not up to that.'

She flattened the book open and frowned at him, considering. They were doing battle together against old age, which he saw as a distinct individual out to get him. They read books or played checkers, pinning his thought to the present moment, hoping to dig a groove too deep for his mind to escape from. His attention span grew shorter every day, but Elizabeth pretended not to notice. 'Isn't it depressing?' people asked when they heard of her job. They were thinking of physical details – the toothlessness, the constant, faltering trips to the bathroom. But all that depressed Elizabeth was that he knew what he was coming to. He could feel the skipped rhythms of his brain. He raged over memory lapses, even the small ones other people might take for granted. 'The man who built this house was named Beacham,' he would say. 'Joe Beacham. Was it Joe? Was it John? Oh, a common name, I have it right here. Was it John? Don't help me. What's the matter with me? What's happening here?' When he awoke in a wet bed, he suffered silent, fierce embarrassment and turned his face to the wall while she changed his sheets. He viewed his body as an acquaintance who had gone over to the enemy. Why had she supposed that people's interiors aged with the rest of them? She had often wished, when things went wrong, that she were old and wise and settled, preferably in some nice nursing home. Well, not any longer. She sighed and creased the book's binding with her fingernail.

'We can read tomorrow,' Mr Cunningham said. 'Today, just sum things up.'

'If that's what you want,' said Elizabeth.

She turned to the first page and scanned it. 'It seems to be about someone named Bartlett. He starts out getting chased by a posse. He's riding through this gulch.'

'What's he wanted for?' Mr Cunningham asked.

'Well, let's see. They say, "In the course of his career as a gunman . . . " Probably one of those guys that hires out. Now he's coming to a shanty, there's a woman hanging out the wash. Her hair is the color of a sunset.'

'Red, they mean,' Mr Cunningham said dreamily.

'Who knows? Maybe purple.' Elizabeth snorted, and then caught herself. All these westerns were getting on her nerves. 'He asks her for a dipper of water from the well. Then when the posse comes up she hides him away, she tells them she hasn't seen a soul. Shs brings him beef stew and a canteen, and he sits there eating and admiring her.'

'This talk about water is making me thirsty,' Mr Cunningham said.

She laid the book on its face and poured him water from an earthenware pitcher. 'Can you sit up?' she asked him.

'I just don't know.'

She helped him, raising his head in the crook of her arm while he took small, noisy gulps. His head was strangely light, like a gourd that was drying out. When he had finished he slid down and wiped his mouth with the back of his hand. Even that much movement had been an effort for him. Resettling himself among the sheets, he gasped out the beginnings of defeated protests. 'I can't get – ' 'It don't seem – ' Elizabeth smoothed her denim skirt and sat back down. She was conscious of the easy way her joints bent and the straightness of her back fitting into the chair. Wouldn't he think of it as a mockery – even such a simple act as her sitting down in a Boston rocker? But it didn't seem to occur to him. He stared at the ceiling, flicking his eyes rapidly across it like a man checking faces in a crowd. Sometimes it seemed to her there *was* a crowd, packing the room until she felt out of place – dead people, living people, long ago stages of living people, all gathered at once into a single moment. She waited for him to call out some name she had never heard of, but he was still with her. 'Go on,' he told her. 'Get to the good part.'

'Okay.' She turned pages, several at a time. 'He's boarding with this woman, taking care of her livestock and such. He goes into town for provisions. Now he's – ' she skimmed the paragraphs. 'He's in the saloon, getting challenged by a tough guy.'

'What about?'

'They don't make it clear.'

'People in those days were so *cranky,*' Mr Cunningham said.

'They have this fistfight.'

'Where, out in the street?'

'Right in the saloon.'

'Oh, good.'

'Bottles smashing,' said Elizabeth. 'Mirrors breaking. Chairs going through the windows.'

'*That's* right.'

'Well, in the end he knocks the other guy out,' Elizabeth said. 'Then he has about a page and a half of bad mood, wondering why people will never allow him to go straight and lead a peaceful life. Let's see. But they don't know he's thinking that, they offer him a sheriff's badge.'

'Don't want the responsibility,' said Mr Cunningham.

Elizabeth glanced over at him and turned another page. 'He has to be argued into it, there's quite a stretch of arguing. Then – '

'I couldn't be expected to take on that kind of burden,' Mr Cunningham said.

'Well, it would be quite a job. But this is only a story. We're reading a story now.'

'*Oh,* yes. I knew that.'

'Where was I? They want him to be sheriff.'

'It's too much. It's too much. It's too much.'

'I'll just lower the shades,' said Elizabeth. She set the

book down and went over to the window. Mr Cunningham rolled his head from side to side. 'It's time to sleep,' Elizabeth told him.

'I'm too little.'

Elizabeth stayed at the window, looking down into the front yard. Heat waves shimmered up from the pavement, and the grass had an ashy, flat, washed-out look. She was glad to be here in the dimness. She pulled the paper shade, darkening the room even more, and then looked back at Mr Cunningham. His eyes were blinking shut. He kept his face set toward her. In the night, Mrs Stimson said, he sometimes woke and called her name – 'Elizabeth? Where'd you get to?' – turning her into another ghost, one more among the crowd whose old-fashioned faces and summer dresses filled this room. 'He just dotes on you,' Mrs Stimson said, and Elizabeth had smiled, but underneath she was worried: Wasn't he sinking awfully *fast?* Just since she had come here? Maybe, having found her to lean on, he had stopped making an effort. Maybe she was the worst thing in the world for him. When she read aloud so patiently, and pulled his mind back to the checkers, and fought so hard against his invisible, grinning, white-haired enemy in the corner, it was all because of that worry. She was fighting for herself as well – for her picture of herself as someone who was being of use, and who would never cause an old man harm.

She watched him drop off like this a dozen times a day, maybe more. He swam in again and out again. Mrs Stimson would say, 'Oh, bless his heart, he's sound asleep,' but there was nothing sound about that sleep. He seemed to have gone somewhere else, but always with a backward glance; returning, he glanced backward too, and mentioned recent experiences that he had never had.

His eyes were flinching beneath the lids. His mouth was open. Short breaths fluttered the hollows of his cheeks. The fingers of one hand clutched and loosened on a tuft in the bedspread.

Now was her time for just sitting. She had sat more this summer than in all the rest of her life put together, and when she bothered to think about it she wondered why she didn't mind. Day after day she rocked in her chair, staring

152

into space, while the flattened old man on the bed stirred and muttered in his sleep. Sometimes her eyes seemed *hooked* in space; to focus them took real effort, so that she would be conscious of a pulling sensation when Mr Cunningham woke again. Her mind was unfocused as well. She thought about nothing, nothing at all. She was not always conscious of the passage of time. It would have been possible to start a woodcarving, or to read some book of her own, but whenever she considered it she forgot to do anything about it. She would think of her whittling knives, which she had brought here on her first day of work along with two blocks of wood. She would picture the set of motions necessary to rise and fetch them, and then the wood itself: how the first slash along the grain would leave a gleaming white strip behind it. But from there her thoughts blurred and vanished, and when the old man awoke he would find her rocking steadily with her empty hands locked in her lap. It was as if she were asleep herself, or in that space on the edge of sleep where people make plans for some action but only dream they have carried it out.

The doorbell rang. Elizabeth rocked on. The doorbell rang again, and she gathered her muscles together to rise from the chair. 'Coming,' she called. Then she glanced at Mr Cunningham, but he only frowned slightly and stirred in his sleep.

The front door was open, so that as she came down the stairs she could see who stood behind the screen. But it took her several seconds, even so, to realize who it was. He was too much out of context. She had to assemble him piece by piece – first that stooped, hesitant posture, then the frayed jeans, finally the tangle of black hair and the smudged glasses. She stopped dead still in the hallway. 'Matthew,' she said.

'Hello, Elizabeth.'

Then, when she didn't open the door, he said, 'It's August. Here I am.'

' I wasn't expecting you.'

'Is it all right if I come in?'

'I guess so.'

He opened the screen door, but she led him no farther inside the house. If he had tried to kiss her she would have

153

dodged him, but when he didn't there was another awkwardness – how to stand, what to do with her hands, how to pretend that there was nothing new about the cold, blank space between them. 'Did you have any trouble finding me?' she asked.

'Your mother gave me directions?'

'How'd you find *her?*'

'Asked in town.'

He shifted his weight and put his hands in his pockets. 'None of it was easy,' he said. 'Not even locating Ellington. I was wondering if you hoped I would just get lost and never make it.'

'I wrote you not to come.'

'Only the once. You didn't say why. I can't leave things up in the air like this, Elizabeth.'

'Well,' said Elizabeth. 'How's your family?'

'Fine. How's yours.'

'Oh, fine.'

'Is there somewhere we could sit and talk?' Matthew asked.

She scratched her head. Then Mr Cunningham rescued her. Her name creaked down the stairs: 'Elizabeth? Elizabeth?'

'I have to go,' she said. 'He worries if I'm not there.'

'Could I come with you?'

'Maybe you could just meet me somewhere after work.'

'I'd rather stay,' Matthew said. 'I took a summer and seven hours getting here, I'm not going to lose track of you again.'

'Well, for goodness sake. Do you think I would just run off?'

Apparently he did. He only waited, blank-faced, until she said, 'Oh, all right,' and turned to lead him up the stairs.

Mr Cunningham lay motionless in his bed. He was nothing but shades of white – white hair and white pajamas, pale skin, white sheets – so pure and stark that Elizabeth felt happy to see him. 'I'm sorry, Mr Cunningham,' she said.

'I called and called.'

'Here I am. Come in, Matthew. This is Mr Cunningham.'

154

'How do, Mr Cunningham,' the old man said.

'No, this is Matthew Emerson. *You're* Mr Cunningham.'

'Well, I knew that.' He raised his chin, sharply. 'I thought you were pointing out *another* Cunningham. The name's not all that singular.'

'You're right,' Elizabeth said.

'I'm glad to meet you,' Matthew said.

Mr Cunningham frowned at him. 'Are you any kin?'

'Kin? To whom? No.'

'To *me.*'

'No.'

'Do I look like a man that would forget his own name?'

'No, you don't,' said Matthew.

'I keep in pretty good touch, for my age. I'll be eighty-seven in November.'

'That's amazing.'

Mr Cunningham turned his face away, irritably, as if something in Matthew's reply had disappointed him. 'I'd like more water,' he told Elizabeth.

'All right.'

'Believe you salted that egg too much.'

She poured the water and helped him raise his head to drink it. When he was finished she wiped the dribble off his chin. 'I'll just raise the shade now,' she told him.

'What's it down for?'

'You were asleep.'

'You *thought* I was asleep.'

She rolled the shade up. Sunlight poured into the room. When she turned back, Matthew had settled himself on the cane chair at the foot of the bed and was watching her. She had forgotten how open his face looked when he was staring at something steadily. Other people, returning from the past, could make her wonder what she had seen in them; with Matthew, she *knew* what she had seen. It was still there, even if it didn't reach out to her any more. He studied her gently, from a distance, puzzling over something in his mind but not troubling her with questions. All he said was, 'I never expected to see you in this kind of job.'

'This here is a very good nurse,' Mr Cunningham said.

'Yes, but –'

'When I'm well we're going on a trip together. Get

155

Abigail to arrange that, will you?' he said to Elizabeth. 'Maybe Luray Caverns.'

'All right,' she said. There was no telling who Abigail was. She bent close to his ear, so that a wisp of his silvery hair feathered her lips. 'Mr Cunningham,' she whispered, careful of his dignity. 'Would you like to go to the – '

'Later, later,' he said, with his eyes on Matthew. 'I can hold out. I have a guest. Hand me my teeth.'

She passed him the glass. He dabbled in the water a minute with shaky fingers, but he didn't take the teeth out. Maybe he thought he did; he rearranged his lips and gave her back the glass. 'Now then,' he said. 'Just imagine, a relation I didn't even know about. How's your family, boy?'

'Mr Cunningham,' said Matthew, 'I'm not – '

'Family all right?'

'Yes, fine,' Matthew said.

'Parents okay?'

'Oh, yes.'

Mr Cunningham looked at him a minute, and then he gave a cross little laugh. 'You ain't exactly *colorful*, are you?' he said. 'Are you shy? What grade you in, anyhow?'

Matthew threw a quick glance at Elizabeth – asking for help, maybe, or wondering how soon he could get out of this.

'Matthew is a grownup, Mr Cunningham,' she said.

'Is that so. Why? How old are you?'

'Twenty-eight,' said Matthew.

'*That* all you are? Call *that* grown up? The real growing up is between twenty and thirty. That's what I meant. I knew you weren't no *child*.' He hugged himself suddenly, as if he were cold. 'How's that pretty aunt of yours doing?' he asked.

'Uh, fine.'

'She should take better care of herself,' Mr Cunningham said.

'I'll tell her that.'

'Summer or no summer. Those skimpy little bathing suits are ruining the nation's health. You can get pneumonia in August, did you know that?'

'No, I didn't,' Matthew said.

'Quick summer pneumonia, they call it. Now who did I –? Yes. Took my little brother when he was two. Not a thing they knew could save him. How old would he be today, I wonder? What was his name?'

He was about to start fretting over his memory again, Elizabeth thought. She leaned forward, but before she could change the subject he shook his head. 'It don't matter anyway,' he said. 'He'd be an old man. What's the difference? I want a piece of whole-wheat toast, Elizabeth.'

She had been hoping he would go on forever, wearing Matthew down till he left without saying what he had come for. So she tried not answering (he might forget) but Mr Cunningham gave her a sharp look from beneath his pleated lids. 'Toast,' he said.

'Buttered?'

'Dry, just dry. I want things back to simple.'

She nodded and left, and Matthew followed just as she had known he would. 'You could stay here, if you like,' she told him.

He didn't bothering answering that. In the kitchen he said, 'Where are your blue jeans?'

'Mr Cunningham doesn't like women in pants,' she told him. She heaved a cat off the breadbox.

'You look so different.'

She concentrated on making toast, plugging the toaster in and emptying its crumb tray and carefully rolling the cellophane bag after she had taken out a slice of bread. Matthew sat down in a kitchen chair. 'Would you like something to eat?' she asked him.

'Everything about you has changed. I don't understand it. There's something muffled about you.'

'Oh well, I'm taking care of a very old man,' she said.

'Elizabeth.'

She jammed the toaster lever down.

'Look, this is such a *waste,*' Matthew said. 'What are you doing in this hot little house?'

'I like being here,' Elizabeth said. 'I like Mr Cunningham. I'm going to miss him when I leave for school.'

'For school. You're not coming back with me, then.'

'No,' said Elizabeth.

157

'Well, I knew that when I came, I guess. But I thought – and I never expected to see you like *this*.'

'Like what?'

'You're so changed.'

'You *said* that,' Elizabeth told him.

He was quiet for a moment, looking down at his hands. 'Well, I didn't want to fight about it,' he said finally.

'Who's fighting?'

'I came to get things straightened out. I didn't know what to think, way off in Baltimore. You weren't much help. You don't say what you feel, you *never* say what you feel.' He looked up, sending her one sudden spark of anger. 'Why is it that sometimes the things I like most about you make me dislike you?'

'Oh, well, don't let it bother you,' Elizabeth said. 'Other people have told me that.'

What she liked best about *him* was that slow, careful way of doing things – tracing the rim of a plate, now, stilling his hand when she laid the toast down. He had treated people just as carefully. He had never crowded her in any way. Watching her once in an argument with his mother, he had held back from protecting either one of them, although she had seen him lean forward slightly and start to speak before he caught himself. She could remember that moment clearly, along with the sudden ache of love that had made her stop in mid-sentence to turn to him, open-mouthed. Now the only feeling she had was tiredness. She sat down in the chair opposite him and set her hands on the table.

'I know I should have written again,' she said.

'Then why didn't you?'

'It wasn't on purpose. I just seemed to be going through some laziness of mind.'

'Try *now*, then,' Matthew said. 'Tell me why you left.'

She didn't look at him. She waited till the words had formed themselves, and then she said, 'That day with Timothy – ' Then she raised her eyes, and she saw the fear that jumped into his face. What she had planned to tell him, relieving herself of a burden, was going to weigh him down. She changed directions, without seeming to. 'That day after Timothy died,' she said. 'I stopped feeling comfortable there. I felt just bruised, as if I'd made a mess of things.' She kept her eyes on his, to see if he understood. 'Everything I'd been happy about before,' she said, 'seemed silly and pathetic.'

'Do you mean me?'

'Well, yes.'

'Did you stop loving me?'

'Yes.'

'And you aren't the type who'd just say that. Just as some kind of sacrifice to make up for, for anything that might have happened.'

'No, I'm not,' Elizabeth said.

Matthew sat back.

'I should have said it in that letter, I know,' she said. 'Only I was trying to do it roundabout, and ended up making a bigger mess than ever.'

'Don't you think you could change?' Matthew said.

'I know I won't,' she said. 'It's permanent. I'm sorry.'

Then she was just anxious to have him go, to get the last little dangling threads tucked away. She watched him gather himself together too slowly, rise too slowly, scratch his head. There were things she wanted to ask him – Would he drive all the way back now? Was he angry? Was he all *right?* Even when she didn't love him, he could still cause a stab of worry and concern. But questions would prolong his going; she didn't want that. 'I'll see you to the door,' she said, and she walked very fast out to the hallway.

'I can find my way.'

'No, I want to.'

When they reached the screen door she went out first and held it wide open for him. He stopped on the braided mat to shake her hand. He held it formally, as if they were just meeting, but she couldn't see his expression because the light was reflected off his glasses. They shone like liquid, the plastic rims pinkish and dulled with fingerprints. 'Well,' he said. 'I hope school goes all right.'

'Thank you.'

'Are you really *going* to school?'

'Well, of course.'

'I can picture you not ever getting out of here,' he said, and he gave her another long, stunned look so that she was suddenly conscious of her wrinkled denim skirt and the prison pallor of her skin. 'Maybe I'll see you again some-time. Do you think so?'

'Maybe.'

'And if you ever change your mind,' he said, 'or see things in a new light –'

'Okay.'

'I won't have married anyone else.'

She smiled, and nodded, and waved him down the walk, but she could picture him married to someone else as clearly as if it had already happened. She saw his life as a piece of strong twine, with his mother and his brothers and sisters knotting their tangled threads into every twist of it and his wife another thread, linked to him and to all his family by long, frayed ropes.

Elizabeth never did go back to school. By September Mr Cunningham was much worse, and he cried when he heard she was leaving and clung to her hands. She stayed on. She failed him more every day in their battle against the enemy. Then a year and a half later he died, on a weekend so that she wasn't even with him. The last thing he asked, Mrs Stimson said, was where Elizabeth was.

But she heard no more from Matthew. He never wrote her again.

9

1963

The trouble began on a Sunday morning in June. Margaret woke early, before her husband. She lay in bed feeling pleasantly hungry but too lazy to do anything about it, and she spent some time making pictures out of a complicated crack in the ceiling while she tried to remember a dream she had had. None of it came back to her. Only vague sensations – the smell of parsley in a brown paper bag, the feel of some rough fabric against her cheek. Then the crack in the ceiling dimmed, and she found herself looking directly into the face of her first husband. He was laughing at something she had just said. His black eyes were narrowed and sparkling; his mouth was open, lengthening his pointed chin. He had the carelessly put together look that is often found in very young boys. While she watched he stopped laughing and grew serious, but deliberately, exaggerating the effort, making a mockery of it, as if the laughter were still bubbling within him. He pretended to frown. All she saw in his eyes was love.

She buried her face in her pillow and started crying. Beside her, Brady stirred, and a minute later he had propped himself on one elbow and was trying to turn her over. 'Margaret? Margaret?' he said. She kept her face in the pillow. She cried on and on, while Brady first asked questions and then watched helplessly. When her tears seemed to be used up, she stopped. She sat against the headboard and brushed away the damp hair that was plastered to her face. 'I'm sorry,' she said. 'I don't know why I'm doing this.'

'You don't *know?* You've been crying for a quarter of an hour.'

'It must have been a bad dream,' Margaret said.

She watched him pacing the bedroom in his striped pajamas – a big, square, red-headed man with a kind face that screwed up into question marks when he was puzzled. In the sunlight, his hair turned orange and his eyelashes were white. He laid a hand on her forehead. 'You sure you feel all right,' he said.

'I'm fine.'

'I think you have a fever.'

'That's just from crying,' Margaret said. Then she reached for a Kleenex and got up to fix Sunday breakfast.

He kept a close eye on her all that day, and every time she caught him looking at her she smiled. By evening he seemed satisfied that she was all right again. He might have forgotten all about it, if it weren't that from then on – every two or three days, just when neither of them were expecting it – the tears returned. She would be breaking an egg into a frying pan, and all of a sudden her face would crumple and she would sink into the nearest chair. 'Margaret?' Brady said. 'Honey? What's wrong?' She never told him. She didn't *know* what was wrong. Why should Jimmy Joe come back like this? (Even his *name* seemed unrelated to her.) Why just now, when she was finally settled and happy and in love with someone who loved her back? She kept picturing Jimmy Joe's ducktail haircut, and the baggy, gray delivery coat he had worn the first time they met. Pieces of their apartment would suddenly appear before her – a dusty basement room in which they had lived out the five weeks of their marriage. Antimacassars on the sagging chairs, red checked oilcloth thumbtacked to the table. Turning the page of a book, she would see instead Jimmy Joe's bony, childish hands, with the nails bitten and the shiny new wedding ring much too loose once it got past the bulge of his knuckle. She ate breakfast staring blurrily at the sugarbowl, which had turned into the music box he brought her in a Kresge bag the night that they eloped. Subway wheels spun out the sound of his reedy voice, mocking lady customers, asking Little Moron riddles, telling her he loved her. 'Honey? Honey?' Brady said. She looked at him from a distance, unable to remember for a moment what he had to do with her.

She gave him lists of reasons to explain away the tears. She had a headache. She had her period. She must be coming down with something. Brady didn't listen. He watched her constantly, wearing on her nerves until she snapped at him, which made her feel terrible and then she started crying all over again for a different reason. If she said what was in her mind, he would think she had stopped loving him. She kept it to herself. She began watching him as closely as he watched her. They were so careful of each other, so quick to protect each other, that even while she slept Margaret was conscious of a tense alertness arching between them in the dark. She would wake and reach toward his hand, or move to lay her head on his shoulder, and then stop herself. Let him sleep. One touch and he would spring awake, asking, 'Are you all right? Are you happy?'

Over and over, Margaret's mother clicked through a long-ago shaft of sunlight in the basement room. She wore a cream wool dress. She lifted an antimacassar to stare at it and then plunked it down again, lopsided. 'Margaret darling,' she said. 'I'm sure you *think* you're in love. But you're only children! If it were really love would you be doing things this way – hidey-corner, fly-by-night?' And Margaret was crumbling, particle by particle, inch by inch, while she waited for Jimmy Joe to make a stand for her. He didn't. He never said a word. He sat on the arm of a chair with one sneaker propped on a radiator. His shoulders were hunched, his elbows were close to his sides, he chewed on a thumbnail and looked up at Mrs Emerson beneath eyebrows that met in the middle. Other images – the music box, their dimestore goldfish, the pack of Marlboros by Jimmy Joe's side of the bed – came and went fleetingly, sometimes no more than once. The scene with her mother returned, and remained, and left only to return again. Mrs Emerson's kid shoe prodded an issue of *House Beautiful*. Jimmy Joe chewed his thumbnail and did nothing, said nothing, allowed Margaret to be taken away from him and never saw her again.

'What you need is a trip somewhere,' Brady said. She started to disagree. Travel? When even in her own apartment she was feeling worn out by the roots? But then she saw his face, which was strained and tired. 'You're probably right,' she told him. They dragged out road maps and travel brochures and puzzled over where to go. No place looked just right. Finally they flew to California to visit friends, and they spent a week lying on beaches and smiling at each other too often. Brady got sunburned. His back peeled, his nose was bright pink, but there were still smudges beneath his eyes. And Margaret sat on a towel in a black bathing suit, her skin eternally a pasty white, and imagined Jimmy Joe stalking toward her across the sand. She began to feel angry; the anger was so strong it caused ripples in everything she looked at. Why was Jimmy Joe doing this to her? If he was going to hang around then why hadn't he stuck up for her all those years ago, when she needed him? She could feel the hurt and the shock all over again; she could see her mother repacking her clothes while

Margaret herself stood numbly by. 'This we can just leave behind, I believe,' her mother said, and she lifted a black lace nightgown between thumb and forefinger and let it slip to the closet floor.

At the end of July, Brady's patience was beginning to show the strain. He suggested a minister, a doctor, a visit home. Margaret refused them all. 'What *do* you want?' he said, and she said, 'Nothing.' What she wanted was a trip on her own, but at the same time she wanted to stay close to Brady. She shifted from one decision to the other, sometimes within minutes, without ever mentioning what was going through her mind. Then a chance for a trip rose all by itself: a wedding invitation. She met him at the door with it one evening when he came home from work. 'Guess what,' she said. 'Elizabeth Abbott is getting married.'

'Is that someone I'm supposed to know?'

'No, maybe not. She's just a friend of the family. I thought I might hop down,' she said, speaking rapidly, slurring over what she was telling him. 'It's just in North Carolina, I wouldn't be gone long.'

'Are you saying you're going alone?'

'Well, I thought, *you* know –'

'Maybe you should,' he said. 'Do you good to get away a while.'

She didn't know whether to feel relieved or worried, now that he had let her leave so easily.

The wedding was the second week in August. It was to be held in a Baptist church in Ellington. On the invitation, Elizabeth appeared as Elizabeth Priscilla – a middle name so unsuitable that Margaret had trouble making the connection. The groom's name was Dominick Benjamin Whitehill. Margaret had never heard of him, but then there was no reason why she should have. Elizabeth's letters weren't that informative. She wrote only two or three times a year – always briefly, in direct answer to letters from Margaret. Mainly she just asked how Margaret was and said that she was fine. She gave no more details than a fifth-grader might. She was working in a shop, her last letter had said. But what kind of shop, what was she doing there? She was living in Raleigh. She was getting along okay. And then, out of the blue, this invitation, with one

164

hand-written sentence scrawled on the bottom margin: 'Come if you want to – E.' As if she placed no real faith in all that copperplate engraving cordially inviting Margaret to attend.

Margaret couldn't locate Ellington on any Esso map. She called Elizabeth at her Raleigh address to find out how to get there, and Elizabeth said, 'Oh, you're coming, are you?' Her voice was lower than Margaret had remembered it. And her face she could barely picture any more. After all, they didn't really know each other. Uncertainty made Margaret clench the receiver more tightly. 'If you still *want* me – ' she said.

'Well, sure.'

'But I can't find Ellington.'

'Just look for – no. Wait. This thing is taking place in the morning. If you're coming from New York, you'd better get to Raleigh the night before. I can put you up at my apartment.'

'Won't I be in the way?'

'No, you'll solve the car problem. I can ride over with you in the morning.'

'Well, if you're sure,' Margaret said.

That was on Wednesday, her day for lunch with Andrew and Melissa. She avoided mentioning Elizabeth in front of Andrew, but when she and Melissa were leaving together she said, 'You'll never guess who's getting married.'

'Everyone but me already *is* married,' Melissa said.

'Elizabeth Abbott. Remember her?'

'No.'

'*Elizabeth.* Mother's Elizabeth.'

'Oh, her,' Melissa said. She stopped in the middle of the block to peer into her compact. 'Not to anyone in the family, I trust,' she said.

'No, someone named Whitehall.'

'Well, more power to her.' She snapped her compact shut and continued walking.

'I thought I might go to the wedding,' Margaret said. 'It's down in North Carolina.'

'Are you driving? You could give me a ride to Raleigh, if you're going near there.'

'What for?'

165

'I need to see a woman in Raleigh who makes patchwork evening skirts. It's for the boutique.'

'Oh, that,' Margaret said. The boutique was a vague, half-hearted plan that Melissa had first mentioned last April, on her twenty-sixth birthday. She had short bursts of enthusiasm, where she spilled swatches and drawings from her purse and talked about leather and velvet and Marimekko, but then her modeling engagements picked up again and she would forget all about it. This must be one of her slack periods. It was always a bad sign when she looked in her compact too often. 'This woman in Raleigh,' she said, 'sells her skirts for twenty dollars. We could get fifty, easily, if we could only pin her down. She hasn't got a phone and she doesn't answer letters. Just give me a lift there, will you?'

'I was thinking of going alone,' Margaret said.

'Well, *go* alone, I'm not crashing the wedding. Just take me as far as Raliegh.' She hailed a taxi, which coasted to a stop at the curb. 'When was it?' she asked.

'Saturday after next,' said Margaret, giving up. 'I'm going down that Friday.'

'Well, give me a ring beforehand, then.' And she slid into the cab, pulling her long, netted legs in last, and slammed the door. Margaret continued down the sidewalk with her handbag hugged to her chest. She was rearranging her vision of the trip to include Melissa. She pictured driving down hot southern highways with all the windows rolled up for the sake of Melissa's hairdo. Passing up Howard Johnson's (her favorite restaurant, with its peppermint ice cream) because Melissa would not be caught dead in such a place. Suffering through a hundred of those sharp, conclusive clicks Melissa's florentined compact made when she shut it. Then she thought, I'll just call her up and tell her I'm going alone, I don't want anyone with me. But she kept putting the call off from day to day, until it was too late.

Which was lucky, as it turned out. Because as soon as they had set off, on a bright Friday morning, with Brady still solitary and desolate in the rear-view mirror, Margaret started crying. She drove on until the car was out of his sight, and then she parked by the curb. '*You* drive,' she told Melissa. 'I can't.'

'Margaret, what in the world?'

'*Drive,* will you?'

Melissa muttered something and got out of the car. When she was back in, behind the wheel, she said, 'There's something you're not telling me. Have you had a fight with Brady? Is that why you're going off like this?'

'No, of course not,' Margaret said. She blew her nose, but went on crying. Melissa, without a glance behind her, nosed the car into traffic again. Horns honked, brakes squealed. She fluttered a hand out the window. 'You're getting a divorce,' she said.

'Oh, don't be silly.'

'Well, *what* then?'

But Margaret only buried her face in a Kleenex. She cried until they were well into New Jersey; she cried her way through half the Kleenex box, building a pile of soggy tissues on the seat beside her. She topped all the records she had set in the last two months. 'Margaret, would you *mind?*' Melissa said. 'Is this what you have planned for our whole *trip?*' Margaret turned further toward the window. She should have gone by train. This car was Brady's, and everything about it – the smudged radio dial, the leathery smell, the masculine-looking tangle of stray coins and matchbooks and tobacco flecks in the dashboard tray – made her wonder how she could have thought of leaving him. If she were alone, she would have turned the car around. (But then, when he opened the door and saw her, wouldn't that patient look cross his face again? He would shepherd her into the room, saying, 'There, now,' and making her wish she had just headed on south and never come back.)

In the middle of the New Jersey oilfields, she blew her nose a final time and blotted her eyes. 'I'm sorry,' she told Melissa. Melissa pushed the gas pedal and sailed past a Porsche. 'Think nothing of it,' she said.

'I just keep having these crying spells.'

'Oh well,' Melissa said, 'so do we all.'

Margaret, glancing sideways at her face, believed her. Melissa's mouth was a downward curve, dissatisfied-looking. Even behind her enormous sunglasses, fine lines showed at the corners of her eyes. 'Everyone,' Melissa

167

said, 'should have one day a month for nothing but crying. We'd all be a lot better off. Crime would stop, wars would stop, generals would lay down their arms –'

'But not *unreasonable* crying,' Margaret said.

Melissa only shrugged and passed another car.

In Pennsylvania they changed seats. Margaret drove, and Melissa filed her fingernails and polished her sunglasses and yawned at the huge, tidy farms that slid past them. 'I could never live in the country,' she said. 'God, it's hot. I wish your car was air-conditioned.'

'Roll down the windows,' Margaret told her.

'Never. We're going to the *sticks*, there won't be a decent beauty parlor in the state.'

Margaret didn't press her. She wasn't feeling the heat at all. She felt sealed in, immune. She was watching Jimmy Joe teach her how to drive, and he was laughing at her tense, forward-huddled posture behind the wheel until she lost her temper and they had their first and only argument. Jimmy Joe's left hand corrected her steering. A frayed gray Band-Aid looped his thumb.

They bypassed Baltimore. The countryside around it – more farms, pastureland, clumps of trees – reminded her of Matthew's place, and her mourning was extended to include him as well. He was the most loving of all her brothers. She might even have been able to tell him what was bothering her, except that it would just upset him. 'Why can't we stop off at Matthew's?' she asked Melissa. 'It isn't that far.'

'He would be at work.'

'Do you suppose he knows about Elizabeth?'

Melissa didn't answer.

'*Do* you?'

'Oh, I don't think they were all that serious, anyway,' Melissa said.

'Well, maybe not.'

'Even so, I hope he hasn't heard. Weddings do funny things to people.'

'I've hardly ever been to one,' Margaret said.

'Well, I have. Dozens. Always a bridesmaid, never a – especially when the minister says to show cause why they shouldn't get married. *You* know. "Speak now, or forever hold your peace" and sometimes the silence is so long, I start worrying I'll jump up and say something silly just to fill it.'

In the back of her mind, Margaret's second wedding was moved into a church and it was Jimmy Joe's voice that broke the silence. '*I* can, I can show cause,' he would say. 'I still love her.' 'You should have thought of that twelve years ago,' Margaret would tell him, and she would turn her back and take a closer hold on Brady's arm, shutting Jimmy Joe away forever.

In the afternoon they stopped at a restaurant Melissa approved of and ordered a late lunch. They sat across the table from each other, looking drained and frazzled, their ears humming in the sudden quiet. Melissa kept her sunglasses on. The tip of her nose poked out from beneath them, cool and white. 'For someone you barely know,' she said, 'you're certainly going to a lot of trouble. A wedding? In this heat? Or was it just to get away a while.'

'Both, I guess,' Margaret said. 'But I *would* like to see Elizabeth. I try to keep up a correspondence with her, not that she makes it all that easy.'

'Andrew goes into a mental state if he even hears her name. He says it was her fault what happened with Timothy.'

'That's ridiculous,' Margaret said.

'I'm just saying what he told me.'

'Well, don't.'

'Why take it so personally? You only saw her the once.'

'Whatever else she may have done,' Margaret said, 'she kept Mother company that whole awful year after Daddy died. Which was more than *we* did, any of us. I knew I should have, but I just couldn't. You should be thanking your stars she was around.'

'Well, it's not as if there was nothing in it for *her*.' Melissa said.

'Oh, stop,' said Margaret.

After that, they ate in silence.

They entered North Carolina late in the afternoon. They seemed to have come during a dry spell; the red soil was baked, the pines were harsh and scrubby, the unpainted barns had a parched look. 'KEEP NORTH CAROLINA

169

GREEN,' Melissa read off. '*Get* it green, first.' She pulled out her compact and a zippered bag full of bottles and tubes. It took her half an hour to remove all her make-up and put on fresh – an intricate task which she performed without speaking. Margaret drove in a daze of exhaustion. She barely winced when Melissa snapped her compact shut.

In Raleigh, they found a hotel for Melissa and unloaded her suitcase. 'Now, don't forget,' said Melissa, standing on the curb. 'The minute that wedding is over, I want to get *out* of here. Don't hang around all day. I plan on seeing this woman tonight; after that I'll just be twiddling my thumbs.'

'All right.'

'Don't go to any receptions or anything.'

'All *right*,' Margaret said, and she slammed the door shut and zoomed off.

Elizabeth lived in a green, wooded area that reminded Margaret of Roland Park, on the top floor of someone's garage. When Margaret climbed out of her car, twilight had just fallen and the lights in the garage windows were clicking on. She stood in the driveway, smoothing her rumpled dress, and then she pulled her suitcase from the trunk and headed for the wooden staircase that ran up the outside of the building. She felt large and pale and awkward, top-heavy on the rickety steps. As she climbed she wiped her damp forehead and ran her fingers through her hair, and when she reached the top she paused a moment to catch her breath. Through the screen door she could see a bright, cluttered room, pine-panelled, sparsely furnished. Elizabeth was just crossing toward her. 'Come on in,' she said. 'I heard you on the steps. Need a hand?'

She opened the door and reached out to take the suitcase. In two and a half years she had hardly changed at all. She wore jeans and a white shirt and moccasins; she might have been just about to go out and prune Mrs Emerson's poplar tree. Only her hair was short – hacked off raggedly, at ear level, making her look like a bushier version of Christopher Robin. A little sprig of a cowlick stood on the back of her head, as precise as the stem of a beret. 'I'm making you some supper,' she told Margaret.

'Oh, don't do that.'

'Why not? I have to eat myself.'

She slid the suitcase onto the daybed, which was already heaped with unironed clothes and a dozen blocks of wood. It must have been the wood that gave the place its workshop smell. Sawdust and shavings sprinkled the grass rug, and a stack of sandpaper sat on the table. In one corner was a large, mysterious object that turned out later to be a potter's wheel. 'Sorry about the mess,' Elizabeth said. 'I have to pack tonight.'

'*Tonight?* Don't you have to rehearse?'

'It's not going to be that complicated a wedding.' Elizabeth picked up a head of lettuce and took it over to the sink. 'At least, I hope it isn't,' she said. 'This whole thing is getting out of my control. Well, *they* know how it goes, I'll let them handle it. Want a beer?'

'Yes, thank you,' said Margaret.

Elizabeth got her one from the refrigerator and then hooked a chair with the toe of her moccasin and pulled it out from the table. 'Sit and rest,' she said. 'I hope you like hamburgers.'

'I do. It's nice of you to put me up like this. I know how busy you must be.'

'Me?' she laughed. 'No, I can use the lift to Ellington.'

'Is that where you'll live? Ellington?'

'Mmhmm.' She was cutting the lettuce into a wooden bowl. Margaret watched her and took sips from her beer, which instantly started to numb her. If she had any sense, she would stop drinking right now. Instead she kept on, dreamily fixing her eyes on Elizabeth's quick hands. Elizabeth poured dressing over the salad, slapped out some meat patties, dumped a can of beans into a saucepan. 'I'm trying to use up most of the food,' she said. 'Then I'll give what's left to a guy I work with.'

'Where *do* you work?' Margaret asked.

'In this handicrafts shop, over a tavern. I wait on customers and stuff. And they stock some of my carvings.'

'Do many people buy them?'

'No,' said Elizabeth. She looked toward the blocks on the daybed. 'They keep coming in and picking them up, they say, "Oh, I like this *type* of thing, do you have any more?" Then I show them more. They like that type, too, but they don't often buy them.' She laughed. 'I'm glad I'm quitting. I never did like waiting on customers.'

'It's different from being a handyman,' Margaret said.

'Yes.'

'Did you like *that* job?'

'Oh, yes.'

But she didn't say anything more about it. She hadn't even asked how Margaret's family was, and Margaret didn't want to bring them up on her own.

The whole of that evening, as it turned out, was centered on packing. Elizabeth packed the strangest things. Five cardboard boxes were filled with broken odds and ends – cabinet knobs, empty spools, lengths of wire, wooden finials. 'What are they *for?*' Margaret asked, and Elizabeth said, 'I may want to make something out of them.' She dumped a handful of clock parts into a suitcase, and folded yards and yards of burlap down on top of them. Margaret watched in a beery haze. She was never able to remember much of her visit later – only in patches, out of chronological order. She remembered Elizabeth striding through a jumble of paint cans, munching on a hamburger. And her own trips from couch to refrigerator, and back to the couch with another beer. She sat in a slumped position, like something washed up on a beach and left to dry out and recover. Her shoes were abandoned on the rug; her dress became sprinkled with breadcrumbs and sawdust and bits of potato chips. 'Oh, I feel so *relaxed,*' she said once, an Elizabeth stopped work to laugh at her. 'You look it,' she said.

'I'll never get up for the wedding tomorrow. Are there going to be many guests?'

'No. I don't know. Just whoever they invited.'

'Why was *I* invited?' Margaret said – something she never would have asked sober. But Elizabeth didn't seem to mind. She straightened up from a pile of books, thought a while, and then said, 'I don't know,' and went back to work again. Margaret decided it was better than a lot of answers she could have been given.

Twice some people stopped by – a married couple with a gift, two boys with a bottle of champagne. The couple stayed only a minute and kissed Elizabeth when they left. The boys sat down for a beer. Margaret couldn't remember seeing them go.

And meanwhile Elizabeth worked steadily on, clearing the room. Her clothes were the last thing she packed. She threw them into a steamer trunk and slammed the lid. 'Done,' she said.

'How are you getting all this to Ellington?' Margaret asked.

'Dommie will move it in a truck, later on.'

'Dommie? Oh. You haven't said anything about him,' Margaret said. 'What's he like? What's he do?'

'He's a pharmacist. He's taking over his father's drugstore.'

'Well, that'll be nice.'

'How's your family?' Elizabeth asked suddenly.

'They're fine.'

'Everything going all right? Everyone the same as usual?'

'Oh, yes.'

Margaret's mind was still on Dommie, trying to picture him. It wasn't until several minutes later that Elizabeth's questions sunk in. Had she wanted to hear about Matthew? There was no way of knowing. By then Elizabeth was making up the daybed, moving around with sheets and army blankets while Margaret watched dimly and sipped the last can of beer. 'On the way down here,' Margaret said finally, 'we passed so close to Matthew's house I was tempted to stop in and see him.'

Elizabeth folded the daybed cover, slowly and silently.

'He never married, you know,' Margaret told her.

But all Elizabeth said was, 'Didn't he?' Then she put a pillowcase on a pillow and laid it at the head of the daybed. 'Well, here's where you sleep.'

'How about you?' Margaret said.

'I have a sleeping bag.'

She brought it out from the closet and unrolled it – a red one, so new that a label still dangled from the zipper-pull. 'We're supposed to go camping on our honeymoon,' she said.

'But you can't just sleep on the floor. Why don't we change places? You need to rest up for tomorrow.'

'I don't mind the floor, it's the *ground* that's going to

173

bother me,' Elizabeth said. 'Old roots and stobs and crackling leaves.'

'Why are you going, then?'

'Dommie likes nature.'

'Doesn't the bride have some say?'

'I did. I chose camping,' Elizabeth said. 'You don't know Dommie. He's so *sweet*. He makes you want to give him things.'

'Well, still –'

'You want first go at the bathroom?'

'Oh. All right.'

She had thought she would fall into a stupor the minute she was in bed, but she didn't. She lay on her back in the dark, watching the windowpane pattern that slanted across the ceiling. Music and faint voices drifted over from the main house. A screen door slammed; crickets chirped. On the floor Elizabeth breathed evenly, asleep or at least very relaxed, as if tomorrow were any ordinary day. Her white pajamas showed up blurred and gray – the same pajamas, probably, that she had worn back in Baltimore. There they had slept in Margaret's old twin beds, with fragments of Margaret's childhood lining the bookshelves and stuffed in the closet. And she had lain awake, just as now. She had been going over and over Timothy's death – not yet wondering *why* he died, or picturing how, but just trying to realize that she would never again set eyes on him. Tonight he seemed faded and distant. The sadness that washed over her wasn't because she missed him but because she *didn't* miss him; he was so long ago, so forgotten, a tiny bright figure waving pathetically a long way off while his family moved on without him. They were caught up in things he had never imagined. He had never met Brady, or Mary's daughters, or Peter's strange girlfriend. And he wouldn't know what to make of it if he could see her here, in a garage in North Carolina the night before Elizabeth's wedding.

She flowed from Timothy to Jimmy Joe, to what would happen if *he* should see her here. Anywhere she went, after all, it was possible to run into him. Anywhere but Baltimore – he must surely have moved on. Maybe to New York, to materialize beside her at a counter in Bloomingdale's. Maybe to that beach in California. Maybe to Raleigh. He would come sauntering down the street with his windbreaker collar turned up, soundlessly whistling. His eyes would flick over her, veer away, and then return. 'Oh,' he would say, and she would stop beside him, poised to rush on to somewhere important as soon as she had said hello. 'How are you?' she would ask him, smiling a social smile. 'Oh, *how* could you just let me go, as if five weeks of me were all you wanted.'

She saw his mouth starting to frame an answer. His lips were slightly chapped, his shoulders were thin and high, and his hands were knotted in his windbreaker pockets. This time when the tears came she thought of them as a continuation, interrupted on some days by dry-eyed periods. She rolled to a sitting position, disguising her sniffs as long deep breaths, and reached for her purse at the foot of the bed. Beneath the window, Elizabeth stirred.

'Are you in some kind of trouble?' she asked.

She must have been awake all along; her voice was firm and clear.

Margaret said, 'No, I think it's an allergy.'

She fumbled for a Kleenex. Then she said, 'I seem to keep having these crying spells.'

'Anything I can get you?'

'No, thank you.'

'Well, if you should think of something.'

'I'm really very happy,' Margaret said. 'I'm not just saying that. I *felt* so happy. Everything was going so well. Now all of a sudden I've started thinking about my first husband, someone I don't even love any more.'

'Oh, well, he'll go away again,' Elizabeth said.

Margaret stopped in the middle of refolding a Kleenex and looked over at her. All she saw was a dim gray blur.

'You don't know what it's like,' she said. 'Nobody does. I keep remembering things I'd forgotten. I keep thinking about the last time I saw him, when my mother walked in and just took me away and he never said a word.'

'Took you *away*? How did she do that?'

'Just – oh, and he *allowed* it. I've never been so mistaken about anyone in my life. She packed me off to an aunt in Chicago. But do you think he even lifted a finger?'

'How did she find you?' Elizabeth asked.

'I'd written her a note once we got settled, telling her not to worry.'

'But took you away! She's so little.'

Through her tears, Margaret laughed. 'No, not by force,' she said. 'She didn't drag me out by the hair or anything.'

'How, then?'

'Oh, well – ' Margaret stared past Elizabeth and out the window, where the sky was a deep, blotting-paper blue. Her tears had stopped. She zipped her purse and set it at the foot of the bed. 'I feel much better now,' she said. 'I hope I didn't keep you from sleeping.'

Elizabeth said nothing. Margaret lay down and watched the ceiling. It tilted a little from all the beer she had drunk. She was conscious of an alert, unsettled silence – Elizabeth still wakeful, still not saying, 'That's all right,' or 'This could happen to anyone,' or some other soothing remark to round off the conversation. 'You must think our family is pretty crazy,' Margaret said after a while.

'More or less.'

It wasn't the answer she had expected. 'They aren't *really,*' she said, too loudly. Then she sighed and said, 'Oh well, I guess they *could* wear on your nerves quite a bit.'

Elizabeth stayed quiet.

'Dragging you into all our troubles that way. It must – '

'Ha,' said Elizabeth.

'What?'

'They didn't drag me *in,* they wanted me for an audience.' She clipped off the ends of her words, as if she were angry. 'I finally saw that,' she said. 'I was hired to watch. I couldn't have helped if I'd tried. I wasn't supposed to.'

'Oh no, I think Mother just liked having you around,' Margaret said.

'That's what I'm saying.'

'But I don't *see* what you're saying.'

'They were always asking me to do something,' Elizabeth said. 'Step in. Take some action, pour out some feeling. And when I didn't, they got mad. Then once, one time, I did do something. And what a mess. It was like I'd blundered onto the stage in the middle of a play. What a

176

mess it made!'

'I think you must be talking about Timothy,' Margaret said.

Elizabeth only rolled over and plumped her pillow up.

'But *you* didn't do anything,' Margaret said. 'Nobody thinks you're to blame.'

'Talk to your mother about that.'

'Why? Because she never kept in touch? Well, you have to see *that* – she just doesn't want to be reminded. If there's anyone she blames it's herself.'

'Not that I ever heard,' Elizabeth said.

'She blames herself for telling Timothy that you were taking Matthew home with you.'

'Well, she — what?' Elizabeth sat up. 'When did she tell him that?'

'Before he left the house, I guess,' Margaret said. 'That morning. She says she should have let *you* do it, however you were planning to.'

'Before he left with *me*? Before we went to his place?'

'Sure, I guess so.'

'He knew all along, then,' Elizabeth said. 'All the while he was asking to come with me. He *planned* it that way. He was trying to make me feel bad.'

'Maybe so,' said Margaret. 'Anyway, I don't know how — '

'If I never see another Emerson in all my life,' Elizabeth said. 'I'll die happy.'

Which should have hurt Margaret's feelings, but it didn't. She was feeling too sleepy. Sleep took her by surprise, dropping the bottom out of her mind, and suddenly she was blinking and floating, losing track of what they were talking about, spinning off into blurry unrelated thoughts. She was barely conscious of the sound of a match striking. She heard Elizabeth inhaling on a cigarette and crumpling cellophane – wakeful, daytime sounds, but they only made her sink further away. She slept deeply, feeling trustful and protected, as if Elizabeth sitting alert on the floor were a sentry who would keep watch for her through the night.

The wedding was held in a red brick church in the middle of nowhere. Elizabeth directed Margaret there, along glaring highways. She wore her jeans, and her hair was not combed; it blew out like a haystack in the wind. She was going to change at her parents' house, she said. In the back seat were her suitcase and her sleeping bag. A linen suit hung from a hook by the window. 'Oh, you're not wearing a long dress,' Margaret said. 'No,' said Elizabeth. All her answers this morning were brief and vague. Her mind must be on the wedding. She watched the road with narrow gray eyes that looked nearly white in the sunlight. Her face was calm and expressionless, and her hands, curled around her pocketbook, remained perfectly still.

'Here's where my family lives,' she said finally, and Margaret pulled over to the side of the road. The driveway was choked with cars, each one crinkling the air with heat waves. A woman stood on the cement stoop of the ranch-house, and as soon as the car doors opened she called, 'Happy wedding day, honey!' and started down the steps. Margaret hung back, although it was she who carried the white suit. She hated to be the only stranger in someone's family gathering. 'I'll just go straight to the church,' she told Elizabeth.

'Come in, if you want to.'

'No, I'll just – '

She pushed the suit on top of Elizabeth's sleeping bag and turned toward the church, barely taking time to wave at the woman. It must have been Elizabeth's mother. She was saying, 'You haven't got much time, honey. Oh! Won't your friend stay? Mrs Howard's already at the organ, you can hear her if you'll listen. Your flowers are in the icebox but don't you dare get them out till the very last thing, you know how they'll – where are your *shoes,* Elizabeth? Are you planning to get married in moccasins?' If Elizabeth said anything, Margaret didn't hear her.

She walked along the highway to the church, which had only one car in front of it and a Sunday school bus to the side. Although she felt awkward going in so early, it was too hot to stand out in the sun. She climbed the steps and entered through the arched door. Inside, she smelled lemon oil and hymn books. The light was so dim that she stood in the back of the nave for a moment, blinking and widening her eyes, listening to the organ music that wound its way down from the choir loft. The pews were empty, their backs long polished slashes. In front of the altar was a spray of white flowers. The windows were rose-colored and stippled with asterisks. Margaret crossed to the nearest one and opened the lower pane. Then she sat down in the pew beneath it, but still no breeze came to cool her. She picked up a cardboard fan stapled to a popsicle stick and stirred the warm air before her face.

At Elizabeth's house, now, they would all be gathered around and fussing over her, straightening her veil and brushing her suit. Margaret imagined her standing like a totem pole, dead center, allowing herself to be decorated. But she couldn't picture her coming down this aisle. She turned in her seat, looking toward the doorway, and saw the ushers just stepping inside with carnations in their buttonholes. They looked back at her, all out of the same perplexed brown eyes. Was she on the correct side of the church? Which was the bride's side? She couldn't remember. She stayed where she was, to the right of the altar, and whisked her fan more rapidly.

People began filing in – old ladies, a few awkward men, women who took command of the church the moment they stepped inside. They clutched the ushers' arms and beamed at them, whispering as they walked ('How's your mama? How's that pretty little sister?'), while the ushers stayed remote and self-conscious, and the women's husbands, a few steps behind, carried their hats like breakable objects. The organ grew more sure of itself. A fat lady slid into Margaret's pew, trailing long wisps of Arpege. 'I finally did make the Greyhound,' she said.

'Oh, good,' said Margaret.

The fat lady frilled out the ruffles at her elbows, touched both earlobes, and pivoted each foot to peer down at her stocking seams. Margaret turned and looked out the window. If she ducked her head, she got a horizontal slice of grass, ranch-house, and the lower halves of several pastel dresses and two black suits heading toward the church. In the center was Elizabeth's white skirt, drawing nearer – a sight that startled and scared her, as if she herself were involved in this wedding and nervous about its going well.

The fat lady had started talking, apparently to Margaret.

'You knew Hannah couldn't make it,' she said. 'She's having such a lot of trouble with Everett. But *Nellie* will be here. "Oh," she told me, "I wouldn't miss it for the world. Been waiting a long time to see that boy get married." Well, *you* know. It came as quite a surprise. I had always thought he would marry Alice Gail Pruitt. I expected to see Liz Abbott die an old maid, to tell you the truth.'

'Why is that?' Margaret asked.

'Well, she's been mighty difficult. Wouldn't you say?' She kept looking around the church while she spoke, as if she had lost something. 'Didn't they do a nice job with the flowers, now. A few more wouldn't hurt, but – *we* had thought she'd lost Dommie forever, but then he broke off with Alice Gail and came right back here where his heart had been all along. Talk about patient! That boy has the patience of a saint. I just hope Liz knows how lucky she is. And her parents! They've been angels to her. I said to Harry, I said, speaking for myself I just don't know how John and Julia do it. "If it were me, Julia," I told her once – '

As if on cue, Mrs Abbott started up the aisle on the arm of an usher. She was an older, heavier Elizabeth, but her speech was a continuation of the fat lady's. Margaret could hear her clearly as she passed. 'That child's *hair!*' she told the usher. 'Oh, I begged her to leave it long. "Just till after the wedding," I told her, "that's all I ask." But wouldn't you know . . . ' She passed on by, a whispering blue shadow wearing white roses and absently patting the usher's hand. He kept his eyes on his shoes.

Then the organ paused, and a door at the front creaked open and the minister came out. If she hadn't known ahead of time, Margaret would never have guessed that he was Elizabeth's father. He was tall and handsome and frightening, dressed in black with a small black book between his clasped hands. He was followed by two young men. When they had arranged themselves at the front, so that Margaret could tell which was the groom, she sat forward to take a closer look. She had noticed how Elizabeth described him. 'Sweet,' she had said – not a word that Margaret would have expected from her. But now she saw that nothing else would have been accurate. Dommie Whitehill's face was the kind that would stay young and

180

trusting till the day he died; his eyes were wide and dark, his chin was round, his face was pale and scrubbed and hopeful. His short brown hair was neatly flattened with water. If he had any last-minute doubts, none showed in the clear, shining gaze he directed toward the back of the church.

The organ started up, louder this time. What it played was not the traditional march, but then it couldn't be what Margaret thought it was either – the wedding music from *Lieutenant Kije*. She looked toward the aisle and saw a frilly blonde in pink – Elizabeth's sister, it must be, but softer and prettier – keeping pace with some more dignified music in her head and carrying a nosegay. Behind her came Elizabeth, on the arm of a young man whom Margaret assumed to be the brother-in-law. Elizabeth's white suit was crisp and trim, but without her dungarees she seemed to lose all her style. She walked as if her shoes were too big for her. A short veil stuck out around her face like a peasant's kerchief. Her escort scowled at the carpet, but Elizabeth's face was serene and the music had brought out one of her private half-smiles. They passed Margaret and continued forward, beyond a multitude of flowered hats and whisking fans.

When everyone was in place, Margaret sat back and wiped her damp palms on her skirt. 'Things are going to be all right, I believe,' the fat lady whispered. Margaret watched Elizabeth's father open his black book and carefully lay aside a ribbon marker. 'Dearly beloved . . . ' he said. He was one of those ministers who develop a whole new tone of voice in front of a congregation. His words rolled over each other, hollow and doomed. Margaret forgot to listen and watched Elizabeth's straight white back.

But Elizabeth wasn't listening either. The moment her father started reading she turned toward Dommie, as if the ceremony were some commercial she already knew by heart. She spoke, not whispering but in a low, clear voice. Margaret was too far away to hear what she said. Dommie turned toward Elizabeth and parted his lips; Elizabeth waited; but when he said nothing she went on speaking. Her father's voice crashed above their heads, unnoticed.

Now *no* one was listening. Everyone watched Elizabeth. Whispers traveled down the pews. 'You would think just this *once* – ' the fat lady said. Even Elizabeth's father seemed to have stopped hearing what he was saying. He spoke with his eyes on Elizabeth, his finger traveling lower on the page, line by line, without his following it. He was going faster and faster, as if he were running some sort of race. 'Do you, Dominick Benjamin . . . ' Dommie's face turned reluctantly from Elizabeth. 'I do,' he said, after a pause. He had the strained, pre-occupied look of someone interrupted in the middle of more important things. 'Do you, Elizabeth Priscilla . . . '

Elizabeth's pause was even longer. A fly spiraled toward the ceiling; someone coughed. Elizabeth drew herself up until she was straight and thin, with her elbows pressed to her sides and her feet close together.

'I don't,' she said.

No one breathed. Elizabeth's father snapped his book shut.

'I'm sorry, I just don't,' she said.

Then she turned around, and the organ gave a start and wheezed into *Lieutenant Kije* again. Elizabeth came down the aisle slowly and steadily with her nosegay held exactly right and her head perfectly level. Oh, why didn't she just turn and run out that little door at the front? How could she bear to travel all that long way by herself? Margaret thought of leaping up and shouting something, anything, just to pull people's eyes from Elizabeth. But she didn't. She stayed silent. After one glance at Dommie, frozen before the pulpit, she stared down the aisle as hard as anyone.

It took several minutes for people to realize what had happened. They just sat there – even the fat lady. Then the organ dwindled out in the middle of a note, and whispers and rustles started up. Mrs Abbott rose and marched firmly toward her husband. She looped one arm through his and the other through Dommie's, and led them back out the little door.

'Did you ever?' all the women were asking, rising and clustering together. 'Did you ever *hear* of such a thing?' the fat lady said. 'I always did want to see somebody do that,' a

182

man told Margaret. She smiled and sidled out of the pew. In the doorway, Elizabeth's sister stood circled by more flowered hats. She looked dazed. 'I don't understand, I just don't understand,' she kept saying. A woman with feather earrings said, 'Now tell me this, Polly. Had they had a little quarrel or something?'

'*Dommie* wouldn't quarrel,' an old lady said.

'Did they – '

'She *told* us she'd changed her mind,' Polly said. 'Told us just as we left the house. Father said no. He said, "Liz, now all the guests are here," he said, "and you owe them a wedding," and she said, "Well, all right, if a wedding's what you want." But we never thought, I mean, we thought she meant – and Father said she was sure to feel differently, once she was standing at the altar.'

'Well, of course. Of course she would,' someone said. '*All* brides get cold feet.'

'That's what he told her,' Polly said, ' "And they forget about it an hour later," he told her, but Liz said, "How do *you* know? Maybe they're just saying that, and they regret it all their lives. It's a conspiracy," she said – oh, but still I never thought – Mother asked if there were anyone else. I mean, anyone, *you* know, but she said no, and you could tell she meant it, she looked so surprised – '

'Excuse me,' Margaret said. She slid sideways through the crowd until she reached the front steps. Then she shaded her eyes and looked all around her. The sun had bleached everything – the grass, the walk, the highway – but in all that whiteness there was no sign of Elizabeth's wedding suit. She had vanished. All she had left behind were two high-heeled shoes placed neatly side by side on the bottom step.

Margaret walked to her car very slowly. She wanted to give Elizabeth a chance to catch her, in case she needed a ride. But no one called her name. By the time she reached the highway she was feeling a letdown. Now I suppose I'll never hear from her again, she thought. I'll never know how this turned out. Then she opened her car door, and there was Elizabeth on the front seat.

She was slouched so far down that she couldn't be seen from outside, but she didn't have a fugitive look. She seemed flattened, exhausted, as if her sitting so low were merely poor posture. 'Hi there,' she said.

'Elizabeth!'

'You think you could get me out of here?'

Marglaret slid in and slammed the door and started the car, all in one motion. When she pulled onto the highway she left streaks of rubber. Anyone watching would have known it was a get-away car. 'Elizabeth,' she said, 'are you all right?'

'More or less,' said Elizabeth.

But from the stoniness of her face, Margaret guessed that she wanted to be left in peace.

They flew down the highway, across mirages of water that streaked its surface. Margaret wanted to make sure where they were going, but she was afraid to break the silence. Then they entered Ellington, and Elizabeth sat up straighter and looked out the window. 'There's where I went voting,' she said.

'Boating?' Margaret asked. There was no water anywhere, but she couldn't believe that Elizabeth would mention voting at a time like this.

'Voting. Voting,' said Elizabeth. 'Polly's husband said I ought to.' She sighed and trailed a hand out the window. 'There were all these people lined up. Shopkeepers and housewives and people, just waiting and waiting. So *responsible*. I bet you anything they wait like that every voting day, and put in their single votes that hardly matter and go back to their jobs and do the same chores over and over. Just on and on. Just plodding along. Just getting through till they die. You have to admire that. Don't you? Before then I never thought of it.'

'I admire *you*,' Margaret said.

'What for?' said Elizabeth, absently. 'But when I was waiting to vote I thought, Wouldn't you think I could do that much? Make some decisions? Get my life in order? Let my parents breathe easy for once? Well, I tried, and you see what happened. Just before the finish line I think no, what if I'm making a mistake? Sometimes I worry that everyone but me knows something I don't know: they set out their lives without *wondering*, as if they had a few extras stashed away somewhere. Well, I've tried to believe it, but

I can't. Things are so permanent. There's damage you can't repair.'

'But it took a lot of courage, doing what you did today,' Margaret said.

'*Flashes* of courage are easy,' said Elizabeth, with her mind on something else. Then suddenly she spun around and said, 'What's the matter with you? What are you admiring so much? If I was so brave, how'd I get into that wedding in the *first* place? Oh, think about Dommie, he's always so sweet and patient. And my family doing all that arranging, and people coming all that way for the wedding. But *Dommie*. He's never said a mean thing in his life, or done anything but hope to be loved. What am I going to tell him now?'

From far back in Margaret's mind, where she hadn't even known it existed, came the picture of Dommie's face as he watched Elizabeth leaving him. His eyes were blank and stricken; his mouth was closed, unprotesting. He hadn't yet realized what was happening to him. He unfolded before her eyes as complete and as finely detailed as if the glance she had given him had taken whole minutes, as if she had known him for years and had memorized that picture of him line by line and dreamed of it every night. She blinked and widened her eyes, tightening her hands on the wheel as she drove.

'Well, shoot, Margaret,' said Elizabeth. 'It's weddings you cry at, not the escapes from them.'

'So,' said Melissa, settling herself in the car. 'How'd the wedding go?'

'It didn't.'

'It didn't? What happened?'

'She got to the altar and said, "I don't," ' said Margaret. She laughed, surprising herself. 'Well, it really wasn't funny, of course.'

'Sounds funny to *me*,' Melissa said. She frowned, briefly interested. Then she said, 'Well, anyway, this patchwork skirt woman. She's a *nut*. I'm sorry I ever came down. Do you know what she said to me? I said, "Look, you're getting twenty dollars for these things. I'll give you twenty-five apiece," I said, "if you'll supply me with a dozen now and all you can make from now on." "Twenty-five?" she said. "Well, I don't know, there's something fishy about that." You'd think I was trying to sell *her* something. "Look," I told her . . . '

Margaret gazed through a traffic light. She was thinking of Jimmy Joe, who might be sauntering down the sidewalk just a block from here. His collar would be turned up, he would be whistling beneath his breath. When he saw her, he would stop and wait. She reached out and touched his wrist, which was frail and bony. 'Jimmy Joe,' she said, 'I'm sorry I left you the way I did.' He smiled down at her and nodded, and then he walked on. If he ever came back it would be dimly, for only a second, in the company of others whose parts in her life were finished.

' "How do I know I'll *feel* like making all those skirts?" she asked me. *Feel* like it! What next? "Oh, I believe I'll just go my own little way," she said. Teeny old scrawny woman living all alone, you'd think she'd be jumping at the chance. In her front yard she'd set a bathtub on end and turned it into an icon.'

Margaret laughed.

'Why do you keep laughing?' Melissa said. 'I think you've spent too much time with Elizabeth.'

'Elizabeth? No. She wasn't laughing at all.'

'Oh, that doesn't matter,' Melissa said. 'She's all in the mind anyway. Margaret, what am I going to do? I was counting on patchwork skirts. What can I do instead?'

Margaret didn't answer. She was out on the highway now, concentrating on driving, trying to get home before nightfall.

10

Mary's letter said, 'Good news, Morris and I are going off for a week in July. Just the two of us, no children. Finally we'll be able to finish a conversation, I told him . . . . '

Mrs Emerson read it several times, trying to figure out what was expected of her. Was this a hint? Was Mary hoping her mother would babysit? No, probably not. The last time she visited Mary she had overstayed her welcome. Only four and a half days, and she had overstayed. She had replaced a scummy plastic juice pitcher with a nice glass one – nothing special, just something she picked up in downtown Dayton – and Mary had thrown a fit. 'What is my juice pitcher doing in the garbage?' she had said. 'What is this new thing doing here? Who *asked* you? What right did you have?' Mrs Emerson had packed and left, and held off writing for three weeks. Then just a bread-and-butter note, brief, formal, apologizing for waiting so long but life had been so cram-*packed* lately, she said. And now what?

She wandered through the house carrying the letter, pressing her fingers to her lips while she thought things over. If she didn't offer to babysit she would be missing a chance to see her grandchildren. If she did offer, she might be turned down. The insult pricked her already; imagine how much worse if it actually happened! But if she didn't offer . . .

She climbed the stairs to her bedroom. Lately her legs had grown stiff. She moved like an old lady, which she had promised herself she would never do, and although her shoes were still frail and spiky she had lately been eying the thick, black walking shoes in store windows. If she wore

187

sheer stockings with them, after all, if she bought the kind of shoe with a fringed flap so that people thought she had merely changed into a tweedy type . . . . Her hand rested heavily on the banister, and when she reached the top she had to pause to catch her breath before she went into her bedroom.

Dear Mary, she wrote on cream notepaper. *How nice to hear about the vacation. It will do you a world of good. You don't mention a babysitter, and maybe you've already found one, but I did want to let you know that just in case you haven't –*

She stopped to read over what she had written. Although she had chosen her words carefully, her handwriting was deliberately a little more slapdash than usual. Let it look casual, spur-of-the-moment. But when she took up her pen again, she paused and read the letter a second time. She was thinking of her grandchildren. Four of them, three girls and a boy, and she would like to know where people got the idea that girls were quieter. Oh, they ran her ragged. Climbing too high, jumping too far, running too fast. Talking in their high-pitched voices with excited gulps for air. Always hiding her things and giving shrieks of laughter when she missed them. Was she even sure she *wanted* to do this?

Grandchildren were not all they were cracked up to be. She held onto that thought a minute, enjoying it, before she flicked it away again. Grandchildren were wonderful. What *else* did she have to live for? Her committee work was fading out; her friends were turning into droning old ladies or even, some of them, dying. Mornings, when she came downstairs in a fresh crisp dress and looked all around her at the high ceilings dripping cobwebs, she sometimes wondered why she had bothered to get up. The house seemed thinner-walled, like an old and brittle shell, and she was a little dried-up scrap of seaweed rattling around in its vastness. But then she would remember her children, who descended and spread out from her like a fan, and *their* children spreading out further; and she felt grand and deep and bountiful, a creamy feeling that she held to tightly all through her empty mornings. She felt it now. She rose and made her way to the hall again, for no other purpose than to fill all the other rooms with her richness while it lasted.

Down the stairs, which was harder on her legs than coming up but not so bad for her chest. Through the lower hall, touching pieces of furniture meaninglessly as she passed them. And into the kitchen, where she put a piece of bread in the toaster because it was possible that she had skipped lunch. While she waited for the toast she gathered dirty dishes and set them into the sink. Alvareen had not been by for a week. It looked as if she had finally quit, and all over a little spat that had no importance whatsoever. She had claimed she ought to be paid for her sick-days. 'Seeing as you always save up what work I missed, every rag and tag,' she said, 'and I got to do it then when I get back, you ought to at least pay me for it.' 'That's rubbish, that's ridiculous,' said Mrs Emerson. 'I don't have to stand for any smart talk, Alvareen, I can always find some clean hard-working girl to bring in from the country.' 'Suit your-self,' said Alvareen. What Mrs Emerson couldn't bring herself to tell her was that it wasn't just *work* she paid Alvareen for, it was her presence in the house, something to drive the echoes away. But try letting her know that: she would puff up immediately, maybe ask for a raise. Mrs Emerson would not even give her the satisfaction of a telephone call. If she quit, she quit. There *were* no more clean hard-working girls in the country (where had they got to, anyway?) but good riddance, even so. She'd make do without.

The toaster clicked. Mrs Emerson took the last clean plate from a cabinet and went over to the table, but then she saw that the toast had not come up. It was caught down inside by one bent corner. Mrs Emerson poked it with a finger, and nothing happened. She circled the table thoughtfully. 'Never put a fork in a toaster,' people were always saying. It might have been the only advice she had ever been given; it came in a chorus, from somewhere above her head. Lately she had been noticing how many opportunities there were for painful deaths. Anything was possible; gas heaters exploding, teenaged drivers running her down, flying roof slates beheading her in a windstorm, and cancer – oh, cancer most of all. Several nights she had awakened with the certain, heart-stopping knowledge that when she died it would be in some horrible way. She had pushed it off, but the knowledge sank in and became accepted. In the daytime she often found herself surveying her actions from some distant point in the future. This was me, before it happened, she would say, going about my business blissfully unaware, never dreaming how it would end. The thought gave a new tone to everything she did. Measuring out tea leaves or folding back her bedspread was tinged with a lurking horror, like the sunlit village scenes in vampire movies. And where there was actually some danger – getting this toast out, for instance – she became nearly helpless. She spent minutes just staring at the toaster, plotting courses of action. A wooden spoon, maybe – something non-conductive. But how did she *know* it was non-conductive? She had only the scientists' word for it. Finally a channel seemed to break through in her brain, and she clicked her tongue at herself and bent to unplug the toaster. Even then, she didn't put her fingers in. She turned the toaster upside down and shook it, scattering crumbs all across the kitchen table.

When she had buttered the toast, she took it with her into the hallway. There she picked up the telephone and dialed Mary's number. Lines whirred and snapped into action halfway across the continent. The phone rang several times at the other end, and then Mary said, 'Hello?'

'Oh, Mary,' said Mrs Emerson, as if she had forgotten whom she was calling. 'How are you, dear?'

'Oh, fine,' said Mary, and waited.

'How wonderful about the vacation,' said her mother.

'Yes, isn't it?'

'And no children along.'

'No.'

'You'll be leaving them behind.'

'Well, I don't see what's so wrong about *that*,' Mary said. 'You and *Daddy* went off sometimes. It's not as if – '

'No, no, it's a fine idea,' said Mrs Emerson. 'I think it's just fine.'

'Well, then.'

'Now that you mention it though,' Mrs Emerson said, 'do you have someone to stay with the children?'

'Oh, yes, that's all taken care of.'

'No problem there, then.'

'Oh, no.'

'I see. Of course, if it's *settled,*' Mrs Emerson said. 'But you know I'm willing to help out with them if I'm needed.'

'Thank you, Mother. I think we can manage.'

'Oh. All right.'

'We'll leave them with Morris's mother, and that way there'll be less – '

'*Morris's* mother!' Mrs Emerson said. She put her other hand to the receiver. 'But *she* gets to see them all the time!'

'All the more reason,' said Mary. 'They're more used to her. We have to think of the children's side of this.'

'But I am,' Mrs Emerson said. She picked up a ballpoint pen and bent over the telephone pad, although there was nothing she wanted to write down. Her voice was soft and feathery. No one hearing it would have guessed how tightly she held the pen. 'It's for the children that I want to come, after all,' she said

'Yes, but with Pammie in this nightmare-stage, one more trauma is all she – '

Mrs Emerson drew a straight slash across the pad and straightened up. 'You have just said a word which I utterly despise,' she said.

'Now, Mother – '

'I loathe it. I detest it. *Traumas.* How much harm can it do them to see their grandmother once in a while? How long has it *been*, after all? I so seldom – '

'It's been seven weeks,' said Mary. 'In the past year you've paid us four visits, and all but one lasted nearly a month.'

'There, now. See?' said Mrs Emerson. 'You don't make sense. First you say the children aren't used to me and then you say I'm around all the time.'

She smiled brightly at her wavery yellowed reflection in the antique mirror. Her hair clung to her forehead, which was damp. Although she wasn't hot, a flush of some sort was rising from her collarbones. She undid the top button of her blouse.

'It's not *my* fault I'm not making sense,' Mary said. Her voice was younger and higher; she sounded as if she were back at that terrible time in her teens, when all she seemed

191

to do was cry and throw tantrums and pick out her mother's niggling faults. 'Mother, can't you stand on your own *feet* any more? You're out here all the time, and every visit you make I have the feeling you might not go home again. You get so *settled*. You seem so *permanent*. You act as if you're taking over my household.'

'Why, Mary,' Mrs Emerson said. She laid her fingers to her throat, which was tightening and cutting off her breathing. 'Where could you get such a thought? Don't you see how careful I am to be a good guest? I help out with the chores, I give you and Morris a little time alone when he comes home in the evenings – '

'You circle around whatever room we're in, clearing your throat. You throw out all our food and buy new stuff from the health store. You make a point of learning the mailman's name and the milkman's schedule and the garbage days, as if you were moving in. You send my clothes to the laundry to save me ironing when ironing is something I enjoy, you buy curtains I can't live with and hang them in the dining room, you string Geritol bottles and constipation remedies all across my kitchen table – '

'Well, if I'd only – '

'*Then* you go off to Margaret's and spoil little Susan rotten. She told me so.'

'Oh, this is unfair!' said Mrs Emerson. 'How was I to know, if no one tells me?'

'Why should we *have* to tell you?'

'Well, now that I've heard,' said Mrs Emerson, getting a tighter grip on her voice, 'you'll have no further cause for complaint. I certainly won't be troubling you again.'

'I might have known you'd take it that way,' said Mary.

'Well, what am I supposed to say? Anything I do is wrong. I shouldn't visit, I shouldn't *not* visit. What, then, Mary? Why are my children so un – un – ?'

Her tongue stopped working. It jerked and died. Her throat made an involuntary clicking sound that horrified her. She dropped the receiver, letting it swing over the edge of the table. 'Mother?' Mary's voice said, tinnily. Long cold fingers of fear were closing around Mrs Emerson's chest. She buckled her shaking knees and slid to the floor. Then, like a very poor actor performing an artificial death, she felt her way to a prone position and lay staring at the underside of the table. 'Mother, what *is* it?' Mary said. The swinging receiver was nauseating to watch. Mrs Emerson closed her eyes and felt herself draining away.

When she looked up at the table again it seemed darker, clustered with spinning black specks. Was she going blind? She tried to work her arms, but only one responded. It moved to touch the other, which felt dead and cold and disgusting. She was dying in pieces, then. How fortunate that she had got the children grown before this happened. They *were* grown, weren't they? Weren't they? There seemed to be one baby left over. But when she tried to picture him she realized that she had never seen him; he was that poor little soul born dead, between Melissa and Peter. Well, but it was logical that she should have thought of him; she was going to heaven to meet him, after all. So some people said. Only he had managed alone so long, and the ones left here needed her so much more. How could she bear to look down and see her poor, unsatisfied children struggling on without her? And don't tell her she *wouldn't* see them. If heaven was where people stopped being concerned with such things then no woman would be happy there.

The undersurface of the table was rough and unfinished, a cheat. From above, it had always been so beautifully polished. In one corner a carpenter's pencil had scrawled the number 83, and she spent a long time considering its significance. Her mind kept floating away from the problem, like a while balloon. She kept reaching out and grabbing it back by the string. Then she saw a small gray brain, a convoluted bulb growning on the inner side of one table leg. Shock caused new chills to grip her chest, before she realized that she was looking at a chewed piece of gum. Chewing gum. She saw cheerful rows of green and pink and yellow packets strung across the candy counter at the Tuxedo Pharmacy. She saw her children snapping gum as they came in for supper, a nasty habit. Chewing open-mouthed, on only one side, their faces peaceful and dreamy. Laying little gray wads on the rims of their plates before they unfolded their napkins. How often had she told them not to do that? The wads cooled and hardened; Margaret, her sloppiest child, would pry hers off the plate and pop it back in her mouth when she had finished eating. Was it Margaret who had stuck chewing gum to her mother's walnut table?

The children swam up from the darkness at the edges of the hallway. Not I, not I, they all said. They were happy and glowing, as if they had just come in from outdoors. Matthew and Timothy and Andrew, their voices newly changed, their hands newly squared and hardened so that she kept having an impulse to reach out and touch them. Teenaged boys are so difficult to live with, a friend whispered. Yes, difficult, Mrs Emerson said politely, and she smiled and nodded, rubbing the back of her head against the floor, but inwardly she disagreed. She was layered around with teenaged boys, all huge and gangling, making her feel small and frivolous and well-protected. In the middle of their circle she spun, laughing. She was going to stay at this moment in time forever.

It was some trouble with Mary that caused her to be lying here. She remembered now.

She was arguing with her husband, something about the baby. Matthew. This is the wrong one, she said. In the hospital he was fairer. How could I have such a dark-headed baby? She had made him drive her back to the hospital, she had carried the baby in naked, the way he had arrived, rolled in a blue receiving blanket. Would she ever forget how the nurses had laughed? They had called in doctors, orderlies, cleaning ladies, to share the joke with them. In their center she stood looking at the unwrapped baby and saw that he was her after all – those level, considering eyes, wondering how much to expect from her. She had started crying. 'Why honey,' her husband said. 'This isn't like you.' And it wasn't. She had never been like herself again. All the rush of life in this house, that had carried her along protesting and making pushing-off gestures with both hands. All the mountains out of mole-hills, the molehills out of mountains. 'The trifles I've seen swelled and magnified!' she said, possibly out loud. 'The horrors I've seen taken for granted!'

She opened her eyes, although she had thought they

194

were open already. There was something she had to do. Feed someone? Take care of someone? Was one of the children sick? No, only herself. She had to call for help. She framed the word 'Mama' and discarded it – too strange a mouthful, it must be inappropriate. Her husband? She worried over his name, which was almost certainly Billy. But would she have married a Billy? Oh, after all the hesitation and excitement, the plans, the doubts, the final earth-shaking decision of whom to marry – and now look. She couldn't remember which man she had ended up with. It was all the same in the end.

She circled Billy, looked at him and then away again, finally made up her mind to speak. 'But!' she said aloud. Her tongue was playing tricks on her. She tried again, making such an effort that her forehead tightened. 'But!' she called, and saw Billy dead in his bed, his profile barely denting the pillow. Without taking time to mourn she went on to Richard. Would he help? But Richard was tinkling in the rosebushes. Men! His broad, sloping back reminded her of some sorrow. There was no one left. When she awoke in the night, the bed beside hers glowed white and leaped to her eyes at first glance as if it had something to tell her. So there! it said. She rocked her head from side to side.

Now, that clicking sound. Was it her throat again? Her heart? Her brain? No, only the telephone company, reminding her to hang up. She nearly laughed. Then she grew serious and gathered her thoughts together. It was necessary to call a doctor. She was quite clear about it now. She tensed her neck muscles and raised her head. Far away her feet pointed upward, side by side, ludicrous-looking, the feet of the wicked witch in *The Wizard of Oz*. Her good arm moved to support her. She was just fine; she could do anything. She sank back again and stared up at the table. Beneath it, wooden braces ran diagonally at each corner. They were held in place by screws, which were sunk in round holes so that the heads were flush with the wood. Wasn't it wonderful how the holes were so round? How the slant of the braces fit so well to the table angles? There was a word for that; she had heard it once.

'Mitering,' Elizabeth said.

Elizabeth, she said silently but briskly, I'm going to want

a new backing for that picture of the head of the stairs. Mend the glass in the bookcase. Coil the hose, please. I can't go getting sued if it trips someone. Do you know how to restring a venetian blind?

Elizabeth's voice came in on a muffled jumble of sound, like a loudspeaker in a railroad station. She spoke in fragments. 'The what?' she said. 'What would he do *that* for?' 'Oh, well – ' She laughed. 'If I have time, maybe,' she said.

We are falling to pieces around here, Mrs Emerson told her.

Elizabeth laughed. 'So are most people,' she said.

Elizabeth, we are -

'All right, all right.'

Mrs Emerson prepared to sleep, with everything taken care of. Then some irritating thought began drilling her left temple. She had forgotten: she'd stopped liking that girl a long time ago. Shiftless. Untrustworthy. The world was made up of people forever happy, wastefully happy, laughing at something too far away for Mrs Emerson to see even when she stood on tiptoe. She craned her neck. She clutched at Andrew's elbow for support. What do you want from me? she asked him.

'Let us in,' he said.

He left. She was all alone. She was back before the children, before her husband, back to the single, narrow-boned girl that had been looking out of her aging body all these years.

'Let us in,' a man said. He rattled the front doorknob. 'Mrs Emerson? Are you there? Can you hear us? Let us in!'

She meant to answer, but forgot. Voices brushed against each other on her front porch. They were wonderful men, just wonderful. They were here for her. Love and trust washed over her in a flood, and she closed her eyes and smiled.

They broke the window of the front door. Now, why would they do such a thing? Large pieces of glass clanged on the floor while she screwed up her face, trying to figure it out. Then she found the answer. She was pleased with the rapid way her mind was working. She turned her head to watch a blue-sleeved arm reach in and unsnap the lock. The door opened and two policemen entered, dressed in full uniform just for her. 'Mrs Emerson?' one said.

'Ham,' she said, and then she went to sleep, finally in the care of someone competent.

11

Matthew sat by the hospital bed, looking at a *Saturday Evening Post* while his mother slept. He ran his eyes down a couple of lines, broke off in the middle, and turned the page. He glanced at a few more lines, turned another page. None of what he read was coming through to him. His mind was on his mother, who lay on her back with her hands by her sides. Her face seemed young and unlined. Her eyes moved beneath the veined lids, following dreams. When Matthew was small, coming in to wake her on a Sunday morning, he had watched her in just this way – jealous, back then, of her dreams, which might not be concerned with him at all. Now he hoped that he was farthest from her mind. 'Don't give her anything to worry about,' the doctor had said. 'Let her sleep as much as she wants, keep her calm and quiet.' Which made Matthew consider, and re-consider, before he even opened his mouth. The most trivial small talk might lead to something disturbing. When she slept, he was relieved. He willed her into dreams of a long-ago time when she was young and untroubled. He sent her thought-waves of her youth, which for some reason he pictured against a sunlit, windy meadow sprinkled with daisies. 'Before you were born . . . ' she used to tell him, and that meadow would rise in front of him, with his mother running through it dressed in white and laughing, free of quarrels and tears and insufficiencies of love.

He glanced across the bed at Mary, who was knitting a child's sweater. Every time she came to the end of a row she reeled more yarn off the ball with a long, sweeping motion and frowned into space a moment, as if she were trying to remember something. Once she sighed. 'You must be tired,' Matthew said. 'Why don't you go on home?'

'Oh, no.'

And then she returned to her knitting. She had spent more time here than Matthew, even – two full days, planted in that armchair. And at night, when he took her home, her mind was still back with her mother. 'If only I hadn't *quarreled* with her,' she kept saying. 'I mean, stated my case, but quietly. Put her off a little instead of coming right out with things. Do you think she blames me?'

'No, of course not.'

But there was no real way of telling. Their mother's speech was difficult; she could talk, but only after false starts and hesitations. To save effort she kept to the bare essentials. 'Water,' she said, and it could have been a polite request or a surly order, no one knew. Yet the doctor said she would be back to normal in no time. Already the paralysis was lifting. Her face merely had a numb look, as if she were under Novocain. Her hand was beginning to respond to massage, and she was anxious to try walking. 'Your mother's a remarkable woman,' the doctor said. Mary frowned, as if he had told her something she didn't want to hear.

Margaret had come, but she had had to bring the baby. She only visited the hospital when Mary was home to babysit. And Andrew had arrived on the bus the day before, still pale and shocked over the news. 'She's fine, she's going to be fine,' they told him. But he barely heard. In the hospital room he prowled nervously, stopping every now and then to lay a hand on his mother's forehead, and finally they had sent him home in a cab. 'But I want to be *with* her,' he kept saying. 'Hush, now,' Mary told him, 'you'll only make her worse, going on like this.'

'Can I come back this evening?'

'She'll be *home* day after tomorrow, Andrew.'

'Who will stay with her later on? Are you all going to leave her alone again?'

'No, no.'

'*I'll* stay. I'll come here to live, I've been meaning to for years.'

198

'No, Andrew.'

But who *would* stay with her? It was on all their minds. The girls had to go home soon. Matthew was planning to spend his nights there for a while, but his mother needed someone in the daytime. 'Where is Alvareen?' Mary asked. No one had thought to wonder before. They looked at the house, which seemed stale and dusty. Not even Alvareen would have let it get that way. Had she quit? They asked Mrs Emerson, who merely closed her eyes. 'What's her last name?' Mary said. 'Do you have her phone number? We want her to come look after you.'

'No,' said Mrs Emerson.

'No, what? You don't have her number? Or you don't want her to come.'

'I don't want – '

'You don't need a nurse, exactly,' Mary said.

'No.'

'Is there someone *you* can think of?'

Mrs Emerson raised her good hand to her lips and frowned. She sighed, apparently about to give up, and then just as she was turning her head away she said, 'Gillespie.'

Mary looked at Matthew, puzzled. 'Gillespie?'

'Gil – ' Mrs Emerson struggled to a half-sitting position. She looked irritated. '*Gillespie*,' she said.

'Elizabeth,' Matthew said suddenly.

'Elizabeth? The handyman?'

Mrs Emerson sank down again. Mary raised her eyebrows at Matthew.

'She'd be good if she'd do it,' Matthew said. 'I saw her taking care of a sick old man once.'

'But you don't think she'd do it,' Mary said.

'I don't know.'

'You know better than anyone else.'

'What makes you say that?' Matthew asked. 'Do you think I keep in touch with her or something?'

'Well, excuse *me*,' said Mary.

'Sorry,' Matthew said. 'Well, give it a try, if you want. I don't know what she'll say.'

Mary tracked down Elizabeth's parents right then, from the phone in the hospital room. She had the operator place the call person-to-person to Elizabeth. While she waited

Matthew stood at the window with his back to the room, pretending to be looking at the view. He wound a venetian blind cord around his fist. 'Lots of visitors today,' he told his mother. Mrs Emerson made some small, impatient gesture that rustled the sheets. Then Mary tensed, listening, 'I see,' she said. 'Well, place the call there, then. Thank you.' She cupped the receiver and turned to Matthew. 'They say she lives in Virginia now. They gave us the number to call her at work – some kind of children's school.'

'School? *Elizabeth?*'

'They said – ' She uncupped the receiver. 'Yes? All right, I'll hang on. They're trying to reach her now,' she told Matthew.

But Matthew didn't stay to hear. He had a sudden urge to get away, as far as he could from Elizabeth and even from the phone that connected her. 'Think I'll buy a cup of coffee,' he said, and he bolted from the room while Mary stared at him. Once he was outside he took several deep breaths. He pressed the elevator button, and then when it didn't arrive immediately he pushed out the swinging door beside it and started down the stairs.

Elizabeth would never come. He didn't even want her to. He had stopped thinking about her long ago. The hole she left, after the last time he saw her, had made him realize that he wasn't happy living alone; and he had conscientiously taken out several other girls in that first empty year. One he had grown serious about. He had considered asking her to marry him. Then Elizabeth had unfolded herself from a dim corner in the back of his mind, shaken the dust off her jeans and stretched her legs. Her face was bright, threaded across with wisps of blond hair blowing in the wind. She was laughing with a careless kind of joy that took itself for granted. But once he had made his decision – broken off with the other girl, although he sometimes regretted it – he was no longer troubled by Elizabeth. His life had solidified. He was a man in his thirties who lived by himself, encased in a comfortable set of habits and a plodding, easy-going job. He liked things the way they were. Change of any kind he carefully avoided.

He bought a cup of coffee from a vending machine and

drank it very slowly. Then he returned to his mother's floor using the stairs again, and when he got back Mary was peacefully knitting in her armchair. 'Sssh,' she told him. 'Mother's asleep.'

He went over to the window. 'Sun's out,' he said.

'Is it?'

'The forecast was rain.'

'I talked to Elizabeth,' Mary told him.

He stayed quiet. Mary untwined another length from her ball of yarn.

'I asked if she could come, but she said no. She's not interested.'

'Oh. Well, then,' Matthew said.

'Then I thought of Emmeline. Remember her? Do you happen to know what her last name might have been?'

'Why are you asking *me* all these things?' Matthew said. 'Ask Mother, she's the one who keeps using people up and throwing them out. Wouldn't you think she could just once *keep* someone?'

'There, now,' Mary said. 'Keep your voice down, Matthew.' And she went on serenely knitting that endless sweater.

Mrs Emerson came home in an ambulance, pale and mysterious on a wheeled stretcher. Mary rode with her; the others stayed at the house to meet her. As soon as the ambulance drew up to the curb Mary leaped out, all energy and efficiency. 'Coming through! Coming through!' she called, and chased Matthew from the front door so that she could open it wider. 'Is the room ready? Are the sheets turned down?' The men bore the stretcher up the steps. Mrs Emerson stared straight into the sunlight with the corners of her mouth slightly curled. 'Where is the *door-stop?*' Mary asked. Beside her, the others seemed drab and subdued. Margaret stood next to Matthew, with little Susan over her shoulder. Andrew waited just inside. His face loomed out of the dimness like a sliver of moon on a cloudy night. 'Out of the *way*, Andrew,' Mary told him, but he paid no attention. 'Should you be so loud?' he ased. 'Mother? Are they going too fast?' The men navigated the stretcher through the house, calling out warnings and cursing panel posts and doorframes. Mrs Emerson's smile seemed to be apologizing for her sudden awkwardness. She had been so small, all her life. Now she had grown to the size of a bed, with four square corners to catch on furniture.

She was taken to the sunporch, which Mary had converted to a sickroom. Her twin bed filled one wall, with a table beside it already bearing a tumbler and a water pitcher, flowers in a vase, a pile of slick new magazines. At the other end were all the chairs that had once been scattered through the room. They were placed in a double row, as if Mary had planned on the family's sitting there as rigid and watchful as an audience. Beneath one window was the television, its face newly Windexed, waiting to be depended upon.

'Easy, easy now,' one of the men said, and they lifted Mrs Emerson from the stretcher. She held her neck stiff and clutched at her bathrobe. Matthew, watching her face, could tell when she tried to move her paralyzed hand and failed. There was a shift in her expression, a momentary distance in her eyes, as if she were surprised all over again at the failure and was just recollecting how it had come about. Then she was settled. Her lips moved, and firmed themselves, but instead of speaking she merely nodded to the men. They backed out of the room with the stretcher between them.

For the first hour, there was a concentrated flurry centered in the sunporch. A servant's bell was brought in, and a reading lamp. Andrew put ice in the water. Susan was set on the bed but she cried and had to be taken away again. And everyone, without intending to, kept speaking for Mrs Emerson. 'How nice to be *home!*' Mary said. Then she caught herself, and laughed. Mrs Emerson raised her head. 'It fools – ' she said.

'Feels? Feels too hot?' said Matthew.

'Too cold,' said Mary.

'Strange,' said Andrew.

Mrs Emerson brushed them all away. 'Summery,' she said. Then she closed her eyes, as if she were disappointed at such a pointless remark after all that effort. Everyone rushed to make a fuss over it. 'It *does,*' Mary said, and Andrew said, 'It's June now, you know. Good time to be on

202

the sunporch.' They fell silent and looked at the slant of yellow light. 'Tomorrow,' said Mary.'I'll get the window washers in.'

Mrs Emerson didn't open her eyes.

Pianists, Matthew thought, are the ones that get arthritis, and artists go blind and composers go deaf. And his mother, who pulled all the family strings by words alone, was reduced to stammering and to letting others finish her sentences. All morning they supplied her words for her – never exactly the right ones, never in the proper tone. Tears of frustration kept slipping out of the corners of her eyes and forming gray discs on the pillow. Her chin trembled and her mouth turned downward. She gave her children the feeling that it was they who had failed.

They found her a memo pad, and closed her fingers around a ballpoint pen. But what good was that? Even writing letters to her children, she had preferred using a dictaphone first to try out the words on her tongue. She threw the pen away, with such a jerky movement that it landed in the bedclothes. Then she shook her head, over and over again. 'Sorry,' she told them.

'It's all *right,*' said Mary. 'Nobody blames you at all. Do we? We know how hard it must be.'

Lunch was eaten in the sunporch, with Mary beside the bed helping her mother and the others in the lined-up chairs. Susan was put on the windowseat, where she popped all her peas with one finger and babbled to herself. Everyone was grateful to have her there. During breaks in the conversation they watched her intently, implying that there was much more they could be saying if only she hadn't distracted them.

Supper was easier; their mother was asleep. But by then they were all exhausted. They ate sandwiches by a dim light in the dining room, on a table cluttered with bills and playing cards which no one had the energy to move. 'How do *nurses* do it?' Margaret asked. 'There are four of us. Wouldn't you think we could manage better than this?'

Mary raised her chin from her hand and said, 'Margaret, do you know Emmeline's last name?'

'Emmeline. Emmeline – it will come to me. Why?'

'We figured she might take care of Mother after we

leave.'

'Well, that's a thought,' Margaret said.

'*Mother* knows her name, I'm sure of it, but she pretends she doesn't. She's latched onto the idea of Elizabeth.'

Andrew lowered his sandwich carefully to his plate, and Margaret shot a glance at him. 'Then why *not* Elizabeth?' she asked.

'Margaret?' Andrew said.

'She won't come,' said Mary, ignoring him.

'Did you try her?' Margaret asked.

'We called her this morning.'

'Really? Where's she at?'

'Virginia,' said Mary. 'I thought you kept in touch with her.'

'Oh, no. Not since, not for years. I wrote but she never answered. What'd you say to her?'

'This conversation is pointless,' Andrew said. 'I would never allow her to come back here.'

'Well, she isn't, so don't go into a stew over it,' Mary said.

'Stew? Who's stewing? I merely feel –'

'She isn't *coming,* Andrew.'

'Can you guarantee that?' Andrew said. 'She's packing her bags right now, I can feel it. Wild horses couldn't keep her away. Well, if necessary I'll bar all the doors and lock the windows. I won't allow it. *Mother* wouldn't allow it.'

'Mother's the one who asked for her,' Matthew said.

'There are other people she likes in this world.'

'But not that she asked for.'

'I'm surprised at her. I don't understand her, she used to not even want to hear her name. Are you sure she said *Elizabeth?* Does she *remember?*'

'*Mary,*' said Margaret, 'what did you *say* to her?'

'Just asked if she could help out with Mother a while. She said no.'

'Did you say it would only be for a short time? Did you tell her we'd just need her till Mother's herself again?'

'She didn't give me a –'

'Did you say all we wanted was a nurse, pure and simple? No other problems dumped on her? Did you tell you we'd let her go back afterward to her old life?'

'Well, of *course* we'd let her go back,' said Mary. 'Why should I bother telling her *that?*'

'You did it all wrong, then,' Margaret told her.

'I did the best I knew how.'

'We should call her again and give her a limit. Six weeks, say. Tell her six weeks is all she'd – '

'Margaret,' said Andrew, very quietly, 'I'd like to state a preference, please.'

'*You* get sick and you can state your preferences,' Margaret told him. 'This time it's Mother that's sick. Shall I call Elizabeth now? Matthew?'

'Babcock,' said Matthew.

They stared at him.

'I just remembered Emmeline's last name. Babcock.'

'You're right,' Mary said.

But Margaret said, '*Emmeline's* not the one Mother asked for.'

'She's much superior, though,' Andrew said.

'Emmeline wouldn't even *come!* I'm sure of it! She never forgave Mother for firing her like that. Can't I call Elizabeth?'

It was Matthew who settled it. 'No,' he said. 'I'm too tired. I don't feel like any more complications.'

They finished their supper in silence. Even Andrew wore a defeated look.

At night they watched television. Mrs Emerson had awakened but refused to eat. She stared at the ceiling while her children watched westerns they had no interest in, and when the picture grew poor no one had the strength to do anything about it. The frames rolled vertically; their eyes rolled too, following the bar that sliced the screen. 'I'm sorry,' Mary said finally. 'I seem to be sleepy. I don't know why.' She kissed her mother good night. 'Well, Susan will be up so early in the morning – ' Margaret said, and she left too. Matthew followed shortly afterward. Andrew stayed behind, gazing at them reproachfully, but before Matthew was even in his pajamas he heard Andrew's feet on the stairs.

Matthew slept in his old room on the second floor. He associated the room only with his early childhood; in his

205

teens he had moved to the third floor with the others. The fingerprints on the walls here reached no higher than his waist, and the scars were from years and years ago – crayon marks, dart punctures, red slashes of modeling clay rubbed into the screens. Even the bed, which was full size, seemed hollowed to fit a much smaller body. He sank down on it and stretched out, without bothering to turn down the blankets.

There was some disappointment far in the back of his mind, a dull ache. Elizabeth. Had he really wanted her to come, then? But even thinking of her name deepened his tiredness. He pictured all the strains she would have brought – his own love and anger, knotted together, and Andrew's bitterness. 'I hate her,' Andrew had once told him. 'She killed my twin brother.' 'That's ridiculous,' Matthew had said, but he had had no proof of it. He had spent years wondering exactly how Timothy's death had happened; yet the one time Elizabeth seemed likely to tell him, down in Mr Cunningham's kitchen, he had been afraid to hear. Now he felt grateful to her for keeping it to herself. The worst strain, if she came, he thought, would be Elizabeth's own. At least she had been spared that. Then he relaxed and slept.

When he woke it was still dark, but he heard noises downstairs. He switched on a lamp and checked his watch. One-thirty. Someone was running water. After a moment of struggling against sleep he rose, felt for his glasses, and made his way down the stairs. It was Mary in the kitchen, heating something in a saucepan. She looked blowsy and plump in a terry-cloth bathrobe, with metal curlers bobbing on her head. 'What are you doing here?' he asked her.

'Mother wants hot milk.'

'Have you been up long?'

'All night, off and on,' Mary said. 'Didn't you hear the bell? She wanted water, and then a bedpan, and then another blanket –'

'Why didn't you wake me?'

'Oh, we're *all* tired,' said Mary. 'You too. And each time I thought it would be the last. It's not even two o'clock yet. Do you think this will go on all night?'

'Maybe she's uncomfortable,' Matthew said.

206

'She's nervous. She wants someone to talk to. That water she didn't even drink, and I bet it will be the same with the milk. Oh, I don't know.' She slumped over the stove, stirring the milk steadily with a silver spoon. 'I ended up getting cross with her, and now I feel bad about it,' she said. 'There's too much on my mind. I worry how the children are doing. And Morris, he can barely tie his own *shoelaces,* and his mother will be feeding him all that starchy food – '

'Go to bed,' said Matthew. 'Let me take over.'

'Oh, no, I – '

But she gave up, before she had even finished her sentence, and handed him the spoon and turned to leave. Her terrycloth slippers scuffed across the linoleum, and the grayed end of her bathrobe sash followed her like a tail.

He filled a mug with hot milk and brought it in to his mother, who lay rigid in the circle of light from the reading lamp. 'Oh,' she said when she saw him. Since the stroke, she had not spoken his name. She must be afraid that it wouldn't come out right. She hadn't said Margaret's or Andrew's names, either, and although he could see why – they were all such a mouthful – still he wished she would try. The only one she mentioned was Mary. Was there some significance in that? Was it because Mary was the only one who hadn't eloped or had a breakdown or refused to give her mother grandchildren?

He propped up a pillow for her and handed her the milk, but after one sip she gave it back to him. 'I hear you're having trouble sleeping,' he said. 'Would you like me to read to you?'

She shook her head. 'When – ' she said, and then struggled with her lips. 'When you were – '

'When we were children,' Matthew said, knowing how often she began things that way.

She nodded and frowned. 'I, *I* read to – '

'To us,' said Matthew.

She nodded again.

'I remember you did.'

'I never – '

'You never?'

'I never – '

'You never refused?' said Matthew. 'You never got

207

tired? You never – '

'*No.*'

He waited, while she took a deep breath. 'I never asked, asked *you* to – '

'You never asked *us* to read to *you,*' said Matthew. But that made so little sense that he was surprised when she seemed satisfied. He turned the sentence over in his mind. 'Well, no,' he said finally, 'you didn't.'

'Money, *Mary*, Mary nooting, knitting – '

'Mary knitting,' said Matthew. 'Beside your bed? In the hospital?'

'Gave my life,' his mother said.

'Oh. Saved your life. By calling the police.'

'*Gave.*'

'*Gave* your life?'

'Like a mud, a mother,' his mother said.

Matthew puzzled over that for a long time. Finally he said, 'Are you worried that it's us taking care of *you* now?' She nodded.

'Oh, well, we don't mind,' he said.

His mother didn't speak again, but she might as well have. The words locked in her head crossed the night air, crisp and perfectly formed: *I* do. *I* mind. But all she did was turn on her side, away from him. Matthew switched off the lamp, unfolded an afghan, and settled himself in an easy chair at the other end of the room. Shortly afterward he heard her deep, even breaths as she fell asleep.

In this sunporch, where the family had always gathered, Mrs Emerson's long-ago voice rang and echoed. 'Children? I mean it now. *Children!* Where is your father? When will you be back? I have a right to know your whereabouts, every mother does. Have you finished what I told you? Do you see what you've done?' On Timothy's old oscilloscope, she would have made peaks and valleys while her children were mere ripples, always trying to match up to her, never succeeding. Melissa was a stretch of rick-rack; Andrew's giggles were tiny sparks that flew across ·the screen. Margaret only turned the pages of her book and tore the corners off them. She was a low curved line, but Matthew was even lower – the EKG of a dying patient. He pulled the afghan up closer around him. His mother slept on, her moonlit profile sharp and strained, her mouth pulled downward with the effort of accepting when she had always been the one to pour things out.

He slept, and she woke him three times – once for water, once for the sound of his voice, once for a bedpan. For the bedpan she insisted that he call one of the girls. He climbed the stairs in the dark, hesitated at Mary's door, and then woke Margaret. While she helped her mother he stayed in the living room and kept himself awake by watching a pattern of leaves moving over the Persian rug. Then Margaret came back out and tapped him on the shoulder. 'Do you want me to take over?' she asked. 'You look dead on your feet?'

'No, I'm all right.'

'I called Emmeline. She won't come,' Margaret said.

'We'll find someone.'

'Matthew, you *know* that I could change Elizabeth's mind. Mary didn't put it to her right.'

'No,' Matthew said.

'I could have her here in an hour, if she took a plane.'

'There are agencies all over Baltimore that can help us out with Mother,' Matthew said.

He went back to the easy chair. Its rough fabric had started prickling through his pajamas, and he kept shifting and turning and rearranging the afghan while his mother lay tense and wakeful at the other end of the room. 'I want –' she said. But in her pause, while he was waiting for her to finish, Matthew fell asleep.

He awoke at dawn. Every muscle in his body ached. 'Oh, Matthew,' someone said, and for a moment he thought it was his mother, finally getting around to saying his name; but it was Margaret. She stood over him, fully dressed, holding Susan. Susan wore a romper suit and straddled her mother's hip with small round legs still curved like parentheses. She looked down at him solemnly. 'Hi there,' he told her. 'Matthew, you look terrible,' Margaret said.

'I'm okay.'

He looked over at his mother. She was watching them out of eyes the same as Susan's – round and pale blue and worried. 'How you doing?' Matthew asked her.

'I fool –'

'You feel?'

'I fool I'm –'

She flattened the back of her hand across her mouth. Tears rolled down her stony face, while she stared straight ahead of her. 'Mother?' Matthew said. He struggled up out of his chair, but then there was nowhere to go, nothing to say. He and Margaret stood there in silence, already defeated by the day that lay ahead of them.

Everyone agreed that Matthew should go to bed now – even Matthew himself. But first Mary brought him a breakfast tray in the sunporch, and while he was buttering a roll his head grew so heavy that he laid his knife down and leaned back and closed his eyes. He felt the tray being lifted from his knees – a falling sensation, that made him jerk and clutch at air. 'You should go upstairs, Matthew,' Mary said. But he only slid lower in his seat and lost track of her voice.

He dreamed that he was in a forest which was very hot and smelled of pine sap. He was walking soundlessly on a floor of brown needles. He came upon someone chopping wood, and he stood watching the arc of the axe and the flying white chips, but he didn't say anything. Then he felt himself rising out of sleep. He knew where he was: on his mother's sunporch, swimming in the bright, dusty heat of mid-afternoon. But he still smelled the pine forest. And when he opened his eyes, the first thing he saw was Elizabeth in a straight-backed chair beside his mother's bed, whittling on a block of wood and scattering chips like fragments of sunlight across her jeans and onto the floor.

12

The first thing Elizabeth did with Mrs Emerson was teach her how to play chess. It wasn't Mrs Emerson's game at all – too slow, too inward-turned – but it would give her an excuse to sit silent for long periods of time without feeling self-conscious about it. 'This is the knight, he moves in an L-shape,' Elizabeth said, and she flicked the knight into all possible squares although she knew that Mrs Emerson watched in a trance, her mind on something else, the kind of woman who would forever call a knight a horse and try to move it diagonally.

She set up game after game and won them all, even giving Mrs Emerson every advantage, but at least they passed the time. Mrs Emerson cultivated the chess expert's frown, with her chin in her hands. 'Hmmm,' she said – perhaps copying some memory of Timothy – but she said it while watching her hands or the clock, just tossing Elizabeth a bone in order to give herself more empty minutes. Elizabeth never hurried her. Mary, passing through the room once, said, 'Hit a tough spot?' And then, after a glance at the game, 'Why, the board's wide open! All that's out is one little pawn.' 'She doesn't like standard first moves,' Elizabeth explained. Although eventually, when Mrs Emerson had collected herself, all she did was set her own king pawn out.

Every time Elizabeth looked up, Mary was somewhere in the background watching her. Margaret was standing in the doorway hitching her baby higher on her hip. Well, Margaret she had always liked, but still, she kept having the feeling that she was being checked out. Were they afraid she would make some new mistake? Under their gaze she felt inept and self-conscious. She plumped Mrs Emerson's pillow too heartily, spoke to her too loudly and cheerfully. All of Thursday passed, long and slow and tedious. No one mentioned going home.

For them – for Margaret, who had sounded desperate and offered double pay and a six-week limit and a promise of no strings attached – she had taken a leave of absence from her job with only ten minutes' notice and flown to Baltimore when she had never planned on seeing it again. She had minded leaving her job. She was a crafts teacher in a girls' reform school, which was work that she loved and did well. The only mistake she had made there was this one: that she had left so suddenly, and lied about the reason. Told them her mother was sick. Oh, even the briefest contact with the Emersons, even a long distance phone call, was enough to make things start going wrong. She should have kept on saying no. She should be back in Virginia, doing what felt right to her. Instead here she was pretending to play chess, and all because she liked to picture herself coming to people's rescue.

She moved out pawns, lazily, making designs with them, sustaining over several turns the image of some fanciful pattern that she wanted them to form. No need to watch out for attacks. Mrs Emerson would never attack; all she did was buckle, at the end, when she found her king accidentally surrounded by half a dozen men for whom Elizabeth had forgotten to say, 'Check.'

'Could I bring you two some tea?' Mary asked, hovering. 'Does anyone want the television on?' Margaret said. 'If you'd like a breath of air, Elizabeth, I can stay with Mother. Feel free to go to the library, or draw up lesson plans.' They thought she was a teacher in a regular school. Elizabeth hadn't set them straight. She kept meaning to, but something felt wrong about it – as if maybe the Emersons would imagine her students' crimes clinging to her like lint, once they knew. She wondered if the school smell – damp concrete and Pine-Sol disinfectant – was still permeating her clothes. While Mrs Emerson struggled for a word Elizabeth's mind was on the paper towel roll on the nightstand: two more towels and the roll would be empty, and she could hoard it in her suitcase for an art project she had planned for her students. 'I want – ' Mrs Emerson said, and Elizabeth's thoughts returned to her, but only partially. Piecemeal. Neither here nor there. She felt suddenly, four years younger, confused and disorganized and uncertain about what she could expect of herself.

Mrs Emerson said, 'Gillespie. Gillespie.' Elizabeth jumped and said, 'Oh,' She wasn't used to this new name yet. She wondered how it felt to have Mrs Emerson's trouble. Did the words start out correctly in her head, and then emerge jumbled? Did she hear her mistakes? She didn't seem to; she appeared content with 'Gillespie.' 'I'm – ' she said. 'I'm – ' Her tongue made precise T sounds far forward in her mouth. Elizabeth waited. 'Tired,' Mrs Emerson said.

'I'll put the board away.'

'I want – '

'I'll lay your pillow flat and leave you alone a while.'

'No!' said Mrs Emerson.

Elizabeth thought a minute. 'Do you want to sleep?' she asked.

Mrs Emerson nodded.

'But you'd rather I stayed here.'

'Yes.'

Elizabeth put the chess pieces in their box, tipped her chair back, and looked out the window. She kept her hands still in her lap. From her months with Mr Cunningham she had learned to lull people to sleep by being motionless and faceless, like one of those cardboard silhouettes set up to scare burglars away. Even when Mrs Emerson tossed among the sheets, Elizabeth didn't look at her. If she did, more words would struggle out. She imagined that coming back would have been much harder if Mrs Emerson could speak the way she used to. I think of what she might have felt compelled to say: rehashing Timothy, explaining those years of silence, asking personal questions. She shot Mrs Emerson a sideways glance, trying to read in her eyes what bottled-up words might be waiting there. But all she saw were the white, papery lids. Mrs Emerson slept, nothing but a small, worn-out old lady trying to gather up her lost strength. Her hair was growing out gray at the roots. The front of her bathrobe was spotted with tea-stains – a sight so sad and surprising that for a moment Elizabeth forgot all about those students that she was missing. She rocked forward in her chair and stood up, but she watched Mrs Emerson a moment longer before she left the room.

Matthew was in the kitchen, eating what was probably his breakfast. He had shaved and dressed. He no longer had that uncared-for look that he had worn asleep in the armchair, but his face was older than she remembered and a piece of adhesive tape was wrapped around one earpiece of his glasses. 'Can I pour you some coffee?' he asked her.

'No, thank you.'

'How's Mother?'

'She's asleep.'

'How does she seem to you?' he asked her.

213

'Oh, I don't know. Older.' She wandered around the kitchen with her arms folded, avoiding his eyes. She didn't feel comfortable with him anymore. She had thought it would be easy – just act cheerful, matter-of-fact – but she hadn't counted on his watching her so steadily. 'Why are you staring?' she asked him.

'I'm not staring, you are.'

'Oh,' Elizabeth said. She stopped pacing. 'Well, the *house* seems *terrible* to me,' she said. 'Much worse off than your mother. How did it get so rundown? Look. Look at that.' She waved to a strip of wallpaper that was curling and buckling over the stove. 'And the porch rail. And the lawn. And the roof gutters have whole *branches* in them, I'm going to have to see to those.'

'You're not the handyman here anymore,' Matthew said.

She thought for a moment that he had meant to hurt her feelings, but then she looked up and found him smiling. 'You have your hands full as it is,' he told her.

'When she's napping, though. Or has visitors.'

'I've been trying to do things during the weekends. I mow the grass, rake leaves. But it's a full-time job, I never quite catch up.' He looked down at his plate, where an egg lay nearly untouched. 'Before she got sick I'd just finished cleaning out the basement,' he said. '*Shoveling* it out. All that junk. Remember our wine?'

'Yes.'

'I found it in the basement six months after you left. White scum on the top and the worst smell you can imagine.'

'I wondered what you'd done with it,' Elizabeth said.

A younger, shinier Matthew flashed through her mind. 'When the wine has aged we'll go on a picnic,' he had said. 'I'll bring a chicken, you bring a . . . ' As if that picnic had actually come about, she seemed to remember the sunlight on a riverbank and the flattened grass they sat on and the feel of Matthew's shirt, rough and warm behind her as she leaned back to drink from a stoneware jug.

'What would it have tasted like, I wonder,' Matthew said.

She knew she should never have come back here.

214

The first time she realized that Andrew was home was at supper. They ate in the dining room – Elizabeth, the two sisters, Matthew, and Susan. Elizabeth kept hearing clinking sounds coming from the kitchen, separated by long intervals of silence. 'What's that?' she asked, and Mary said, 'Oh, Andrew.'

'Andrew? I didn't even know he was here.'

'He's going back on Sunday.'

Nobody pretended to find it odd that he should be eating in the kitchen.

That night, from the army cot that had been set up for her on the sunporch, she heard Andrew cruising the house in the dark. He slammed the refrigerator door, creaked across the floorboards, scraped back a dining room chair. He carried some kind of radio with him that poured out music from the fifties – late-night, slow-dance, crooning songs swelling and fading as he passed through rooms, like a bell on a cat's collar. In the morning when she went upstairs his door was tightly shut, sealed-looking. When she returned from the library with a stack of historical romances for Mrs Emerson she found florist's roses by the bed – nothing any of the others would have thought of buying – and the smell of an unfamiliar aftershave in the air. He ate his lunch in the kitchen. That weighty, surreptitious clinking cast a gloom over the dining room, but no one mentioned it. 'We seem to be missing the butter,' Elizabeth said, and Mary rose at once, letting a fork clatter to her plate, as if she feared that Elizabeth would go out to the kitchen herself. 'Sit still, I'll get it,' she said. But Elizabeth hadn't even thought of going. She avoided Andrew as much as he did her. Otherwise, even in a house so large, they would have had to bump into each other *sometime*. She kept an ear tuned for the sound of his approach, and circled rooms where he might be. Why should she bother him, she asked herself, if he didn't want her around? But she knew there was more to it than that. She didn't want *him* around, either. He had passed judgement on her. Once or twice, during the afternoon, she caught glimpses of him as he crossed the living room – a flash of his faded blue shirt, a color she associated with

215

institutions – and she averted her face and hunched lower in her chair beside Mrs Emerson. She should have gone right out to him, of course. 'Look here,' she should have said. 'Here I am. Elizabeth. You *know* I'm in the house with you. I feel so silly pretending I'm not. Why are you doing this? Or why not just go back to New York, if you can't bear to see me?' But she already knew why. He had summed her up. He was afraid to leave his family in her hands. He alone, of all the Emersons, knew that she was the kind of person who went through life causing clatter and spills and permanent damage.

A man from an orthopedic supply house delivered an aluminum walker. It sat by Mrs Emerson's bed most of Friday afternoon, but she made no move to use it. 'Try, just try it,' Mary said. Mrs Emerson only sent it slit-eyed glances full of distrust. She felt strongly enough about it to frame a very complicated sentence about walkers reminding her of fat old ladies in side-laced shoes, which made Elizabeth laugh. 'You're right, come to think of it,' she said. Mary frowned at her. When they were alone she said, 'Elizabeth, I hope you'll *encourage* Mother a little. The doctor says she'll be back to normal in no time if she'll just take things step by step.' 'Oh, she'll be all right,' Elizabeth said. And she was. With no one watching, with Elizabeth's back deliberately turned, Mrs Emerson looked at the walker more closly and finally reached out to test its weight with one hand. Within a few hours, she had allowed herself to be lifted to a standing position. She clomped around the sunporch, leaning heavily on the walker and puffing. Elizabeth read a magazine. 'I think – ' Mrs Emerson said.

'You should probably get some rest,' Elizabeth said. She had figured out by now how to carry on their conversations. As soon as she got the gist of a sentence she interrupted, which sounded rude but spared Mrs Emerson the humiliation of long delays or having words supplied for her. It seemed to work. Mrs Emerson released the walker, and Elizabeth closed her magazine, helped Mrs Emerson back to bed, and took her slippers off. 'Before supper we'll try it again,' she said.

'But I – '

'Yes, but the more you practice the sooner you'll be free of the walker.'

Mrs Emerson closed her mouth and nodded.

Matthew and his mother and Elizabeth went over Mrs Emerson's checkbook. Mrs Emerson wanted Elizabeth to pay bills and keep her records; she had had Elizabeth's signature cleared at the bank. 'But why?' Elizabeth asked her. '*You* can write *that* much. Why me?' She felt herself sinking into some kind of trap, the trap she had been afraid of when she first said no to coming back. 'I'll only be here six weeks, remember,' she said.

'Oh, well,' said Matthew. 'I suppose it's tiring for her, dealing with all this.'

But Elizabeth was still watching Mrs Emerson. 'Six weeks is all the leave I have,' she said. 'That's understood. Margaret told me so.'

Mrs Emerson merely aligned a stack of envelopes. She moved her lips, forming no words, pretending it was the stroke that kept her from speaking.

Matthew smoothed open the pages of the budget book and explained how it was kept – a page for every month, an entry for every expense, however small. Matches, stamps, cleaning fluid. Her children thought of the book as a joke. Matthew showed Elizabeth the first page, started two years ago: 'This book, 69c; envelope for this book 2c.' He pointed it out silently, smiling. Elizabeth barely glanced at it. 'Why couldn't *you* do this?' she asked him. 'You're here all the time.'

'But I won't be after Sunday.'

'Why? Where are you going?'

'Well, I have to get back to work. I can only stop by in the evenings.'

She looked up and found him watching her. His glasses had slipped down his nose again. His shoulder just brushed hers. He smelled like bread baking, and always had, but until now she had forgotten that. Caught off guard, she smiled back at him. Then Mrs Emerson cleared her throat, and Elizabeth moved over to sit on the foot of the bed.

All Friday evening she worked on the bills, staying close by Mrs Emerson in case questions arose. 'Who is this Mr Robbins? Why the two dollars? Where is this bill they say

217

you've overlooked?' She decided that budget books were more revealing than diaries. Mrs Emerson, who had been born rich, worried more about money than Elizabeth ever had. Her business correspondence was full of suspicion and penny-counting, quibbling over labor hours, threatening to take her business elsewhere, reminding everyone of contracts and estimates and guarantees. Her bills were from discount stores and cut-rate drug companies, some of them clear across the country, and to their trifling amounts interest rates and penalties had been tacked on month after month while Mrs Emerson hesitated over paying them. Her checks were from an inconvenient bank at the other end of town – lower service charges, Matthew said. Yet Elizabeth found a seventy-dollar receipt from a health food store, and a sixty-dollar bill for a bathrobe. She whistled. Mrs Emerson said, 'What, what – '

'Your spending is all cock-eyed,' Elizabeth told her.

'I worry – '

'I would, too. What kind of bathrobe costs sixty dollars? *Health* food! You can live in perfect health on forty-nine cents a day, did you know that? For breakfast you have an envelope of plain gelatin in a glass of Tang, that's protein and vitamin C, only you have to drink it fast before the gelatin sets. For lunch – '

'But stone-ground – '

'Fiddle,' said Elizabeth. 'And forty-watt lightbulbs, so you'll ruin your eyes and need to buy new glasses. I'll have to change all the bulbs in this house, now. And five cents postage to save four cents on aspirin.'

'I worry – '

'But what *for*? You never used to.'

'I don't know,' Mrs Emerson said clearly. Then she slumped against the pillow and started plucking at her sheet. Worry radiated from her in zig-zags that Elizabeth could almost see. Crotchety lines were digging in across her forehead – just what Mr Emerson had set up all these trust funds to keep her from, never dreaming that they would be no comfort. 'Oh, well,' said Elizabeth, sighing. She tapped Mrs Emerson's hand lightly and then went back to the bills. She wrote out neat columns of numbers, as if by her careful printing alone she could salvage all Mrs Emerson's hours of fretting and hand-twisting and helplessness.

By Saturday morning, Mrs Emerson had grown more adept with the walker. She had turned it into an extension of herself, like her little gold pen or her tortoise-shell reading glasses – lifting it delicately, with her fingertips, setting it down almost soundlessly. 'Now we can go out,' Elizabeth told her. She flung open the double doors off the sunporch and then went ahead, without looking back at Mrs Emerson. 'I think – ' Mrs Emerson said.

'Aren't you planting any annuals this year?'

Mrs Emerson moved out into the yard. Elizabeth heard the barely perceptible clink of screws against aluminum, but still she didn't look around. She walked on ahead, sauntering in an aimless way so that it wouldn't seem she was deliberately slowing down. 'We *could* pick up some marigolds,' she called back.

'I fool so – so – '

Unseen, Mrs Emerson's struggle for words seemed more difficult. Elizabeth winced and held herself rigid, staring at a flowerbed.

'Gillespie. I fool so – '

'Take your time,' Elizabeth told her. 'I'm not in any hurry.'

'I fool so *clumsy,*' Mrs Emerson said.

'Oh, well. That'll pass.'

She ambled toward the trellis, poking stray weeds with her toe. 'Plantain is taking your yard over. Something's wrong with your grass. Don't you ever feed it anymore?'

She turned and found Mrs Emerson smiling at her, with the pale yellow sunlight softening her face.

While Mrs Emerson napped, Elizabeth wound all the clocks. She nailed up a kitchen spice rack that was dangling crazily by one corner. She dragged the aluminum ladder out from under the veranda and stood on it to clean the gutters, until Matthew found her there. 'I thought I told you not to do that,' he said. He held onto the ladder, steadying it, while she took swipes at damp black leaves that had rotted into solid clumps. 'This isn't your job any more,' he said. 'And it isn't safe. Will you let me take over, now?' The force he put into his words travelled through his hands and shook the rungs, so that she felt she was standing on something alive. When she descended with an armload of twigs it was he who moved the ladder to a new position and climbed it, and Elizabeth who held it steady. 'You were supposed to be mowing the grass,' she called up to him.

'Never mind, I'll get to it later.'

They were at the back of the house, above the steepest part of the lawn, and when she looked down the hill and then up at Matthew he seemed dizzyingly high. How old was this ladder, anyway? She leaned forward until she was braced full length along its slant, with her arms woven through the rungs and her head hanging down to study her feet. When Matthew shifted his weight, a tremor ran through the metal like a pulse.

For supper that night, Mrs Emerson came into the dining room. They lit candles to celebrate. She sat in her old chair at the head of the table, her back beautifully straight, her right hand folded in her lap while she managed her fork with her left. If she was surprised to see Andrew's place empty, she didn't show it. When Matthew offered her more meat she said, 'No. Ask – ask – 'and waved her hand toward the kitchen. Mary went out and there were low murmurs; then she came back in. 'No, thank you,' she told Matthew. She threw a quick, embarrassed look at Elizabeth, who hardly noticed. Now that she had spent the afternoon repairing things, Elizabeth was thinking like a handyman again. She was making a mental note of the knobs on the corner cupboard, both of which had come off. They were sure to be in the silver candy bowl on the top shelf. How many times had she fished them out of that bowl and fitted them back on? She knew exactly how they would feel in her hand, the chipped, rounded edges pressing into her thumb and the way the left one always went on crooked unless she was very careful. She seemed to have memorized this house without knowing it. Between the main course and dessert she slipped out of her chair and stood on tiptoe to feel in the candy bowl, and sure enough, there they were. A little dirtier, a little more chipped. She squatted by the lower door and screwed the first one on. 'Elizabeth?' Mary said. 'Would you care for coffee?' Elizabeth turned and said,

220

'Oh, no thanks.' Mary's face was puzzled and courteous. 'If you have things to do,' she said, 'maybe you want to be excused.' But Matthew was smiling at Elizabeth as if she'd done exactly what he'd always known she would.

In the night Mrs Emerson kept calling for things. She wanted food brought in, or errands run, or the sound of someone's voice in the dark. 'Gillespie. Gillespie,' she said. Elizabeth, on her cot, slept on, incorporating Mrs Emerson's voice into her dreams. 'Gillespie.' Then she opened her eyes, and struggled up among a tangle of sheets.

'What,' she said.

'Water.'

She lifted the pitcher on the nightstand, found it empty, and padded off to the kitchen. While she was waiting for the water to run cold she nearly went to sleep on her feet. The name Gillespie rang in her ears – the new person Mrs Emerson was changing her into, someone effective and managerial who was summoned by her last name, like a WAC. Now Mary had started calling her Gillespie too. It was contagious. She jerked awake, filled the pitcher, and brought it to the sunporch. 'Here,' she said, and dropped into bed again.

'Gillespie.'

'What.'

'A blanket.'

The third call was for pills. 'Pills?' Elizabeth said blurrily. 'Sleeping pills? You've had them.'

'I can't –'

'The doctor said no more than two. Remember?'

'But I can't –'

Elizabeth sighed and climbed out of her cot. 'How about warm milk,' she said.

'No.'

'Would you like a glass of wine?'

'No.'

'*What*, then.'

'Talk,' said Mrs Emerson.

Elizabeth sat down on the foot of the bed, and for a minute she only frowned at the moonlit squares on the floor. Soft night air, as warm as bath water, drifted in the

221

open windows. Her pajamas smelled of Ivory soap and clean sheets, a dreamy, comforting smell. But Mrs Emerson said, 'Talk,' and sat straighter, waiting.

'When you called, I was asleep,' Elizabeth said.

'Sorry,' said Mrs Emerson.

'I dreamed that your voice was a little gold wire. I was chasing a butterfly with my fourth-grade science class. My fingers would just brush the butterfly; then the wire pulled it away again. There was gold in the butterfly, too. Threads of it, across the wings.'

She pulled her feet off the cold slate floor and tucked them under her. 'You may be scared of the dark,' she said.

'No.'

'Why not? What would be so strange about that? Look at all the dark corners there are, and the moonlight makes them look darker. I used to think that skinny ladies in bathrobes were waiting in corners to get me. I don't know why. My father had a lady like that in his church – sick for years, about to die, always wore a pink chenille bathrobe. Whenever my mother said "they" – meaning other people, just anyone – that's who I pictured. "They've put a stop sign on Burdette Road," she'd say, and I would picture a whole flock of ladies in pink bathrobes, all ghostly and sure of themselves, hammering down a stop sign in the dead of night. Funny thing to be scared of. They weren't only in corners, they were in the back of closets, and under beds, and in the slanty space below the stairs. Now I'm grown up and don't think of them so much, but if something is worrying me, dark corners can still make me wonder what's in them. Possibilities, maybe. All the bad things that can happen to people. Or if I'm worried *enough*, ladies in pink bathrobes all over again.'

'Yes,' said Mrs Emerson. But she didn't seem to be dropping off to sleep yet.

'When you're independent again it won't be so bad,' Elizabeth told her. 'It's feeling helpless that scares you.'

'But I won't – '

Elizabeth waited.

'I won't *be* _ '

'Of course you will. Wait and see. By the time I leave you'll be running this house again.'

'Gillespie.'

Elizabeth stiffened.

'Can't you – '

'No,' said Elizabeth. 'I have a job now. One I like.'

'You never *used* to – '

'Now I do, though,' Elizabeth said. 'I stay with things more. I don't go flitting off whenever I'm asked nowadays.'

But she hadn't guessed the words correctly. 'Never used to like, like *children,'* Mrs Emerson said.

'Oh. Well, not as a group, no. I still don't. But these I like.'

She passed a hand across her eyes, which felt dry and hot. She was going to be exhausted by morning. 'Are you sleepy?' she asked.

'Talk,' said Mrs Emerson.

'I *have* talked. What more is there to say?' She wound a loose thread around her index finger. 'Well,' she said finally, 'I'll tell you how I happened to start working at the school. I was leaning out the window of this crafts shop where I used to sell things, watching a parade go by. There were people crammed on both sidewalks, mothers with babies and little children, fathers with children on their shoulders. And suddenly I was so *surprised* by them. Isn't it amazing how hard people work to raise their children? Human beings are born so helpless, and stay helpless so long. For every grownup you see, you know there must have been at least one person who had the patience to lug them around, and feed them, and walk them nights and keep them out of danger for years and years, without a break. Teaching them how to fit into civilization and how to talk back and forth with other people, taking them to zoos and parades and educational events, telling them all those nursery rhymes and word-of-mouth fairy tales. Isn't that surprising? People you wouldn't trust your purse with five minutes, maybe, but still they put in years and years of time tending their children along and they don't even make a fuss about it. Even if it's a criminal they turn out, or some other kind of failure – still, he managed to get grown, didn't he? Isn't that something?'

Mrs Emerson didn't answer.

'Well, there I was hanging out the window,' Elizabeth

said, 'thinking all this over. Then I thought, "What am I doing up here, anyway? Up in this shop where I'm bored stiff? And never moving on into something else, for fear of some harm I might cause? You'd think I was some kind of special case," I thought, "but I'm not! I'm like all the people I'm sitting here gawking at, and I might just as well stumble on out and join them!" So right that day I quit my job, and started casting about for new work. And found it – teaching crafts in a reform school. Well, *you* might not think the girls there would be all that great, but I like them. Wasn't that something? Just from one little old parade?'

'Yes,' said Mrs Emerson. Then she was silent.

'Mrs Emerson?'

But all Elizabeth heard was her soft, steady breathing. She slid off the bed and found her way back to the cot. She stretched out and pulled the cool sheets over her, but then she couldn't sleep. She stayed wide awake and thoughtful. She was awake when Andrew's shadow crossed a moonbeam, heading all alone to the gazebo. When she propped herself on an elbow to look at him, he had stopped close beside the sunporch. A thin silvery line traced the top of his head and slid down the slope of his shoulders, stopping at the white shirt whose collar was pressed open in a flat, old-fashioned style. Although he was looking toward the windows, he couldn't see her. His face was a blank oval, pale and accusing. After a moment he turned and wandered off behind the tangled rosebushes.

'Look,' Matthew said. 'From here you would think the house was on fire.'

Elizabeth followed the line of his arm. They were in the gazebo, balanced precariously on a rotten railing, and from where they sat they could look up and see the house reflecting the sunset from every window. Not as if it were on fire, Elizabeth thought, so much as *empty*. The windows were glaring orange rectangles, giving no sign of the life behind them. The scene had a flat, painted look. 'I wonder why she keeps the place,' Matthew said.

'Maybe for her children to come home to.'

'We never come all at once anymore.'

He picked up her hand and turned it over. Elizabeth

224

wasn't surprised. At this time of day, in this stillness, it seemed as if she had never been away; his hardened palm was as familiar as if she had last held it minutes ago. She rested lightly against his side, which felt warm on her bare arm. Matthew was in a suit. He was dressed to take Andrew to the bus station and the girls to the airport. Elizabeth wore only jeans and a short-sleeved shirt. When she shivered he said, 'Do you want my jacket?'

'No, thanks. It's time for you to be going.'

But Matthew didn't move. 'My father bought this house when they were married,' he said. 'Before they even had children. They moved in with nothing more than Grandmother Carter's parlor furniture, in all this space. He said they were going to live here till they died. He expected to have a long life, I guess. They were going to celebrate their golden anniversary here, all white-haired and settled with the third floor closed off except when children and grandchildren came to spend their summer vacations.'

'Vacations in *Baltimore?*'

'If you were to marry me,' Matthew said, 'we could stay in this house, if you liked.'

Which surprised her no more than his hand had. Why should it? Life seemed to be a constant collision and recollison of bodies on the move in the universe; everything recurred. She would keep running into Emersons until the day she died; and she and Matthew would keep falling in love and out again. If it snowed, wouldn't Timothy be waiting for her to shovel him a path? Wouldn't he emerge from those bushes if she took it in her head to walk another turkey?

'When I picture *our* golden anniversary,' Matthew said, 'I think of us in a supermarket. One of those cozy old couples you see telling each other what food they like. "Here's some nice plums, Mother," I'd say, and you'd say, "Now Pa, you know what plums do to your digestion. Remember back in '82," you'd say, "I fixed stewed plums for supper and you never got a wink of sleep. Remember?" ' He made his voice old and crotchety, but Elizabeth didn't laugh.

'It's funny,' she said. 'I picture us with your family tangled up in everything you do, and me brought in to

225

watch. Your mother living with us, and long distance phone calls from sisters divorcing and brothers having breakdowns, and quarrels among the lot of you every evening over the supper table. And me on the outside, wondering what next. Putting on the Band-Aids. Someone to impress.'

'Is *that* how you see yourself?' Matthew asked. 'On the outside?'

'Of course I do.'

'Then what are you doing here now?'

'Putting on the Band-Aids,' Elizabeth said.

'But who *asked* you to do it? Mother. She didn't want anyone else. She thinks of you as family. They all do.'

'Mighty strange family,' Elizabeth said. 'She didn't write for four years, I never once got one of those little letters of hers all rehearsed on the dictaphone. What do you say to that? I used to think of *them* as family too, I always did want a little more sinful family than the one I've got. But then I caused all that trouble with Timothy, and your mother didn't write and we all went our separate ways. Now I'm back for six weeks. Period.'

'You and I don't see things the same,' Matthew said. 'Do you think you're just standing off aloof from us?'

'Well, I'm surely not collecting guns,' Elizabeth said, 'or eloping, or having spells of insanity or shouting quarrels.'

'We're having a shouting quarrel right now.'

'Matthew, will you go? Your sisters are going to miss their planes.'

'There's plenty of time.' But even as he spoke, the back door slammed and Mary called, 'Matthew? Are you coming?'

'Go on, Matthew,' Elizabeth said.

'In a minute. We haven't – '

'*Matthew!*' Mary called.

'Oh, all right,' he said. He slid off the rail and stood there a minute, scratching his head. 'Tomorrow I go back to work,' he told Elizabeth.

'All right.'

'I can only come here in the evenings. Will you be here?'

'Where else?' Elizabeth said.

She watched his loose-boned figure shambling up the hill

226

toward Mary, with his awkward suit that looked too short and his hair shaggy and ruffled. Then Margaret came out of the house, carrying Susan, and Mary started speaking. Whatever it was she said – scolding Matthew, or asking where Andrew was, or worrying about plane schedules – Elizabeth couldn't catch, but she heard her thin, sharp voice and Susan's irritable fussing. The scraps of their quarrel and the fluttering of Mary's skirt in the breeze made them seem remote like little figures under glass. They stood with their backs to Elizabeth. In a minute Andrew would come out and they would leave, confident that Elizabeth would keep things going somehow while they were away. Elizabeth slid off the railing and wandered through the grass, feeling cold and tired. She ought to say goodbye. Instead she moved in a wide slow circle around the gazebo, picking up twigs and fallen branches out of habit although she had nowhere to put them.

One long branch refused to be lifted, and when she tugged at it, it broke off in her hands. It was weighted at the other end by a pair of shoes, slim and elegant but scuffed across the toes; above them, a gray suit, and a faded blue shirt pressed open at the collar.

She straightened, holding the branches close to her chest, and looked squarely into Andrew's long, sad face. 'Well,' she said.

Andrew said nothing. He held a little steel pistol whose eye was pointed at her heart.

Now, why should that make her want to laugh? The blue of the steel was lethal-looking, and she was holding the branches so tightly that her muscles were trembling. And above all, she had been through this before; she knew now that it was something to take seriously. Laughter tended to set explosions off. 'Why is everything you say so *inconsequential?*' Timothy had asked, but now the most inconsequential remark of all came into her head, and she said it in spite of herself.

'Where did you get *that* gun, I wonder,' she said.

Andrew winced, as if he knew what a mistake she had made.

'Plucked it off a tree? Found it in your mother's sewing box?'

'It was left with me by a friend,' said Andrew. 'He went to Europe.'

'Funny friend,' Elizabeth said.

'Things always come to you somehow, if you want them badly enough.'

She had never heard his voice before, except above the noise of the bus station. It was light and frail, breakable-sounding. There was a pulse ticking in his forehead. The hand that held the pistol was shaking, which gave her some hope that his aim might be poor. 'Andrew,' she said, 'give me the gun now.'

'I can't. I didn't *want* to do this. I warned you and warned you, I wrote you letters. Nothing stops you. I know what you were up to in the gazebo.'

'Really? What was I up to?' Elizabeth asked.

'You'd better take this seriously. I mean it.'

'I am. I know you do,' said Elizabeth. And she did. It was beginning to seem possible that this was the way she would die – in a numb, unreal situation in the orange half-light of a Sunday evening. How could she have guessed, when she woke up this morning and brushed her teeth and chose what shirt to wear? She didn't even know what date it was. 'What's today's date?' she asked.

'June seventh,' said Andrew.

She thought it over. June seventh had never had any significance before. She pushed her mind back to Timothy, who had died one day in April because of mistakes that she had made and had rehashed again and again since then, but she had never been sure what she should have done instead. Started crying? Run away? Said she would take him south with her after all?

She made up her mind. She said, 'Well, I can see how you feel. Shall I leave Baltimore and not come back?'

Then she spun away from him to start toward the house. She had completed the turn already (she saw Matthew with a suitcase, his back to her, his sisters straggling behind him) and she was just wondering what to do with these dead branches when the gun went off.

The sound had nothing to do with her. It was as distant as the diminished figure of Matthew, who pivoted in midstep without a pause and dropped the suitcase and started running toward her. The others were a motionless, horror-struck audience; then they came running too. But the first to reach her was Andrew himself. He knocked away the branches and picked up her arm. Blood was soaking through the cuff of her sleeve. She felt a hot stab like a bee-sting, exactly where her smallpox vaccination would be.

'Oh, Elizabeth,' Andrew said. 'Did I hurt you?'

When Matthew reached her she was laughing. He thought she was having hysterics.

They took her to old Dr Felson, who wouldn't make trouble. He had a dusty, cluttered office opening off his wife's kitchen. It smelled of leather and rubbing alcohol. And Dr Felson, as he hunted for gauze, talked like someone out of a western. 'A graze,' he said. 'A flesh wound. Would you happen to be sitting on my scissors? I've seen you here before, I believe.'

'You sewed up a cut for me,' Elizabeth said. 'A knife wound on my wrist.'

'Came with young Timothy, didn't you?' He straightened up from a desk drawer and scowled at Matthew, who was holding tight to Elizabeth's bleeding arm. 'Don't go getting germs on that,' he said. 'Well, Lord. Who was it cut your wrist now? I forget.'

'I cut my wrist,' Elizabeth said.

'You Emersons could support me single-handed.'

'I'm not an –'

'Mind if your blouse is torn?'

'No.'

He slit her sleeve and put something on her arm that burned. Elizabeth hardly noticed. She felt silly and light-headed, and the pain in her arm was getting mixed up with the stab of light that cut through her brain: Now we are even, no Emersons will look at me ever again as if I owe them something; now I know nothing I can do will change a bullet in its course. 'This'll throb a little tonight,' the doctor said, but Elizabeth only smiled at him. Anyone would have thought Matthew was the one in pain. He held her wrist too tightly, and his face was white. 'Don't worry,' Elizabeth told him. 'It looks a lot worse than it feels.'

'Of course it does,' said Dr Felson. He was wrapping her arm in gauze, which felt warm and tight. 'But how about next time? You may not be so lucky.'

'*Next* time!' Elizabeth said.

'What does Andrew have to say about this? I've looked the other way quite a few times in my life, but that boy's beginning to bother me.'

'Oh, well, he's apologized,' Elizabeth said.

Dr Felson snorted and stood up. 'If it gets to hurting, take aspirin,' he told her.

'Okay.'

She let Matthew lead her out again, across the wooden porch and into the street. He guided her steps as if she were an old lady. 'I'm all *right*. Really I am,' she said, but he only tightened his arm around her shoulders. His car was waiting beside the curb, packed with people who had missed their travel connections all on account of her. Mary in the front seat, Margaret and Susan and Andrew in the back – peering out of the dusk, their faces pale and anxious, waiting to hear the outcome. 'What's he say?' said Andrew. 'Is she all right? Will you be all right?' He loomed out through the window to take a better look, and at the sight of him bubbles of laughter started rising up again in her chest. 'Of course I will,' she said, and laughed out loud, and opened the door to pile in among a tangle of other Emersons.

13

1970

While Peter drove P.J. slept, curled in the front seat with her head in his lap. Long skeins of tow hair strung across his knees, twined around the steering wheel and got caught between his fingers. He kept shaking his hands loose, as if he had dipped them in syrup. Then the hot wind blew up new strands. 'P.J.?' he said. 'Look, P.J., can't you stretch out in the back?' P.J. slept on, smiling faintly, while blocks of sunlight crossed her face like dreams.

They were driving back to New Jersey after a week with P.J.'s parents – an old tobacco farmer and his wife who lived on a rutted clay road in Georgia. The visit had not been a success. The gulf between Peter and the Grindstaffs had widened and deepened until P.J., the go-between, could cause a panic if she so much as left the room for a glass of water. She had ricocheted from one side to the other all week, determinedly cheerful and oblivious. Now her head was a weight on his right knee every time he braked; she was limp and exhausted, refilling her supplies of love and gaiety while she slept.

Just past Washington, he pulled into a service station and woke her up. 'Would you like a Coke?' he asked her. P.J. lived on Cokes. And she was a great believer in breaking up trips – for sandwiches, rest rooms, Stuckey's pecan logs, white elephant sales, caged bears and boa constrictors – but now she only looked at him dimly. 'A what?' she said.

'A Coke.'

'Oh. Well, I guess so.'

She yawned and reached for the door handle. While the attendant scraped bugs off the windshield Peter watched her cross the concrete apron – a thin, tanned, rubber-boned girl with red plastic rings like chicken-bands dangling from her ears. She swung her purse by its strap and tugged at her shorts, which were brief enough to show where her tan left off. The attendant stopped work for a moment to watch her go.

From the glove compartment Peter took stacks of maps – Georgia, New England, even eastern Canada, and finally Baltimore. He had promised P.J. they would stop over to see his family. It was three years since he had last been there. When he opened the map to check the best route the half-forgotten names of streets – St Paul and North Charles, criss-crossed now with grimy folds that were beginning to tear – gave him the sudden, depressing feeling that he was a teenager again. He remembered hitchhiking on North Charles, sweating in the damp heavy heat, fully aware that his mother would go to pieces if she ever saw him doing this. He pictured Baltimore in an eternal summer, its trademark the white china cats, looking fearfully over their shoulders, which poor people riveted to their shutters and porch roofs. And then his mother's house – closed, dim rooms. Gleaming tabletops. What was the point of going back?

P.J. came in sight, picking her way across the cement on narrow bare feet. When she caught the attendant watching her she grinned and raised her Coke bottle in a toast. Then she leaned in the window and said, 'Come on, Petey, get out and stretch your legs.'

'I'm comfortable here.'

'Out back they have garden statues, and birdbaths and flowerpots. Want to take a look?'

'I'd rather get going,' Peter said.

She climbed into the car, wincing when the backs of her thighs hit the hot vinyl. Down her cheek were the stripes of Peter's corduroy slacks. Her eyes were still sleepy and rumpled-looking. 'They have the cutest little plaster gnomes,' she said. 'On spikes. You just stick them into the grass. I bet Mama would love one of those.'

'I bet she would,' said Peter.

She looked at him sideways, and then took a sip of her Coke. 'Shall I get her one?' she asked.

'Why not?'

'As a sort of making-up present?'

Peter handed a credit card to the attendant. '*You* don't have to make up,' he said.

'I was thinking of sending it in your name.'

'Well, don't.'

She drank off the last of the Coke, wiped the rim of the bottle, and set off toward the case of empties beside the vending machine. The minute she was gone Peter felt sorry. 'P.J.!' he called.

She turned, still cheerful. He slid out of his seat and ran to catch up with her. 'Of course we can buy one,' he said. 'Put my name all over it, if you like.'

'Oh, good,' P.J. said. 'I'll do the wrapping and mailing and all, you won't have to lift a finger, Petey.'

She led him around the back of the filling station toward

a field of plaster flamingos and sundials and birdbaths. The gnomes stood in a huddle, their paint already flaking, grinning at a cluster of little black boys who held out hitching-rings. The saleslady wore a straw hat and a huge flowered smock that blazed in the sunlight. 'Aren't they darling?' P.J. said. 'Or would she rather have an eentsy wheelbarrow to plant her flowers in. Which do you think?'

'You know her best,' Peter said.

'Or then these deer. *They're* nice.' She wandered through the field, unable to make up her mind, patting the heads of little painted animals and returning the smile of any statue that smiled at her. Her bare feet stepped delicately between the grass blades, as if she had no weight at all. 'How much do you reckon it would cost to mail a sundial?' she asked. The saleslady said, 'Oh, no, honey, you don't want to *mail* them, it'd take a fortune.' Peter hated people who called their customers 'honey.' But P.J. only shifted her smile to the saleslady's face, and the two of them stood beaming at each other like very dear friends. Oh, it would take a lot to make P.J. start frowning. He thought of all this last week, all the times her parents must have whispered, 'Paula Jean, what's the *matter* with that boy?' all the children who, coming upon him unexpectedly, lost their bounce and seemed to sag under the weight of his gloom. Yet P.J. had continued smiling. She had led him by the hand through the barnyard, hoping that he would make friends with the animals. She had introduced a hundred topics of conversation that Peter and her family might seize on. 'Petey's just got out of the Army, Daddy, you and him ought to compare experiences. Petey, don't you want to see Mama's herb garden?' Peter had tried, but nothing came to his mind to say. He floated in a weariness that made him want to escape to some hotel and sleep for days. 'Petey, darling,' P.J. said, 'don't you *like* them?' I do,' he said truthfully, 'but I just can't – ' 'Talk about the crops. Daddy likes that. Talk about baseball, or what's on the television.' So then, back among the others, Peter said, 'How're the crops, Mr Grindstaff?' 'Just fine,' said Mr Grindstaff, and Peter said, 'Oh, good,' and subsided, unable to think of what came next.

'He's just back from Vietnam,' P.J. would tell people.

233

Everyone murmured, as if that explained things. But Peter had been gloomy long before the Army. War only added a touch of fear and the sense of being out of place, neither of which seemed to leave him when he came back. He was still afraid. He still felt out of place. He had a job now, teaching chemistry in a second-rate girls' school, where the pupils whispered and giggled and knit argyle socks while he lectured. 'All of you,' he would tell them, 'missed the second equation on the last hour quiz. Now I would like to go over that with you.' The girls looked up at him, still moving their lips to count stitches, and Peter fell silent. *Why* would he like to go over it? What difference did it make? How had he come to be here?

P.J. settled on a gnome with a pointed red cap, cradled it in her arms all the way to the car and rolled it in a picnic blanket in the trunk. 'I just know she's going to love it,' she said. And then, when they had pulled out into traffic again, 'I know things will work out all right. Won't they? Everything will be just fine now.'

'Of course,' said Peter, but he had no idea what she was talking about. This trip? The two of them? He and her family? If he found out he might have to disagree. He kept quiet, and smiled steadily at the stream of oncoming cars while P.J. slid down and set both feet against the dashboard. Her hair blew out behind her, knotting itself and slipping out of the knots. She seemed to glint and shimmer. When Peter first met her, in the school cafeteria, she had stood out among the pasty dull students like a flash of silver. She had worn a white uniform and collected dirty dishes off the tables with pointed, darting hands. He took her for a student with a part-time job. When she turned out to be a real waitress he was relieved, since it was against school rules to date students. Then later, after they had begun to grow serious, he had some doubts. A *waitress?* What would his family say? He pushed the thought away, ashamed that it had come up. He started seeing her daily; he fit himself into her motionless, shadowless life: lying oiled and passive on a beach towel for hours at a stretch, watching television straight through till sign-off, sitting all afternoon in dusky taverns dreamily peeling the labels off beer bottles. She gave him the feeling that she could never

234

be used up. Whenever he looked her way she smiled at him.

The rush hour was beginning. Traffic was bumper-to-bumper, and the flashes of sunlight off chrome stung his eyes. 'Where are we now?' P.J. asked.

'Close to – just past Washington.'

'Close to Baltimore.'

'Well, yes.'

'How much longer to your mother's?'

'Well, I've been thinking,' Peter said.

'Oh, Petey, don't say we can't go. After all this time that I've been counting on it?'

'If we drove straight through, we could be home by bedtime,' Peter said. 'Besides, she might not even be there.'

'Didn't you tell her we were coming?'

'I meant to drop a postcard, but then I forgot.'

'You're ashamed to show me to her.'

'No, Lord,' he said. 'I've kept away long before *you* were around.'

'That's just not natural, Petey. Not and you living so close.'

'But I wasn't always close, I was in the Army.'

'When Barney Winters went overseas, down home,' P.J. said, 'they let him have some time with his folks after basic training. Then when he came back he spent a month there, just filling up on that good home cooking he said. Fat? In that one month he must have gained thirty pounds. You never would've known him.'

'I went to New York after basic training,' Peter said.

'Gunther Jones, too, *he* visited home before he left. And would have after, I reckon, if he hadn't gone and got killed.'

'Well, we all do our own thing,' Peter said. 'I went and saw a lot of art galleries.'

'Before, you mean. I don't know how much you enjoyed it but afterward I *know,* you told me yourself. Up until the new semester opened you didn't do a thing but lay around a old rented room reading the beginnings of books. Call that a rest? Call that a recuperation? When you could have been home all that time eating your mother's good home cooking?'

'I can cook better than my mother does,' Peter said.

'Petey, do you have some *reason* not to want to go there?'

'None at all,' said Peter. Which was true, but he should have made something up – some feud or family quarrel that would have satisfied her. As it was, she thought he was putting her off. She considered the subject still open for discussion. 'Barney *Winters*' mother met him when he landed,' she said. 'Bringing a whole chess pie that he ate right there by the plane.'

'Oh, Lord,' said Peter.

'Myself, I'm a family-type person. Just made that way, I don't know why. We always were close-knit. Now I want to meet *your* family too, but if you think I wouldn't match up to them – '

'No, P.J. We'll go, if you're set on it. But just for one night, is that understood? No hanging around. No getting caught up in anything.'

'Whatever you like, Petey,' P.J. said.

By the time they reached Baltimore, Peter had a long ache of tiredness running down his spine. He drove irritably, one hand always ready at the horn. Row houses slipped past him in endless chains, with clusters of women slumped on all the stoops, fans turning lazily behind lace curtains, parlor windows full of madonnas and globe lamps and plastic flowers alternating with windows boarded up and CONDEMNED signs on the doors. Children were drinking grape Nehis. Men scuttled out from package stores with brown paper bags clutched to their chests. 'Are you still sure you want to stop in Baltimore?' Peter asked.

P.J. didn't bother answering. She was neatening the edges of her lipstick with the tip of a little finger. 'Should I put my hair up?' she said.

'You look okay.'

'My wig is right handy.'

'*No*, P.J.'

P.J. dumped her pocketbook on the seat and riffled through ticket stubs and loose change and wadded-up hair ribbons until she found the little plastic case containing her eyelashes. They were cut in a style called 'Innocence' – spiky black lashes widely spaced, so that when she had put them on she looked as if she had just finished crying over some brief, childish tragedy. She blinked and turned to him. 'How's that?' she asked.

'Very nice.'

'Is it far to go?'

'Another fifteen minutes or so.'

'Well, is there something I should *know* first. I mean, subjects not to bring up? People not to mention? You never tell me things, Petey. I want to do this right, now.'

'Oh, just be yourself,' Peter said. Which were her exact words on the way to Georgia, but she missed that. If he were to list forbidden subjects it would take him all night.

Once out of the downtown areas they drove faster, through streets that grew steadily greener and cooler. Then they entered Roland Park, and Peter suddenly felt eager to be home. He forgot all the misgivings he had had. There was the old locked water tower, which he had once tried to break into. There was the Women's Club where his mother went for luncheons, always in a hat and gloves. And now the wooded road that led to the house, dark and cool and dappled with sunshine. He hid his eagerness from P.J. as carefully as if she might mock him for it, although he knew she wouldn't. 'We're almost there,' he told her, keeping his face blank. P.J. nodded and sat up straighter and wet her lips.

In this neighborhood, people stayed out of sight more. All he saw was one lone maid with a shopping bag, heading toward the bus stop. And his mother's house, when he drew up in front of it, was closed and silent. The curtains hung still, the veranda chairs were empty. A water sprinkler spun dreamily in the right side yard.

'Well,' said Peter. He let his hands drop from the wheel. P.J. said nothing. She was looking at the house, taking in the rows of gleaming windows and the wide expanse of grass, the multitude of chimneys rising from the slate roof.

'You never told me it was a *big* house,' she said finally.

'Shall we go in?'

P.J. began gathering up her possessions. She had a purse, sandals, a scarf, a sack of licorice shoestrings which had already lined her lips with black although Peter didn't tell her so. When she had climbed out of the car she tugged

at her shorts and slid into her sandals – leather soles with
yards of straps which would have twined all the way to her
knees if she had tied them. She shuffled up the front walk,
curling her toes to keep the sandals on. She looked like a
seal on dry land. Peter stayed where he was, watching her.
He didn't even open his door until she turned to look for
him. 'Aren't you coming?' she asked.

'Sure.'

He had expected his mother to burst out of the house the
moment he cut the engine, ending a three-year vigil at the
front window.

It wasn't until he was halfway up the walk that he became
aware of the noise. A clattering sound, like millions of
enormous metal zippers stickily opening and shutting. It
rose from every bush. It was so steady and monotonous
that it could pass unnoticed, like a clock's ticking. 'What *is*
it?' he asked, and P.J. only looked at him blankly. 'That
noise,' he said.

'Chickens? Locusts?'

A buzzing black lump zoomed into his face, and then
veered and swooped away. He ducked, seconds after it had
gone.

'Seventeen-year locusts,' he said.

'Never heard of them,' said P.J.

'Cicadas, in point of actual fact.'

The words were Timothy's, dredged up from a long-ago
summer, and so was the tone – dry and scientific, so unlike
Peter that even P.J. noticed and looked surprised. The last
time the locusts had been here, Peter was twelve. He
remembered the fact of their presence, and Timothy's
lecture on them, but not what they were really *like* – not
these viciously buzzing objects which, he saw now, swung
through the air on invisible strings and hung like glittering
fruit from all the bushes. P.J. had one on her shoulder; it
rattled menacingly when he brushed it away. When he
stepped on the sidewalk, he crunched countless pupa shells
which lay curled and hollow, small beige shrimps with all
their legs folded tightly inward.

They crossed the shiny gray floorboards of the veranda.
P.J. knocked at the door. 'Knock, knock!' she called out
gaily. She always did that, but today Peter found it

238

irritating. 'There *is* a doorbell,' he said, and reached around her to press it. P.J. looked up at him, her eyes like round, rayed suns in her Innocence eyelashes.

It was a child who opened the door for them. A squat little blond boy with a solemn face, wearing miniature Levis. 'Hi,' he said.

'Hi there,' said Peter, too heartily. 'I'm your Uncle Peter. Remember me?'

'No.'

'So there, Peter Emerson,' P.J. said. She laughed and bent down to the little boy's level. 'I'm P.J.. What's your name?'

He studied her. Peter cleared his throat. 'This is George, I believe,' he said. 'Matthew's boy. Is your grandma home, George?'

'Yup.'

'Could we see her?'

'She's in the kitchen,' George said.

He turned back in the direction he had come from. The cuffs of his Levis dragged on the floor. 'Well,' said Peter. 'Shall we go in?'

They followed George across the hallway – Peter leading P.J. as if she were another child, clutching her by the arm while she looked all around her. They went through the butler's pantry, windowless and stale, and then into the sudden brightness of the kitchen.

His mother was standing just as he had imagined her – wearing soft colors, her hair a clear gold, surrounded by her family. The only thing wrong was that she and all the others had their backs turned. They were facing squarely away from him, watching something out the rear door. 'It's the screens, they will have to be mended in the morning,' his mother said. 'Look at those holes! *Anything* could get through them.'

'Hello, Mother.'

She turned, but even when she looked directly at him she seemed distracted. 'What?' she said. 'What – *Peter!*'

Everyone turned. Their faces were momentarily surprised and unguarded.

'Peter, what are you *doing* here?'

'Oh, just passing through. Mother, this is P.J. P.J., this is

239

my brother Andrew, my brother Matthew's wife Gillespie – where's Matthew?'

'He's still at work,' his mother said. 'Are you staying long? Why didn't you tell us? Have you eaten supper?'

'We were heading back from Georgia – ' Peter said. His mother stood on tiptoe to kiss him. Her cheek felt withered and too soft, but she still wore the same light, powdery perfume, and she held her back as beautifully straight as ever. Her speech was slower now than her children's – as slow as Gillespie's southern drawl, and hesitating over consonants. 'Georgia?' she said. 'What would you go to *Georgia* for?'

'You look older,' said Andrew. He looked older himself, but happy. His hair was thinning, and below his concave chest a paunch had started. Someone's apron was tied around his middle. 'If I'd known you were coming – ' he said, and then P.J. stuck her hand out to him. He looked at it a moment before accepting it.

'I'm very glad to meet you all,' said P.J.

Andrew frowned. He was nervous with strangers – something Peter had forgotten to warn her about. But before the silence grew noticeable, his sister-in-law stepped in. 'We're glad to meet *you*,' she said. 'Good to see you again,' she told Peter, and she shifted the diapered baby who rode her hip and held out her hand. Peter took it with relief; her cool, hard palm seemed to steady him.

'We were just on this trip, you see,' he told her. 'Passing through Baltimore. Thought we'd stop in. I wasn't sure you'd – are we interrupting something?'

'Oh, of *course* not!' his mother said gaily.

'But with everyone at the back door there, I didn't know – '

'It was a locust. Gillespie was shooing it out of the house for us. Oh, these locusts, Peter, you can't imagine. We keep the house just *sealed*, and still they get in. Will this screen be seen to, *now?*'

'I'll mend it in the morning,' Gillespie said.

'Mother is scared of locusts,' Andrew said.

'You're none too fond of them yourself, Andrew dear,' his mother told him.

'Well, no.'

And meanwhile P.J. stood smiling, hopefully, with her

240

belongings still clutched to her chest, looking from one face to another and settling finally on the baby, who was playing with a long strand of hair that had straggled from Gillespie's bun. 'Oh, isn't it *darling*,' she said. 'What's its name?'

'She isn't an it, she's a she,' Andrew said stiffly.

'Well, how could anyone tell?' Gillespie asked him. 'All she's got on is a diaper.'

'Her *face* is a girl's face. No one should mistake it.'

'Oh, hush, Andrew, I never heard of such a thing.'

Peter waited for Andrew to get insulted, to collapse in a kitchen chair or turn on his heel and leave, but he didn't. He had changed – a fact that Peter forgot all over again each time he left home. He was the only person in this house who had changed. His mother remained a gilded pink and white and Gillespie continued shuffling around in dungarees, her face a little broader and more settled-looking but her fingers still nicked by whittling knives and her manner with babies still as offhand as if she were carrying a load of firewood. But Andrew had mellowed; he had calmed and softened. ('Andrew is in such a state,' Mrs Emerson had written last winter. 'You know how he gets when Gillespie's expecting, I believe he'd go through the labor pains *for* her if only he could.' Only Peter seemed to remember the day after Timothy's funeral, when Andrew had paced the living room saying, 'Where is that girl? Where? I'll get her for this.') Now instead of taking offence Andrew smiled, first at Gillespie and then at the baby, whose cheek he lightly touched. 'Her name is Jenny,' he told P.J.

'Oh,' said P.J. She looked bewildered, but after a moment she smiled too.

'Now then,' Mrs Emerson said. 'Shall we go into the living room where it's cool?'

She led the way, calming her skirt with her hands as if it were a long and stately gown. If the kitchen had become Gillespie's, with its wood chips across the table and its scatter of tools beside the breadbox, the living room was still Mrs Emerson's. The same vases marched across the mantel; the same dusty gray smell rose from the upholstery. The red tin locomotive under the coffee-table could have been Peter's own, back in the days when he was a child here anxiously studying the grownups' faces.

His mother settled in her wing chair, across from Andrew, and Gillespie sat in the high-backed rocker with both children nestled against her. Peter chose the couch, beside P.J. He felt she needed some support. She was nervously twisting her purse strap, and the licorice bag rustled on her knees like something alive. 'I just love old houses,' she said.

'How long can you stay?' his mother asked Peter. 'And don't say you're just passing through. I want you to plan on a nice long visit this time.'

'I have a lot of work to get back to,' Peter said.

'In the summer? What kind of work would you do in the summer?'

But then, remembering her social duties, her face became all upward lines and she turned to P.J. 'I hope you're not tired from the trip, J.C.' she said.

'P.J.' said P.J. 'No ma'am, I'm not a bit tired. I'm just so happy to finally *meet* you all. I feel like I know you already, Petey's told me so much about you.'

A lie. Peter had told her next to nothing. And he hadn't even mentioned her to his family, but Mrs Emerson continued wearing her bright hostess look and leaning forward in that hovering posture she always assumed to show an open mind. 'Where are you from, dear?' she asked.

'Well, New Jersey *now*. Before it was Georgia.'

'Isn't that nice?'

P.J. shifted in her seat, deftly smoothing the backs of her thighs as if she wore a dress. 'You look just like I thought you would,' she said – oh, always trying to get down to the personal, but she was no match for Mrs Emerson.

'I suppose this heat is no trouble to you at all then,' Mrs Emerson said.

'Ma'am?'

'Coming from Georgia.'

'Oh. No ma'am.'

'Peter darling,' Mrs Emerson said, 'I want you to tell me *everything*. What have you been up to, now?'

'Well, I – '

'Where are my cigarettes?' She slid her fingers between

242

the arm of the chair and the cushion. Peter, who hadn't been going to tell her anything anyway, felt irritated at being cut off. He kept a pointed silence, with his arms folded tightly across his chest. He thought his mother was like a hunter who set traps and coaxed and baited until the animal was safely caught, and then she forgot she had wanted him and went off to some new project. 'Nothing is where it should be in this house,' she said. 'Gillespie, I think we could do with some iced tea to drink.'

'Oh. Okay.'

Gillespie handed the baby to Andrew and went to the kitchen, with George tailing her. P.J. sat back and smiled around the room. The only sound to be heard was the clatter of locusts. Finally P.J. said, 'Mrs Emerson, have you got a family album?'

'Album?'

'I'd like to see pictures of Peter when he was a baby.'

'Oh, there are hundreds,' Mrs Emerson said. She had filled more albums than any coffee-table could hold – rows upon rows of snapshots precisely dated – but she didn't offer to bring them out. '*Somewhere* around,' she said vaguely, and she turned to stare out a window. What connection did this girl have with Emersons?

What connection did *Peter* have? He sat plucking the knees of his slacks, as empty of things to say as he had been in Georgia, as hopeful of acceptance as P.J. From the kitchen came the smells of supper cooking, roast beef and baked potatoes. There was nothing like cooking smells to make you feel out of place in someone else's house. While he was on the open highway life here had been going on in a pattern he could only guess at – meat basted, knife sharpened, bustling hunts for misplaced spoons, systems and rituals and habits they never had to think about. Mrs Emerson lit her cigarette and reached without looking for an ashtray, which was exactly where she had known it would be. A silvery strand of baby-spit spun down onto Andrew's hand, and out of nowhere Andrew produced a folded diaper and neatly wiped Jenny's chin. P.J. was telling Mrs Emerson how she just loved this section of Baltimore. (She just loved *everything*. What was the matter with her?) At her first pause, Andrew turned to Peter.

243

'How's the job going?' he asked. Mrs Emerson said, 'Do you like New Jersey?' To counterbalance P.J., he was blunter than he should have been. 'I hate it,' he said.

'Oh, Peter.'

'If there was another job open *anywhere,* I'd take it in a flash.'

'Why don't you then?'

He peered at his mother. She was perfectly serious. Jobs nowadays were scarce and money scarcer, and no one was interested in chemists any more, but what did she know about that? It was possible that she wasn't even aware there was a war on. Since he first left home there had been upheavals of every kind – assassinations, riots, not once referred to in letters from his mother. Oh well, once: 'Mrs Bittern was just here collecting food for riot victims. I gave her a can of pitted black olives . . . ' 'I had hoped you might teach in some university,' she told him now. 'Well, times are hard,' was all he said. She frowned at him, distantly, secure in her sealed weightless bubble floating through time. While he was in Vietnam, she had kept writing to ask if he had visited any tourist sights. And could he bring home some sort of native craft to solve her Christmas problems?'

'Petey's school is just a *real* nice place,' P.J. said. 'He couldn't hope for a better job.'

'That's all *you* know,' Andrew said.

'What?'

'Peter made straight A's all through school. Are you qualified to say he should stay in some mediocrity in New Jersey?'

'Oh! Well!'

She looked at Peter to defend her, but he didn't. He was irritated by the soft, hurt look on her face. It was his mother who stepped in. 'Now, Andrew,' she said. 'You mustn't mind Andrew, J.C. He's hard on outsiders. The second time he met *Gillespie,* he shot her.' She laughed, and so did Andrew – a contented, easy sound. Peter heard her without surprise, although he had never been told about any shooting, but P.J. gave a little gasp and drew closer to him. 'With a *gun?*' she said.

'Oh, Mother, now – ' said Andrew.

But he was saved by a noise from the fireplace – a rattle as steady and senseless as some wind-up toy. Mrs Emerson screamed. Her cigarette flew out of her hand and landed on the rug, and when Peter leaped up to stamp it out he collided with P.J., who reached the spot before he did but then tripped over one of her long twisted sandal straps. 'Gillespie!' Mrs Emerson screamed. 'Gillespie, a locust!'

Then out came Gillespie, skating along levelly with a brim-full pitcher. She poured a dollop of tea on the cigarette and set the pitcher down on the coffee-table. 'Where?' she said.

'In the fireplace!' said Mrs Emerson, already scuttling toward the dining room. 'Oh, I *told* you you should stuff that chimney up! Anything, I said, could get down inside it and the flue handle came off in Matthew's hands two years ago – ' Andrew followed her out of the room, shielding the baby, and Peter rose but had nowhere to go. He didn't feel up to helping out. He could imagine how cold and heavy a locust must be, slithering down the back of his neck, and he was relieved to see that Gillespie seemed to have the situation in control. She crouched before the fireplace with a rolled-up magazine. George stood by with the poker, scratching the front of his grimy T-shirt and looking bored. 'Here, buddy,' Gillespie told the locust. She poked at the ashes. 'Come on, *come* on.' The whirring grew louder. The magazine rattled as if a fan blade had hit it and then up swooped the locust, evading Gillespie, zooming toward the ceiling with an angry buzz. Mrs Emerson screamed again. She ducked behind Andrew, clutching him by the sides. 'Will I survive this summer?' she asked.

Andrew said, 'There, Jenny, there, Jenny,' although Jenny was happily gnawing his shirt collar without a care in the world.

'I will *never* get used to these creatures, never,' said Mrs Emerson. 'I haven't stepped out of the house since they arrived. Gillespie? Why are you just standing there?'

'I'm waiting for him to come down,' Gillespie said.

'Down? Where *is* he? Oh, on my damask curtains, I'm sure of it.' She stepped back and sank into one of the dining room chairs. From the table behind her she took a bottle of vitamin C, uncapped it and gulped two pills, like a man downing a glass of whiskey. Her hands were shaking. 'They're everywhere,' she said. 'Chattering all day, bombing into people, and at night it's no better. They're silent then but it's a *planning* silence, they hang from all the leaves plotting how to get me in the morning.'

'It's the oak trees,' Gillespie said. 'They favour oaks.'

Her voice was calm and unemphatic, reducing monsters to mere scientific fact. But then the locust whirred up from the curtains and lit on the lampshade, and when George swung at it with the poker all he did was knock the lamp over. 'Damn,' said Gillespie.

'We're like in jail,' Andrew said. 'Matthew and Gillespie and George are the trusties, they get to go out for mail and food. Mother and I stay inside.'

'I spend a summer in the house every seventeen years,' said Mrs Emerson. She thought that over a minute. Then she said, 'The next time they come, I'll be dead.'

'Oh, Mrs *Emerson!*' P.J. said.

But Mrs Emerson only looked at her as if she wondered where P.J. had come from. She said, 'Peter, do you remember when they were here before? You were, oh, twelve, I suppose. You were *hopeless*. You made a necklace out of the shells and wore it everywhere. You had bottles in your closet packed full of locusts. *Black* with them.'

'I did?' Peter said.

'You kept one on a string and took it for walks down Cold Spring Lane.'

He still couldn't picture it. Like most youngest children, he had trouble remembering his own past. The older ones did it so well for him, why should he bother? They had built him a second-hand memory that included the years before he existed, even. He had a distinct recollection of Melissa's running away from home with a peanut butter sandwich and a pomegranate, two years before he was born; but he himself, with his locust on a leash, had vanished.

There was another whir. George leaped straight up in the air, as if he were catching a fly ball, and came to earth with his hands cupped tightly around a rattling black shape. 'Ha!' he said.

'Now, when I open the door,' Gillespie told him, 'throw

him outside. *Far* out, Georgie. Don't let him fly back in or Grandma will have a fit.'

They all went to the hallway – even Mrs Emerson, hanging back a little. Gillespie opened the door and stood ready with the magazine. When George tossed the locust up it seemed to hang in mid-air a minute, and then Gillespie reached out and batted it on its way so violently that she lost her balance. It was Matthew who caught her. He was just crossing the porch with a folded newspaper.

'Not *another* one,' he said, setting her on her feet.

'She says we'll have to stop up the chimney. Look who's come for a visit.'

Matthew looked over Gillespie's head and said, 'Peter! I wondered whose car that was.'

'I was just driving through,' Peter said.

'He brought a girlfriend, and we're going to get him to stay a good long time.'

Peter said, 'Oh, well, I don't – '

'Come on, we've got plenty of room,' Matthew said. 'Well! Looks like the Army's changed you a little.'

But Matthew hadn't changed. He was still black-haired and stooped and skinny, still continually readjusting his glasses on the bridge of his long narrow nose. Gillespie, sheltered under his arm, smiled up at him and said, 'You look tired.'

'I am. Old Smodgett was drunk again.'

He kissed his mother, who had come to the doorway but not an inch beyond it. He clapped Andrew on the shoulder and ran a finger down the curve of the baby's cheek. P.J. stood waiting, next in line. 'Oh,' said Gillespie, 'this is P.J. P.J. – what's your last name, anyway?'

'What?' said P.J. 'Emerson.'

'Oh, isn't that funny.'

'What's funny about it?'

Peter cleared his throat.

'It's *customary* to have your husband's last name,' P.J. said.

'Husband?' said Mrs Emerson.

P.J. spun around and stared at Peter.

'Guess I forgot to mention it,' Peter said.

'Mention what?' asked Mrs Emerson. 'What's going on?'

247

'Well, P.J. and I got married last month.'

He had startled everyone, but P.J. most of all. 'Oh, Peter,' she said. 'Didn't you *tell* them?'

Then his mother's voice rose over hers to say, 'I can't believe it. I just can't. Could this be happening to me *again?*'

'I thought they knew,' P.J. said.

'Peter, I assumed she was a *friend*. Someone you had picked up along the way somehow. Is it just a joke? Are you making this up just to tease me?'

'Well, why? What would be funny about it?' P.J. said. She looked ready to run, but there was nowhere she knew of to run to. Mrs Emerson ignored her.

'Is she pregnant?' she asked.

'Well!' said P.J.

'Now, Mother,' Matthew said, 'I believe the best thing might be to sit down and – '

But it was Gillespie who rescued P.J. 'Well, that's one problem solved,' she said cheerfully. 'I didn't have two extra beds made up anyway. Do you want to see your room, P.J.?'

'Yes, please,' said P.J. Her voice was thin and muffled. She followed Gillespie up the stairs without a backward glance at Peter.

'I never expected this of you, Peter,' his mother said.

'Now, let's sit down,' Matthew told her. 'What's that on the coffee-table? Iced tea? We can all have a – '

'I have five married children now. Five. And six weddings between them. Do you know how many I was invited to? One, just one. Mary's. Not Melissa's, not Matthew's, not Margaret's two. Just secrets! Scandals! Elopements! I can't understand it. Don't girls dream of big church weddings any more?'

'Sit down, Mother,' Matthew said. 'Do you want lemon?'

They grouped themselves around her on the edges of chairs, all uneasily aware of the footsteps over their heads. Matthew poured tea and passed out the glasses. Each time he crossed the rug he had to step over his mother's soggy cigarette, afloat in a puddle of tea, but he didn't seem to find it odd. 'Well, now,' he said, and he settled himself on the couch and began chafing his bony wrists. 'What have you been up to, Peter?'

'We were just discussing that,' said his mother.

'I meant –'

'I believe I'm going to be sick,' Andrew said.

'Oh, Andrew. Pass me the baby.'

But he only clutched her tighter, and Jenny squirmed in his arms and screwed her face up. She started crying, beginning with a little protesting sound and working toward a wail. Gillespie entered the room, scooped her up, and passed on through. 'Supper will be ready in a minute,' she called back.

'None for me,' Andrew said.

She didn't answer him.

Peter rose and went upstairs, with the feeling that everyone's eyes were on his back. He found P.J. in Melissa's old room. She was in front of a skirted vanity table. Tears were running down her cheeks in straight, fine lines.

'P.J., I was *going* to tell them,' he said.

'I don't believe you.'

'You know how seldom I write them. I just hadn't got around to –'

'You wouldn't have told them. You'd have let them give us separate rooms, never said a word. Or asked to *share* a room, that's more like you. Let them think we were living in sin. That's your idea of a joke. And me just going on not realizing, thinking you had told them. Oh, I feel like such a *fool!* Here I was trying so hard, asking for baby pictures – they must have thought I was the pushiest girlfriend you ever had. I wondered why they kept mixing my name up. Did you even tell them I existed?'

'I might have. I forget,' Peter said.

'You didn't, did you?'

He put his hands in his pockets and circled the room. It had the musty, dead feeling of a guest room – furniture bare and polished but thinly filmed with dust, bedspread perfectly smooth, all traces of Melissa gone except for perfume stains on the vanity table. When he reached the window he pulled it open and leaned out into the twilight. 'Hot in here,' he said.

'You never even told them you were dating me,' P.J.

said. 'You kept us so separate you never even told *me* about *them*, not hardly enough to count. Not even their names, just sets of words – the Nervous Case, the Sister that Elopes, the Handyman's Husband. Like you'd met them only once or twice, and had to think up labels to keep them straight. And if you'll pardon me for saying so I get the feeling they do you the same way. Which will you be, now? The Georgia Cracker's Husband? And not a word about we wish you a happy life together, or we hope you'll be like one of us –'

Peter watched her lips, which were puffy from crying. The paint was flaking off her ear-bangles. All he seemed able to think of was her grammatical mistakes, which chalked themselves up in his mind like a grocery list.

'Why, there I was with a wedding ring on!' P.J. said. 'Did they think to notice? No. They were too busy chasing bugs around. That crazy old lady locking herself away from the bugs.'

'Well, wait, P.J.,' Peter said. 'This is my *family* you're talking about.'

'What do I care?'

'This afternoon you were going to be their long-lost sister.'

'Me? Not now, boy. Not for a million dollars. That little closed-up family of yours is closed around *nothing*, thin air, all huddled up together scared to go out. Depending on someone that is like the old-maid failure poor relation you find some places, mending their screens and cooking their supper and fixing their chimneys and making peace – oh, she ended up worse off than *them*. I wouldn't move into this family for anything you paid me. You can just go on down to them and leave me be.'

'P.J. –'

'Will you *go?*'

He made a grab for her – a mistake. He felt a cool smoothness slipping through his fingers and then she was gone, flashing white through the doorway and clattering down the stairs with her sandals flapping. The front door slammed. 'Peter?' his mother called. 'Is that you? Was that him?' The door spring twanged and hummed, and then fell silent.

250

Peter didn't go after her. He had been through this too many times – not the quarrels, she had never quarreled before, but the running away whenever his moods grew too much for her. She would stay gone for two or three hours before she wandered in, cheerful again. 'What do you do when you're gone?' he had once asked her, and she had laughed and looked down at her hands. 'Oh, walk around,' she said. 'Sit on park benches. Check the time every now and then to see if I've been away long enough to worry you.' She should never have told him. Now he could afford to stay home and wait for her. Before, he had run after her in a panic at the thought of being left with no company but his own forever more.

He descended the stairs slowly, and found his family still sitting in the living room. There was no sign of supper yet, not even any silver on the dining room table, but they didn't seem concerned. In the kitchen, Gillespie whistled a tune; they waited, confident that food would arrive somehow, sometime.

'Where's P.J.?' Matthew asked him.

'She's taking a walk.'

'I didn't warm to her,' said Andrew.

'You don't warm to anyone.'

'When I was married,' Mrs Emerson said, 'my family disapproved very strongly. They said, "Oh, certainly he's nice enough, and we have no doubt he can support you. But don't you want more than that? Pamela, he's not your *type*," they said. "He doesn't have, he has a different – " Well, I didn't listen. I will say this, though: I told them to their faces. I never snuck around. We had a perfectly beautiful church wedding with all my family in attendance, acting very civilized. Then later I thought, Well, now I know what they meant. I know what my parents meant. They had my best interests at heart, after all. But I only thought that later.'

Andrew looked up from the asterisk he was drawing in a tea-ring. 'What are you saying?' he asked. 'Are you telling us that you and Dad didn't get along?'

'Oh, we got *along*,' said his mother. 'But there was so much – we were so far apart. Never understood each other. And I thought you children would take after my side. Even

251

Billy wanted that. Why, it was he who named you – Matthew Carter Emerson, Peter Carter Emerson, every last one of you had my maiden name in the middle. "It gives them something to be proud of," Billy said. "The whole world knows who the Carters are." Oh, I had such *expectations* of you all! How did things turn out so differently? You're pure Emerson. You're all like Billy's brothers, separate and silent and with failure just built into you, and now looking back I can't even pinpoint the time when you shifted sides. Why did it work out this way?'

As if she were discussing some abstract problem, something that had nothing to do with them, her three sons sat looking detached and interested. Them Matthew said, 'Oh, I don't know. I kind of liked Dad's brothers.'

'You would,' said his mother. 'You most of all.'

'They *were* sort of rednecks, Matthew,' Andrew said.

'Well, wait a minute – '

Before it became an argument, Peter escaped. He went out to the kitchen, where he found George playing with a locust on the floor and Gillespie nursing the baby, sitting peacefully with her blouse unbuttoned like a broad golden madonna. The roast was cooling on the counter, but she didn't seem in any hurry. 'Where's P.J.?' she asked.

'Gone out.'

'Well, I wish you'd go get her. Supper will be on as soon as I'm through here.'

'Maybe we could start without her,' Peter said. A picture of never finding P.J. at all flashed through his head. He might jump in his car now and leave alone, light-hearted and full of a pure, free joy. Then hours later P.J. would come straggling in, with grass stains on the back of her shorts. 'Where's Petey?' 'He's gone.' 'Well,' she would say, trying to remain dignified, acting as if this were all according to plan – 'I believe I'll be getting along too now. I just loved meeting you all.' He imagined her out on the street thumbing rides, with her purse hitched over her shoulder and her bare legs flashing like knife blades in the darkness. Yet how could he be sure that, halfway to New Jersey, he wouldn't start feeling lonely and remorseful? Then too, he could stay here. This house could expand like an accordian, with its children safe and happy inside and

252

Gillespie to take care of them. Why not?

Gillespie hoisted the baby on her shoulder and went to the refrigerator for a carton of milk. She poured a saucer full and set it out on the back porch. 'Kitty, kitty?' she called. Then she returned and checked the biscuits in the oven, and after that she placed the baby on the other breast. Jenny screwed her face sideways, searching for the nipple. Gillespie hummed beneath her breath – a juggler of supplies, obtaining and distributing all her family needed. But when she caught Peter watching her, she said, 'I'd wish you'd go find P.J., Peter.'

'I'd rather not,' he said.

'*Emersons,*' said Gillespie, but without much force. She brushed back a wisp of Jenny's hair. In this position, with her eyes lowered, with her mouth curved for the baby, she looked younger than he had expected. He had pictured her as some kind of family retainer, ageless, faceless, present for as long as he could remember, although in fact she hadn't arrived till he was in college and she was only a few years older than he was. Now she stuck out a moccasin to stop the locust's progress across the floor, and when she grinned at George she looked like another child. 'You better not let that in where Grandma is,' she told him.

'I'm going to teach him how to fly,' George said.

'Don't you think he already knows?'

But George was wandering out of the kitchen now, toward the front door. Peter frowned after him.

'They think I've made a mistake,' he told Gillespie.

Gillespie stayed quiet. The baby, intent on nursing, rolled her eyes up to study him.

'Maybe they're right,' he said. 'You shouldn't hope for anything from someone that much different from your family.'

'You should if your family doesn't *have* it,' said Gillespie.

Then she rose, with the baby clinging like a barnacle, and went to check the oven again.

Peter stood still a moment, watching her, but she seemed to have nothing more to say to him. Finally he went out of the kitchen, down the hallway, avoiding the rest of the family. He passed so close that he could hear his mother in the living room. 'Why are my children always leaving?' she asked. Peter stopped, afraid for an instant that it was him she was speaking to. 'Why are they always coming *back?*' Andrew asked her. 'Scratching their heads and saying, *'What* was it you wanted me to do?' Mrs Emerson murmured something Peter couldn't understand. Then a newspaper crackled, drowning out their voices, and under the cover of its noise he went out the front door and eased it shut behind him.

The dry, bitter smell of locusts hung in the dark, but they were silent now. The only locust to be seen was the one on the porch which George flung out, caught, and flung once again, never causing more than a buzzing sound and a dazed whirring of wings. 'Bye, fellow,' Peter said. He rumpled George's hair.

'Bye,' said George, without surprise. He caught the locust again and looked at Peter absently, as if, every day of his life, he saw people arriving and leaving and getting sidetracked from their travels.

Peter went out to his car, looked up and down the dark street, and then got in and started the engine. He rolled slowly and almost soundlessly, peering at everything his headlights touched. After a few hundred feet he stopped and leaned over to open the door. 'Want a ride?' he asked.

'Might as well,' said P.J.

She climbed in. When she slid over next to him her skin felt cooler than the night air, but the hand she laid on his knee was warm and she warmed the length of his side. By the time they had reached the main road again, she was asleep with her head in his lap.

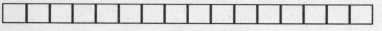